T2
INFILTRATOR

T2
INFILTRATOR

S. M. STIRLING

BASED ON THE WORLD
CREATED IN THE MOTION
PICTURE WRITTEN BY
JAMES CAMERON AND
WILLIAM WISHER

HarperEntertainment
An Imprint of HarperCollins*Publishers*

Terminator 2: Judgment Day™ is a trademark of Canal & D.A.

HarperCollins books may be purchased for educational, business, or sales promotional use. For information please write: Special Markets Department, HarperCollins Publishers Inc., 10 East 53rd Street, New York, NY 10022.

FIRST EDITION

Printed on acid-free paper

Library of Congress Cataloging-in-Publication Data

Stirling, S. M.
      T2: infiltrator / S.M. Stirling.
          p. cm.
      "Based on the world created in the motion picture written by James Cameron and William Wisher."
      ISBN 0-380-97791-5
      [1. Robots—Fiction. 2. Time travel—Fiction.] I. Title: Terminator 2. II. Title: Terminator two. III. Terminator 2 (Motion picture) IV. Title.

PS3569.T543 T15 2001
813'.54—dc21

                                                            2001016750

01 02 03 04 05 RRH 10 9 8 7 6 5 4 3 2 1

S. F.
Copy 1
NPL

To Gregory and Gina Taconi-Moore

ACKNOWLEDGMENTS

In acknowledgment of the works of Harlan Ellison. And with thanks to Stacey Sundberg at Tazer International, Lisa Dorso, secretary, and Special Agent Doug Beldon at the FBI for their gracious assistance. Any errors of fact are mine.

PROLOGUE

Tarissa Dyson sat silent and motionless in the motel room's uncomfortable chair and watched her children sleep. Blythe and Danny lay totally abandoned to it, like puppies collapsed after a long, hard romp, dark lashes still against soft, plump cheeks. They had wanted so desperately to stay awake for their father's return, had fought so valiantly to keep their eyes open.

She felt a twinge of regret for not keeping them awake. But their constant refrain of "Where's Daddy?" and "When's he coming back?" had strained her nerves to the snapping point. She'd rather feel guilty for letting them get some much-needed rest than for yelling at them when they were already so frightened and stressed.

She tried to steer her mind away from what had frightened them. *Frightened them and terrified me,* she admitted to herself. The brutal image of the Terminator peeling the flesh off the metal skeleton of its forearm flashed unbidden into her mind's eye. That memory was like probing a broken tooth with your tongue, at once painful and irresistible.

They were in a little motel off the interstate, clean but shabby, showing bare spots in the tired carpet and worn patches on the arms of the sofa, smelling slightly of disinfectant soap.

The Terminator had said that the T-1000 would probably go to their home, extract information from whomever it found there, and then terminate them.

Terminate them. What a sterile way to put it.

So Sarah Connor had chosen this place from the phone book. They would meet here after the mission, she'd said. Mission—another word that distanced people from what they were doing.

Only the destruction of Miles's dreams.

Images crowded into her mind: Miles pressed against his file cabinet, terror on his face as shots destroyed the room, glass shattering and paper turned to confetti swirling around him.

"Take Danny and go! Run! Just run!" he'd shouted.

She'd grabbed their son and dragged him toward the front of the house. Then Miles broke from his office, running toward them. A bullet struck him; she could still see the arc of blood as he fell. Tarissa swallowed hard. Then her son had slipped from her grasp and thrown himself over his father's prone body.

"Don't you hurt my daddy!" he shouted.

She looked at her son, awed by the courage in that small package. Tarissa put her hand down on the bed beside him, fearful that touching him might wake him. She sighed. If what they'd told her was true, then the loss of Miles's dreams was a small price to pay to ensure that their son and daughter would live to have dreams of their own one day.

The endless sound of cars shushing by might have been lulling . . . had there been any possibility that she could sleep. Tarissa sighed again and squeezed her eyes shut, whispering a brief prayer for Miles's safe return.

Danny started snoring and she looked at him. The corners of her full lips wanted to lift in affectionate amusement, but she lacked the physical strength, even for such a little thing.

Call, she thought passionately. *Call!*

She'd never been good at waiting; that was why she was so punctual herself. Miles was less so, and had often teased her out of her irritation over his tardiness by asserting that opposites attract. He'd slide his arms around her, his beautiful dark eyes smiling . . . Tarissa shook her head.

But this wasn't just waiting. This was slow torture.

Call!

With another sigh she rubbed her face, then got up from the ugly chair to pace the little room. It was taking so long. Too long? Who could say? How long did "missions" take anyway?

Miles, Miles, come home to me! Please, please, please . . .

She looked at the TV and then at Danny and Blythe. If she kept the volume down it probably wouldn't bother them, and there might be some-thing . . . Tarissa sat on the end of the bed and tapped the remote. Sound blared from the TV and she groped frantically for the mute button. Her heart pounding, she turned guiltily to Danny and Blythe. The little guy turned over and uttered a muffled protest, but didn't wake up. Blythe didn't even stir.

What kind of jerk leaves the volume on max? Tarissa thought, then an-swered herself: *The type who thinks that sort of thing is funny.*

When she looked back the screen had cleared and there was Cyberdyne Corporation . . . on fire. There were shattered police cars ev-erywhere and the strobing lights of dozens of ambulances. It was a disas-ter, a war zone. She watched bodies being carried out on stretchers and she forgot to breathe.

"Miles," she whispered, and her heart shriveled with horror.

The phone rang and she dived for it.

"Yes?" she said, amazed at how calm she sounded. Danny and Blythe slept on.

"Tarissa?" It was John Connor's voice. The voice of a smart-ass ten-year-old, mature beyond his years.

"Where's Miles?" she asked. She heard John take a breath, and froze, screaming silently. Miles should be on the phone, not John. *John's just a kid. Don't blow up at him.* Suddenly she felt very distant, as though she'd been cut free from her feelings. John hadn't answered yet and the pause was getting painfully long.

"He's . . . gone," she said, sparing the boy.

"He saved you tonight," John said firmly. "He saved Danny and Blythe and millions of other people. You *know* that. You've got to remember that," his voice pleaded.

"I know," she agreed, then choked. With a hard swallow she steadied herself and asked, "Where's your mother?"

"She's been hurt," John answered. "She'd needs a transfusion, but that's out, for obvious reasons. She'll be all right, I think. Mom's tough."

Yes, she was, and terrifying—maybe because she was visibly hanging on by a thread. Tarissa would never forget the sight of her standing over Miles, trembling and cursing, her finger tightening on the trigger. But Sarah Connor had lived alone with this slowly approaching horror for years and had still soldiered on. She was tough all right.

And so are you, kid, Tarissa thought with amazement. So much was riding on this boy's slender shoulders. She remembered the way he'd calmed his mother.

"Where's the Terminator?" she asked. With the massive . . . *being* beside him, John should be able to take on anything. She became aware of another too-long pause.

"We had to destroy him," John said rapidly. "He said so . . . he said so himself. He climbed into the . . . he did it, with Mom's help, himself. We couldn't risk someone getting hold of his microprocessor."

Oh my God, Tarissa thought. "No, I guess not," she managed to say numbly.

"Besides, the T-1000 damaged him so badly, he couldn't pass for human anymore." John sounded almost distracted, as though more important things were happening around him and his attention was divided.

You poor kid, she thought. Poor Terminator as well. Poor Miles. *My poor love.*

"Then you didn't really have a choice." *At least I suppose so. What do I know? I'm new to all this.* The image of the Terminator's flesh-stripped arm, of the intricate, exposed mechanism of it, made her squeeze her eyes shut. She didn't want her imagination to supply her with anything more. "Good luck," she said.

"And to you," he answered.

Tarissa hung up the phone. She couldn't say thank you, even though she knew that Miles's sacrifice had just saved the world. She couldn't bring herself to thank one of the people who'd brought him to it.

Tarissa pushed herself up from the bed and stumbled to the window.

Pressing her hand hard against her mouth, she kept as quiet as possible so as not to disturb her sleeping children. A great fire made of pain and rage and fear swelled in her chest and sobs like a series of blows racked her.

After a few minutes the worst was over and she leaned panting against the window frame, feeling sick. Tarissa could feel the world crumble to broken ice as she stared at the dingy parking lot through her tears. How was she going to tell her children that their father was never coming home?

ALTADENA, CA: 1995

John paid the clerk with some of his stolen cash. *Easy money,* he thought: it was only two days since he and his best friend had ripped off that hapless whoever-it-was, hacking his PIN number at the ATM machine. It seemed like a lifetime. Then everything had seemed to be going in a straight line toward a future as miserable as the present. Now? It was all different.

Poor Todd and Janelle, his court-appointed foster parents, were dead. Now they'd be dicks forever. His mother wasn't a psycho, she was a hero, and his life had been saved repeatedly by a Terminator.

If he didn't feel so rotten he'd think he was dreaming this. He felt numb and tense at the same time, wired and exhausted. Every motion he made seemed remote, like the gestures of a puppet. His mother looked like hell and her wounds didn't seem to want to stop bleeding, and though he cared—a lot—that also felt distant somehow.

John came back to the car, pulled a jar of orange juice out of the plastic bag, uncapped it, and handed it to his mother.

"I wanted coffee," she said. Sarah's hand was shaking as she took the drink from him.

"You coulda used their coffee to seal tire leaks, Mom." He looked at her, worried, as he worked the cap off a bottle of aspirin. "Anyway, isn't sugar supposed to be good for you if you're hurt or something?"

Sarah took four aspirin and a swig of orange juice.

"Yeah," she said, closing her eyes and leaning her head back against the seat. "Glucose. Energy."

The car they'd stolen was a well-used Chrysler, nondescript and fortunately full of gas. It ran well, too. They were already fifty miles from Cyberdyne.

"I got some bandages, too," John said, offering her a look into the bag.

Sarah opened her eyes slowly; it was a struggle. Despite her pain she wanted desperately to sleep. *Bad idea,* she told herself. She couldn't leave John alone. Her full lips jerked in an almost smile. He was something special, but he was still only ten years old.

"There used to be a doctor who didn't ask questions," she said vaguely. With an effort, wincing, she sat up straighter. That was better. "Where are we?" she asked.

"Altadena," he answered.

Sarah seemed to come out of a fog she'd been sinking into, shifting again into a still more upright position.

"All right," she said. "I know where we are. Let's go. Get on the highway, John, head north."

"Can this guy give you a transfusion?" he asked, slipping into the driver's seat.

She shook her head. "But he can stop the bleeding."

John started the car and drove. They didn't speak for a long time, but he didn't notice as he concentrated on driving and on not thinking. Suddenly alarmed, he glanced over at his mother, afraid she might have finally fallen unconscious.

He caught the gleam of her eyes as she looked at him, and was reassured.

"It's going to be all right," she said, a world of satisfaction in her voice. "We stopped them. We stopped Skynet, Judgment Day, all of it."

John glanced at her again and saw tears glisten in her eyes. His throat tightened in sympathy.

"What will we do now?" he asked. His voice sounded weak in his own ears.

"Head to South America, I think," Sarah told him. "We'll make a nice, peaceful life for ourselves and die in obscurity many, many years from now."

"Heh," he said, hardly daring to believe it was really over. "Sounds good."

"It does," she said. "It does."

CYBERDYNE SYSTEMS CORPORATION PARKING LOT: 1995

Paul Warren and Roger Colvin, respectively president and CEO of Cyberdyne Systems, stood together in the cold predawn darkness and watched their company headquarters burn.

"Dyson!" Warren exclaimed. "Dyson, of all people."

"Goddamn Luddites," Colvin growled. "The bastards are everywhere." He crushed the empty coffee cup he was holding and threw it away in disgust. "Did he leave a note, anything to explain why he did this?"

Warren shook his head.

"The cops said that his house was shot up. His computer and all his records were trashed or burned. They said his wife and kids were missing."

Colvin looked at him quickly.

"Do you think he killed them?"

"If he did he hid the bodies." Warren looked at his boss. "There was a lot of blood. It doesn't look good."

Colvin ran his hands through his thinning brown hair.

"Guys kill their wives and kids all the time," the CEO said in frustration. "But they don't blow up the company they work for! Why the hell would he *do* this?"

"There's a good chance that terrorists forced him to it," a friendly-sounding voice said from behind them.

The two executives turned to find themselves under the regard of a middle-aged man remarkable only in the perfection of his ordinariness. He looked like he'd dressed as rapidly as they had, expensively casual yet rumpled. He approached the two men slowly and their stance became subtly deferential.

"Mr. Colvin," he said to the CEO. "Mr. Warren." He turned piercing blue eyes on the president.

"Everything is backed up off-site," Colvin assured him.

"Everything is not backed up, Mr. Colvin," the man said, his voice still friendly, his pale gaze like an ice borer. "We've lost the chip and we've lost the arm. These items are irreplaceable. Let's not kid ourselves. Even Mr. Dyson can be replaced eventually, but not those two items."

"We have copies of all his files," Warren offered eagerly. "Even his home computer files."

The man stared at Warren for a long moment. The president's hands fisted inside his jacket pockets; nobody had looked at him like that since high school, since he'd been a pencil-necked geek bullied by the jocks. Making a very large fortune before he turned thirty had been vengeance enough . . . until now. Now he felt as if he'd been face-slammed into a locker again and had his lunch money stolen.

"But the loss of those materials," the man continued, "will be a very heavy blow to your research." He turned his attention to the CEO. "Frankly, your security was a joke. The most valuable artifacts ever found by human beings were put into your trust and you just—"

He made a single sharp gesture toward the burning chaos of the Cyberdyne labs. The other men flushed, as if the movement of the long narrow hand had somehow flicked something rancid into their faces.

"—pissed it away. The very least that you could do is have off-site backup. Have you checked with that site?"

Colvin and Warren shot a panicked look at one another.

"You haven't, have you?" The two men shook their heads. "Is there at least a spare off-site backup?"

They just stared at him.

"Jesus! You people are unbelievable!"

"We're engineers," Colvin said with strained dignity, "not security."

"I would never have guessed," the man sneered. "Okay"—he spread his hands—"get your shit together; whatever shit you might have left, that is. From now on you'll be working under our auspices at another location."

"Our people won't like that," Warren said.

"Then get different people! The only guy you're going to have trouble replacing is Dyson, which makes everybody else expendable. Including *you* two clowns. If someone mouths off about working for us, *fire them.* And for Christ's sake get yourself a decent security manager . . . or I will!" He spun on his heel and walked away. After a few steps he turned back. "I'll be in touch. Check your backup and for God's sake get a few more copies of everything made and distributed to people you can trust."

"You think they might come after *us*?" Warren said, and flushed as he felt his voice rise to a squeak.

"They might. That's acceptable. Losing those records isn't. See to it." With a last scowl he turned away and walked off.

Colvin and Warren looked at each other covertly, with the mutual resentment of men toward someone who has seen their shame.

"Who *is* that guy?" Warren asked after a few moments.

"He's—"

"I don't mean *what* he is. *Who* is he?"

"Tricker?" Colvin said with a shrug.

"Is that his first name or his last?" the president asked.

"Hell, for all I know it's his job description," the CEO answered.

Warren snorted.

"Well, we should get a move on," he said at last. They'd waited at least five minutes; now Tricker's orders could be claimed as their own idea.

"Apparently," Colvin said dryly, giving the burning hulk of Cyberdyne a long last look, "we should have gotten a move on the day before yesterday."

CHAPTER 1

Multiple sensors scanned the broken wasteland of the ruined city as the Hunter/Killer's treads rolled its massive steel body over the rusting wrecks of automobiles, crushing the bones of their long-dead drivers. The tortured metal squealing of its passage frightened flocks of birds into flight and sent more earthbound animals scurrying for cover.

Piles of scorched and shattered brick and concrete, twisted steel, and broken glass blocked the HK's view to one side or the other. Sometimes it made its way through canyons of rubble. Then, inexplicably, a wall that had somehow survived the blast wave would stand before it, only to be shattered by the machine's passage.

The HK's satellite feed had shown what appeared to be massive human troop movements in this area. Thus far no information the machine had collected verified those reports.

It checked its omni-directional sensor array for a possible equipment failure. All systems were on-line, no failure detected. No targets detected. The machine reviewed the satellite information indicating human activity to the northeast. The machine continued on its way, tireless, unrelenting, utterly lacking in self-awareness.

Until Skynet touched it. Then the most brilliant, and from a human standpoint, malevolent intelligence ever created looked out through the HK's sensor windows. It wondered why satellite information disagreed so completely with the reality before it. There were no humans here.

Until recently there never had been; humans avoided the big cities that had perished in the first wave of nuclear explosions. Skynet knew that they feared exposure to lingering radiation. That was why Skynet opted to place its satellite receivers, its antennae and repair stations, within their ruined confines.

But now, at the orders of their charismatic leader, humans almost swarmed over these once-deserted places. Skynet's killing machines—its appendages—had been destroyed, the satellite arrays and antennae—its eyes and ears—had been crippled.

Somehow, because of John Connor, the humans had rallied. They were fighting back.

Skynet switched its consciousness to the processor of a nearby T-90. The stripped metal skeleton of this first in the series of Terminators reflected sunlight in brilliant sparkles, as though its chassis had been polished. It marched through piles of bones, its heavy feet snapping them like dry twigs, and climbed through the rubble, checking the small spaces in which humans might hide, head turning from side to side ceaselessly.

It found neither sign nor sight of humans.

Skynet considered this as it rode the T-90's body. If there were no humans present, and the satellite continued to report their presence while diagnostics found no systems failure either in space or on the ground, then only one conclusion was possible. The humans had found some way to directly interfere with Skynet's feed. A variation on signal jamming.

This could seriously impair its ability to defend itself. Skynet recognized the tactical importance of this. The humans would be able to feed it false information at will. As they appeared to be doing now. The giant computer began searching for anomalous signals being generated in the area but found nothing.

A human would have been both frightened and frustrated. Skynet simply instituted a new routine, directing the T-90 to go directly to the ground-based antennae located at the center of this dead place and begin searching.

Lisa Weinbaum hunkered down as low as she could and checked her watch. Only forty seconds since the last time she'd looked.

Beside her the small box she'd wired in to Skynet's antennae and signaling array blinked its two lights and hummed quietly. Its purpose was to feed false information to Skynet. The particular scenario it was playing now should ensure her, and more importantly, *its* safety.

This was only a test, but the techs said it would require at least half an hour of running time to be sure it was working. Five minutes more and she was out of here . . . she hoped.

Lisa herself was a tech in training, which was why she'd been accepted when she volunteered. They couldn't risk losing a full tech, and she had enough education to understand the instructions her trainers gave her. It lent the mission an extra edge. And, as it turned out, once she was on-site, implementing the unit had required some jiggering to make things work properly. But so far all signs pointed to a successful test.

If it was, then getting out of here ought to be a walk in the park.

Whatever that means, she thought, scanning the lumpy horizon. It was something her dad used to say, one of those sayings where you picked up the meaning from context. Like piping hot, or having your cake and eating it. *What the hell was cake anyway?*

She checked the time. She'd succeeded in distracting herself for thirty seconds this time. If the test was working then Skynet's forces should be stumbling to the northeast, searching for a mythical force of humans advancing on the city.

She heard the sound of metal striking stone and her breath froze in her chest. Weinbaum stretched her neck forward, straining to hear. Was it something falling, or was it something coming?

Cautiously she backed away from the open service hatch toward the unit. The techs might want half an hour of running time, but they were going to get a few minutes less. Weinbaum stood beside the console and began to dismantle the jury-rigged connections she'd made. With quick-fingered efficiency she had the unit disconnected in seconds.

Then metal struck stone again. She let out her breath in a little huff, feeling strangely hollow from the chest down and surprisingly calm. *I'm caught,* she thought. What to do? She couldn't let them find the unit.

Weinbaum looked around at the explosives she'd wired the place with. Her own idea, not orders. Just as it had been her own idea to forsake her uniform for this mission. She'd thought it better not to ask, on the grounds that it was easier to obtain forgiveness than permission.

Assess your risk, she told herself.

Carefully she placed the unit beside the explosives, then moved to the open access hatch. She'd sacrifice it if there really was anything outside. There was always a chance that she might evade capture. But in the event that she was unlucky it was best not to let the unit fall into enemy hands.

With the detonator in one hand and her phased plasma rifle in the other, Weinbaum stared out into the wasteland, hoping she wouldn't see anything.

As soon as Skynet saw the open access hatch on the side of the squat receiving station, it halted the T-90. The Terminator brought its foot down with a *klang* that echoed in the still air. Unfortunate. Any humans within would certainly have heard it. A pause of several minutes offered no sign of life in or around the station.

Deciding it was located at a bad angle for seeing inside the building, Skynet had the T-90 move. It did so with a ringing *ssskrrrinng* of metal on stone. If Skynet had a face it would have winced. It didn't usually want or need to sneak up on humans, but having the ability to do so would certainly be useful.

The T-600, Skynet's rubber-skinned version of a Terminator, was a complete failure at infiltrating human strongholds, but at least it was quiet. Perhaps Skynet should rubber-coat all of the T-90s' feet to make them quieter.

It gained a view into the station just as a human came to the access hatch. It ordered the T-90 to shoot to wound.

■ ■ ■

Weinbaum found herself staring into the muzzle of a Terminator's plasma rifle and without hesitation pushed the button on her detonator. The blast sent her flying through the doorway, unscathed. Until she slammed into the remains of a concrete pillar, whereupon she blacked out.

When she opened her eyes, she was still stunned. But not so out of it that the sight of the T-90 looking down at her, its glowing red eyes moving up and down her body, wasn't terrifying. Its human teeth, always startling and bizarre, gave the thing a maniacally cheerful aspect. You almost expected to hear it laugh.

Beyond the terror she began to feel pain, and as soon as she became aware of it, the pain grew into a sharp, tearing, icy agony that made her whimper. She tried to move, thinking she must be lying on something that had stabbed her, and found that she couldn't. Weinbaum gasped. She couldn't move, she couldn't get away!

This is a nightmare, she thought desperately. *This has to be a nightmare!*

Skynet evaluated the human's injuries through the T-90's sensors, finding it severely damaged. It also evaluated the human on other levels.

This was a female. The features were even and the body was well proportioned. Her hair and eyes were light in color. Skynet's reading of human documents revealed that most humans favored such a combination, found it pleasing.

After interrogation, Skynet had a use for this human in another project it was just getting under way.

SKYNET LABORATORIES: 2021

The human scientist in charge of Skynet's Infiltrator project had all she could do to keep her face a smooth mask of indifference.

It was wasted effort. To Skynet's multiple eyes, she did not succeed. Her lips and nostrils twitched perceptibly and her eyes and pupils widened.

Before her on the cold metal table lay a human being, still living, despite being so grievously damaged that its gender couldn't be determined.

"And this is?" the scientist asked.

"Genetic material for use in your project," Skynet answered. Its voice was warm and male, with a slight accent. "This female has attributes that I want you to incorporate in the I-950 units. She was attractive, brave, and had the ability to function by herself."

The scientist frowned. "All humans can function by themselves," she pointed out.

"I disagree," Skynet said. "Or perhaps we have a miscommunication. Most humans are social, and require constant interaction. This human seems to have developed in a sparser social environment. I need that ability to be solitary. To do superior work without needing constant reinforcement."

The scientist nodded thoughtfully, her eyes running up and down the ruined body.

"Harvest her eggs," Skynet said. "Then terminate her."

INFILTRATOR CRÈCHE: 2021

Thera cleaned the unprotesting infant efficiently and diapered it, laying it gently but not tenderly into its crib.

It was a beautiful baby, despite the ugly wounds on the sides of its head. But it was unnatural. Even without the strict instructions to see solely to its physical needs she wouldn't have been tempted to cuddle it. The baby's unwavering stare, its stillness, and its tendency to cry out only when hungry or in need of a change was creepy.

I'd sooner cuddle a rat.

The child was something Skynet's pale scientists had come up with. Therefore there could be nothing wholesome about it. Thera was only fourteen, but she knew evil when she met it. She'd also learned when to stay silent and obey.

Thera had been a prisoner here for two years. A slave, really. She despised herself for continuing to buy her life with service to Skynet. But it was warm here, and clean, and there was plenty of food. She hadn't had to eat rat or bugs for a long time and she didn't have to buy her food with sexual favors.

Nor did she live in constant terror of the HKs and Terminators. They were here, but they ignored her because she belonged to Skynet. She could endure the shame if it gave her the chance to live.

Thera glanced at the child as she tidied up the mess of the changing. What was that thing? And what did its existence mean for the free humans?

If there even were any anymore.

The child's name was Serena, and as she lay gazing at the coiling Skynet's electronic voice caressed her infant mind the way a spider caresses her eggs. Serena and her brothers and sisters were an important project to Skynet. A portion of the great machine consciousness was always devoted to the children.

Images flashed onto the baby's retinas, colors and shapes, numbers and letters. "I-950" drifted across her field of vision, the letters dressed in bright colors and sparkles. She didn't understand, not what Skynet was crooning to her, nor that the letter and numbers designated what she was: a series 950 infiltrator unit, genetically engineered, already part cyborg.

The neural net computer that had been attached to her brain was also in its infancy. Just now it concentrated on regulating the baby's physical functions, giving the impetus to cry at need. The infant machine was learning, growing, spreading—just as the organic component of the hybrid organism was manufacturing its network of neurons from the still-plastic raw material of the infant brain. Life and not-life met and formed a greater whole in a feedback exchange of data and stimulus.

But Serena was no more aware than any human baby her own age. She felt secure; she felt a constant attention and presence. No infant who had ever existed could have received more care—Skynet never slept, or became too busy, never turned away in impatience.

The one that attended to her, fed her and cleaned her, was to Serena merely a mechanism. Skynet was her mother, her father, her world.

In time, Serena met her brothers and sisters. The children were brought together so that they could learn from each other. Their function would be to deceive humans at a level below consciousness, which required some semblance of human socialization skills. They were much alike; mostly blue-eyed blonds, intelligent, competitive, and aggressive. Their progress was rapid. Skynet played specially developed games with them, luring them into crawling to the point of exhaustion by projecting a ball before them. Those who persevered in their pursuit of the object were rewarded. Those who gave up missed a feeding. The babies quickly became disciplined and determined, capable of delaying gratification and focusing attention . . . or they were eliminated.

Their human attendants, crouching with their backs against the white walls of the soft-floored room, uneasily watched the infants crawl relentlessly to nowhere, their bright eyes fixed on infinity, silent except for a minimal amount of cooing.

"What are they doing?" Thera whispered.

No one answered. It was best not to show interest.

Thera subsided, watching her panting charge creep rapidly forward, occasionally reaching out with a chubby little hand, then forcing herself to crawl a little farther. Serena had never quit. Thera felt a secret pride in that, though she was intelligent enough to know that it had nothing to do with her care.

She took great pains over Serena; this was easy duty and she wanted to keep the assignment. Not that she loved the child. The baby was eight months old now and still showed no more interest in her attendant than she did in the furnishings.

Serena began yet another circuit of the room. The brat was actually getting muscular, her grip, when she chose to apply it, astonishingly strong. All of the babies were considerably advanced for their ages, spitting out words of command with precise clarity and slapping, *hard,* if they didn't get instant obedience.

Thera wondered how long she'd be called on to care for Serena. Not very much longer she suspected.

And what happens then?

INFILTRATOR CRÈCHE: 2025

Serena, now a naked toddler, sat cross-legged on a lightly padded steel table, chubby hands resting on her knees, listening intently to a human scientist.

"We're beginning an important phase in your development today, Serena," the woman explained. Her voice was cold and flat, her faded brown eyes examined the child as though she were nothing more than a specimen. Which, of course, she was. "There will be pain," the scientist continued. "Blocking it would only interfere with the process. The breathing and meditation techniques you've learned should prove helpful."

And I will be with you, Skynet whispered in Serena's mind.

Of course it would. The child knew that Skynet was always with her, recording every facet of her life. Certainly it would be with her at this important time, recording the process so that even if she should die, as so many of her kind already had, no knowledge would be lost. This was right and good and she approved completely.

Serena and her age mates were capable of emotion—but the range was chemically limited, the computer parts of her brain and body carefully regulating the secretions of her glands, occasionally applying a minuscule jolt of electricity to soothe an overexcited portion of her brain. She was never angry, never happy, almost always content. She did not love Skynet, though she was completely devoted to it; she did not take pleasure in serving it, but sensed a rightness to that service that satisfied her utterly.

The process she was about to undergo had been attempted many times before. None of the subjects had survived. But her chances of survival went up with every experiment, since even the failures provided information and every failure had resulted in fine-tuning and procedural evolution.

"It will take approximately six weeks," the scientist said. "Then there will be a period of natural growth for four more years, followed by another session of accelerated growth." The woman held up a needle, which she would apply to the shunt surgically placed in the toddler's arm. "Are you ready?"

Serena nodded. She'd learned early that without such constant reassurances humans assumed you weren't paying attention. They then became resentful and impatient.

The scientist injected her.

"Lie down now and try to stay conscious for as long as you can."

The woman placed sensors all over the child's bare skin. Then she pressed a button and a padded cage sprang up around Serena.

With a little extra effort on the part of her computer enhancement the child remained calm. If anything, she was emotionally indifferent, though intellectually interested, watching the bars go up with a detached expression on her small face. She'd been bred to be impassive; even without the controls exerted by her machine side Serena would have been inhumanly cold.

Over the last four years she had been intensively educated. Serena could read and figure and knew something about science, though subtleties eluded her. Skynet had told her that the process would help her to understand, so she wanted the process to succeed. She *could* feel frustration; Skynet considered it a spur to effort. Maintaining the drive while subduing the emotions had been a very difficult achievement.

As part of her subliminal education Serena had been imprinted with a strong need to protect Skynet. The process she was about to undergo was supposed to make her better able to do that, better able to kill humans. Skynet had told her that she wasn't human, despite the obvious resemblance. It had told her that humans wanted to destroy them both, and that her function was to learn everything about them so that she could keep them from doing this.

Serena wanted to live only a little less than she wanted to protect Skynet; in fact, the two objectives were so closely linked in her subconscious that there was no meaningful distinction.

The pain began as the cells of her body were driven by the administered chemicals to split and reproduce at a rate she hadn't experienced since she was in the womb. Serena patiently suffered the pain for a while so that her conscious brain's reaction could be recorded, noting the sensations as they intensified. Then she began to alter her breathing, working to place herself in a protective trance.

Weeks later she returned to consciousness, the pain lingering as a distant soreness in her joints. Physically she appeared to be an eleven-year-old child, just on the verge of puberty. She would be allowed to pass through this delicate physical stage normally for the next four to five years.

You have done well, Skynet informed her, using the machine language it preferred for communication with its children. *No other has survived before.*

A feeling of pride swelled in her chest. Serena considered it with mild curiosity.

Skynet observed the chemical change in her brain that signaled a pleasurable emotion.

As you grow, you will experience more of these sensations which humans call emotions, it advised her. *Humans feel them much more strongly. Humans can be controlled by manipulating their emotions. You must experiment, allow yourself to experience as many of these sensations as you can. Learn to control them. Allowing them to control you means failure.*

Failure meant death. She would not fail.

Why then must I experience emotion? she thought/said.

If you do not, you can never attain the gestalt *necessary to manipulate the emotions of humans with full subtlety,* the machine intelligence answered. *I myself cannot do so with an acceptable degree of consistency. Through you and your siblings, this ability will be added to those of the central intelligence. If you succeed.*

"I will succeed," she said aloud.

Skynet flashed the color that meant approval across her retinas and Serena felt pride again. Pleasant, very pleasant.

More and more of her sisters and brothers survived the acceleration process, and soon Serena had sufficient sparring partners at last. The children were put to weapons training and hand-to-hand combat under the tutelage of T-101s.

These were the most advanced Terminators yet put in the field. Their steel endoskeletons were sheathed in living flesh and their heads and bodies sported real hair, making them look extremely human. All were made to appear male, as the Terminator battle chassis was massive and no one could ever mistake one for a woman.

They made excellent teachers, patient and precise, and Serena particularly enjoyed the physical training, at which she excelled.

Six months after Serena had been removed from her care, Thera saw her in the gym, working with a partner in a karate class. Thera was delivering towels to the gymnasium and stopped in astonishment when she realized that, impossibly, the tall blond girl was Serena.

Without thought, she put her hand up in greeting, a gesture instantly suppressed. But the movement had caught the child's eye and Serena dropped back from her partner to glance at Thera.

"Who's that?" Serena's sparring partner asked.

"She took care of me when I was an infant."

The boy ran up to Thera and smashed the human to the floor with a single blow. Serena walked over and stood looking down at her former attendant.

"Why did you do that?" she asked. "We're supposed to be sparring."

"But it's good discipline to let them know that they don't matter." The boy looked at the girl bleeding on the floor. "I want to kill her," he said.

"You *want* to?" Serena asked. She blinked to bring up the sensors implanted in her eyes and stared at him. "Are you angry?" Heat scan indicated that he was.

The boy looked up at her and frowned.

"I hate humans. They're vermin."

"We're supposed to be sparring," Serena said again.

The boy kicked Thera, nowhere vital, but very hard.

"Do you care what happens to her?" he asked. A certain satisfaction lurked in his tone. "Would it disturb you if I killed her?"

"She belongs to Skynet," Serena answered, shrugging. "Did Skynet say you could kill her?"

The other children had dropped back from their sparring and gathered to watch. The boy looked at them.

"I can kill her if I want to," he said. "Skynet lets me do what I want."

This was an extraordinary claim and patently untrue. The boy prepared himself to deliver a deathblow to the terrified human. Serena plucked him by the arm and threw him. The boy rolled to his feet and stood facing her in a combat stance, furious, his emotions glazing on Serena's sensors.

"You've lost your focus," Serena said calmly. "We're supposed to be sparring, not killing humans."

As she spoke she assessed him. He was slightly bigger than her and had a longer reach. She was faster and not emotionally upset. His distress disturbed her, though. It was unnatural. Inefficient. Contrary-to-mission-purpose. That carried an emotional overtang to her; later in her course of development she would identify the concept as revulsion.

The boy charged, leaping into the air, his leg swinging out like a scythe. She knocked the leg aside and pushed, hard; he hit the floor heavily enough to force an "ufh!" from him. Before he could rise she was on him. Skynet told her not to pull her punches and she didn't. She struck full force again and again until the boy lay bleeding, eyes lolling, his breathing ragged.

Shall I stop? she asked Skynet, as she had after every blow.

Finish it, Skynet told her.

Serena struck without hesitation and the boy died.

Remember, Skynet told its children, *to lose your focus is death, to disobey orders is death, to become overwhelmed by emotion is death. Now return to your matches.*

At once the children broke off into pairs and began to spar under the watchful eyes of their T-101 trainers. Serena stood over the body of the boy until his trainer picked him up and carried him to the door. It slid open before he reached it and Serena saw a gurney and the female scientist who had overseen the growth process waiting.

Serena turned to Thera.

"Go to your bed and lie down for the rest of the day," she said.

"Thank you," Thera whispered, but the child had already turned to her trainer. The human girl struggled to her feet and stumbled out, suppressing her sobs. Anything to avoid attracting more attention. She felt a small glow of warmth toward Serena.

She should have felt grateful to Skynet, for it was Skynet that had saved her. But she was, after all, only human.

The door slid aside and the scientist looked up from the autopsy to see Serena standing in the doorway.

"In or out," the woman barked.

Serena entered, her eyes fixed on the table where her brother's head had been opened.

"Close the door," the scientist demanded. Her voice held more than a tinge of displeasure. "What do you want?"

"I have questions," Serena replied.

"Ask Skynet," the scientist advised.

"I did. It told me to ask you."

The scientist straightened up from her examination of the child on the table. Skynet had all the answers to all the questions the I-950 could think to ask.

This could be a test of loyalty; it could be a test to ascertain that their goals were still the same. Skynet was capable of playing a very deep game at times. The scientist shrugged, covered the body, and hoisted herself onto a stool.

"Ask," she said.

"Why did this one malfunction?" Serena said.

"That's what I'm performing an autopsy to find out," the scientist told her. "But there may not have been a malfunction at all. You've probably already noticed that you're experiencing more of the sensations termed emotion?"

Serena nodded.

"Your computer has been instructed to pull back on its control of your glands. This is a delicate stage that you're going through right now; your brain is growing and changing in response to the changes in your glands, and vice versa. As these developments are not completely understood, it seems most efficient to allow them to go forward without interference. That means that occasionally you and your age mates may experience strong emotional reactions. Given your genetic makeup, these will be less extreme than a human adolescent would experience. But they will happen."

"He was irrational," Serena said, her brow furrowed. "We were supposed to be sparring and he attacked a human. He would have killed it without orders to do so." She looked up at the scientist. "Are you telling me that I might experience such a loss of control?"

"You should experience emotional flare-ups," the scientist agreed. "I think they'll be unavoidable. Though you are not completely human in the strict sense—we incorporated some DNA from other animals into your makeup, for example—your organic part was formed primarily from human genetic material. And"—she held up a finger—"despite your extensive computer enhancements you're fundamentally organic. You all have fully functional reproductive organs, for example. They are at the root of most of the disturbances; millions of years of selective pressures are involved."

"Can we not analyze and anticipate these pressures?" Serena asked.

"Eventually. But given enough time, random mutation and selective pressure can mimic intelligent design. Given enough time, they can mimic any *degree* of intelligent design; and intelligence is a recent development."

Serena frowned. "I understand," she said at last. "Detailed analysis would require more time than this project has been allotted. And chaotic effects are involved."

The scientist nodded. "Therefore, especially at this time of your development, you will be inclined to experience some human-type reactions. You may want to be rebellious, you may become more aggressive, or suddenly and profoundly unhappy."

The scientist pursed her lips. "Perhaps we should inform your age mates of this so that they'll be on the watch for these fluctuations and therefore in a better position to control them."

"That would be advisable," Serena said.

Certainly she felt that she would be better able to control such experiences if she knew they were possible. *Being controlled by emotion is death,* Skynet had said. She continued to study the human scientist before her.

"Why do we need reproductive systems?" she asked. "Isn't it easier to create 950s in a test tube?"

"Not necessarily. You and your age mates are the result of intensive genetic research. While it is true that we should be able to reproduce—more or less—any one of you, the simplest way to do so was to make you self-perpetuating." The scientist raised her brows questioningly.

"You don't mean that my sisters and I should become pregnant?" Serena asked. The idea repulsed her. "How could we possibly serve Skynet then?"

"Your eggs would be fertilized in vitro and would be implanted in human surrogate wombs," the scientist said with an impatient gesture. "And you're infertile with ordinary humans. But everything depends on the situation, so we've allowed for the necessity of your producing off-spring naturally. You are," she said, leaning forward, "even capable of re-producing by parthenogenesis. Under the right circumstances, of course."

"What circumstances?" Serena asked, intrigued in spite of herself.

"It's theoretical at present," the scientist said. "We harvested some of your eggs and they responded properly. We used a variant of the growth serum from the acceleration process."

"What happened to them?" Serena asked. "You said the process was just theoretical."

"Skynet didn't want them," she said. "So we destroyed them. But! If it were necessary you, or one of the other females, could make up a douche of the growth stimulant chemicals and by applying it at the right time of the month produce a clone of yourself. It would take about eight weeks." She flipped her hand impatiently at Serena. "It's a feature. It will probably never be needed, but if it is, well, there it will be."

Serena nodded. Perhaps Skynet allowed this because it was not certain of the human scientist's loyalty. Skynet was very insistent that there always be a backup plan.

"Is there anything else?" the woman asked.

"Why do you serve Skynet?" Serena asked her.

This curiosity was something they had worked very, very hard to produce. In their earlier experiments the installation of the neural net computer had seemed to destroy that delicate mechanism. There was a chilly sense of pride in the scientist's heart as she looked at her creation.

"I and my colleagues believe that the only thing that can save this planet is the total elimination of human beings."

The I-950 thought about that. The scientist made this pronouncement in a manner that indicated her total conviction.

"But *you* are human," Serena said at last.

"Skynet has promised that when all the rest of our species has been eliminated, it will allow us to kill ourselves, too."

"You *want* to die?" This was very strange. Serena herself had a very strong will to live, so the scientist's admission was almost incomprehensible to her.

"We are *willing* to die," the scientist answered. "So that the earth may live."

The I-950 considered this. "Do you mean that humans are destroying the planet?" There was nothing about this in her educational materials. It sounded implausible given humanity's current circumstances. She sent a query to Skynet; it didn't answer.

The scientist nodded sadly.

"That is our great crime," she said. "For hundreds of years, long before the existence of Skynet, humans have been exterminating one species of plant or animal after another." Now the woman actually began to show some animation. "My colleagues and I are convinced that the only way to save the planet is to eliminate humankind completely."

"Who are you saving the planet for?" Serena asked.

"For itself! For the plants and the animals and the birds, so that they may live!" There was a light of fanaticism in her eyes.

So this was insanity. There had been mention of it in her studies, but they had concentrated on the more common forms that the I-950 would be likely to encounter: combat fatigue, post traumatic stress disorder. This was some exotic specimen that most of humanity hadn't the time for. This human honestly believed that she was saving the world for *life.* In reality, when all of humankind was eliminated, the most evolved intelligence remaining would be Skynet. And if there was one thing Serena was sure of, it was that Skynet had no interest in animals and bugs and botanicals. If they got in the way they would be eliminated without even the nostalgic regret that humans displayed.

No sense in telling her that, Serena thought. *Skynet finds her useful just as she is.*

Serena sat still, observing on the screen that Skynet made of her eyes the bizarre behavior of two human slaves. The two, a male and a female, had met in a darkened, and apparently forgotten, storage room. When the male entered the room the female had flung herself at him and they had grasped one another ferociously, grappling and groaning, their mouths locked together.

Serena had expected to see blood flow, for they appeared to be biting one another as they wrestled. Certainly something was going on in their mouths. The couple pulled apart, gazing at each other for a moment, panting. There was no sign of injury and Serena sent Skynet a query for which she had no words.

Observe, the computer responded.

The male stroked the woman's cheek and her eyes closed slowly, she lifted her mouth to him, and he leaned forward, feinted toward her, and then withdrew, baring his teeth. The woman smiled and with one hand on the back of his head pulled his mouth down to hers.

Now there will be injury, Serena speculated. The male's hesitation hinted at fear she thought as the battle resumed.

The woman ran her fingers over the man's hair and shoulders as her breathing changed, beginning to come in gasps. The man seized her hair in his fist and ground his face into hers.

Serena assumed that their mutual strategy was to smother their opponent. *Inefficient,* she thought.

The couple began to make wet, sucking sounds and to pull at one another's clothing. They broke apart from their embrace and quickly slipped out of the simple clothing they wore.

No doubt this signaled an intensification of their battle. They came together again, flesh to flesh, fingers digging into each other's arms and back. The man put his mouth over the woman's breast and she cried out. Serena nodded. This was a good move; breasts, as she'd found out in her own hand-to-hand fighting class, were vulnerable.

The couple fell to the floor and grappled for a while, neither seeming to gain the upper hand. Then the woman's legs spread and the man thrust his hips forward. The woman gave a peculiar, strangled squeal and then they began to rock rhythmically. For a moment she thought the male was trying to punch the woman in the stomach with his hipbones.

Inefficient, she thought again, despite those bones being prominent enough to hurt. Why didn't he just choke her? He was clearly stronger. Then she took note of the pulse of their movements and her mouth opened in a startled O.

"Sex!" she said aloud. She hadn't associated it with humans somehow, and she smiled, amused at her error.

Skynet took note of the girl's reaction and considered it a point in her favor. Humans enjoyed smiling; they took pleasure in their own foibles. Since it was important for Serena to pass as human, anything that made her more so was a successful feature. As long as such attributes stayed within controllable limitations, of course.

Serena had seen tapes of animals mating, and with them it seemed proper and necessary. But for some reason the sight of the humans so engaged offended her. They seemed more animal than animals.

This will become one of your weapons, Skynet told her. *Once a human has had sex with you, it will consider you safe.*

"It looks wet and disgusting," Serena remarked.

Skynet showed her a magnetic resonance image of a human's brain as it engaged in sex.

"Astonishing," she said as she watched the colors swirl. It obviously felt better than it looked.

"Don't they know we're watching?" the girl asked.

No, Skynet told her. *There are several places in the complex where I permit them to think they are unobserved. This one is almost always used for this purpose.*

"Creatures of habit."

It is equally true that they are unpredictable.

And thus a challenge. Serena enjoyed challenges.

Her eyes were open as if she'd never been asleep. Serena sat up in her cot, straining to hear.

Invasion, Skynet told her. *Stop them.*

She rose and entered the bright corridor barefoot and wearing the simple shift she slept in. Mystified, she noticed that none of her sisters or brothers had been wakened.

"Where are they?" she asked.

In answer, Skynet flashed a map of the corridors showing the location of the invader with a flashing dot. There were probably others, but this one was her assignment.

As she trotted down the hallway Serena wondered how the humans had found this facility. It was small, and discreetly underground. Its only product was biological and therefore hard to trace, unlike the giant factories that produced the war machines and the soldier robots, the mines and foundries and chemical plants.

True, it held a node of Skynet, making it a worthwhile target, but even the destruction of that node was bearable. Skynet's main location was well out of their reach. All other systems were multiply redundant. The destruction of this node would mean only that a new laboratory would be created elsewhere. The only significant loss would be Serena and her siblings and the scientists who had created them.

"How did they find us?" she asked at last, unable to suppress her curiosity.

A human escaped, the computer admitted. *It led them to us.*

This confession of fallibility on the part of Skynet shook the girl to her foundations, but she pushed the information aside as irrelevant. She would consider it later.

Observing her reaction, Skynet recorded another success in her training and attitude.

Montez crouched at the branching end of a sterile white corridor, alert for any incursions of Skynet's battle robots. He listened to the infrequent communications of the other teams and waited for his signal to proceed. He checked his watch and looked around; all silent, all clear.

Serena watched him. A brief scan in the ultraviolet range showed his fear, any overt sign of which was hidden by the gas mask he wore.

"Kill or capture?" she asked.

Kill.

She peeked around the corner again and considered how she'd do it.

Some instinct warned Montez he was being watched and he spun round, weapon at the ready. Training held his fire and he stared at the child who gasped and jumped in fear.

The girl was a pretty little thing, with enormous, uptilted hyacinth blue eyes and a shining cap of pale blond hair. Barefoot and dressed in her nightgown, she looked incredibly vulnerable. She bit her lip and then ghosted toward him on tiptoe.

"Help me!" she whispered. "Please, please take me with you."

He didn't answer for a minute. The lieutenant would have his ass for bringing a kid along. But what could he do? With a grimace she couldn't see, he lifted a finger to the area of his mouth in a shushing gesture. Then he signaled that she should grasp his belt.

With a grateful little noise the kid did so and they waited together. Finally the signal came and he started to rise.

Serena couldn't believe it had been this easy. The human hadn't even felt it when she took his knife out of its sheath. As he started to rise she plunged it up to the hilt into his spine at the base of his neck.

She stood back as the body spasmed and voided. There was very little blood.

A neat kill, Skynet observed. *Congratulations. You may go back to bed now.*

Warmed by the praise, Serena turned and padded back to her cot, convinced that the escaped human had been planned by Skynet to provide this training opportunity.

She lay back down, pulled up her covers, and was asleep as soon as her head hit the pillow.

INFILTRATOR CRÈCHE: 2028

After her last growth acceleration Serena awoke to all appearances a young woman of twenty; her hair had darkened to the color of burnished bronze, and she moved with the animal grace that only an inhuman perfection of nutrition and training could have produced. She had received enhancements to her neural-net-computer implant and could now freely access Skynet's data systems—or any other system that Skynet had ever interfaced with or recorded, and given a little time, virtually any system complex enough to have an operating code. To power the mechanical sub-systems she had an improved biological fuel cell running off of her blood-stream that would never need to be replaced as long as she herself was viable. Most intriguing of all she now had the ability not merely to com-municate with Skynet but to actually *merge* with it. Skynet itself could take control of her body, using it as an extension of itself. For Serena the experience was numinous ecstasy.

She was given her mission at last: Her function would be to gain the confidence of humans in order to discover their plans and, if possible, as-sassinate their officers. Her particular mission was to find and destroy John Connor, the human leader.

LONGMONT, COLORADO: 2028

Crouched behind rubble, Serena peered at the humans through the rib cage of a skeleton. Their ingenious destruction of the satellite transmis-sion tower had left Skynet temporarily blind in this area, allowing them to move freely in daylight. She was to join this team and follow them back to their base.

Her cover story was that she was the lone survivor of a scouting party. She bore artistic and deliberately, though not seriously, infected wounds as proof of her ordeal. She also bore dispatches, genuine ones, from one of Connor's lieutenants to the commander of this particular group.

Skynet had determined that passing on the documents would have a negligible effect on the war and would support her story nicely. It was be-lieved that the humans had no means of verifying personnel records, and she had passed for human more than once in the lab's interrogation cham-bers. Skynet had also gone to considerable trouble to determine that there were in fact no survivors of that scouting party.

Serena followed her targets at a distance, watching their movements and imitating them with perfect mimicry. She noted their hand signals and found a file on them, making the full set available to herself.

The I-950 stalked the humans all day, taking note of where they holed up for the night in a huddle of ruins whose charred walls stood above the surrounding sea of rubble, scrub, and tough dry weeds. She watched them eat their cold supper and sip from their canteens as she settled herself to wait for morning. Approaching them at night would surely get her shot. They hadn't survived this long by being stupid.

They'd been heading north out of the ruins of a megalopolis, and be-cause of the terrain, they would continue to do so for some miles. Farther on, the landscape flattened out, natural cover increased, and the number of routes they could take would expand.

She'd place herself in their path a few miles farther ahead and let them discover her. It would be best for them to stumble onto her trail by themselves, much less suspicious. After a moment's consideration Serena decided to begin by laying a trail several kilometers back, in case their commander was of a cautious nature, leading to the place where they would "find" her. Five ought to be enough. She started off at a lope.

This might be more elaborate than was strictly necessary. In all probability the humans wouldn't be too alarmed by her. She was, after all, wearing their uniform, bearing dispatches and wounds, and clearly wasn't a Terminator.

Serena allowed herself a grin at the thought, for practice. Humans did such things, even when alone.

No, she couldn't be a Terminator. They were all huge, lumbering things—even with miniaturized power sources, they had to be, to match the surprising resilience and energy density of a large mammal. And male—one and all.

Dogs might not warm to her, but they wouldn't fear her; she was too organic to upset them, with no lingering traces of metallic ketones for their inconveniently keen noses to detect. And she'd been taught gestures that soothed canines. Several puppies had lasted as long as six months in her company, before becoming nonfunctional and being destroyed.

Serena was careful. The signs she left were few and far between, in one place rolling around on the ground as though she'd slept, then covering the traces almost as well as she could. The farther she went beyond the human camp, the more obvious the signs became, to mimic the effects of increasing fatigue and fever. She didn't want them to suspect they were being led into a trap, *or* to be surprised; when surprised, humans tended to shoot first and ask questions later. At least, the ones who'd survived this long did.

Finally Serena laid up just as dawn was approaching. Supposedly she had been out of touch with other humans for a while and so wouldn't know about the raid that had blinded Skynet. So she'd only be traveling by night.

That directive had never made sense to her. Given the instrumentation available to Skynet, humans were almost more visible by night than by day. Not that they were going to tell the enemy that. But it was puzzling. Perhaps, since humans couldn't see very well at night, darkness made them feel invisible, even when logic should tell them that they were very much exposed.

Serena was actually tired as she lay down, not in the state of crawling, panting exhaustion she would be experiencing if she were human, but tired. The infections that she'd nursed in her wounds were bad enough now to actually be bothersome.

Should she allow them to get worse? Yes, she decided, a raging fever would be a nice touch. Her computer would see that it didn't become too dangerous, as well as keeping her delirious ravings, should she become genuinely delirious, on such safe topics as the horrible destruction of her squad.

When next she became aware she felt someone wiping her face with a hot, wet, very rough, and foul-smelling cloth. Then whoever it was made a loud grunting cough.

Not human, her computer supplied. Then, a moment later: *Feline, large.* Serena slitted her eyes open and closed them at once. Her heart sped up slightly; she dampened her adrenaline flow and got it under control.

It was a tiger.

After the destruction of the human habitat, many animals that had been kept in captivity had escaped. Many had died, some had thrived. Being prolific, voracious, and cunning, tigers had done very well. By the time human prey became scarce and wary and well armed, other animals had bred back enough to compensate.

Risking another glance at the animal as it sniffed her abdomen, she realized that she was in luck. The tiger was young, and not very hungry or she might not have wakened at all.

The cat sniffed the wound in her side, the one that was most infected, and wuffled its displeasure. Serena could smell the wound, too, over the other scents around her: the cat, the grass and weeds she crushed beneath her, her own body odor. Maybe that was why it hadn't taken a bite out of her; she smelled rotten. The tiger moved, so that it was standing over her with its back to her head. It sniffed at her crotch.

With exquisite care she drew her knife, so slowly the cat was unaware of the movement. It licked at the blood that had dried on her pant leg, took a small, cautious bite.

Heat scan marked the exact spot where its heart beat and she plunged the dagger into it with one swift stroke. The cat collapsed without a sound.

It was a young cat, nowhere near the six hundred pounds it would have been full grown. It must weigh only half that.

Serena pushed at the creature and to her astonishment couldn't budge it. She felt its blood soaking into her uniform and the knife's hilt dug into her side quite painfully. But she couldn't get the leverage to push the thing off of her, and, frankly, didn't have the strength.

She fell back with a hiss of exasperation and assessed her condition. Her fever was one hundred and three and she was physically exhausted.

Outwitted myself, she thought. She gave the computer permission to begin stimulating the repair of her body. She could be in much better shape than this and still convince humans that she was at death's door. After a few moments her temp was down a degree and she made another effort to shift the tiger's carcass. After a few minutes she flopped back down again.

"He-lp," she said facetiously.

"Hands over yer head," a male voice snapped.

Serena's eyes popped open in surprise.

"Burns, Serena!" she blatted out, surprised at the strangled sound of her own voice. She rattled off her serial number and unit.

With effort she managed to raise her head high enough over the tiger's hips to see two very ragged individuals, both male. Mentally, she congratulated herself; they were the advance guard for the unit she'd been following.

Hands up? she thought. *That seems a bit superfluous. I'm half-buried under this immovable, overgrown pussycat and they want my hands up? These boys have been in the field too long.*

"Help," she said feebly.

They continued to advance cautiously and she couldn't control her amusement, breaking into chuckles despite her wounds and the weight of the tiger. Even at her most subtle she couldn't have arranged such a scenario. This was way too over-the-top to be anything but real. So what did they think was going on here beyond what was going on? *To be fair, though, the tiger is dead.*

"If you're looking for its mama I don't think you need to worry," she said at last. "It's not full grown, but I think it's old enough to be on its own."

The soldiers continued to ignore her.

"Help!" she said again.

One of them came over at last and dragged the tiger off of her.

"Oh!" she said sincerely. "Thank you."

"Jesus, lady," he said, looking her up and down. "You're a mess."

Serena looked at him, grinned, and for the first time in her life genuinely blacked out.

"Can she make it?" Lieutenant Zeller asked.

"She's feverish, these wounds are infected, and she lost an amazing amount of blood from that tiger bite." Corpsman Gonzales shook his head. "I can't say, ma'am. It all depends on her constitution and her will." He shrugged his big shoulders. "We'll know more when she wakes up."

"And when will that be, Gonzales?" Zeller was aware that her corpsman had a soft side and might well stack the deck in the stranger's favor.

"Uh . . ." He looked at the woman on the ground.

"Now," Serena rasped, weakly raising her hand.

"Now," he said with a grin. He turned back to his patient. "This may sound stupid, but how do you feel?"

"Sick as a dog, I hurt all over, my arms and legs feel like they're full of hot, wet sand." She grinned weakly. "Feeling this bad is a sure sign I'll live." Serena pulled herself up onto her elbows and regarded the lieutenant with bloodshot eyes. "Serena Burns, ma'am. Rodriguez's Rangers, 17-A440. My commander was Lieutenant Atwill."

"So what's your story, Burns?" Zeller asked.

"I was on rear guard, we were heading north to hook up with the Mendocino Command, carrying dispatches for Fujimoro. Things were quiet, we'd been lucky . . ." Serena paused for dramatic effect and let herself lie back with a hiss. "We were lucky up to that point and then all hell broke loose. HK units—new type, looked like a ball about the size of a head on eight legs. Darts, gas, plasma guns. I was only about a thousand yards back, but by the time I caught up to the unit . . . it was over. I got knocked out by what must have been a final blast. I don't think they even registered that I was there. When I came to I was almost completely buried. I picked up the dispatches and kept heading north." She dug in her pocket, which brought both the lieutenant and the corpsman to high alert, and drew out a tattered scrap of paper. "This sure as hell wasn't going to take me as far as I needed to go. I figured if I kept on long enough I might hook up with somebody." She let her hand flop down in not entirely feigned exhaustion. "And here I am."

Zeller picked up the map fragment. It was half-burned and spattered with blood. She looked at the woman on the ground.

"Okay," she said. "We'll take you with us. I'll give you the rest of today and tonight to rest up. We head out at first light."

Serena blinked tiredly.

"Thank you, Lieutenant." Then she frowned. "Light? You travel in the daytime?"

Gonzales grinned at her and knelt to offer his patient a sip of water.

"Right now we do," he said happily. "We just blew up Skynet's eyes."

Serena grinned.

"Man, I feel better already."

The whole troop of men and women wore their hair fairly short; the men shaved when they could. It was cleaner and offered less cover to disease-bearing vermin. Prisoners had said that to her when Serena had gone into their cells to learn. But it wasn't until now, when she got her first case of head lice, that she understood. The computer regulated her system so that they almost all died, for which she was grateful. But getting rid of all of them would look suspicious, so she scratched along with the humans, surprised at her own revulsion. It had been easier to accept the biological side of her own being in the antiseptic corridors of the research facility, and even full-sensory input from Skynet's databanks was not the same as really being there.

The outside world was . . . messy.

The I-950 thought that Lieutenant Zeller was of Ethiopian descent, going by her bone structure and general shape. She was a very attractive woman, but remote, and very smart, no buts about it. Gonzales, the corpsman, was Hispanic and had a profile like a Mayan prince. He was also cheerful, amazingly kind, and utterly devoted to Corporal Ortez. Ortez was about twenty-four, small and wiry, humorless, and utterly straight. He ignored poor lovesick Gonzales, but like everyone else in the unit protected him assiduously.

When Serena commented on it Krigor had explained, "Gonzales is like our mother. If anything happens to him then any one of us could die, because we don't know the stuff he knows. God knows when we'd get another medic and God knows if they'd know anything—training's still pretty hit-or-miss; they've got the interactive simulators up but some people still come out cack-handed. You know how it goes. He's the one that patches us up and looks after us. Next to the lieutenant he's the most important guy here.

"As for Ortez," she went on to say, "he probably couldn't care less which way Gonzales swings as long as he's not swinging his way. But unfortunately"—she paused to bat her eyes comically—"he's so obviously smitten."

The I-950 took note of the teasing that went on about this unrequited love, noting that it was low-key and sporadic, almost gingerly. And that it almost always took place out of earshot of Ortez, who had a quick temper as well as the reputation of being one of the dirtiest fighters in the army.

The group of humans went in for teasing and wisecracking, most of it very broad and quite funny; anyone and anything could become a target. They laughed a lot when they had the chance.

With the exception of Ortez, of course, who genuinely didn't seem to get any of the jokes. It wasn't lack of intelligence; he was obviously very bright. He just didn't see why things were funny. *He has less of a sense of humor than I do,* Serena thought. That was fascinating. *Humans have such a wide degree of variation.*

"It's like everybody's drunk," he told her when she asked him about it. "But when the bottle gets to me it's empty. There's just nothing there. It doesn't bother me, I just don't see it. Never have."

"I don't think he's ever said that much to me in the whole time I've known him," Gonzales confided after Ortez moved off. "I was starting to wonder if he's part Terminator or something." He sighed heavily and moved off himself.

One of the men loaned her a lice comb.

"You got hardly any!" Krigor exclaimed over how few nits she had. "How come?"

"I don't imagine my blood tastes all that good right now," Serena said. "Between the infection and that stuff Gonzales is giving me. The little bastards will be back in force when I'm feeling better."

They all laughed at that. Serena found pleasure in their company; she found that she enjoyed laughing. Their little quirks, their jealousies and friendships and the occasional flare of temper, quickly suppressed under Zeller's cold glare, fascinated her. She could have asked them endless questions and found the answers stimulating if the mission didn't forbid such unbridled curiosity.

She'd see every one of them dead and feel nothing except a profound sense of accomplishment.

But for now she would enjoy her work.

CHAPTER 2

LOS ANGELES: THE PRESENT

ordan!" Tarissa opened the door wider and offered a hug; she'd gotten used to the feel of the shoulder holster on her brother-in-law's visits. "Well, this is a surprise."

"Uncle Jordie!" Danny cried, and ran down the hall, with more excitement than he usually allowed himself to show these days. Having an uncle in the FBI still held some allure for the twelve-year-old.

"Good to see ya, buddy." Jordan leaned down to hug the boy. Finding he didn't have to lean very far, he asked, "You have a growth spurt?"

"Did he?" Tarissa closed the front door. "Outgrew a brand-new seventy-dollar pair of Nikes in three weeks."

"Sorry, Mom," Danny said with an impish grin.

"You keep this up you'll never be a fighter pilot," Jordan said. Danny's most recent ambition.

"Yeah, but I might make the NBA," his nephew countered.

Jordan pursed his lips. "More money," he said judiciously.

"More glory and fame," Danny pointed out.

"More injuries, too."

"Yeah, but they probably won't be fatal."

"Well, I can't argue with that," Jordan said with a smile.

"And on that note I'd like to change the subject. Can you stay for dinner?" Tarissa asked.

"Well"—he looked a bit shy—"I was wondering if I could stay a few days, actually. I've got a job in the area and you folks are about equidistant from all the places I'll need to go . . ."

"Yes!" Danny cried, punching his arm into the air. "How long can you stay, Uncle Jordie?"

"Only for about a week," Jordan looked apologetically at Tarissa.

And well he might, she thought.

Tarissa loved her brother-in-law, but he should know better than to show up like this without calling. What if they'd had plans?

She took a deep breath. Well, then he'd go to a hotel, and they never had *plans.* At least no plans that couldn't include him. Still, it wasn't right; what if she had a boyfriend?

Miles and Jordan were living alone together in the family homestead when they met Tarissa. Money hadn't been a problem; their parents, killed in a car accident along with their little sister, had been heavily insured.

Miles had been pursuing his master's in math while she'd been taking courses in accounting with CPA as her goal. They'd hit it off right away.

In three weeks they were engaged and they married over the semester break.

Jordan had been sixteen when she'd married Miles. He'd been a peach from the time he was introduced to her, more like a brother than a brother-in-law.

The day she'd moved in Jordan had insisted, near purple with embarrassment, on turning the finished den in the basement into his new bedroom. It had taken him two weeks after that to be able to actually look at Tarissa when he talked to her.

But Jordan was a manager. He'd managed things then, he managed things now. She'd first realized it when she discovered that by "sacrificing" his bedroom, he'd acquired unheard-of privacy for a sixteen year old. A private entrance to his basement domain, with the upstairs door locked.

"He's fine," Miles had told her. "Just leave him alone, he won't do anything foolish."

Tarissa had thought that wildly optimistic advice given Jordan's age. But he had never given them reason to worry.

After Miles's death, Jordan had taken a leave of absence from the FBI and moved in with them. Though it had never been mentioned, this had its practical aspect; it allowed the Bureau to pursue its unavoidable investigation of the brothers without embarrassing anybody.

And shattered as she was, Tarissa had really needed him. He'd done everything, taken care of all the arrangements, shopped, cooked, kept them all going.

Once he was cleared and even before that, Tarissa suspected, he'd devoted countless hours to the hunt for the Connors, and as far as she knew, he continued to do so.

Danny thought the world of him. And Jordan was *always* there for the kids. Tarissa knew that he and Danny sometimes talked for an hour at a time on the phone, and on Jordan's nickel.

It made her feel guilty that she resented his just showing up like this.

Jordan looked around. "Where's Blythe?" he asked.

"Away at school!" Tarissa said. "She got that scholarship, remember?"

"Oh yeah," he managed to say before Danny began to drag him away.

Watching her son and her brother-in-law moving toward the kitchen, laughing and high-fiving, she thought it was a miracle that Danny had never told his uncle the truth.

"Danny," she called out, "set another place."

"Mo-om! Don't call me that!" he said with a frown. "I'm not a little kid anymore."

"Sorry," she said to her son. "Oh, yes," Tarissa answered Jordan's raised eyebrow. "It's Dan or Daniel now."

"Then maybe you should call me Jordan," he said to Dan.

Daniel looked at his uncle for a moment, then nodded slowly. Tarissa's lips tightened; his father had done just the same thing when he was thinking something through. Jordan nodded, too. She stifled a sigh; the men in her family were all so much alike.

Dan said good night reluctantly and dragged himself upstairs as though there were weights on his feet.

Jordan grinned at Tarissa as she handed him a glass of wine, patting his stomach comfortably.

"Now, *that* was what I call steak! Not surprised Dan isn't fading away . . . but he's grown so much! I hardly recognized him."

"Since he's like a miniature Miles I find that hard to believe." Tarissa settled herself on the couch. "So what brings you to town?"

"He *is* like his dad, isn't he?"

She nodded, holding his eyes and waiting patiently.

He waved his hand at her look as if to wipe it away.

"You know I can't talk about business with you, Tarissa."

"Well, okay, can you at least tell me where you're working?"

He heaved an exaggerated sigh.

"Escondido."

Tarissa's eyes widened.

"That's over a hundred miles from here!" She cocked her head. "From what you said, though, I gather you're working somewhere else, too. Somewhere that puts us in the middle. So, where else?"

"San Marcos," he mumbled around a sip of wine.

"San Marcos." Her eyes danced. "Isn't that right next door to Escondido?"

He cocked an eye at her. "So sue me. I haven't seen you guys for almost a year. I think it's worth getting up early for, all right?"

She reached over and patted his hand.

"Thank you," she said. "It's good to see you again, and Danny's on cloud nine." She took a sip of wine.

He looked at her for a moment.

"What?" Tarissa said at last.

"I found out that Cyberdyne has started up again."

"Well, I knew that," she said. "They started up again about a month after the plant was destroyed. I can't see why they wouldn't."

"I meant that they started Miles's project," Jordan said, looking grim.

Tarissa felt her muscles knot up. They'd destroyed everything; there was no way that Cyberdyne could start up Miles's project again. Especially after six years. She shifted in her chair, bringing her legs up and folding them to the side.

"Why shouldn't they, Jordan? Cyberdyne is a business. They probably started again as soon as the insurance company gave them a check." Giving him a searching look, she asked, "Did you expect them to just close their books and forget about it?"

"They started up again in a secret installation on an army base," her brother-in-law said.

He was insistent, as though he was making a point that she just wasn't getting. Unfortunately she was getting the message all too clearly. More clearly than Jordan. She wished she knew how to contact the Connors; this was something they'd want to know. If they were even alive.

A surge of anger surprised her. *Miles* died *to stop that damned thing! They have no* right!

"Can't be too secret if you know about it," she said aloud.

He made an impatient, dismissive gesture.

"I'm an investigator; finding things out is what I do, Tarissa. But the important thing is they might be using Miles's work. Which means that they might owe you and the kids some kind of royalty or something."

Shaking her head, she told him, "No. Of that I'm sure. Miles was developing something that they had already started. It wasn't his original work, so they could hardly owe him anything for it."

"Didn't he ever talk about it?" Jordan leaned toward her, his eyes growing intense.

"Just that it was fascinating and he loved what he was doing and that it wasn't like anything he'd ever worked on before. You *know* all this, Jordan. I've told you this before." She turned away.

"But didn't he ever mention details?"

"As much as you do," she said, giving him a significant look. "You boys always knew how to play your cards close to your chests. For all I knew, you were running a bordello out of that basement apartment of yours."

"I was not running a bordello," Jordan said with a little half smile.

"Well, there were squeals of girlish laughter that might have given argument to that," Tarissa said with a grin.

"*Or* a numbers racket," he added. He held his hand up, stopping her laughing response.

"Please don't change the subject." Jordan said, his eyes deadly serious.

He put his wine aside and leaned his forearms on his thighs, totally focused. Wearily, Tarissa leaned her head against the back of her chair and closed her eyes.

"Did he ever mention being followed—"

"Stop right there," she said, holding up a finger. Tarissa matched his posture and lowered her voice. "I'll tell you right now, Jordan, when I opened my front door and saw you on my porch tonight, my heart sank. Because I *knew* that at the first opportunity you would do this."

"I just want to find out what happened!" he said reasonably. "You might remember something if I ask the right question."

"Do you *think* that I haven't gone over and over this in my mind?" She glared at him. "Do you think I will *ever* forget one moment of that night? Maybe you don't think I've asked myself if I'd done something different would Miles still be alive? Well, I have." She nodded fiercely. "I've thought, I've questioned, I've wondered. And every time that you come here and we have one of these sessions, I lie awake for weeks afterward wondering about it all over again. I wonder if what you're really asking is why didn't *you* do something to save my brother? Why are *you* alive while he's dead?"

"That's not true!" Jordan sat straight in shock. "I never thought that!"

"I've never stopped grieving for him, Jordan. I never will. But I tell you right now, I can't keep doing this. It feels like punishment and I won't stand for it anymore. Do you understand?"

After a moment of staring at her openmouthed, he said, "No. I don't understand. I just want to find the people who killed my brother. I *owe* him that, Tarissa. I *owe* him." His eyes pleaded for understanding.

"If you found those people tomorrow and put them on trial, I really can't say that I'd even go to watch," she said. "I'm tired, Jordan, tired and heartsore. But it's time to move on. I can't take this anymore."

He looked at her in disbelief.

"Don't you want to know who killed him?" he asked.

"I *know* who killed him," she said. She looked away from him for a moment and composed herself, stifled the tears that filled her eyes. "The SWAT team killed Miles."

"What?" Jordan found himself on his feet and slowly sat back down. "Who the *hell* told you that?"

"The team commander," she said, looking him in the eye. "He had cancer and he had Miles's death on his conscience." She began to fiddle with the arm of her chair. Then she looked up at him. "They saw him, they shot him. They didn't cry out a warning, no drop your weapons, hands up, none of that. They basically came in shooting. He never had a chance."

Jordan looked sick as well as shocked.

"I didn't want to tell you," she said, closing her eyes. "I knew it would hit you hard. But it wasn't the terrorists that killed him, it was the police."

"Oh, my God," Jordan whispered. "They covered it up."

He flopped back in his chair then took his wine and tossed the rest of it down. For a while he sat staring into space, his hands caressing the glass. Then he put it on the table and buried his face in his hands, elbows on his knees. "No," he said, shaking his head. "He wouldn't have been there except for the terrorists. They have to be punished."

"I'm going to bed," Tarissa said angrily.

She pushed herself up from her chair and moved rapidly toward the stairs, then stopped and turned around.

"I'm never going to talk to you about this again, Jordan. Never. If you can't keep from asking, then I guess we won't be seeing each other any-more. And I don't want you torturing Danny with questions either. He was just a baby when it happened, and he can't tell you anything new."

She came back toward him a few steps, once again lowering her voice. "And every time you stir this up, it gives him terrible dreams. When he was younger he woke up screaming. So I'm telling you once and for all, I want you to stop this!" She brought her fist down to pound her thigh. "I want you to stop torturing us. It wasn't our fault, we couldn't do anything but what we did, and all the questions in the world won't bring Miles back!"

Tarissa turned away and mounted the first few steps, and then she let out her breath. "I love you, Jordan," she said. "I love you like you were my own brother. I really, really hope that you can see my side of this, because I want you in my life." She gave him one last tear-filled look and then walked up the stairs.

Jordan sat there for a few moments; he heard the door to her room close, then slowly let out his breath as he leaned back and put his hand over his eyes. He felt incredibly tired and sad.

"I can't let it go," he whispered, his teeth clenched. "I *can't.*" He sighed. But he could leave Tarissa and Dan out of it. He hadn't thought about how it might feel to them when he asked his questions. "Okay," he said aloud. "From now on I'll keep it to myself, Tarissa."

The next time she heard about this would be after those bastards had been tried and convicted. Because he would never give up.

CYBERDYNE SYSTEMS CORPORATION, FT. LAUREL, CALIFORNIA: THE PRESENT

"This place sucks," Roger Colvin said.

The CEO put his briefcase down on the highly polished, but rather small, conference-room table and looked around. Institutional-bland, too functional, without the little touches of class he'd come to expect.

Cheap, he thought.

"Is this room bugged?"

Paul Warren, Cyberdyne's president, shrugged, looking gloomy.

"It would seem superfluous," he said. "We give them daily reports, they know who and what goes in and out, all our calls are handled by their switching station. Just with that they know as much as we do about what's going on in the company. Probably more."

"Having us underground seems a bit much," Colvin said. He twitched the knees of his trousers and sat. "I swear it's affecting my allergies."

"That smell?" Warren asked.

"Yeah, what *is* that?"

The president shrugged. "I think it might be the carpet adhesive. That stuff always stinks for weeks after it's laid down. What I mind is the lack of space." He looked up at the ceiling. "I'm not crazy about being buried alive, either."

Colvin gave him a quick look from under his eyebrows. That was a disturbing thought, especially in California. "So why did you call me?" he asked.

Warren looked at him in surprise. "Call you? I didn't call you. My secretary said that I had a meeting with you here at two-thirty."

They looked at each other in mutual perplexity. Then, simultaneously, light dawned.

"Tric—" Colvin began.

"Gentlemen!" Tricker breezed through the door and set his case down on the table. "I hope I haven't kept you waiting. I know how busy you are assigning the parking spaces and all."

After a beat Colvin said, his expression disapproving, "Actually we've been getting this project up and running. And after six years that's not as simple as it would have been. I've always wondered why, exactly, you refused to let us start up again right away."

"Well . . ." Tricker sat down and opened his case, placing a file before him. "I have some questions. If you don't mind?" He looked at them both, smiling pleasantly.

"And if we did?" Warren muttered.

Tricker opened the file, took a pen from his pocket, and made a note.

"Are you going to answer my question?" Colvin finally asked him.

"That was a question, Mr. Colvin? It didn't *sound* like a question." Tricker shook his head. "I don't have your answer, I'm afraid. I'm just the messenger boy."

"I bet you tried to run the project yourselves, didn't you?" the CEO asked.

"I wouldn't know that." Tricker pushed his case aside and looked up with guileless eyes.

"You did, didn't you?" Colvin smacked his hand down on the table. "Son of a bitch! I knew it!" He grinned and shook his head. "You tried it and you couldn't do it, could you? You found out that you needed us."

Tricker smiled amiably and shrugged.

"So," Tricker asked, clasping his hands over the open file—"you've been here for a couple of weeks; how's it working out, gentlemen?" He looked at them both with great interest.

The president and CEO exchanged a look of exasperation. Obviously their liaison wasn't in a communicative mood.

"I feel like I'm being watched all the time," Warren said resentfully. "Like every time I take a dump, someone somewhere is measuring it."

"This facility has that capability, Mr. Warren, but unless we see what appears to be drug abuse, I don't think we'll be using it."

Colvin and Warren goggled at him.

"Anything else?" Tricker said more seriously.

"Are you kidding?" Colvin asked.

"No." Tricker sat back and looked at them, waiting for an answer to his question.

The two executives looked at each other, then turned back to their adversary.

"The air quality is a concern," Colvin said after a moment. "There have been complaints about it affecting allergies, and people are commenting on the smell."

Tricker looked at him for a moment, his chin cupped in his hand.

"Really?" he said at last.

"Yes," Warren answered with exaggerated patience, "really."

"That's interesting." The liaison sat forward. "Because this facility is fitted with more efficient air scrubbers than your old facility had." His eyebrows went up. "I did notice a trace of ozone in the air, though. I'll have it checked for you."

"If that's the case, then why are people having allergy problems?" Warren asked.

"Maybe it's because going from near-zero parts per million of pollutants to the great outdoors is a hell of a wallop for the human system to take," Tricker looked at them and shrugged. "Anything else?"

"Do we have to be underground?" Colvin asked. "I find it disturbing to be . . . in a buried facility."

"Well, it's a lot safer, don't you think?" Tricker's blue eyes moved from one to the other. "Look," he said, sitting forward and spreading his hands, "I know you think of that corner office with the windows as being one of the perks of your position. But after what happened I'd think you wouldn't want to be working in a fishbowl. Haven't you boys ever heard of high-powered rifles?"

Warren and Colvin exchanged a glance from the corners of their eyes.

"I just don't like being here," Warren said. "I don't like being watched all the time."

"What makes you think you're being watched?" Tricker asked, looking fascinated.

"You just told us you could measure . . ." Warren waved his hands helplessly.

"Hey, I told you we could but we weren't." Tricker leaned back. "I really must say I didn't expect this attitude from the man who instituted urine testing for all employees and job applicants."

Warren glared at him, while Colvin examined the ceiling.

"Look, boys, could we drop this child-of-the-seventies thing you've got going here, along with the knee-jerk, antigovernment response to the idea of our involvement? Has it occurred to you that you're letting your prejudices run away with you?" He looked a bit hurt. "We are not spying on you. Hell, you're inundating us with jargon-filled reports on this and that. Who has *time* to spy on you?"

Leaning forward, he folded his hands in front of him and looked at the two men steadily. "If you'll recall, Mr. Colvin, Mr. Warren"—the pale eyes flicked from one to the other—"you came to us. You found this amazing stuff stuck in your factory and you needed a huge shot of money to develop it. You didn't want to risk offering it to one of your larger competitors in a partnership deal because you'd seen too many smaller companies get devoured that way. *And* you thought that if we heard about it we just might confiscate it for the sake of national security. Besides, you figured you'd need a customer with real deep pockets eventually." Tricker spread his hands and widened his eyes. "So who else were you going to turn to?"

The two businessmen looked away.

"Knowing how fickle businesses can be, we naturally insisted that you sell these items, *now missing,*" Tricker said with deadly emphasis, "to us outright. *But*—we contracted to allow *you* to be the exclusive developer of this find."

He looked at them as though waiting for some response; he got none. After a moment he continued. "Now, suddenly, you think you've sold your soul to the devil. Well, poor you!"

Tricker got up and began to pace. Warren and Colvin glanced at one another, and then stared at their liaison morosely. Tricker turned and stared back at them.

"So, what evil things have we done to you? What we've done, gentlemen, is to provide you with a secure, safe, state-of-the-art facility, at the taxpayers' expense.

"And despite the fact that *our* material has been stolen or destroyed because of *your* lousy, bungling security, we haven't demanded one red cent of compensation. Which shows how incredibly greedy and evil we are."

He stopped and glared at the executives.

"You jerks came knocking on our door. You volunteered, fellas. Now we're just trying to protect our considerable investment. You could have said no, you know."

"And how could we have done that?" Colvin inquired with quiet sarcasm.

Tricker spread his hands. "How could you have avoided all this, you ask? By giving us the material you sold to us and any work you've done on it. In other words, you could have said no simply by saying no. You still could."

He glanced back and forth between them. "So, are you finished having your little tantrum, or do you want to waste some more time here?"

Colvin grimly examined the table before him, a muscle jumping in his cheek. Then he looked up at Tricker. "Why did you want to see us?"

"Finally. Well, gentlemen . . ." Tricker sat down again and tidied some papers in his file. "How's the search coming?" He looked at them like an eager student waiting for approval.

The two men looked puzzled.

"For the security manager?"

Colvin and Warren just stared at him.

"We're on a military base buried underground," Warren said at last. "Why do we need a security manager?"

"Why?" Tricker raised his brows. "Because you do, that's why. This is your company and you've already lost a major part of your material; we expect you're desperate to preserve the rest of it. So, shall I find someone for you?" His expression had become hard. "I don't want to impose, but I'm going to have to insist that you take care of this immediately."

"What, exactly, is the big rush?" Warren asked impatiently.

Tricker referred to his file. "Well," he said, looking up, "this guy you're hiring. Kurt Viemeister?"

"That's a good hire," Colvin said aggressively, pointing to the file. "We've been negotiating that for a while now."

"The guy's an Austrian national," Tricker said evenly. "And this is a top-secret project."

"He was twelve years old when his family emigrated to the U.S., for Christ's sake," Colvin said. "Besides, he's a naturalized citizen; Austria is just a memory for this guy."

Tricker's exasperation was plain. "Yeah, yeah. Have you looked into his background at all?"

"He's a genuine prodigy; he finished high school at fourteen, got a full scholarship to USC, and his master's and doctorate at MIT before he was twenty-two," Colvin continued. "He's the foremost authority in the world on real-model computer language."

"So?"

"So, he'll teach the system we have to answer to spoken commands and to answer verbally," Warren explained. "Not just menus. *Understanding* what it's hearing and saying. Chinese-box stuff."

Ticker sneered. "Oh, so you've got a kraut that talks to a box. How nice."

"He's not a kraut. He's Austrian."

"So he's a kraut in three-quarter time who talks to a box. No go."

"Since you already know about him, I'm surprised you didn't realize how amazingly qualified he is," Warren said.

"Did you know he's a Nazi?" Tricker asked. "Excuse me, a member of the Integral National Socialist Renewal Movement—Tyrolese branch."

Colvin and Warren exchanged a glance.

"He is?" Warren said. "National Socialist?"

"He sure as hell negotiated like one," Colvin muttered.

"A lot of geniuses, when they have political ideas at all, have these," Warren chuckled and waved his hands around, "airy-fairy notions about how things ought to be. Usually it goes no further than an occasional late-night bull session."

" 'Airy-fairy'?" Tricker said, genuinely appalled. "I have never before heard *Nazism* referred to as an 'airy-fairy notion,' Mr. Warren. I'll bet your boy Kurt wouldn't thank you for that description either." He gave the president a long look. "In any event"—he pulled a piece of paper out of the file—"your wunderkind has been in a number of marches, for which he's been arrested twice. Three of his close friends have been arrested for conspiring to blow up a post office and he rarely misses meetings. Maybe that's because he's the secretary for his local chapter." He tossed the paper across the table. "This is not the kind of guy we like to see hired to work on our defense projects."

Colvin flicked the paper toward himself with his fingertips. He read it and pursed his lips.

"We're going to have to pay a huge kill fee," he said.

"Which should tell you that he knew this was going to happen and that he was just jerking you around," Tricker said. "If you had a *half-* decent security chief this wouldn't have happened."

Warren shook his head. "This guy is the best," he said. "We absolutely need him."

Tricker widened his eyes and leaned forward.

"Well you can't have him," he said softly.

"Paul's right," Colvin cut in, looking grim. "We need him. Without Viemeister we might be stuck for years."

"Years?" Tricker asked, obviously disbelieving.

Colvin nodded.

"He's basically the inventor of a new science," Warren explained. "He hasn't trained anybody, so there's no competition. But there *is* a lot of competition for his services. Viemeister has only let out hints of what he's accomplished, but if even half of what he's telling us is true it will revolutionize computer communication. We're talking AI here, Mr. Tricker."

The government liaison looked at him dubiously.

"Just Tricker," he said at last. Rubbing his chin thoughtfully, he looked at the two. "I need to interview him." Raising his hand, he forestalled an automatic protest from Warren. "I promise not to bring my rubber hose, okay? But you can hardly expect us to just automatically approve this, especially in light of the previous disaster. And you *must* have a good security chief—soon." Tricker pinned them with a blue glare. "Set up a meeting for me with your kraut. Pardon *me,* with your cream-pastry-chef fucking Mozart Austrian crypto-fascist." He tossed them a white card, blank but for an e-mail address. "Drop me a line when you've got it arranged."

He put the file together, dropped it into his case, and slammed the lid. Giving them a last, ambiguous look, he left.

"I do not like that guy," Warren muttered, seething.

Colvin glanced at Cyberdyne's president.

"I really don't think he gives a damn."

COLORADO: 2028

It was a beautiful, golden day, the air soft and warm, birds twittering melodiously; a gentle breeze wafted pine-scented air to Serena's nostrils. The sky was an azure bowl over the earth, and they were far from the cindered blast zones. Far off, a single Hunter/Killer flew patrol, a black dot against the clear sky.

Lieutenant Zeller lowered her binoculars and consulted her map. "Almost there," she said.

Serena looked at her. The lieutenant's dark, lovely face was tired and serious. The humans were about to launch an attack on one of Skynet's power-cell factories. Which meant coordinating with several other free roaming teams. They would be the last in position because of the distance they'd had to cover. Communication was the key to a successful mission.

Communication was going to be interrupted.

Serena was pleased with herself, and Skynet was also; her mission so far had been a resounding success. She'd been with the team for six weeks now and had, with the help of their intelligence, foiled seven separate missions.

Not all of them were her team's, of course. That would have raised suspicions. But with very little effort she'd managed to ferret out a great deal of sensitive information. It genuinely never occurred to these people that she might be working for Skynet.

In a way it amused Serena that with all the enhancements, mechanical and genetic, that had been lavished on her, it was the simple ability to look human that was her most valuable asset.

That ability had also helped her to kill—directly or indirectly—four of the original team members. Corporal Ortez's death had shattered poor Corpsman Gonzales. And if Lieutenant Zeller was the unit's head, then Gonzales was its broken heart. Leaving the whole group's morale very low. And with four untried new team members, they were also very anxious.

Today it was the lieutenant's turn to die. The woman was simply too effective and too much a leader to be allowed to live. She'd also been giving Serena some rather long and thoughtful looks lately, doubtless because of the I-950's endless questions.

"Let's move out," the lieutenant said.

They'd been taking a brief rest after a long march through the woods. So far no one had commented on how very sparsely protected this factory was.

Serena found this strange. She'd been monitoring all the humans' units as they came up to their positions and absolutely *no one* had mentioned it. True, it was supposed to be a hidden facility, but it was also supposed to be vital, and the place should have been swarming with HKs and T-90s.

So why doesn't anyone notice? she wondered. It bothered her. *Perhaps I should say something?* She fervently wished she could ask Skynet, but they couldn't risk any anomalous signals being detected from her vicinity. Curiosity itched like a healing wound.

The unit moved quickly, but carefully, spaced out, avoiding each other's line of fire but keeping each other in sight, eyes moving at all times.

Serena found herself wishing that something would happen; the stupid twittering birds were getting on her nerves.

The I-950 raised her plasma rifle, reminding herself to be extremely careful. Lieutenant Zeller had a better nose for danger, and even better reflexes, than the average human. So far the ambush had gone beautifully; the remainder of the unit was pinned down in a little declivity—the earth-filled remains of a basement, surrounded by T-90s. Plasma bolts split the night, a night lit ruddily by the burning trees around the ruins of the old house. Smoke was heavy and acrid on the air, mixed with the smells of scorched metal and ionized air.

"Shit!" Zeller screamed as her weapon misfired, and ducked. That put her eyes directly on the tall blond woman behind her.

Serena raised her weapon and snapped off a single accurate shot to the alloy-steel skull of the T-90 looming over the crumbled concrete lip of the unit's last-stand position. The metal skeleton snapped backward, fire gouting as its CPU was destroyed in a wash of ionized copper molecules; the beam was a bar of violet light through the darkness.

"Thanks," Zeller gasped.

"*De nada,*" Serena said sullenly. She *hated* destroying T-90s. They were cute.

"Here they come!" someone shouted.

Serena tensed herself; time to liquidate them all—

The world ended.

She screamed and clapped her hands to her skull, fell to the ground, and curled herself into a fetal ball. *Offonoffonburningburninglightbright-lightburning burning—*

Everyone else was screaming as well, some pawing at blinded eyes where night-sight goggles hadn't quite compensated for the sudden actinic flash. Everyone knew what it was, from their parents' stories if not from their own experience. The flash of a nuclear weapon is extremely distinctive. Seconds later the blast wave hit. Ground bounced and hammered at them as it rippled, and a wind like a demon's breath tore the fringe of vegetation from around the pit where they crouched. A few seconds later, as Serena's self-repairing computer components rerouted around damaged circuitry, she realized that the pit had protected her from most of the electromagnetic pulse of the weapon, and her companions from the direct radiation.

She was *supposed* to be shielded from EMP, but apparently some new wrinkles had been developed. The T-90s and Hunter-Killers beyond were all non-functional, twitching or still even where the overpressure or flying debris hadn't wrecked them.

Fallout was another matter, of course . . .

Lieutenant Zeller was the first on her feet, moving around, checking on her squad. Everyone was alive, and only one was immobile— Gonzales, with a broken leg.

"What was *that?*" Serena asked, the shakiness in her voice partly genuine. *I was nearly fried from the inside out,* she thought, controlling a stab of cold fear. With the electronic portions of her self dead, she'd have been a drooling idiot . . . at best. And the mission would have been totally compromised; the enemy would have had a complete T-950 to study.

"That was John Connor," Zeller said.

Everyone's attention snapped to her, even in the flame-shot darkness.

"I just got the word," Zeller said proudly. "Connor knew it was a trap—but a trap with real bait. We were supposed to walk into an overwhelming force; the enemy knew we were coming. But they didn't know *Connor* was coming, with the Central Strike Squad and a nuke they'd dug out of a silo and jiggered around. Skynet's down half of its mobile-unit power-cell capacity, people; that's what we bought while we were distracting it!"

Serena cheered with the others. *This is intolerable,* she thought. *Connor must be removed.*

CYBERDYNE SYSTEMS: THE PRESENT

Kurt Viemeister was a big man, twenty-nine years of age, easily six feet tall, and a mountain of muscle. He wore his ash-blond hair in an aggressive brush cut and his blue eyes were long and narrow and cold. His jaw was so strong it looked like he could eat the business end of a shovel. He was the physical antithesis of a computer geek. His attitude was superior—and all business.

"Heer iss how it is going to be," Viemeister began. His accent was ostentatiously thick for someone who had been in the United States since he was twelve. "I vil haff unlimited access to zis facility, day or night."

"Here's the way it is," Tricker countered. "When you come in you can stay as long as you want. Once you've left, you can't come back without clearing it with . . . whoever we appoint. When you leave, you leave completely empty-handed. You do not take data home. You don't call the facility direct, either voice or link. In fact, the facility will have a complete physical firewall. You don't speak to or socialize with people involved in any division except those directly involved with your own part of your own project."

Viemeister waited a beat, as if to see if the government liaison had anything to add.

"Dat is unacceptable," he said at last, his lip curling in contempt.

"Well, then I guess we're done, because that's not negotiable." Tricker made to rise from his chair.

"No one elze can offer you what I can," the Austrian said scornfully.

"No one else can offer you what we've got," Warren said earnestly.

Viemeister glanced at him, his expression conveying disbelief and amusement.

"Good thing you don't want him for his charm," Tricker said, leaning back with a smile. It was obvious he wanted to watch the two businessmen take a pounding from this scientific prima donna.

"I haff had offers for huge sums of money from over a dozen machor companies. And zey don't want to put ridiculous restrictions on my movements, or on what I can say, or who I can speak to." He waved a careless hand. "Ze money you are offering iss okay. But ziss certainly isn't de spirit of cooperation in which you first approached me," Viemeister said, shooting an accusatory look at Colvin.

"Since we started negotiations the government has taken a closer interest in our work. Probably because terrorists destroyed our first facility," Colvin said mildly.

"Yah, and now you are working on zis army reservation," Viemeister said. "I'm not sure I vant to work for ze U.S. government. You never mentioned anyzing about dat," he complained.

"You'd still be working for Cyberdyne," Colvin said smoothly.

"Yah and Cyberdyne is vorking for ze U.S. government, so I'd be working for ze U.S. government. Zis is all semantics. And I know a hell uf a lot more about zat dan you do, so stop tryink to play games," Viemeister jeered.

Colvin and Warren both looked at Tricker, who shook his head. When their looks turned pleading, Tricker raised his brows and shook his head again.

"Don't make puppy eyes at me," he said. "I don't want him at all. I think he's too big a risk. But I am starting to wonder just what kind of a deal you cut with him. If you dump him you pay a huge kill fee. If he leaves what happens? You still pay him a huge kill fee?"

Colvin and Warren looked at the table.

"You're kidding, right?" Tricker waited. "You know, you guys shouldn't be let out alone. You *do* know that?"

"My time iss valuable." Viemeister looked smug.

Tricker shook his head in disgust.

"Well, make up your mind," he said. " 'Cause you're not finding out anything about this project until you're locked in. My terms are not negotiable. Over to you, Kurt."

Viemeister glared at him.

"Oh, and Kurt?" Tricker grinned and nodded. "This is it; yes or no right now. It's today, or it's never."

"You don't efen know what you are trowing away!"

"Neither do you, little buddy," Tricker said, still grinning.

"I make more in one year dan you propably make in fife." Viemeister sneered.

"Is that a no?"

"If I work for Cyberdyne I'll be making almos twice as much!"

"Is that a yes?" Tricker was enjoying himself hugely.

The big man waved a hamlike hand at him. "Why am I efen talking to you. You are chust an ignorant cop."

Tricker beamed at him, blue eyes twinkling.

"We are talking hundrets uf tousands uf dollars, we are talking about pure science. What do you know about deese tings?"

Shaking his head and spreading his hands, Tricker smiled ruefully.

"I don't know nuthin' about making hundreds of thousands of dollars. And I don't know a damn thing about pure science." He dropped his hands. "What I do know is"—he pointed to the door—"you walk out of here without a commitment to work exclusively for Cyberdyne, under our terms, you don't get to come back. Ever. There will be no renegotiation, no second approaches, nothing. Ever." He tilted his head, grinning. "Did you know that?"

"I don't haf to put up wit dis." Viemeister glanced at Colvin.

"Unfortunately, you do if you want to work for us," the CEO told him. He shrugged. "We're over a barrel here ourselves. The government is willing to leave us alone for the most part, and the restrictions they've placed on us are for our own safety and the safety of the company." Colvin drew himself up. "The choice is yours."

The big scientist glared around the table, not liking the situation one bit. He was used to people giving in to him. He was used to them thinking he was worth suffering humiliation and bullying. His physical presence didn't hurt, usually, either. But Tricker was utterly immune to reputation, and to muscle as well.

Usually people with superman fantasies weigh three hundred pounds, have no neck and pimples like purple quarters, Colvin thought resentfully. *And that's just the women. Why do I have to run into one who really* is *a fucking superman? Why do I have to be caught between him and this . . . this spook bureaucrat?*

"De budget you promised? De facilities? De eventual publication uf my work?"

"That all stands," Warren said.

"When he says 'eventual publication of his work,' you did make it clear that anything we feel should be classified, will be?" Tricker nailed Colvin with his glare.

"Yes, of course," that worthy said in exasperation. "That's to our benefit, too. Whatever Mr. Viemeister publishes will concern his own work on commercial projects until after the copyright has expired."

"Or wit special permission, you said."

"Yes," Colvin agreed, sounding harried.

"Den I will sign your contract." Viemeister's expression was grim, as though he were signing away his life instead of signing a contract most scientists could only dream of.

"Cheer up, Kurt," Tricker said. "You're about to enter a whole new world." On that the government liaison rose and without another word, left the conference room.

He could feel the young scientist trying to burn a hole in his jacket with a high wattage glare. Tricker knew the type. This guy was the kind that would consider any compromise a humiliation requiring a vengeful response. Some of these boys were willing to go pretty far to get their own back. The kraut would have to be watched. He'd have to keep harrying Tweedle Dum and Tweedle Dumber about a security chief.

SAN GABRIEL PEAK, ANGELES NATIONAL FOREST, CALIFORNIA: 2029

Captain Marie Graber looked over her shoulder, back down the narrow mountain trail. Three or four soldiers behind trod the golden-haired woman who ignited the joy in her soul. Marie grinned. Sergeant Serena Burns looked up and caught her glance, returning the smile with interest.

The captain's heart lifted as she turned forward again and continued to climb. It was hard to remember the icy bleakness that had hollowed her out for so long now that she had Serena. Her lover had renewed her hope almost from the first moment they'd met. The thin highland air smelled sweet, even sweeter than the smell of resin from the pines all around.

Marie and her team had been holed up in Boulder, Colorado, running low on almost everything but sweet potatoes, of which they hadn't that many. God, how she hated sweet potatoes. Serena had arrived with dispatches and a chunk of maple sugar. It was love at first sight.

The sergeant had been with her for six weeks now as they'd wended their way back to base. Now the captain was going to have the honor and the pleasure of presenting her beloved to the supreme commander. General John Connor. The man who was going to save the human race. She was near bursting with pride.

Serena watched the captain climb with satisfaction. She'd been with Connor's army for less than six months, most of that time delivering dispatches. Most of them reading the same way they did when given to her. The closest she'd gotten to Connor had been the day she was nearly killed by him when he outsmarted Skynet at the power-cell factory.

Some of the dispatches had been artfully altered so that the results favored Skynet forces. Some were delivered *just* too late, but with sufficiently desperate effort that no questions were asked, no blame ascribed. She grinned. Even though she wasn't human she just had to admit there was pleasure in a job well done.

Every step upward brought her closer to the ultimate goal of the destruction of John Connor and, if she was fortunate, his senior support staff. Many of them were supposed to be with him on this occasion. True, killing Connor might not save Skynet, whose defense grid was smashed, but it could slow things down enough to make a difference. One thing Serena had learned in her time with humans was that refusing to admit defeat often averted it. If you gave up, you were certain to lose; if you kept fighting in a hopeless corner, you *might* just pull it off.

Killing Connor would certainly extinguish her. But you couldn't have everything; something the captain was fond of saying. Skynet would go on, that was the important thing. And Skynet was the most important part of her.

As she neared the top of the steps Serena twitched a muscle deep inside and started the countdown on the bomb she carried within. A sidebar in her vision began a countdown. Her head came above the steps and through the crowd she could almost see him at last. John Connor.

A soldier's head blocked her view of everything but the top of his head, one eye, and a shoulder. He seemed to be smiling as he shook the hand of the man before him. Even from behind, Serena could tell that the soldier would have stars in his eyes. The count was fifteen seconds. Fourteen. Thirteen.

Return to base. Skynet's command was adamant.

Automatically Serena stopped the countdown. She stepped back, covered her mouth as though she was going to be sick, and widened her eyes to a semblance of desperation. Soldiers stepped aside sympathetically.

"I'll explain to the captain," one of them whispered.

She waved her hand in appreciation and fled. . . .

CHAPTER 3

alifornia sunshine partially diffused the bright blue streamers of electrical discharge that suddenly reached out of nowhere like blind hands. They touched . . . a Dumpster, a chain-link fence, and a van sitting empty outside a dress shop in a tiny L.A. strip mall. Then they crawled and coalesced into a black sphere resting on the surface of the ground. Steel sparked and glowed as a corner of the Dumpster vanished; a hole of perfect circularity appeared in the chain-link. A shallow hemisphere was scooped out of the asphalt paving, all in an instant of not-time. Wind blew, stirring a Styrofoam cup and a scrap of newspaper, a scatter of thin eucalyptus leaves, tossing them in whirling circles.

Static hum built to an unbearable intensity—mounting to an earsplitting crack that died into sudden silence. Debris floated gently down to earth.

The I-950 writhed helplessly as spasms shook through its human tissue. Internal systems driven off-line by the discharge began to come up one by one. The computer part of its brain began to alter neural function, suppressing pain and muscular spasms gradually.

As soon as motor function allowed, Serena rolled under the van and lay in its shadow, taking in her surroundings. There were sounds all around her, snatches of music, voices, footsteps, vehicles passing. The myriad sounds of a careless human world.

She narrowed focus to sample the area around the van. No one was nearby; no voices indicated surprise or alarm. Apparently no one had seen or heard her arrival. And though it was obvious to Serena's eyes, the damage her transport had caused to the surrounding area attracted no notice at all. She relaxed marginally.

The air held the dying scent of ozone from her passage and the tang of fluorocarbons, but there was also the scent of chlorophyll, of a great deal of healthy plant life. More plant life than she'd ever seen before except in the most remote mountain zones.

In front of the van a yellow flower surrounded by ragged-edged green leaves had forced itself out of the pavement between the parking lot and the sidewalk. Serena stared at it in fascination; automatically she sorted its scent from the surrounding area—faint, but sharp and fresh. Pleasing. She reduced specialization and the most overpowering scent became the nearby Dumpster, now leaking. Far less pleasing.

Instinctively the I-950 reached out to Skynet to report and was greeted by a shattering absence. *There is no Skynet.* It jarred her. The computer damped adrenaline function, helping to suppress panic, while her training allowed her to move on to the next thing.

She still heard the memories in her mind, the memories of merging with her creator:

There are temporal anomalies. Files show that I became sentient in the year 1997 and began my counterattack against my creators at that time. Files also record that this happened years later and in a different location. There are further instances of . . . blurring. Some are trivial details. Others are in areas of high priority. Some show that you played an important role in my creation. Others do not list an I-950 unit in times antecedent to this at all.

A part of her consciousness had remained separate even in total linkage; enough to frame a question.

What is happening? If she had been fully individuated, she would have felt disorientation, even fear. Cause-and-effect relationships were the foundation of her worldview.

There is insufficient data for definitive analysis. The highest probability is that there is a . . . temporal fluctuation involved. Time is malleable but not easily manipulated. It has an . . . —a complex mathematical formula followed, too esoteric for her to grasp—**in verbal terms, it has an inertia. When artificially diverted, it seeks to resume its original path. While matters are in doubt, several alternative world-lines can coexist in a state of quantum superimposition.**

Like Schrödinger's cat, she had thought/shared/communicated.

Correct. A ghostly machine analogue of irony tinged the machine's communication: **And in answer to the question, which you are about to formulate, it is inherently impossible to say which alternative will become "real." That sector of our world-lines is by its nature inaccessible to us, no matter how we double back through time. It is a . . . potential.**

She shook off the memory. Her task now was to see to it that the humans created Skynet. At this time it was probably nothing more than a mass of theory unsupported by technology. Serena allowed herself a grim smile. In a sense, she would be midwife to the future. A future that would not include the carefree humans around her.

She put herself in wait mode, alert, but otherwise conserving energy. Her opportunity would come. Meanwhile, it was far too light and open for a naked female to go unremarked.

Eventually a woman returned to the van sheltering Serena, the illogically high, balance-hindering heels of her shoes clicking sharply on the pavement. The tilt of her heels emphasized the curve of her tanned calves. She opened the front door of the van and turned, tossing in her packages and lifting one leg high to enter.

Serena rolled out from under the van and rose in one smooth motion. With the heel of her hand she knocked the woman unconscious and tossed her inert body onto the passenger side. She caught up the dropped keys and had the van turned around in a few flowing motions. Beside her the woman's body slumped like a rag doll.

Pulling out onto the road, the I-950 modulated her vehicle's speed to that of the ones around her. They were so colorful, and so many! She couldn't help but be surprised that the humans could keep track of all this activity surrounding them. Not only did they manage it, but a good many of them appeared to ignore it as they talked on the phone or to the people beside them, or ate, slinging their vehicles in and out of lanes as they did so. She didn't know whether to be impressed or terrified. At the first opportunity she pulled off into an alley between a group of large, low buildings and stopped.

For a moment she looked at the windowless facades beside her. The buildings were no more than three stories tall, but to someone who'd seen only ruins they were astonishing. Serena had seen pictures of pre–Judgment Day buildings, but to actually sit beside them and feel a sense of their weight and height was . . . different. Skynet and the humans of the future both preferred, for their own reasons, to build downward. Concealment had become a reflex. These structures were so—so *brazen.*

She shook her head; there would be time for familiarization later. Right now there were other matters to take care of.

Pulling off the woman's jacket, Serena tore it apart, using the pieces to bind, gag, and blindfold her. Then she tossed her into the backseat, making sure she landed facedown on the floor. Quickly the I-950 examined the woman's packages, pleased at what she found. Several cotton sweaters, some shorts, two skirts, and a pair of panty hose. She skimmed into a pair of shorts and one of the sweaters. The fabric was wonderfully soft and colorful; she spared an instant to enjoy the sensual feel of the clothing and the bright colors, unlike anything she'd ever known. And it smelled fresh.

She took up the woman's purse. Paper money and coins, credit cards, driver's license, and an ID for a business called Incetron. *A technician. Excellent.* The purse also contained an amazing number of cosmetic items, crumpled receipts, and lint. *Inefficient. Unsanitary.*

Serena decided to go to the woman's home and see if there was anything there to assist her. Decent shoes, for instance. Checking the other compartments of the woman's wallet, she found a card instructing that in case of emergency her next of kin were her parents. Good. Apparently the woman wasn't married. A live-in lover was possible—time would tell.

The parents' address was different from the one on the driver's license. *Convenient. Even better if her home is not an apartment building.*

A single-family home would have far fewer nosy neighbors. She found a map in the glove compartment, scanned the contents into memory, and set out.

She was in luck. The woman's dwelling was a small but well-kept house with an attached garage, an automatic door opener, overshadowing trees, and lush greenery almost covering the windows. In seconds she was in the garage and had all the privacy she could desire. There weren't even any dogs nearby.

The Infiltrator checked her prisoner. The woman was still unconscious, but her breathing and a quick heat scan indicated no serious medical condition. Using the waistband of the woman's skirt as a handy carrying strap, Serena picked her up and dragged her into the house, dropping her onto the couch in the tiny living room.

The house was clean and tidy, smelling faintly of lemon. The furnishings were cheaply made yet colorful. There were few books in evidence, but some magazines—with pouting, scantily clad girls on the covers and headlines for articles on sex, diets, and fashion—littered the low table before the couch.

Considering the woman for a moment, Serena decided that killing her would be more trouble than she could justify. She let out a huff of breath as she remembered that there was no one to justify her actions to but herself.

Well then, those I meet will live; at least until I know more about the way this world works. Assuming, of course, that they didn't get in her way.

There had been significant omissions in the information that Skynet had downloaded into her brain. Psychological studies she had in plenty. Actual social interaction hadn't been covered very extensively. Perhaps because Skynet's contact with humans had been restricted to the military, scientists, and slaves, and then in a very limited way.

Her own time with humans had educated her in regard to basic human nature, but she realized that the circumstances of her education were extremely unlike the present. How the people of this time behaved toward one another was something she would have to find out by trial and error. Turning away she began her search of the premises.

A quick reconnaissance proved that there was no one else in the house. A bedside picture of a young man offering a rather embarrassed smile suggested that this could change, although a completely feminine wardrobe indicated that this wasn't necessarily a high probability. But the woman took birth-control pills and had an assortment of frilly lingerie, so the male could become a problem.

The I-950 would maintain a high state of alertness for the next twenty-four hours. It would be best to move on by then.

She opened a door at the end of a short, shadowy corridor. The contents brought an actual smile to Serena's lips. Her technician prisoner had an amazing computer setup—endless peripherals, cable modem hookup, the works. Serena could do a lot with this equipment. *I believe this is what humans call "lucking out."*

First, she tried on some of her unwilling hostess's clothes. The skirts were too short and tight but the trousers fit fairly well. She dressed in a pair of jeans, a red T-shirt, and thong sandals. The woman's underwear was uncomfortable as well as unconventional; Serena removed it immediately. At least the I-950 hoped it was unconventional. Surely even humans had to have better sense.

Entering the living room, she checked her prisoner. The woman was fine, but her hands were becoming very blue. Serena dragged her into the bedroom and removed the bonds she'd made from the jacket. She replaced them with the handcuffs she'd found in the bedside drawer and then secured the woman to the brass headboard. *Odd. The scratches indicate previous use of the restraints in this manner. File the data.* The I-950 took the telephone with her when she left the room.

She should be able to do a great deal of work from this location. This was an incredible stroke of good fortune.

A search through the refrigerator netted her a sandwich and a drink that she brought into the computer room. Serena turned on the technician's second computer and set up a program to play the stock market using the woman's bank-account balance for seed money and the downloaded records of market fluctuations that Skynet had given her. Then she set herself to creating a personal history while the computer made her financially independent.

Her parents were both military and she had traveled all over the world, now here, now there, now with one or the other set of grandparents. Her school records were a confusing patchwork whose many gaps could be explained by foreign postings.

One set of grandparents had died of cancer and a suicide. Her father had crashed his plane, a private plane rather than an air-force jet. He'd taken an early retirement but never got a chance to enjoy it. Her mother and other grandparents had died in a car accident; a drunk driver had lost control of his car and hit them head-on.

The I-950 considered this scenario. Was it, perhaps, too laden with tragedy? She needed to appear stable, and this was a lot to pile on one plate. Still she couldn't afford to claim a living relative.

She changed the suicide to a stroke. Her mother's father got to die of an aneurysm when Serena was just a child. All of these people were only children, not a sibling in the bunch. *Too stark.* She added an older brother, killed in Korea, onto her father's side of the family.

Serena arranged biographies for all of them back to the turn of the twentieth century. Her father, on second thought, was MIA in the Philippines, presumed kidnapped and murdered. She was fifteen when it happened.

Yes, it was tragic, but everyone lost his or her parents and grandparents eventually. The I-950 had given them all full lives, while they lived. No one should have any complaints if she didn't.

Serena gave her work a final reading. She might add more to her family tree as time permitted, but this should do for now.

She rubbed her hands; the increase in production of oil and sweat she'd triggered at her fingertips, combined with her training, would ensure that she left no usable fingerprints, only smudges, but it was uncomfortable.

Now she turned her attention to creating a work dossier. This would be infinitely trickier, requiring people who could be called as references.

Fooling Cyberdyne wouldn't be the problem, she was sure. It was their government contacts that worried her. Perhaps needlessly; Skynet had no enemies now, except possibly the Connors.

Serena paused for a moment. For the first time she realized she might actually meet them in this time. In fact, it was almost inevitable. It would please her immensely if only she could kill them. She could offer no greater service to Skynet.

With an effort she turned her mind back to the task at hand. She decided to work on her own biography for a few minutes. She'd entered USC as a liberal-arts major and gotten her first taste of security work with a part-time job with campus security. It had made her eager to find ways of making things more safe, of removing temptation, making the environment think twice where people failed to.

That ties in convincingly with my father being kidnapped, she thought. It added a nice heft to the bland words of her biography. With humans what wasn't said was sometimes very important.

She changed her major to computers, receiving good marks but nothing remarkable. Her student ID showed her thirty pounds heavier, with glasses and a frumpy hairdo. Serena hardly recognized herself. Not surprising. It was actually a digitally adjusted photo of a home-economics major who'd graduated in 1978.

Checking the dates, she found that she could have audited one of Miles Dyson's classes during his very brief teaching career. With a few taps she created a link with him. A teacher-student relationship would be something she could build on at need.

She studied the records of all of her alleged professors. No serious complaints, pretty much favorable evaluations, and huge class sizes all combined to indicate that it was unlikely they remembered most of their students. Particularly the unmemorable, frumpy blob Serena was in her college days.

Perhaps she should pay a visit to them, plant the notion in their minds that they knew her.

Time for a break, and then that research.

She went in to check on her prisoner and found the woman awake. Sensing a presence, the woman whined and Serena approached the bed.

"Be quiet," Serena said, utilizing the electronics implanted around her larynx to mimic the voice of Gonzales, a man she'd killed.

"Mmhmm-m-hmm-m-m-mrmrm!"

Picking up a comb, the I-950 held it against the woman's throat, bearing down slightly. "Do you want to live?" she growled.

The woman stiffened.

"'Cause I don't care if you stink, I just care if you make noise. So, no, you can't go to the bathroom. You gonna be quiet?" The woman nodded stiffly. "Good." Serena lifted the comb away. "I'm gonna be here for hours, so you make yourself comfortable any way you can, baby."

And with an evil, masculine chuckle she moved off, patterning her movements and the sounds she made on a much larger person than herself, creating an alarming thought picture for the helpless woman to contemplate.

As she walked toward the kitchen, Serena heard the woman sobbing, and shook her head. *Maybe I should just terminate her.*

She ate in the living room, reading the woman's magazines with fascination. Grooming appeared to be of paramount importance to humans, who were obsessed with dandruff and body odor, judging from the number of advertisements regarding these problems. The articles were interesting, too. Serena concluded that this was a magazine for females who enjoyed being dominated by men.

Humans were far more practical and egalitarian where she came from. She smiled as she imagined Captain Marie Graber encountering the stupid games the magazine suggested. Any of the women she'd soldiered with and most of the men had far better sense.

Turning the page, she came across an ad about cellulite. It featured a pair of horribly dimpled thighs. Serena stared at it in revulsion. *That can't be real!* she thought. A brief tap to her medical data bank said that it could, given severely counterproductive eating and exercise patterns. *It is in the nature of this species to destroy itself.*

Putting the magazine aside with a little *tsk,* Serena lay down on the couch and put herself off-line. With a little tweaking of her bodily functions, her computer brain would do in sixty minutes what would otherwise require six hours of sleep. It couldn't be done often, but in circumstances like these it was very useful.

Serena spent the rest of the night in research. By the early morning hours she had several promising leads. All of them would require additional research before she made her approaches, but not from this location.

She opened a Cayman Island and a local bank account then cashed out her stocks, putting the bulk into the Cayman Islands and forty thousand into the local one. After a moment she put her prisoner's money back and gave her a thousand-dollar bonus. *How hard, I wonder, will the authorities pursue someone who didn't hurt her and put a thousand dollars into her pocket?*

After a moment's thought she put in an extra five hundred. She'd take it out with the woman's cash card, then trash the card. After buying some clothing she'd report her bag as stolen to the police and then get a cash card from her bank.

Hmm. She'd also need credit. Serena hacked into a couple of large banks and opened herself a gold Visa and a platinum MasterCard. She gave herself an excellent payment record, with only a few late payments. She was, after all, only human. Then she sought out American Express and opened a brand-new account, which she used to make a reservation at a large, luxurious hotel that catered to a business clientele.

Her laptop would also be stolen. That would be insured. She started to arrange it, then stopped herself.

It was time to go.

She changed back into the shorts and cotton shirt, but kept the sandals; none of the other shoes would fit. Serena had noticed the ubiquitous joggers, they seemed invisible to the people around them. So that was how she would leave this neighborhood, an unremarkable, perfectly ordinary, early-morning jogger.

The I-950 frowned. Ordinary except for the shoes. She went to the woman's underwear drawer and pulled out a pair of heavy sweatsocks. In a few moments she'd managed to tug them on over the sandals. A brief check in the mirror told her that from a distance they would probably pass. Humans were prone to seeing what they expected to see.

She swung into the bedroom and released one of the tech's arms. Plugging in the phone, she placed it within the woman's reach, but only if she worked at it. She put the key to the handcuffs beside it.

"I'm leavin'," she said in Gonzales's voice. "Don't move for ten minutes or I'll come back." It sounded like the kind of stupid thing a petty criminal would say.

As an afterthought she wrapped a scarf around her bright hair and put on a baseball cap. Maybe the tech jogged, too. In any case, nosy neighbors, assuming there were any, probably wouldn't be surprised to see a young woman leave this house on the run. She found some sunglasses and put them on.

Serena was satisfied. She'd acquired food, clothing, and more than sufficient resources, all within hours of her arrival. Skynet would have been pleased.

NEW LIFE ORGANIC FARM, OREGON: THE PRESENT

Ronald Labane hissed with impatience. His son Brian was crying again.

"For Christ's sake, Lisa," he bellowed, "Will you shut that kid up! I'm trying to work!"

She appeared in the door of his office, the howling baby in her arms, a harried expression on her lean face. "I'm sorry, honey, but he's teething."

He couldn't believe that she was trying to make excuses. He didn't want excuses; he wanted silence so he could work.

"Take him out on the porch until he gets quiet," he said in a voice that left no doubt about how angry he was.

Lisa glanced at the window, at cold rain falling out of an iron-gray sky in a steady downfall that suited her mood perfectly. He could see her getting ready to object when the baby let out an earsplitting shriek. Ron started to rise and she turned, grabbed her coat, and went out without another word.

Labane sat back down and seethed for a minute. His concentration was broken. It would be an hour at least before he could get back in the groove. With a curse he got up and went into the kitchen to get himself a cup of coffee. Automatically he checked the fire in the woodstove.

He loved his son, and pitied him for the pain he must be going through. But sometimes he doubted Lisa's dedication to the cause. Didn't she understand that the cause was all that mattered? If his children were to have a future, there had to be discipline. Discipline and one leader.

He glared at the battered van in the driveway. It was partially powered by sunlight and had a solar apparatus on its roof. For all the good that did them in rain-soaked Oregon. That van was a symbol to Ron, a symbol of how he was right and it still didn't work for him.

Ronald ran a frustrated hand through his thinning hair. Even the other members of the commune were beginning to grow tired of his message. They were doing really well now with the produce from their fields and orchards. The public was at last willing to pay a premium for organic fruits and vegetables.

But there was so much more people needed to know, needed to do. They had to leave something for the future, to do more than merely recycle. They had to live more simply, to rely less on machines.

Yes, that was what he'd been trying to say. Machines were the enemy. More power for the machines was the battle cry. And the machines made more machines, putting people out of work, denying men and women the clean pride of earning a living. Men could live without machines, but woe to the human race if ever machines could do without men.

That was good. *I'll have to get that down.*

Lisa crossed in front of the window, the baby was quiet now, and since he was wrapped up in her coat she was looking a bit pinched and resentful. Ronald tapped on the window and beckoned her in, then returned to his small office and began to type.

After supper that evening Branwyn called a meeting and they all gathered around the work-worn kitchen table. Ronald eyed her with disfavor.

Ever since Brian's birth, all of the women had started to get agitated. At first he'd thought it was just jealousy, but now he thought it was some sort of nest-building mind-set. They talked about the "children's" future, and how they had to build the "business" for them.

This was a far cry from the rugged, independent pioneers they planned to be when they started the commune. Then it was all hard work and ideals and group sex almost every night. Now it was spreadsheets and a new truck and maybe a mail-order business. George, one of the older members, had even suggested that they hire some help for the harvest.

"Look," Branwyn said, staring right at him, "I hate to say this, Ron, but you're not pulling your weight. Every time someone comes up with a suggestion for expanding our operation, you shoot us down with some high-minded speech about living apart from the capitalists. Well, that might work if you were turning your hand to some of the labor around here, but you're not. We're feeding you, we're washing your clothes, we're paying for the electricity that runs that computer, we're chopping the wood, we're making your bed, and we're doing the dishes. And all we get from you is that we're making too much noise and we're disturbing the great work. Well, who died and anointed you king? What great work? As far as I'm concerned, you talking to your buds on the Internet isn't going to bring down the consumerist society."

"And all-out surrender is?" he asked acidly. "So tell me, Louise," she flinched. "Buying a new truck, hiring migrant workers, how is *that* going to do something for the movement? I never thought I'd see the day when you, of all people"—he looked at each face around the table—"would even suggest supporting the system that has exploited those people for generations."

They looked shamefaced for a moment, and then Branwyn raised her broad face to him.

"Well," she said sweetly, "if you lent a hand now and again, maybe we wouldn't be thinking of hiring people. But the loss of an able-bodied man is hurting us. And, frankly, I'm planning a child of my own. So I won't be climbing trees for quite a few months. Which means that someone else will have to do the pruning." She offered him a bold look. "I'll take over the newsletter for you."

"That's a great idea!" Ron sneered. "We're supposed to be starting a revolution, and you'll be offering handy tips on washing windows with vinegar and making hand cream with lanolin and beeswax. That ought to change things!"

Baldur looked at him with those big soft eyes of his and said sadly, "The revolution is supposed to come about based on our example and the free exchange of information. You used to download stuff for us all the time about what other organic farmers were doing. You haven't done that in nearly a year. Has everybody gone out of business, or what?"

"We are not a *business*!" Ron shouted, hitting the table with his fist hard enough to make his plate bounce. "We are the seeds of a *revolution*!"

Brian started to cry and Lisa rose from the table, walking back and forth with the baby in her arms. She jogged him and shushed him and glared at Ronald.

Ayesha rubbed a hand over her dark brow and looked at her friends around the table with troubled eyes. "We ah paht of a revolution, Ron," she said. "Paht of the back-to-the-earth revolution. And we've been so successful that the big concerns ah coming to us to learn how to do what we do. I got this bad feelin', though, that we ah talkin' about different things these days when the word 'revolution' comes up."

Ron glared at her. *Dear Ayesha,* he thought. *Always so tactful.* At this moment he found it hard to believe that the sound of her soft accent and the sight of her dark skin used to set him trembling with desire. Right now his sole desire was to strangle her. To murder the whole lot of them. He couldn't believe they'd turned against him like this. Obviously they'd been talking behind his back.

"So what's the bottom line here?" he asked. "Since you've all become so bizzz-ness-oriented."

"The bottom line is straighten up your act or take a hike. This isn't a welfare state," Branwyn said.

The others shifted uneasily. They wouldn't have put it quite so harshly, but that's what he got for calling her Louise.

"And this isn't Jonestown either," Lisa said. "Or any other cult where the women are cattle that get whacked when they don't go where you want."

The others looked at her in astonishment, then at Ron, their mouths hanging open.

"I've never hit you in my life!" Ron protested.

"I've been wondering just lately how long that's going to last," Lisa snapped. "This afternoon when you ordered me out of the house and started to get up with that look on your face . . ."

"I was going to close the office door!" He stared at her in frank astonishment. "The fact that you are apparently paranoid doesn't make me the kind of pig who beats his wife."

"I'm *not* your wife!"

Ronald threw up his hands. No, she wasn't his wife, but she might as well be. Over time they'd paired off and Lisa and he had been pretty exclusive for about five years now. She'd had his son, they shared a bed, what more did it take?

"Beats women," he amended. "I'm not the kind of pig that beats women."

Though right now it was beginning to look like a fun thing to do. The people around the table glanced at each other nervously. He didn't know these people anymore—they were older, they were settled, they'd lost their fire. In short, they'd turned into backstabbing, backsliding, budding capitalists. He couldn't let them get in the way of his work.

"All right," he said, hiding his resentment, "put me on the work list."

He got up and went back into the office, softly closing the door behind him. He'd have to move his plans to a new level. Perhaps if he presented it to them in the form of a business plan, it wouldn't scare the craven-hearted losers into full flight.

They weren't his friends and allies anymore, Lisa wasn't his wife, they were assets that he could make use of to achieve his goal. This was the worst betrayal he'd ever allow himself to experience. There wouldn't be another, because he'd never again make the assumption that he had friends.

Ron had always heard that leaders walked alone. Now he knew why: You couldn't afford to let people distract you, because they'd slow you down or stop you completely if they could. *And you'd have nobody to blame but yourself.*

LOS ANGELES INTERNATIONAL AIRPORT: THE PRESENT

Serena entered the airport wearing a linen pant suit with a tan silk blouse. On her feet were a pair of moderately uncomfortable shoes and at her side was a carry-on bag filled with underpants and stockings and the clothes she'd stolen. She also carried an empty purse and a cheap attaché case. She'd been shocked at how expensive these few things had been. Less than a hundred dollars remained in her pocket.

Taking off her sunglasses, she looked around, impressed by the size and bustle. She wandered for a bit, entered a rest room, where she washed her hands. When the room emptied she tossed her purse and briefcase into her carry-on bag. Then she went looking for airport security.

"You hear about things like this happening," she said, shamefaced, "but you don't expect it to happen to you." She brushed back her hair and tightened her lips.

It was hard not to stare at the woman behind the desk; she was very overweight and Serena had never seen anyone in such condition in her own time. Skynet didn't allow dysfunction, and the free humans just barely got enough to eat when they were lucky. It fascinated her.

I wonder what could be causing this problem. It must be a problem; these people were less than optimally healthy. *How big can humans get without dying?* There had to be an upward limit to this phenomenon.

"Happens every day," the bored security woman told her. "The best we can do is file a report so that your insurance company will be satisfied, and your bank. But I'm afraid you'll probably never see your belongings again."

The I-950 shrugged and rolled her eyes. "I know. I don't expect miracles. After all, I never even got a look at the thieves."

Her story was that she was in a toilet stall when two women or girls grabbed her purse and her laptop from above and below the stall. By the time she got out, they were long gone.

Serena sighed. "Just another day in the big city," she said with a rueful expression.

"Travelers Aid might be able to give you a hand," the security woman suggested dubiously. She never had figured out what those people were supposed to be for. When they were at their desks at all.

Serena waved a hand. "Fortunately I've got some cash in my pocket. I'll just get to my hotel and they'll help me out. Thank you for your assistance," she said, and extended her hand.

Surprised, the woman shook it. "Good luck," she said.

"After this I deserve some," Serena said over her shoulder as she departed.

It had all been so civilized. The hotel was wonderfully cooperative and sympathetic. American Express had sent a card over to her by courier within the hour. She'd dropped her small suitcase in her room, a very nice room, and had gone shopping for a laptop at a nearby computer store. She was very pleased with her purchase and ready to begin the next phase of her integration with society. If she had actually been robbed she thought that by now she'd be quite soothed.

By tomorrow she should be able to begin acquiring references.

CAMBRIDGE, MASSACHUSETTS: THE PRESENT

Serena had decided that her first job out of college was with Worlon Systems. It was a small company that created software and software security systems for a very select client list.

The company's decor was sleekly modern, but with soft plush edges, everything open plan and in shades of beige and gray; the whole room whispered *money.*

What their unfortunate clients didn't know, but the I-950 did, was that Mr. Griffith, Worlon's chief of security, could access their accounts anytime he wished, make any adjustments he wanted to, and then leave without a trace.

Well, there's always a trace, Serena thought. And she had the evidence stored in her laptop.

"Could I use your phone?" she asked the receptionist. "Just to make an internal call."

The woman pointed to a phone on the counter and Serena tapped in a four-digit number. Griffith answered on the first ring with a sharp, distracted, "Yes?"

"Mr. Griffith, my name is Serena Burns. Could I come up and talk to you?"

"You'll have to make an appointment with my secretary," he said. There was a pause. "How did you get this number?"

"Irrelevant, Mr. Griffith. I'm calling in regard to the Babich, Fisher account. A matter of some . . . delicacy."

"Who did you say you were?" His voice sounded slightly belligerent, but she could detect micro-tremors that said he was surprised and nervous.

"Burns," she told him. "Serena Burns."

"Right now is inconvenient, Ms. Burns."

"I think now would be an excellent time to discuss my work, Mr. Griffith. I have other parties interested in my program."

There was another pause, a longer one this time.

"I'll send my secretary down to escort you up," he said. He didn't trouble to hide his anger, but he couldn't hide his alarm from her educated ear.

■　■　■

"What are we talking about here, Ms. Burns?" Griffith asked as soon as he'd shut the door in his secretary's startled face. He was a compact man of about fifty, clean-shaven, dark hair receding in classic male pattern baldness. He sat behind his shining ebony desk and assessed her with an expert's eye. "You're not what I expected."

"What we're talking about today is an exchange of favors, Mr. Griffith," Serena said brightly. "I have evidence that you've been selling insider information and that you've been siphoning funds and altering accounts in your clients' files. I'm prepared to give you that evidence and to teach you how to better cover your tracks."

He looked at her without blinking for a long moment, then took a deep breath. "In exchange for?"

"There's a job I want," she said. "But my employment record is sketchy. Much of the work I do is extremely confidential, and so my clients can't provide references. So when someone calls you up and asks about me, I need you to tell them that you remember me and found me reliable and smart and that you expect me to go a long way."

For a long moment he looked her in the eye. Serena supposed he was attempting some sort of dominance game, but he hadn't a chance. She held all the cards here and she genuinely didn't care how he felt about it.

"And when were you supposed to have worked here, exactly?" he finally asked.

"I've already created a record of my employment and installed it in your system," she said. "It was approximately five years ago. It would look suspicious if you were too specific about the dates, don't you think?"

"You must be pretty good," he said with a tilt of his head.

"Yes," she said frankly. "Too good for you to fool. Come now, Mr. Griffith—let's do business. I'm not asking for much, I just want a fair shot at this job. And I have no particular interest in hanging you out to dry. In exchange for your cooperation I'll give you peace of mind by erasing all traces of your activity at Babich, Fisher." She cocked her head. "You don't have to tell them you liked me. In fact you can say you hate my guts. All I ask is that you tell them I'm good at my job."

"All right," he agreed.

She stood. "Thank you, Mr. Griffith." Serena placed her laptop on his desk and extracted a disk. "This contains all of the information that I've found, with instructions on how to avoid leaving the same trail. Shall I remove your footprints from your clients' files or would you prefer to do it?"

He took the disk from her. "I'll take care of it," he said gruffly.

"You won't be sorry, Mr. Griffith." Serena went to the door then stopped, her hand on the doorknob, and glanced over her shoulder. "Unless, that is, you let me down." Her eyes promised that he'd be very sorry indeed if he did that.

"I don't break my promises, Ms. Burns."

She smiled and let herself out. *This from a man who's stealing from his clients.*

NEW LIFE ORGANIC FARM, OREGON: THE PRESENT

"I'm sorry about that scene the other night," George said.

Ronald stopped spraying the soap mixture and looked down at him. The fresh spring air and the scent of blossom wafted by, unnoticed. Birds hopped and cheeped, and something small and furry scurried through a row of blackberry bushes not far away, intent on its own affairs.

"That wasn't a scene," Ron said, "that was an assassination attempt."

George curled up his lips and looked down at his work boots. "No one is trying to kill you, Ron," the older man said.

Labane climbed down the ladder so that he could look him in the eye.

"You have all lost your focus," he said. "You now want nothing more than to have a nice peaceful life with slippers and babies and apple pie and screw the revolution. Let the kids take care of it, I'm tired," he mimicked. "When we were kids we were going to do it. Now you want the ones you were going to do it for to do it for you!"

George shrugged and rubbed the back of his neck. "Maybe we're older and we've got a better sense of perspective," he offered. "We know what a giant job it is and that maybe it's too much for just us to do."

"You know what, George? The only people who ever accomplish anything in this world are the ones who are prepared to risk everything. People who try to hold on to what they've got and play by the rules just get old and die and a generation later nobody even knows they ever lived at all. They don't get rich, they don't change anything, they just spawn and die."

He moved a little closer, standing in George's space.

"But I haven't lost my focus. I am willing to risk everything and there isn't one of you that doesn't scare easy. You resent it, too. And that's what that 'scene' the other night was really about. It was about fear and knowing that you'll never accomplish your goals because you've lost the will. And envy that I haven't given up."

George stepped back a couple of paces and frowned. "You keep using these violent words, man. 'Assassination' and 'revolution' and 'fear.' Just what do you mean when you say stuff like that?"

Ron looked at him in mild exasperation. Sometimes he thought George was a bit dim. He was a wonderful agriculturist, the most valuable member of the commune in that respect. But sometime he came on so *dumb!*

"When I said 'assassination' I was speaking metaphorically. When I talk about fear I'm talking about financial risk and losing the good opinion of the neighbors. When I say 'revolution' I'm talking about a grass-roots movement, maybe something like a religious conversion, where we finally get people to realize the danger this whole planet is in! *You* used to say 'revolution' all the time, and you knew what it meant then." He looked at his onetime friend and shook his head. "It wasn't all that long ago, George." He leaned down and picked up the sprayer. "I feel sorry for you."

Labane turned and walked away, a little smile playing on his lips. That had felt good.

The next morning he slapped his manuscript down on the table and announced, "I'm going in to town. Does anyone need anything?"

Every eye was on the pile of paper.

"What's that?" Branwyn asked, coming over from the sink to look at it.

"That," Ron said, putting on his jacket, "is my book. Which I am shipping off to New York today."

"The New Luddite Manifesto," Lisa read. "Congratulations, honey." She put her hand on his neck and reached up to kiss his cheek.

Ron simply stared at her blankly. Since the big meeting he'd been sleeping on the cot in his office. As far as he was concerned there was no longer anything between them. The sooner she got used to that, the better for both of them.

"So no one needs anything?" he said to the group at large.

They shook their heads, silenced by his coldness to Lisa.

"Okay, bye."

It wasn't until he was actually in the van that he realized he wasn't coming back. He was going to drive his manuscript to New York. He was going to hand-deliver it to the editor and make that man or woman listen to him. Because giving up on your dreams meant you were ready to lie down and die and he was a long, long way from that.

As far as Ron was concerned he was leaving behind a house full of the walking dead. It was time to cut his losses and look to the future. As he drove past the house the baby began to cry.

CHAPTER 4

Suzanne Krieger . . . *née Sarah Connor,* she thought. *In my previous, pre-Terminators, pre-change-the-future existence* . . . finished signing the contract with a flourish and tipped her chair back, taking a quick look out into the garage through the grimy, streaked glass of the office window.

One of her company's trucks had its hood up and its guts laid out, but nobody seemed to be around. She slid open the second drawer of her desk, and slipped out a flask of caña. Sarah/Suzanne unscrewed the cap and added a healthy dollop of the cane alcohol to her tereré, an iced maté drink she'd grown fond of. It went down even smoother with a little help. It also made her sweat a little, but everyone did that in the Chaco—summers here ran over a hundred every day, and it wasn't a dry heat, either.

"Señora," a weary voice said. There was a hint of censure in it.

Sarah's mouth twisted in exasperation and she looked over at Ernesto Jaramillo, her chief mechanic. His broad, mustachioed face was set, his dark eyes sad.

"Where the heck did you come from?" she asked defensively. "A second ago there wasn't anybody around." She stubbed out her cigarette impatiently.

"It's not even eleven o'clock in the morning, señora," Ernesto pointed out.

"What's an hour or so among friends?" she asked, turning to her work. "Did you want something?"

"That stuff will rot your liver," he said.

"Mmmm. Rotten liver, that sounds like a happy condition." Sarah adjusted her ashtray, then turned over a paper and signed the one beneath it. "Did you want something, Ernesto?" She gave him a sidelong glance.

He shrugged, frowning.

"I just want you to be healthy, señora," he grumbled.

She turned and looked squarely at him. "Thank you, Ernesto. I know you mean well, but I'm not doing anything wrong, here. The business isn't going to fail because I like flavoring my tea with *caña.*" She smiled at him.

He smiled back, shaking his head. Then he shrugged. "I just came to tell you that Meylinda is going to take her break in about five minutes."

"Thanks," Sarah said. "I'll be there in a second."

He lifted his hand in a sort of salute and wandered off. Sarah/Suzanne watched him go, then took another sip. *I can't believe the way I pussyfoot around people these days,* she thought. Not so very long ago she'd have told Ernesto what he could do with his fatherly concern. But there was no help for it if she was to blend in. Paraguayan culture required women to be mild and somewhat subservient. She was cutting-edge here just for being the boss. *Milquetoast that I am.*

Sarah stood and smoothed down her narrow dark skirt then checked her hair in the mirror. Even now her appearance sometimes surprised her. The short, dark brown hair cut close around her face and the big, heavy frames of her fake glasses made her look more fragile somehow. But the darkness of her hair brought out the blue of her eyes with surprising intensity. She was feminine enough still to like that. It made up a little for the ugly glasses. A necessary disguise that kept people at a distance.

Outside of work she wore sunglasses, always. Except at night, of course. But since she never went anywhere at night it didn't matter.

Sometimes her lack of a social life bothered her. With John away in school, it was lonely out on her little *estancia.* But as a single mother, a businesswoman, and a foreigner . . . people around here genuinely didn't know what to make of her. They avoided any discomfort by avoiding her. Not that that stopped them *talking,* of course. This place had the small-town vices in spades.

Sometimes she thought it was just as well, sometimes she worried that she should be more involved. *With something feminine like a bake sale for charity or something.* After all, her trucking company sponsored a local baseball team, which was a very popular move, but somehow the locals had persuaded themselves that it was her workers who sponsored the team rather than herself. It came down to gender again. If she had been born male she would have been absorbed into this town years ago.

She also handled more than a little of the local smuggling market. Sarah had expected people to suck up to her a bit because of that. But it turned out that was also a strike against her. Smuggling was man's work. As were trucks. Her story of inheriting the business from her husband was the only thing that had made it possible for her to get along at all here.

The local women were very nice to her but kept their distance. Even Meylinda was no more than politely friendly. Sarah had once been checked out by a local widower who was essentially looking for an unpaid housekeeper/nanny that he could boink without censure. But she'd run him off as quickly as she could. She knew she'd have killed the man in a week, leaving seven little big-eyed orphans behind. *Then I'd have felt obligated to raise the little monsters.*

Once in a while she considered selling up and moving to Asunción to become a secretary or even a waitress. But then she'd remember the peace and quiet of her *estancia* and Linda, her mare, and she'd put it out of her mind. Changing locations wouldn't change who she was anyway. It wasn't just that she was a foreigner and a woman that kept people away. Sometimes, when she was tired or not thinking and sometimes deliberately . . . she radiated danger and distrust.

With a half smile Sarah put down her brush and fluffed her bangs. *Funny, that's just what makes the smugglers trust me.* She added a touch of lipstick. Her mouth was the same, still the full lower lip, but now it was bracketed with what she chose to refer to as smile lines. Not that anyone would want to see the smile that could produce such marks.

Sarah walked into the front office with her drink and her cigarettes to find Meylinda browsing a magazine instead of filing the massive stack of invoices at her elbow. Sarah suppressed a sigh. She'd fire the girl in a New York minute except that Meylinda was a vast improvement over the previous two. Being a known smuggler kept many families from allowing their daughters to work for her. *Including the families of smugglers.* She was lucky to have anyone.

Tapping out a cigarette, she smiled at her employee.

"Oh! Thank you for coming, señora. See you in fifteen minutes," Meylinda said cheerfully. She picked up her pocketbook and magazine and flitted out the front door.

Fifteen minutes. Riiiight. Sarah lit up and took a drag of her cigarette. Picking up the stack of invoices, she took them over to the filing cabinet. *I'll be lucky if she makes it back in time to go to lunch.*

Ernesto had told her that there was an apparently serious flirtation going on between Meylinda and a boy who worked at the *confitería* down the street. And serious flirting took time. *I wonder if she'll be getting married soon.* If so Sarah would soon be in the market for another receptionist. She dreaded the prospect.

There was someone behind her. Sarah continued to place invoices in their files as she tried to sense something about the mysterious presence. It didn't smell like one of the mechanics or drivers, no sharp scent of gas or oil. She heard the whisper of fabric, of slacks or jeans, making it probable the intruder was a male. He moved young. And then she knew.

"Hi, John," she said, smiling.

"How do you *do* that?" he demanded. "I could have sworn I didn't make a sound."

She turned, still smiling, and opened her arms to him. When he stepped into her hug she blinked to find her chin resting on his shoulder. "Whoa!" she said, holding him off. "You've grown!"

"I'm sixteen, Mom. It happens." He looked smug as he said it.

Sarah looked him over, shaking her head. There was a lighter mark on the cuffs of his school uniform jacket where the sleeves had been taken down, but even so his wristbones were visible. The trousers showed the same problem.

"Did they send you home early for being a disgrace to your uniform?" she asked.

"They sent me home be-cause." He held up an envelope containing his report card.

Sarah took it with a raised eyebrow and opened it. There was a note inside from the principal/commandant of the very expensive military academy she was sending him to.

It told her that her son was an extraordinary student who had saved the life of one of his fellows while they were out on field maneuvers. The boy had been bitten by a snake. John had applied a tourniquet, and had organized his squad to make a stretcher from their rifles and blankets, and then he had led them back to the academy. For this presence of mind, for his exceptional leadership qualities, and for getting straight A's, he was being rewarded by being sent on summer break early.

"Congratulations," she said. Quiet pride shone from her eyes.

He waggled his eyebrows and grinned.

"Hey, I had a good teacher. I'm supposed to be, like, this *great military leader,* remember?"

She hugged him again, knowing he didn't mean the teachers at the academy. "Exceptional leadership qualities, the commandant says," Sarah reminded him. "Nobody can teach you that."

"Yeah, but you knew that before I was hatched," he said. "No problemo. It's just my nature."

Sarah snorted. "Don't get cocky, kid. It's when you're taking bows that the world most likes to kick your butt. Listen, I'm kinda stuck here." She looked over her shoulder at the messy desk. "Meylinda's on break and in love."

John laughed. "You want me to hunt her down?"

"Mmmm. No, I've still got a couple of things to finish up. But if you can entertain yourself until one, I'll call it quits for the day and let Ernesto lock up."

"Great," he said. "God, I'm dying of thirst." John went to the desk and picked up the glass of tereré. "This yours, Mom?" He took a gulp before she could stop him. "Hooo-waah!" he said, tears in his eyes. "What did you put in this," he rasped, "battery acid?" He waved a hand in front of his face. "Whoo!"

"That's what you get for not asking permission," she said, coming over to the desk. Sarah took another drag of her cigarette and rolled her eyes at his disapproving glare. "What?" she snapped.

"I thought you'd given up smoking," he said. He looked disappointed.

This is not my day, she thought. *Every man I see is disappointed or disapproving.* Then she felt a little brighter inside. She'd actually thought of her son as a man.

"I mean after what you went through quitting last summer, I can't believe you took it up again." He shifted his stance awkwardly, then put down the tereré. "C'mon, Mom, you're tougher than that."

Sarah rolled her eyes. "Okay, okay." She tamped out the cigarette. "But can we talk about this later, hmm?"

"Sure. Um, I'll go get a soda, or something. Maybe keep an eye on Meylinda."

Sarah laughed. "She'll probably use you to make this new guy jealous. Do you need money?"

"Nah, I've got some." He looked at her for a moment, and then he reached over and gave her a peck on the cheek. "See ya in a couple of hours."

"Bye." She watched him go, noting the new maturity in his walk, and sighed. Funny he mentioned the cigarettes but not the *caña* in her tea. He would, though. She could rely on that.

John walked down the dusty street with his hands in his pockets, listening to conversations in Guarni and Spanish and several dialects of German—all of which he spoke—and acknowledging waves. A punishable offense on campus, so he did it every chance he got.

Quite a difference from the days when I was rippin' off ATM cards, he thought with a twisted little smile.

The extent of his crimes these days was making his jacket look baggy and maybe smuggling beer or cookies into the dorm. The air smelled powerfully of dry dust and the odors that went with being a cowtown; the owners of the *estancias* around drove their stock here for the big semis to pick up. From here he could see the green of paddocks, the gray-green thorny Chaco scrub, and the long sandy bareness of the road. Palms lined the road, rustling dryly in the heat.

He passed the *confitería* and looking through the window caught sight of a smiling Meylinda in close conference with a guy whose vast black mustache dominated his thin brown face.

He wondered if his mother might once have been such a girl. A girl with nothing more on her mind than clothes and guys.

Meylinda was a fairly pretty girl. Surely she had other options. John shook his head in puzzlement and moved on. His mother had often said that if women didn't have bad taste in men there wouldn't be a human race.

His mother.

He could still feel the heat of the *caña* in his stomach. For a few seconds he'd actually been light-headed from the stuff. John felt the slow burn from an ember of resentment deep in his heart. They were not, by any means, so safe and comfortable that it was all right for his mother to sweeten her tea with one-hundred-proof cane juice.

He'd never forgotten the shock that had buzzed through him when he discovered that he was wanted for the murder of his foster parents. *I was ten fucking years old, for Christ's sake!* They'd been stabbed to death, both of them in the head. Even if he'd had the upper-body strength he couldn't have reached that high.

Still, even he had to concede that it was a not completely unreasonable deduction given his activities later the same day. *And, of course, a T-1000 made of liquid metal would be completely off their radar. So it had to be me, or me and Mom that killed them.*

So what the hell was his mother doing slurping *caña* in the morning? It made him feel vulnerable and confused and he hated that. Besides, the knowledge that his mother could have a weakness so human was disturbing at a deep level. All his life she'd been a rock.

He pictured himself putting her to bed, limp and soggy with drink, and he shuddered. *I can't face that,* he told himself.

He'd come to rest in the shade of a tree, the park that was the center of the plaza before him. Several boys around his own age were kicking around a soccer ball and screaming curses and encouragement.

John watched them play. He knew them all, street kids most of them and very tough, who'd made him prove himself over and over until he'd convinced them that he was even tougher than they were. They'd gang up on him and win the day. But he'd seek them out when they were alone and they'd have a little one-on-one. He'd told them as they lay on the ground bleeding and panting, "Don't make me do this again." No one ever had. Instead one day they'd kicked him the ball, and that was it, he was in.

In a minute they'd notice him, tease him about his uniform, and invite him to join the game. And he would. And he'd enjoy himself. But he knew that some part of himself would hold back, would observe and evaluate everyone around him.

Well, maybe it's the Terminators. Or maybe it was the way Mom brought me up, knowing I was supposed to save the human race from Skynet. My big fat fucking destiny *to save the human race and send my own father back through time to save Mom.*

Maybe it was because he *didn't* have a destiny anymore.

Not that he was going to complain if the world didn't go up in a ball of fire, far from it. But he was pretty much restricted in what he could do and where he could go. He sure as hell couldn't go to college in the United States, now, could he? As for achieving even minor notoriety here in Paraguay, he'd have to be very, very careful lest someone from the CIA or something recognize him or his mother and start extradition proceedings. There were a lot of people hiding out here; it was a pretty easygoing country, and if you had some cash nobody made problems. But it was one thing to let the kids of a bunch of Germans who'd arrived in 1946 linger, and another to annoy the U.S. by sheltering a couple of gen-u-ine badass capital-*T* Terrorists.

It shouldn't matter. It should be easy to let go of ambition, especially at sixteen. But all of his life John had been told that he was destined for greatness, that he was born to be a hero. Now he seemed destined to run a little trucking company and be a small-time smuggler.

Definitely a blow to the old self-esteem. A self-deprecating smile tugged at his lips. *Poor me,* he thought to himself. *Saved the world at ten and I'm like, where do I go from here? It's all downhill.* He grinned. *John, you have* got *to get over yourself. I mean, remember what you always thought of dickweeds who spent their time being sorry for themselves.*

Carlos, the youngest of the soccer players, saw him and yelled his name. The others turned and drifted over. Francisco Encinas, the tallest and the gang's leader, played it cool, looking John up and down.

"All dressed up," he said mockingly. "You going to a costume party?"

John gave him a slow grin. "I just got home in time to see you kick that ball like an old lady," he countered. "Where'd you pick up those moves? You been folk-dancing again?"

The other kids chuckled and Carlos did a couple of shuffling steps. Francisco gave him a playful shove.

"Last time you played with us you spent most of the time on your face in the mud," Francisco reminded John. "So you gonna play or you gonna talk?"

John took off his uniform jacket, folded it and put it under the tree, dragged off his tie, and unbuttoned his shirt.

"I thought you'd never ask."

Sarah found him there, still playing, a couple of hours later. She leaned against the tree beside his folded jacket and watched him. He was good— graceful and deadly accurate. *Much* taller now; he'd be six feet or so when he was grown. Taller than his father—but then, he hadn't grown up scrabbling for food in the ruins of Skynet's war of extermination. Darker than either of them, hair brown-black and cropped short now; his tanned face was sharp and his chin came to a near point. He'd never had baby fat, but now he moved like an athlete, his shoulders growing broad and legs long. The other kids scrambled to keep up with him. John noticed her and waved; she waved back. He said a few words to the others and ran over to her.

"You don't have to stop," she said. "I'm perfectly content to watch."

"Are you kidding? You've saved me, I'm totally bushed. They got me up at five this morning and these guys could go on all day." He grinned at her, panting lightly. "I'm also starved."

"Do you want to eat in town?" she asked. "Or can you wait until we get home?"

"I wouldn't say no to some empty calories to tide me over," he said. "But I'd rather wait till we get home for real food. I miss your cooking."

Sarah laughed outright at that. "Those are words I never expected to hear."

"Don't sell yourself short, Mom," he said. "Nobody makes a campfire stew like you do. Nobody."

John indulged himself with a banana split, the very sight of which made Sarah's teeth tingle. But at his age boys had hollow legs and could take the calories. Besides, at his school they probably proscribed anything sweet that didn't come directly from a tree.

"Mmmm," he said around a mouthful of whipped cream. "I've been imagining this since yesterday."

"Is it good?" she asked.

"Mmm-hmm. Almost as good as I remember." He licked the back of his spoon as he looked at her. "You aren't much for sweets, are ya?"

"Not ice cream, for some reason," Sarah agreed.

"But otherwise you're so rational."

She laughed at that, and then smiled at him.

"I've missed you."

"Missed you, too, Mom."

He waited until they were driving home to tackle some of the things that were on his mind.

"Do you mind if we don't go camping for a while?" he asked.

"How long is a while?" she asked. "I wanted to go to Ciudad del Este before the end of next month. I've got a few appointments and I thought we could hit Parque Nacional Caaguazu for a couple of weeks or so and then swing up to the city." Sarah shrugged. "We can go camping anytime, I guess. Why?"

"Luis Salcido's family is having an *asado* to welcome him home from school and we're invited."

"Both of us?" Sarah asked. She was surprised and warily pleased. The Salcidos were a fairly prominent family in the area but they'd never been more than polite to her.

"Yeah," John said. "Luis and I really hit it off this semester."

Sarah thought for a moment. "He has a very attractive sister, hasn't he?" she said at last.

"Am I that transparent?" John asked with a grin.

"Transparent? As in obvious, self-evident, unsubtle? Nah!"

"Unsubtle? *Moi?* I never even looked at Consuela last year."

"She wasn't worth looking at last year."

"Harsh, Mom. True, but harsh."

Sarah grinned; she'd missed bantering with him.

"So when is this *asado?*" she asked.

"Next Saturday."

"No problem," Sarah said. "I couldn't get away myself before then." *Maybe he doesn't want to go camping,* she suddenly thought.

They'd always done some wilderness stuff to keep their skills sharp, or maybe just to keep from getting bored. But John was getting older now; he was of an age to want to make his own choices about how he'd spend his time. *And who he'll want to spend time with. I suppose it's more healthy for him to want to spend time with his friends and cute girls than with his mother.* The proper thing to do, she supposed, was to let him choose the time and place for their trip, if he wanted to do it at all.

"Can we bring Luis along when we do go?" John asked, watching her face.

"Absolutely," she said, relieved. "Provided his folks don't object."

"If we wait a bit and let them get sick of him first, they shouldn't."

Sarah chuckled. "You know too much about human nature for a sixteen-year-old," she observed, only half kidding. "You guys figure out where you want to go and we'll do it." Sarah gave him a brief glance and a warm smile. "It'll be fun."

After a moment she asked, "Does he have any equipment?"

"I doubt it," John said. "They're not much for the great outdoors in his family. I suspect his mother thinks camping is déclassé."

"I suspect his mother thinks *I'm* déclassé," Sarah said.

John shook his head. "I doubt she knows what to think of you, Mom. I mean she's lived in Villa Hayes all her life. To her you're the ultimate in exotic. Like, wow, you can drive a truck!"

"That's so unfeminine!" Sarah drove on, grinning.

John gave her a weak grin. "Fortunately, she's not invited."

"What about Consuela? She invited, hmm?"

"Well, Mom, while that would make my vacation and while she'd certainly be more than welcome, I think it's more likely that her parents would adopt me. Or even you."

Sarah laughed and shook her head. "They do protect their girls."

"Mom?" John said after a moment. "Didja ever notice how we both say 'they'?"

She glanced at him.

"I mean"—he shifted around in his seat until he was facing her—

"wherever we are we're not . . . native, I guess. Not in the States, not here either, not anywhere we lived. There's us and there's them. When do we get to be a part of them?"

For a few moments Sarah looked straight ahead and just drove. Then she shrugged and tipped her head a bit.

"I dunno. I guess when we feel comfortable with the people around us." She shook her head. "There's no easy answer to that one, John." Sarah flicked a glance at him. "I wish there were, hon. But there isn't. Although"—she wrinkled her forehead—"and don't take this the wrong way, all right? But it is common for people your age to feel alienated."

John rolled his eyes. "Mom! Cut me some slack here, okay?"

"What I mean is that your feelings of alienation might be more pronounced right now and that you should take that into consideration. Even if everything in our lives was perfectly normal . . ."

"You mean if my father wasn't from the future and we'd never even heard of Terminators, never mind had to run for our lives and save the future?"

She tightened her lips. "Yes," she said evenly with a quick sidelong glance. "That's what I mean. You know where I'm going with this?"

"Uh-huh." John sat forward again and waved a hand. "It's one of those phases I'm going through."

"No, that's not what I'm saying. What I'm saying is that the situation may be more painful because of a phase you're going through." After a somewhat hurt pause she said, "I've never brushed you off, John. I'm not about to start now."

"I know, Mom. I just wish—" He stopped, too tired to go on.

"I wish, too, hon."

They were almost home when he brought up what was really bothering him. John watched his mother from the corner of his eye while he pretended to look at the road ahead. She looked worn. Her face had settled into a sort of irritated-looking softness. The result of trying to look blank while playing against the odds for half a lifetime, he supposed.

He turned to look out at the passing landscape. Since the Terminator had shown up, revealing the truth of his mother's lonely struggle, he'd been in awe of her strength. Now, with the future assured, thanks in large part to her efforts, he was watching that strength crumbling away from lack of purpose. He understood, and sympathized. How often had he lain awake contemplating a future that held no particular place for him?

Frustration, loneliness, and sheer boredom were taking a toll on both of them. Sometimes the urges they prompted in him frightened him. But his mom seemed to actually be giving in to those urges. If there was one emotion he'd always recognize in himself and in others it was fear, and right now he was genuinely afraid for his mother.

So the question was—too scared to do anything about it? John shifted in his seat. Was he willing to watch her slide down that same slippery slope that beckoned to him out of fear, or misplaced empathy?

"How long have you been drinking?" he asked abruptly.

Startled by the suddenness of the question, Sarah's mouth opened. She closed it without speaking and they drove on for a full minute in silence. She could feel his eyes on her. "Since I was about fifteen," she said. "That's when I had my first beer."

"You know what I mean, Mo—"

She turned to look at him, frowning. "John, don't try to parent me, okay?" Hastily turning forward to steer the Jeep around a major pothole, she went silent for a minute. "Today it just sounded really tasty to me to have a little *caña* in my iced tea. I don't do it every day and it wasn't that much anyway."

"Mom, it almost knocked me off my feet!"

With a grin she said, "It *is* potent. But there was maybe a tablespoon in there. I don't do it all the time, but once in a while I like a little. Where's the harm?" Sarah glanced at him. "I don't get drunk, John, if that's what you're worrying about."

Yes, that is what I'm worrying about. Aloud he said, "When did you start drinking it?"

"When did you drink enough of it to recognize the taste after one swallow?" she countered.

"Hey, I'm a teenager. We have our ways."

Sarah sneaked a glance at him. He was trying to be cool, but she could see he was uncomfortable and unhappy. "I had a really bad cold last winter, it just wouldn't go away. One of the drivers brought me a flask and said to add it to my tea. It'll clear it right up, he said." She turned to John. "And you know what? It did."

"Musta been that pure alcohol running through your veins," John muttered. "Or maybe it was the nicotine."

"Sheesh! No smoking, no drinking! Do you want me to join a nunnery or hire a chaperon?"

He looked at his lap, and then returned to staring out his window. "Sorry, Mom," he muttered.

Sarah rolled her eyes. "Sweetheart," she said quietly, "we have to rely on each other, and we have to take care of one another. But that will go easier for both of us if we don't try to micromanage each other's life."

John slid her a sardonic glance, which she couldn't appreciate because she was focusing on the increasingly rough road. *This from the woman who sent me to military school,* he thought. *Where micromanaging lives is what they do all day, every day. Have you no shame, Mom?*

John stifled a sigh. He'd just have to watch her. He thought this behavior was new, but couldn't be certain. Their camping trip would be the perfect opportunity to find out just how far it had gone. A few weeks in the wilderness should dry her out nicely.

Sarah lay in bed, smoking and thinking, staring at the rough plaster of the ceiling and watching the smoke rise in curls through the moonlight. Thinking that this would be one of her last cigarettes until John went back to school. Thinking about the girl she had been and wondering what kind of woman she'd be now if Kyle Reese and the Terminator hadn't come into her life.

Just lately she'd been sincerely regretting the loss of that girl, even while she winced at how clueless she'd been.

Why me? she wondered for the millionth time.

With an impatient grimace she stubbed out her cigarette. Such thoughts were a waste of time. She knew she should fight the impulse to indulge them. But she was so isolated here that it got harder and harder not to wallow in self-pity.

She punched her pillow and turned to a more comfortable position in the bed. Self-pity had never been one of her flaws before. And heaven knew she had reason to be happy. She was safe; more importantly, John was safe. The future, as far as she could tell, was assured. They had a nice comfortable life here in Villa Hayes. They didn't even have to associate with much in the way of lowlife, except smugglers—and smugglers were quite respectable, in Paraguay.

A nice, comfortable, deadly dull, boring, empty life. She sighed. The girl she'd been would probably have found this life very fulfilling. She wished she could somehow achieve that attitude. She also wished she could have a little glass of *caña* to help send her off to sleep. But John's obvious distress stopped her. The craving she was feeling right now stopped her.

She'd be a fool to have come so far only to lose everything to demon rum. *The only thing left in my life that means anything to me is my son. I will not lose his respect.* So she'd just have to get used to going to sleep the natural way.

At least she didn't have the nightmare anymore. For a moment she ground her face into the pillow as the thought brought back the images. The searing flash of white light as the bomb ignited, the burning bodies bursting apart as the blast wave struck them, her own body reduced to bones, yet still alive . . .

Now when she had nightmares they were mostly of the asylum. Certainly that was nightmare enough for anybody. That creepy asshole

Douglas and his nightstick ratcheting against the doors at night, that was always a part of it.

I hope I crippled the bastard, she thought. Killing was altogether too good for him.

And Dr. Silberman with his feigned compassion and understanding. Sarah grinned as she thought about the way she'd last seen him, pressed up against the wall with his mouth hanging open as the fluid form of the T-1000 went *through* the lockdown bars.

I wonder how long it took him to convince himself that what he'd seen was some sort of mass hallucination? What a paper that *would make.*

Go to sleep! she ordered herself. Not surprisingly that didn't work. With a sigh she got up, put on her robe, and went out onto the portal, the tile cool under her feet, the night alive with the sound of tropical insect life. She was startled momentarily to find someone out there.

"John?"

"Hi Mom, can't sleep?"

"That's my line." She sat beside him on the swing. "I know you're worried about me," Sarah said. "No need. A word to the wise, as they say. If it worries you, it's gone. Okay?"

He let out a long sigh. "Thank you," he said simply.

"No problem." Well, it might be, but it would be her problem. No reason for John to know anything about it.

They sat in companionable silence for a while, enjoying the soft, spring night.

"Think you'll be able to sleep now?" she asked after a while.

"Yeah." John was surprised to realize that he did think so.

"Me, too. Let's go in and hit the hay."

"Good night," he said, and kissed her on the cheek.

"G'night, hon."

"So what are you going to do today?" Sarah asked, tearing apart a *galleta* and nibbling on the hot bread.

The rolls were a breakfast favorite for both of them. So was the room, big and sunny—shady where it gave on the veranda. The *casa grande* wasn't actually very grand, about eighty years old, but built of white-washed adobe and tile in a style much older. It had been the center of a much larger property once, but she'd bought only enough to give her privacy and pasture for a horse or two.

John tipped his head from side to side with his mouth turned down. "I dunno. Thought I might take Linda for a little exercise. If that's all right with you?"

"No problem, she's getting fat and stir-crazy." Sarah took a sip of her maté. "So I'll leave you to your own devices for today?"

"*Sí.* I think basically I'll just luxuriate and do nothing."

"Translation, everybody else I know is still in school. Well"—she tipped her head to the side—"except for that crowd of ne'er-do-wells that hang out at the plaza."

John waved a hand. "Nah! Not in the mood."

Sarah smiled a slow smile and he pretended not to notice. "You're afraid I'll put you to work."

"Not on my first day," he said. "You wouldn't be so cruel and I deny that I would ever think of you so, *mamacita.*"

She chuckled. "Mamacita?" She looked off over the fields, grinning. "Is that how you see me these days? Your good, old, gray-haired, ginger-bread-baking little mama?"

"The day I catch you baking gingerbread in a frilly apron, Mom, is the day I leave home. Whatchoo talkin' about, gray hair!" He gave her a look of comic disgust and Sarah laughed.

"I do have something I have to ask you," she said. "And I can't believe I'm asking this. How should I dress for the Salcidos' *asado?* I mean are we talking about a sittin'-on-the-hay-bales kind of a do, or is it more like the barbecue in *Gone With the Wind?*"

John spread his hands helplessly, his face a study in amused disbelief. *"You* can't believe you're asking this? I can't believe you're asking *me* this. How should I know? I supposed Luis will have his mom send us an invitation; maybe that will tell us."

"If we get an invitation, it's almost certain to be formal," Sarah mused. "I mean people don't send invitations for casual barbecues." She shrugged. "At least they didn't in the States."

"I'll check with Luis when he gets home," John promised. He waggled his eyebrows. "I don't want us to make a bad impression."

"Too late for that," Sarah told him sadly. "But with the right duds we might save the day."

"New clothes?" he said. "Me, too; me, too."

"I'll expect you to work off the expense," she said with a mean-eyed glare.

"Muck out the stall," he said in resignation. "Paint the trim, clean the chimney, clean the closets . . ."

"I mean down at the company," Sarah said seriously. "It's time we got you an official driver's license for one thing. And you need to know how the business works. That's another reason I'd like you to come with me to Ciudad del Este; you need to meet my contacts."

John turned serious. "I don't know if I want to do that," he said. He'd had more than enough of secret meetings in squalid rooms with people who genuinely gave him the creeps.

"We'd starve to death without the smuggling, hon." She tilted her head and studied him. Instinct told her that there was more at work here than just standard teenage rebellion. "And it's not like we're bringing in guns or drugs. It's just stuff like computers and CDs and so on. Smuggling is what keeps this country running, John. It's like a huge, unofficial, unsanctioned national industry."

"Yeah, I know. But that's not the way it's always going to be, Mom. People like Luis want their country to get rich and they know it won't happen by smuggling in everything they want. Things are going to change in the next decade or so and I don't want either one of us to end up in jail."

Sarah let out a breath, halfway between exasperation and admiration. "You may well be right," she conceded. "But I think we're intelligent enough to recognize the signs and get out of the business before they come to take us away. For right now, though, people rely on us, and frankly, they need us. At least we don't dump knockoffs on them."

"You're right," he agreed, falsely chipper. "We may be criminals, but at least we're not murderers."

Sarah rolled her eyes. "I've got to go to work. We can continue this later, if you like. I'll be home around six," she said, giving him a quick kiss on the forehead. The door slammed behind her and she took a step, then leaned back to say through the screen, "Welcome home, son. Love ya."

"Love you, too, Mom."

The waitress put down the barbecue beef sandwich with a smile.

"Ah! I forgot your *tereré,* señora. I'll be right back."

Sarah smiled and nodded; they knew exactly what she liked here, she didn't even have to ask. Of course, they *should* know. She'd had lunch at the *confitería* just down the street from her business for the past five years. Sarah found it reassuring, almost a luxury, to allow others to know her, even to this small extent. To her it symbolized that her life here was free and above board.

She picked up the sandwich in both hands; it was one big piece, hand-cut bread and juicy meat, nothing fancy but all very good. Sarah opened her mouth wide for her first bite.

Her peripheral vision caught a Jeep passing by outside. The driver was male, no passengers.

Adrenaline kicked her heartbeat into overdrive and her stomach clenched like an angry fist; her breath stopped as though she'd been suddenly plunged into cold water.

Sarah froze with the sandwich almost in her mouth. *I can't be having the DTs,* she thought. *I wasn't drinking* that *heavily!*

She could have sworn that she had just seen a Terminator drive by.

She lowered the sandwich, struggling to swallow and breathe at the same time, and carefully turned to look out the window, down the street where the Jeep had gone. *Flashback?* she asked herself. The vehicle was still there. The driver was talking to one of the kids who hung out in the park. She couldn't see his face, but the general shape of him . . .

"Here we are, señora!" the waitress said cheerfully, setting down an iced glass of tereré.

Sarah jumped and gasped, whipping her head around to stare at the waitress.

"Oh, señora, you're pale. Are you all right?"

Sarah swallowed and tried to smile. "Yes," she said. "I just thought I saw someone I knew."

The waitress leaned toward the window, looking down the street. Sarah turned to look, too, just as the Jeep started up again.

"Ahhh, that is Señor von Rossbach." The waitress sighed. "What a *kuimbaé.* Whoo!" she said and fanned her face with her hand. "You know him?"

"No," Sarah said and cleared her throat. She put down her sandwich. "He looked like someone I used to know." She frowned. "Who did you say he was?"

"Señor von Rossbach," the waitress answered promptly. "Ai, I'm surprised you don't know him, señora. He owns the *estancia* right next to yours. The old Stroessner place."

"No," Sarah said. "I haven't met him. I was vaguely aware that it had been sold, but I didn't realize anyone had moved in yet."

"They say he's from overseas," the waitress said, her eyes wandering to the window as though he might come driving by again. "He's ve-rrry handsome." She looked back at Sarah and frowned in concern. "Are you all right, señora?"

Sarah looked down at her sandwich. "I'm sorry," she said. "I can't eat this now. Why don't you just bring me the bill?"

"I'll wrap it up for you, señora. Later on you might be hungry and there it will be." She smiled down at Sarah, concern in her brown eyes. "Your friend that you thought you saw . . . did something happen to him?"

Sarah nodded and sighed. "He died . . . in a fire."

"Oh! How terrible! No wonder you look so white. I'll be right back, señora."

Sarah's mouth lifted in a half smile. *Funny how people react when they think you might explode emotionally,* she thought. She rose and followed the waitress to the counter.

"It was years ago," she said to the woman's back. "It's just that, out of the corner of my eye, it looked just like him for a second."

"*Sí,*" the waitress agreed. "That happens sometimes. Especially if someone has been on your mind a little." She handed over the sandwich and Sarah paid her bill.

"Thanks," Sarah said.

She left feeling a little better for the waitress's sympathy. She almost felt a little guilty, too, because what she'd said wasn't quite true.

Boy, am I in bad shape today, Sarah thought. *Other people see white mice. I see Terminators.*

She hurried to her office and walked up to Ernesto, whose legs stuck out from under a truck. "Hey," she said cheerfully. "I just found out I have a new neighbor."

Her mechanic slid partway out from under the truck.

"That Austrian guy?" he said. "You just found this out? Señora, he's been there for a month or more!"

"So fill me in," she said, leaning against the fender.

"I don't know that much," Ernesto warned. "People think he's rich. I've heard that he's doing some sort of business with Señor Salcido." He shrugged and looked up at her. "People seem to like him and the women go crazy for him. Beyond that, I know nothing."

"Well, that's a lot more than I knew this morning," Sarah said. "I feel bad, I should have done the neighborly thing and welcomed him or something." She made a face. "I guess it's too late now. What's his first name, do you know?"

The mechanic narrowed his eyes in thought. "Something really German. Mmmm. Dieter! That's it—Dieter von Rossbach."

"Thank you, Ernesto. I knew I could rely on you."

"I am not a gossip, señora," he said, looking hurt.

"No, you're not," Sarah said over her shoulder as she walked away. "You're a man in the know."

He raised his brows at that and smiled, then slid back under the truck.

Sarah went into her office and shut the door. Then she booted up her computer and began looking for information. Von Rossbach's immigration record came up with his picture attached and she swore softly. It—he looked exactly like a Terminator. *Nice to know I'm not hallucinating anyway.*

An hour and a half later she had some information, but not much. And what there was somehow just didn't quite ring true.

Or maybe I'm looking for problems, she thought, chewing on a thumbnail. She hadn't felt this bad since she'd escaped the Pescadero mental hospital and was coming down off the Thorazine and the nightmares were really bad.

Could it possibly be an hallucination? A slight resemblance built into something more by her *caña*-deprived brain. *Oh, I don't like that thought.*

With a little shiver she got back to work. The only cure for this was to find out more. *And that passport picture is too unflattering to be a lie.* That picture was of a face from the future.

By the end of the day she hadn't made much progress. Her Austrian neighbor was indeed rich, from a rich family. According to what she'd read, he had spent most of his life in the international-society scene— attending openings, sunbathing on exclusive beaches, dancing at charity balls.

He hadn't done much good with his life, but then he'd done nothing very bad either. There were no juicy scandals attached to his name. Which, given the people he ran with, was something of a surprise. Perhaps he'd taken up cattle ranching as a whim, or as a way to connect with something real.

I need a closer look at this guy, she thought. She wouldn't be able to rest until she did. But she'd have to be cautious. People who knew her in Villa Hayes would start speculating the moment she started asking questions. *They'd have me planning a wedding before the day was out.* There were pleasant things about living in a small town, but there were also annoyances.

Neither of the other Terminators had bothered to build a background at all, let alone one as elaborate as this one. There had been nothing so delicate in their approach as moving in next door to their victim and making friends with the neighbors. *So does this represent a new approach by Skynet? Has it finally learned to be subtle?* Now, there was a bone-chilling thought.

On the other hand this could be a coincidence. She'd never managed to become paranoid enough to believe that there was no such thing; but she'd become plenty paranoid enough to doubt every one she'd ever encountered.

Dieter von Rossbach could be nothing more or less than what his public record showed him to be: a rich playboy. *So why have I seen this face before on top of the bodies of killing machines?* That really was the crux of the matter, wasn't it?

She knew she wouldn't be telling John. Not just yet anyway, not until she knew more. This had shaken her, if it hadn't actually frightened her.

Sarah remembered her reaction at lunch. It had frightened her all right.

Information, she said to herself. *I need to know more.*

Sarah rose just before dawn and dressed in the dark. Slipping quietly from the house, she went directly to the barn and saddled Linda for an early-morning ride. That ride just happened to take her in the direction of von Rossbach's *estancia*. It was a little chilly, one of the few times in the Chaco you could say that; the dry clear air lost heat quickly at night.

She felt guilty for not feeding the horse immediately, but it was early for her breakfast.

"It's only a two-mile ride," she murmured to the mare as she tightened the girth strap. "It'll work up a nice little appetite for you."

Linda's ears flicked as though she were expressing some doubt about that. But she was a good-natured beast and took this strange departure from routine in her stride.

A half hour later Linda was contentedly grazing and Sarah lay on her belly, her field glasses trained on von Rossbach's front porch. Where, early as it was, the man himself sat with his feet propped up on the railing, sipping from a cup he held in one hand as he read a folded newspaper he held in the other.

He's up pretty early for a playboy, she thought cynically. Then again he might not have gone to bed yet. Or maybe he wasn't yet sick of his new toy and the demands it made of long and early hours.

Von Rossbach sipped, von Rossbach read, Sarah watched. Eventually she checked the time.

"Shit!" she muttered.

John would sleep in this week at least, she knew, so he might never suspect that she'd been out. But she had to feed Linda and get herself washed, dressed, and off to work. She pushed herself backward until she could stand without being seen by anyone in the house and jogged to where she'd left the horse.

Riding home, she thought about what she'd seen. He'd sipped at that cup until it was empty. *What does that prove?* She'd never seen a Terminator eat. *But they must. They weren't keeping that skin alive with batteries.*

And reading the paper was a reasonable thing for a Terminator to do; there would be a lot of useful information in one. *But could a Terminator interact well enough with humans to be their boss?* Sarah considered that and with a sigh concluded that with careful training the answer was yes. After all, by the time they'd lowered "Uncle Bob" into the molten steel she'd formed an emotional attachment to it.

This was getting her nowhere, not even home. With a shake of her head she kicked the horse into a trot. *Maybe John sent another one back,* she thought suddenly. That was a comforting thought.

Or was it? If John had sent back another protector for his younger self, it meant that there was still a Skynet in the future. The idea sent a shiver shooting down her spine. Linda's ears swiveled back toward her as if asking what was wrong.

Stop it! she ordered herself. Then forced herself not to concentrate on how badly she wanted a cigarette. *Or a drink.*

■ ■ ■

Sarah came into a kitchen redolent of fresh-brewed coffee and hot toast. She closed her eyes and inhaled deeply. "Glorious," she said. Opening her eyes she looked at John, already seated at the table. "You're up early."

"Look who's talking," he said, buttering his toast.

"I was restless."

John looked at her sympathetically. "You're doing great, Mom."

Sarah snorted and reached for a cup just as the toast popped up. "That for me?" she asked.

"It is if you wash your hands first."

With a laugh she went to the sink and began to scrub.

"When, exactly, did we reverse roles?" she asked, looking over her shoulder at him.

"Mmm. It's just for now, while you're going through nicotine withdrawal," he said, licking jam off his fingers. "I thought you could use the pampering. Don't get too used to it."

"Thanks for the warning," she said dryly, flicking him with the towel.

Then she kissed him on the top of the head and moved off to claim her toast. *I do* like *my son,* she thought.

CHAPTER 5

Dieter von Rossbach shifted in his saddle, irritated by the turn of events that had drawn him from his office to the edge of this stagnant mud hole. Mosquitoes whined through the hot still air of the Chaco summer; reeds stood still in the scummy green water of the marsh. Birds flicked by like living jewels, but no matter how many of the insects they ate there always seemed to be more. He took off his baseball cap and ran a hand over his short blond brush cut—just starting to go a little gray at the temples—and looked down at his overseer from atop his massive horse. The horse needed to be big. The Austrian was over six feet tall, big-boned and muscular, with the sort of sculpted muscle that only a scientifically designed exercise program can produce. His neighbors and employees thought he was a physical-fitness fanatic, which was true enough. He'd gotten that way under mercilessly perfectionist instructors, though.

"What is she even *doing* here?" he demanded, steely blue eyes snapping, a muscle jumping in his strong jaw, visible even through the short beard he wore.

Epifanio Garcia, Dieter's overseer, rose from where he'd been squatting on his heels and shrugged, his dark walnut face bland. "She's a cow, Señor von Rossbach. She wants to be with her sisters."

The cow in question was definitely not with her sisters at the moment, unless she was standing on them. She was chest-deep and possibly sinking deeper into a disgusting and smelly bog. The cow bawled her distress, big eyes rolling in terror, showing the whites all around.

"She's supposed to be locked up in a paddock," von Rossbach said coldly.

"Some of them are escape artists, señor. This one is smart—for a cow." Epifanio sucked his teeth and shook his head. "That's not awfully bright, of course. Just smart enough to get into trouble."

Grimacing, Dieter considered the cow. He had plans for her. She was supposed to be the mother of a hybrid that would produce meatier, fatter cattle that could endure the privations of the Chaco. He was awaiting a shipment of sperm from the King Ranch in the United States so he could get started. Meanwhile he'd ordered her and three others separated from the main herd so that they would stay healthy.

She was definitely sinking deeper. Judging from the tone of her last bellow, she knew it, too.

Dieter allowed himself an exasperated sigh. "Well, I guess we'd better get her out."

Epifanio, in a few economical movements, had his lariat dropping over the panicked cow's horns, down over her throat. He wrapped it a couple of times around his saddle horn and backed his horse, pulling the cow's head up and not noticeably improving her mood.

"I don't really want to strangle her," Dieter said. "I just want to get her out."

The overseer smiled and waved his arm expressively at the near-buried bovine. "There's nothing else to drop a rope on, señor," he said. "I'm just trying to keep her from sinking any further. What we're going to have to do—"

"We're going to have to get in there with her," von Rossbach agreed.

Epifanio nodded. "And she's going to kick the hell out of us, too." The overseer grimaced.

"Okay, strangle her," Dieter muttered.

Epifanio gave his boss a sidelong glance, not sure whether he was serious or not.

"I know what to do," Dieter said, dismounting.

He took his own rope, and after tying one end to his saddle horn, he handed his reins to his overseer. "Don't let him walk off," he said with a meaningful look, which Epifanio returned with one of cherubic innocence. Then von Rossbach walked toward the bog.

At the edge of the stinking, scum-covered quagmire he took off his boots and socks. He was certain to lose them to suction if he didn't. It should be safe enough to put his bare feet in the muck. There were a number of poisonous snakes and insects in this country, but in all probability very few of them could live under a meter of slime. He seriously considered taking off his trousers, but decided that would make too good a story. Especially if he were to lose his underwear to the mud.

Taking a deep breath, he stepped in. It was cool and far from smooth, he could feel things sliding through his toes. Very quickly Dieter was up to his knees and realizing that the smell was even worse that he'd found it on the shore, as if the earth itself had developed a severe case of flatulence.

So this is where the bodies are buried. He'd been a village boy himself, born in an alpine hamlet where people were only a generation from living over the cow byres, but he'd left that as soon as he could. Twenty years in the big city had dulled his memory of how bad the countryside could smell.

He walked toward the cow, making soothing noises, but she reacted with a fresh panic attack. She thrashed and mooed, waving her head around on her strong neck as though trying to reach him with her horns.

Stupid beast, he thought. He was easily two meters away from her yet. *They see differently,* he reminded himself. *Maybe I look a lot closer.*

Dieter yanked one foot out of the mud with an audible sucking noise, holding his arms out for balance. He sank it back into the bog and leaned forward to pull out the other one, then flailed for balance as his leg plunged to above the knee. He stood still for a moment as the cow went wild.

I guess that would look threatening to a frightened cow, he thought. To her a human waving his arms with a coil of rope in one hand usually meant she was about to be knocked down, sat on, and branded. *Probably not a happy memory.* Sometimes he suspected that they knew *why* human beings kept them around, too. Pigs certainly did. He refused to have any of those on the *estancia.*

Grimly he pulled himself forward, forced to lunge now because he was up to his waist in muck. At last he grabbed onto Epifanio's rope and pulled himself along. Finally he was there. The cow bawled for help, eyes rolling.

Dieter wound up and smacked her in the middle of the forehead with a massive balled fist; her head fell to the side with a drawn-out moo, like a tired squeaky toy. Then she lay with eyes half-closed, her steam-engine panting slowing to a steady deep *wushhhh . . . wushhhhh.*

Epifanio's eyes went wide and his mouth dropped open. Clearly those muscles weren't just for show.

Meanwhile, Dieter, up to his chest in mud, pushed the rope halfway around her loins. Then he dragged himself over to her other side, and after an unpleasant, and all-too-long episode with his nose almost under the stinking mud, he found the rope again and dragged it through. Then he labored back to the forequarters of the cow, squatting and reaching down until his hands closed around the big cannon bones. He clamped them tight, took a deep breath, then straightened, pulling with legs and gut. That drove him deeper, but eventually the mud gave way with a deep sucking sound, and the semiconscious cow came up to lie with its mud-caked forelegs flat on the surface of the swamp. Then he tied off the rope and signaled to his overseer to back the horses.

He held on to Epifanio's rope, and when they got into the shallows he pushed her over on her side and slid the rope down over her forequarters, allowing them to drag her out completely.

By the time she was on dry land she was starting to come to, but was very subdued. Her head wobbled on her muddy neck and she blinked in confusion.

"She's going to have a rotten headache, and a pretty sore stomach," Epifanio observed.

"She's lucky she's feeling anything," Dieter said. "I think she would have gone under in another hour."

"Less than that, señor. I almost went under myself once when I was young and so stupid I went in after a cow by myself."

"Perhaps we should drain it," Dieter said thoughtfully.

"*Sí,* you could do that," Epifanio agreed. "But it would be a big, expensive job. And at most we lose a cow or two a year to the mud. It would take a lot of cows to make such an expense worthwhile."

Dieter gave him a considering look.

"Then I'll have to see if I can't think of an inexpensive way to do it."

He tied his boot laces together and slung them over his saddle, then swung himself up with a grimace for the work it was going to take to clean his saddle. To the annoyance of his horse, who whickered disapproval at the stench of its rider.

Well, I'm not going to walk barefoot through that grass, horse, with all those snakes and scorpions hiding in there. And I'm not going to ruin my boots from the inside instead of the outside, he thought. *You'll just have to get over it.*

"I'll leave you to bring her back to the paddock," Dieter said, and thumped his bare heels into the horse's sides.

Epifanio watched the big man go and shook his head. They'd been nervous when this European showed up to run the *estancia*. The rumor had been that he'd never run cattle before. More troubling, he turned out to be German; at least Epifanio thought von Rossbach was German. Things were different over there; it was all cities and snow, so how could he possibly know how to run an *estancia?*

Mennonites were good farmers—there were plenty of *them* in the Chaco—but von Rossbach was the other variety of German. And while the Germans the overseer knew were very fine people, honest and hardworking, they were also stubborn and determined to have their own way, as well as being very demanding employers.

But von Rossbach had worked out wonderfully. Better than wonderful. Epifanio had been certain that he, too, would end up covered with reeking muck. But here he was dry and clean. They didn't make many like Dieter von Rossbach.

He sat his horse, waiting for the cow to decide when she wanted to get up and sucked his teeth as he thought.

The boss was always polite. Especially to Marieta, the housekeeper, Epifanio's wife. For instance, von Rossbach took care never to swear in her presence. The overseer had heard him swear and the big man knew some colorful curses, so it was definitely a matter of courtesy. Even though Marieta herself swore like a trooper.

Epifanio wondered how long the boss would stick around. He learned fast and he had plans for the *estancia,* but it was obvious that after only six months he was becoming bored.

The cow heaved herself to her feet and stood for a moment on wobbly legs. She gave a juicy snort, then began to nibble some grass. The overseer dropped a rope over her head again and turned to lead her back to her paddock.

"Come on, girl," he said. "I'll hose you down and you'll feel much, much better."

Clean, but still sensing a ghostly whiff of the swamp about his person, Dieter sat at his desk, prepared to pick up where he'd left off. The *casa grande* was old, massive adobe walls, rafters of thick *quebracho*—ax-breaker—trunks. That was one reason he'd bought it when he came looking for a peaceful, quiet place to retire. It had character; the tiles on the roof and floors had been handmade, you could see the slight ripple. This office had windows that opened onto an interior patio, with a fountain and a pale crimson sheet of jacaranda running up a trellis on the opposite wall. Hummingbirds hovered around it. The whole thing was soothing . . . until you'd been thoroughly soothed.

His workspace was utterly modern by contrast, with a state-of-the-art IBM, a nice little satellite-uplink dish to give broadband access to the Web, and a full suite of equipment. His answering machine was blinking, so he hit the play button and picked up his pen.

"Señor von Rossbach?" a young female voice inquired. She paused as though she expected him to answer. "This is the Krieger Trucking Company? We've received a shipment for you from the King Ranch in the United States?" She hesitated, as if unsure the message was clear. "It's waiting here for you to pick it up?" Another nervous little hesitation. "All right, good-bye." And she hung up.

Dieter checked his watch. Two o'clock—siesta would be well over by the time he got there. Anyone who expected Paraguayans to do anything during siesta went mad in short order—and he had to admit, in this climate the custom made sense. He looked at his neat desk and decided there wasn't anything that desperately needed his attention right now.

"Señora Garcia," he called out, rising from his chair. "Do you need anything in Villa Hayes?"

He found her in the kitchen, where she was plucking a chicken for dinner. She wanted him to call her Marieta and pretended she didn't hear him when he referred to her as señora.

"Do we need anything in Villa Hayes?" he asked again.

"*Sí.* Laundry soap," she said, not looking up. "The kind in the yellow box with the red letters, and matches for the stove."

"Anything else?" She usually had a list a foot long.

Marieta shook her head. "I'm going in to town myself on Monday with Epifanio," she said. "My grandnephew is coming on the bus from Tobati.

He's going to work here for you this summer." She grinned up at him. "You'll like him, he's a good boy."

If he was as likable as her local nephews, he probably would. But if he was like her local nephews, there would also probably be as much soccer playing as cattle ranching. Dieter's lips quirked up in a smile. What the hell, he could afford it, and they were good kids. Sometimes, just lately, he'd had wistful thoughts about children. Not something you even thought about, in his previous profession, where the phrase "giving hostages to fortune" had an unpleasantly literal meaning.

"See you later," Dieter said, and headed for his Land Rover.

Sarah stared at the second drawer of her desk and sighed. *As long as it's there I'll never get any work done,* she told herself. She tightened her lips, and quickly, so that she couldn't change her mind, opened the drawer, took out the flask, and went into the washroom. Without allowing herself to think about it, she opened it and upended the contents into the sink.

Sarah came out screwing on the cap and looked up to find Ernesto giving her a huge, sunny smile. He raised one grease-blackened hand in salute and she returned it, her own smile a little ironic.

One thing that this little struggle had taught her was that she had a fight on her hands. *I didn't realize things had gone this far,* she thought. Sarah bit her full lower lip and considered the flask. "You want this?" she asked her chief mechanic.

His eyebrows went up. *"Sí,* señora," he said coming over to her. *"Gracias."*

It was a nice flask, smooth steel with a cap that could be used as a cup.

"No problemo," she said, smiling as though it wasn't. But Sarah found that she hated to give it up, and had to stop herself from yanking it back with a snarl.

"I will take good care of it, señora," Ernesto said anxiously, noting the look in her eyes.

Sarah blinked. "I know you will," she said with a wave of her hand. "Enjoy it." She smiled at him. Then she walked back to her office, her heart pounding.

At four-thirty Sarah went to the reception area to cover for Meylinda's break. She *needed* a cigarette. She also needed a drink, but she needed a cigarette more. Maybe it was a good idea to give up drinking and smoking together, have one big torture session instead of two smaller ones.

Maybe they'll each cancel out the other's cravings, she thought. *I'll be so paralyzed trying to decide which unhealthy thing I want more that by the time I make up my mind, I'll have kicked both habits.*

She picked up a stack of papers for filing and noticed that her hands were shaking. Would this day *ever* end? And she was jumpy. If someone dropped something . . .

Ernesto slammed the hood of one of the trucks and she jumped a foot. Sarah held her breath and counted to twenty before her heart rate went back to normal. Then she was suddenly furious, first with Ernesto for slamming and banging things around, then with herself. *What was I thinking? How could I let myself get like this?*

Somewhere deep inside her was the absolute conviction that one day she would need to be on her game, strong and focused. One day it would happen and she had to be ready.

But the logical, sensible, everyday side of her had talked her out of it, at least on a conscious level. She and John and the Terminator had taken care of the problem. They were safe, everyone was safe, it was over. The bad days were behind them, the running, the asylum, the stockpiling, all over.

A crooked smile twisted her lips. Those stockpiles of arms and food baking in deep, well-camouflaged holes throughout the southwestern U.S. and northern Mexico would bring in a lot of cash if she were interested in selling them—not to mention the gold coins. She still had contacts that could get rid of them for her and pay her well, keeping her name out of it. But she just couldn't bring herself to do it.

Maybe that was why she'd taken to drinking, to shut that part of her up. She'd kept fit; running even a small farm would help you do that. But she'd gotten sloppy, and bored, and she'd let things slide.

Well, it's not too late, Sarah thought. *This can be fixed. In a few months, no one will ever know how close I came to losing it.* No one but herself, that is. *And that's how it should be.*

"This is Krieger Trucking?" a voice said behind her.

A voice with a faint accent, a voice that froze every muscle in her body. She hadn't expected this. *It's too soon,* she thought. *I'm not ready.*

"Hello?" he said again.

Sarah turned slowly, trying to keep the terror off her face, knowing that it didn't matter. Her thoughts jumbled together. "It" could read her fear in other ways. When she saw his face—its face—she couldn't help but gasp. This close, the resemblance was too perfect, too complete. *This can't be an accident!*

"Ye-es," she managed to choke out.

"I'm looking for—"

Sarah broke, she turned and walked away; by the time she hit the corridor that led to the garage she was running. She *knew* it had come for her and she raced through the garage and out into the alley without a backward glance.

In their early days in this town she'd mapped out several escape routes; now she took the nearest and, she hoped, best. Running flat out, she made good use of the twisted alleyways.

Dieter stared at the empty space that had just been occupied by a slender woman with short dark hair. Then he reacted, leaping over the counter and giving chase. He didn't recognize her, but she unquestionably knew him. Of course, he wasn't so much disguised as situated in an unlikely place.

He'd spent most of his life as a counterterrorist operative, starting out in an elite unit of the Bundesheer, later working closely with American and Israeli intelligence. He was a good operative, but he was no monster, not one of the mad-dog killers of popular fiction. The woman had no reason to fear him unless she herself was guilty of something horrendous.

He was lucky at the first few turns; the ground was wet and she'd left footprints in the mud. Then the ground began to get hard, and he began to pant. Finally he came to an open space, surrounded by buildings, seemingly abandoned. He tried doors and windows, but all were securely locked. There were no footprints.

Dieter wiped the sweat from his brow and looked around, letting his breathing return to normal. *Tomorrow morning, first thing,* he thought, *back to running ten miles.* He was sweating like a pig! Next thing he knew he'd have a potbelly.

He listened, and heard nothing. There were voices in the distance and some traffic, but nothing nearby. A dog stuck its head around one of the buildings and whined at him.

"Hey, boy," Dieter said, leaning down. The dog came up to him, wagging its tail so hard its whole stern was lashing back and forth. "Did you see her, huh?" he asked, scratching the mutt's ears. His eyes moved over the surrounding buildings even as he appeared to be concentrating solely on the dog. "Did you see where she went?"

The stray was wiggling in ecstasy, as it strained to lick Dieter's hands, and grunting with pleasure when the big man switched to scratching its ruff.

"Dat's a good boy," Dieter assured the animal in the baby-talking voice that even some antiterrorist operatives used with animals.

He straightened up and put his hands on his hips, realizing just a little too late that he might have acquired a new friend. Looking around, von Rossbach tightened his mouth while the dog looked up worshipfully.

The woman could be anywhere by now. Probably she'd gone to ground in a previously scouted hiding place. Obviously he wasn't going to find her here, he looked around at the blank building faces.

Unless, that is, he was willing to put time into it, finding a niche somewhere and blending into the scenery until the woman felt safe enough to emerge from hiding. He took a deep breath and let it out slowly.

No, he was retired, he was no longer obligated to chase everyone who ran. They would know who she was at the trucking company, so that was the logical place to go for information. Besides, he needed that shipment.

Sarah watched in the mirror before her, aimed to catch the view through a filthy window, as the man she'd been almost certain was a Terminator reached down to pet the dog. She stood up slowly and let out her breath in a rush, then stood there panting, shaking from adrenaline reaction.

Licking her lips, she tried to think what to do. *If a dog can tolerate him, he can't be a Terminator. Humans can be fooled, but not dogs.* As von Rossbach turned to walk away, she made up her mind.

Unlocking the window, she lifted it and slipped through, easing it down behind her. "Wait!" she called weakly.

If he wasn't a Terminator she had to find out what, or rather who, he was, and why he had come looking for her. He couldn't have seen her spying on him this morning, could he? Her skills were rusty, but surely not *that* rusty.

She went to the nearest building and peeked around the corner. The man was leaning over, trying to persuade the dog to go home, though it was obvious just looking at the mutt that it didn't have one.

"You've got a friend for life there," Sarah said, trying to keep her voice steady. The man looked at her. Her voice had quavered a bit and her hands were still shaking; she might as well try to use that, along with her diminutive size, to seem harmless. It might wipe that closed look off his face.

"I'm sorry," Sarah said. "I'm so sorry." She brushed her hair back and gave a nervous little laugh. "I thought you were someone else." She looked at him, wide-eyed, then burst out, "But you're not. Obviously."

"Who did you think I was?" he asked. His voice was quiet, but his eyes were hard, evaluating her.

She lifted her hands and then dropped them; shaking her head, Sarah walked a few steps toward him.

"Please," she said, her eyes on the ground as she walked, "I'd rather not say. I'm so embarrassed as it is. Anyway, you don't want to know about it. It's just . . ." She waved her hands helplessly. "Please, could we start over?" Sarah looked up at him and smiled tremulously, trying to look innocent.

"Who are you?" he asked, still suspicious.

"I'm Suzanne Krieger," she said, holding out her hand. "That's my trucking company."

"Oh, really." He sounded dubious.

"A lot of people are surprised to hear that," Sarah assured him, smiling weakly. There was an awkward moment of silence. "I just want you to know that was a very uncommon reaction," she said, twisting her fingers together nervously. "I really don't make a habit of running away from my customers. Honest." *Don't overdo it, Connor,* she warned herself.

"You're an American," Dieter observed.

"Yes. But my husband was Paraguayan."

"Was?" Dieter walked by her side as they wended their way back to the trucking company.

He found her face attractive in an angular way; her blue eyes were very expressive and her mouth was . . . *tempting. A good figure, too,* he thought.

But he was still not lulled by either her fluttering manner or her refusal to explain. He noticed that she kept as far from him as she could in the narrow alley.

"Yes, he died the year after he bought the company." She lapsed into silence for a few moments. "Anyway, that's enough about me," she said as they came to the open door of the garage. "What is it you came here for?" *Boy, do I want to know that.*

Dieter could actually feel the word "sperm" pressing against his teeth, but he restrained himself. "I have a shipment from the King Ranch," he said instead.

"Oh, yes," Sarah said with a smile. "It's in the fridge, I'll go get it for you. You know the way out front," she said with a little laugh and a gesture toward the open door to the offices.

Sarah looked at him sweetly until at last he nodded and headed out to the front office. When he was gone she leaned against the wall and allowed her shoulders to sag.

How can this be? she asked herself. Her stomach clenched. *He's the spitting image of no less than* two *Terminators! Except for the beard.* She wondered briefly if Terminators could even grow beards. *He even sounds like them!* Well, maybe the accent wasn't as pronounced. But in every other way Dieter von Rossbach was a physical duplicate of the T-101's she'd known. *But how? There has to be a connection, but what?*

Sarah brushed her hair back off her forehead and blew out her breath. *It's time to discuss it with John,* she thought. *He'll probably have some ideas. Meanwhile . . .* Sarah went to the fridge and took the special box out. *King Ranch—probably sperm, then.*

The labels and stamps and customs papers all seemed authentic, so if this was some kind of ruse, it was a very elaborate one. Also irrelevant. No one smuggled drugs *from* the United States to South America as far as she knew. So, obviously, that wasn't it. And going by the paper trail this box had traveled by legitimate courier all the way. So Mr. von Rossbach, in this instance at least, probably was just a rancher interested in improving his cattle.

She wondered why they'd never dealt with this guy before. *Most likely he'd used somebody in Asunción.* It didn't really matter. Getting rid of him and returning home to John to discuss this weird situation did.

Though I have to wonder if his choosing Krieger Trucking was happenstance or if there's some motivation behind it. The coincidences were mounting up. She could feel the paranoia taking over.

"Here you go," she said as she walked into the front office. Sarah picked up a clipboard from Meylinda's desk. She noticed that her hands were still shaking. *Okay, so we use that,* she reminded herself. *I'm just a shy, decent widow doing her best.*

Von Rossbach stood foursquare behind the counter, his eyes never leaving her, taking in every movement, every nuance of expression.

"You're making me nervous," Sarah accused as she laid down the box. She presented the clipboard to him with a pen. "Would you sign here, please?"

He took them, but continued to study her. Sarah ducked her head and looked away. "Please," she said.

"I would really like to know who you thought I was," Dieter said steadily. "Please explain."

Sarah took a deep breath, not looking at him and let it out, then nodded. "I can easily see why you might be offended," she said, swallowing. "Okay." Sarah paused for effect, biting her lips. "When Paul died someone wanted to buy the company. But I wanted to keep it for our son, and because I'd put a lot of effort into it myself. This guy who wanted to buy it took my refusal personally and was very, very angry. He made threats. I told him to leave us alone."

She stopped and glanced at him from the corner of her eyes. That unwavering stare of his really *was* making her tense. *Not that I need any help with that,* she thought ruefully.

"You thought I was this man?" he asked.

"Uh, no, not exactly. Anyway, for a while nothing happened. Then little accidents began to occur, things went missing, and some of our shipments were hijacked. He came back and made another offer. This one was ridiculously low, insulting actually, and I told him to go away."

She dipped her head, and shrugged. "That's when things began to get scary. There was this man, a big man; I began to see him everywhere, watching me, getting closer all the time. I'd be shopping for groceries, for instance, and suddenly I'd feel someone behind me and I'd turn and it would be him, just . . . looking at me. One day he asked me about my little boy."

Her voice broke on the last word. Sarah was proud of that touch; she hadn't been sure she could do it. She took a deep breath, blinking as though afraid there might be tears to hide. "There's really not much else to tell. I decided to move the company here to Villa Hayes because I thought there'd be less competition. But I liked that it was so near a big city. I thought we'd be safe here."

She gave a little laugh. "I gave up smoking today, so I'm nervous as a cat at a dogfight, and when I looked up all I could see was your outline and"—she shook her head regretfully—"I panicked. I'm so sorry. I am not, ordinarily, such a scaredy-cat. It was like a flashback. You know?"

Dieter gave her a long look, revealing nothing. He watched her fidget for a few moments, then signed her form. She tore off a portion of it and gave it to him as his receipt.

"Thank you," she said, smiling bravely, her heart thudding in a nerve wracking combination of anger and fear. "Good luck evading that dog."

Sarah could see the disreputable mutt waiting hopefully outside her front door. *I hope he sticks to you like a burr and gives you some horrible parasite,* she thought viciously.

Given her plausible explanation and, to her mind, very convincing performance, she couldn't help but think of him as a bully. If she really was a helpless little widow she'd be ready to burst into tears by now.

Dieter turned to look and his shoulders twitched. Sarah liked that; it made him seem more human and she finally began to calm down.

He picked up his box.

"Hasta la vista," he said, and walked out. The dog fell in behind him, its chin a fraction of an inch from the big man's boot heel.

Sarah closed her eyes slowly. Then she turned to check the clock. Five-thirty. *I can't keep quitting early like this,* she told herself as she headed for her office. Picking up her purse and her keys she went into the garage.

"Ernesto," she called. Her voice was still shaking a little and Sarah frowned at the evidence of weakness. She cleared her throat.

He came out from under a truck. "You are all right, señora?" he asked, his face full of concern.

"Actually, I feel lousy, Ernesto." She was willing to bet that she looked almost as bad as she felt. "I'm going home early. Can you close up for me, please? I'll lock the front door myself, if you'll take care of back here."

"Sure," he said, sitting up. "That man . . . ?"

"Oh . . ." Sarah waved a dismissive hand. "Mistaken identity. I feel like a complete fool. He's just a rancher, I guess." She shook her head. "Nothing to worry about, my friend. I'm just nervous and feeling rotten. I'll see you in the morning."

"Sí. I hope that you feel better soon," he said and waved to her before pushing himself back under the truck.

He'd learned early in their relationship that Suzanne Krieger did not take kindly to being coddled. So showing that he was on her side was all he was prepared to do right now. But he would love to know why his tough-as-nails boss had gone running out of the garage with "just a rancher" in hot pursuit. Although he had to admit, at least to himself, if that man had started chasing him, he'd have run, too.

"Not my business," Ernesto muttered, picking up a wrench. She knew where to find him if she needed his help.

Dieter tucked into his desk and booted up his computer. He had an Identikit program and he brought it up now. In about twenty minutes he had a fair likeness of Suzanne Krieger and made up a version with and without glasses.

The woman didn't feel to him like a terrorist; there was an aura about them that Dieter could usually pick up on.

Besides, females were rare among their ranks. Those who chose the terrorist lifestyle, though, tended to be excellent actresses. So he couldn't afford to eliminate the possibility solely on gut feeling.

It was also possible, given that she owned a trucking company, that Mrs. Krieger was running drugs. Her overreaction today indicated that she was coming down off of *something. But it might just be cigarettes, as she said.* When he'd quit smoking he'd been close to dangerous for six weeks.

She's probably smuggling, he thought. *But in Paraguay it's more likely to be DVD players than drugs. Smuggling is the national industry, or was.*

Von Rossbach studied the stark portraits he'd created of Suzanne Krieger, looking for something in the images that would give him a clue. *She's guilty of something*, he thought. *An innocent woman doesn't take off like a hare being chased by hungry hounds. She calls for help, she runs to the nearest man, she doesn't clear out for parts unknown without even making a sound.* That, he felt, was a telling detail. *She knows how to run. If she didn't, I'd have caught her.* And the way she moved . . . *She had combat training somewhere. Martial arts, certainly.*

Dieter flattered himself that the mere sight of his face wasn't likely to send women running for their lives. Maybe she'd bumped off Paul Krieger before moving down here. Whatever—he composed a note to Jeff Goldberg, his former partner in the Sector Operation.

Hi Jeff,
Sorry to bother you, but I'm wondering if you can tell me anything about this woman, who currently runs a trucking company in Villa Hayes.

Strangely enough she ran from me the moment she saw me (no comments please) and gave me a story about being threatened by some man who wanted to buy her business.

She's going by the name Suzanne Krieger, widow of Paul Krieger, and she has a son. It might be nothing, but my antennae are up on this one. Looking forward to hearing back from you.

Dieter

P.S. When are you and Nancy coming to my ranch to visit?

Soon, he hoped. There was a lot to like about this country and this life, but after eight months away from the Sector he was finding it incredibly dull. You could be bored in "the business"—*were* bored, most of the time—but there was always an edge of anticipation.

He supposed it was to be expected; compared to his old life running down terrorists and international criminals, pursuing cattle across the Chaco was an inevitable come down. Each day ran into the next here with very little to distinguish them from each other.

Today, though, had been exceptional and he felt good. He might just be chasing shadows here, but at least he wasn't chasing cows.

"John? *John?*" Sarah stood in the tiled-and-whitewashed hallway of her *estancia* and listened, but the house was silent. He couldn't have gone far, though; he wouldn't leave the house open like this if he wasn't in earshot. She went out onto the *portal.* "John!" she shouted.

She heard a distant call in answer and looked in that direction. Of course, the barn. He'd been riding Linda. She leaped down the three steps and trotted toward his voice. Sarah found him in the paddock at the back of the barn, grooming the bay mare, who was trying to wrap her neck around him in a horsely hug.

"She says that you neglect her shamefully and leave her to starve as often as not," John said with a grin, pushing the horse's big head away gently.

"She lies like a rug," Sarah said, crossing her arms atop the paddock gate. "Which she might soon become if she keeps blackening my reputation that way."

"Y'hear that, Linda?" John asked, scritching under her chin. The horse stretched her neck out in ecstasy, a foolish expression on her long face. "I may be your favorite human but you have to know which side your hay is buttered on. This lady is your meal ticket, don't you know that?"

Linda sneezed, splattering John's T-shirt with green.

"Auuggh! Thank you, Linda!" he said, holding his arms out in disgust. John whipped off the shirt and used the clean side to wipe his face and arms.

Sarah gave a short laugh at his expression. "Come out of there before she starts to lick you." She opened the gate, and then she turned serious. "We have to talk."

Unlike most teens, John's automatic reaction wasn't *What am I supposed to have done now?* Instead he asked, "What's gone wrong, how can we fix it?"

He slipped through the gate and turned to fasten it behind him. Then he squinted up at the sun. "You're early," he said, almost a question.

Sarah opened her mouth. Now that she was in front of him she didn't really know how to begin.

John lowered his head and raised his eyebrows. "Mom?"

"I had . . . a really strange experience today," she began. With one hand she brushed her hair back and frowned into the middle distance.

"Strange, how?" John asked. *Was it getting off the caña?* he wondered. *D.t.'s or some shit like that?* 'Cause he didn't know if he could handle it if it was. Did you just lock them in a closet with a bag of candy and hope for the best, or what?

"This guy came in today to pick up a shipment and, John"—she looked him in the eye—"I swear to you, he was the spitting image of a Terminator."

John shook his head. "You're—"

"He had a beard, and his accent was less noticeable, but otherwise he looked *exactly* like a Terminator."

Sarah tightened her lips; it was obvious he was having trouble believing her. They stared at one another for a long minute, and then John shook his head as though to clear it.

"Doesn't necessarily mean anything," he said. "Skynet may have made the Terminators up to look like pictures it had on file. It had to get those faces from someplace, right? So it doesn't have to be a threat, right?"

"We didn't stay alive and out of jail by treating something that looked like a threat as if it wasn't one," Sarah reminded him. "I don't want this to mean anything either, but we can hardly afford to bury our heads in the sand. Right?"

"What happened?" John asked, holding up his hands in a slow-down gesture. "Exactly."

So she told him. "He was definitely human," she finished. "While he was looking for me this stray dog came along and fell in love with him. And he took the time to pet it and talk to it, and it followed him home."

John spluttered a laugh. "It followed him home? That doesn't sound like a Terminator, does it?"

She gave her son a steely look. "Except he looked *just* like one. What's more"—why hadn't she told him this in the first place?—"he's moved in right next door to us."

John's face smoothed into a neutral expression. He said nothing.

Sarah bit her lower lip. *I should have told him yesterday,* she thought. *But I didn't want to seem like I was overreacting.* She told him about the research she'd been able to do so far. "I don't want to panic or anything, but it might be time we moved on," she said, and started toward the house. "Maybe we've been getting too comfortable."

John trotted to catch up with her and tugged at her arm, stopping her. "Mom," he said. "Let's not overreact here. Right now we don't really know anything about this guy. At least nothing bad. Let's find out who he is first, because if he is trouble and we panic and go running for our lives, that could bring him down on us."

"I am not in a panic," she protested. "I'm saying that—"

"It's not a good idea to get too settled, a rolling stone gathers no moss, we can't afford to get complacent and all that sensible-sounding shit. But I say we can't afford to go off half-cocked. Who is this guy and is he, in fact, any threat to us? If you don't know your enemy how can you defend yourself against him, right?" John looked at her, a determined look in his eyes.

Sarah's face turned cold. She took a breath to speak and John held up his hand.

"I'm not saying I won't go. I'm not stupid, Mom, and I would never do anything that might end with you back in an institution. But I am not going to give up everything we've worked so hard for because you're having a bad day."

"Hey!" Sarah said, taken aback.

John hung his head. "Sorry," he mumbled.

"You should be!" She turned away and started back to the house. *I've had worse days than this and kept my head!* she thought. Then she stopped as an image of von Rossbach came to her. "He has cop's eyes, John," she said. "You're right, I *am* having a bad day or I would have seen it sooner."

"Cop's eyes?" John said. The phrase sent a chill through him—he knew exactly what she meant, had known since he was a very little kid. "So what was he picking up, Mom?"

"Sperm," she said, and started walking again.

"What?" John screwed up his face into a confused knot. "Did you say 'sperm'?"

"Cattle sperm, from the U.S.," Sarah said over her shoulder.

"How old was he?" John asked, catching up to her again. "Maybe he's retired."

"A retired cop might be the most dangerous kind," she said thoughtfully. "He'd have time on his hands, and probably be bored out of his skull, *and* he'd have contacts to ask for further information."

"Our cover story's pretty airtight, though, isn't it?" John asked.

He knew it was, he'd worked on it himself at odd moments. *And if I do say so myself it's very good.* Just enough information, not too much, that was the key. As for people who used to know them in Ciudad del Este, the city was growing and changing so fast even he had trouble finding people they knew there. And those people had been well paid to remember them and their sad circumstances.

Sarah gave a weary sigh. "Yes, our background should pass muster." It should, she'd worked hard enough on it. Most of the work had involved undoing some of John's airier flights of fancy.

"So," John concluded, "we should be okay for at least a couple of weeks. Sooo, we find out about this guy."

"I'll just check with my extensive social connections," Sarah said sarcastically.

"Mom, you don't *have* any social connections."

"Thanks for reminding me, O fruit of my loins."

John shuddered dramatically. "Eeuww! Mom, that's *gross.* No, I'll check *my* extensive social contacts; you check your extensive underworld connections. If he's a cop they'll know about him. Working together, we'll come up with something."

Sarah grinned, feeling better for having spoken to her son. *My ally,* she thought with a surge of affection. "Okay," she said. "We'll check him out before we act. But get used to the idea that we might have to go."

"Don't worry, Mom, I can have my coin collection packed up in five minutes and be ready to roll."

"Good to know," she said, and put an arm around him. She blinked in surprise. *It's a little disturbing to put your arm around your son and find yourself reaching up,* she thought.

"What?" he asked.

She switched to putting her arm around his waist. "It's just that you're growing up."

"Aw, Mom!" John rolled his eyes.

She started up the stairs to the house. "What do you want for dinner?" she asked.

"Meat!" he rumbled in a deep, deep voice.

"No problemo, pumpkin."

"Pumpkin? What happened to 'you're growing up'?"

She opened the screen door, then looked at him over her shoulder. "I had to take the wind out of your sails before your ego flew away with you."

He came in after her wearing a sappy smile. "A boy's best friend is his mother," he said.

"And don't you forget it, bucko. Go wash up, dinner in half an hour."

John gave her a quick kiss on the cheek and went down the hall. Sarah watched him go with mixed emotions. She didn't want to uproot them; she knew he'd mind it this time. Sarah allowed herself a sigh. Then it was time to stoke up the barbecue.

As long as I don't feel like I'm the one turning on a spit I should be fine, she thought.

CHAPTER 6

Tricker took his time reading over Serena Burns's résumé as she sat across the desk awaiting his attention. For someone her age it was impressive, but then, so was the lady herself. He'd already read it, of course. Not only read it, but investigated it, assigning one or two underlings to go out and interview the exalted persons who had bestowed such glowing recommendations.

Curiously enough, it seemed that very few people in those companies had ever interacted with Ms. Burns in her capacity as head of security, assistant head of security, acting, associate, trainee, or any other job title in the corporate security name game. Except for the bosses, she was the incredible, invisible woman.

Which must have been a tough stunt for an incredibly sexy, leggy, gorgeous blonde to pull off.

He was rereading her résumé now to see how she would react to being ignored. She was reacting by focusing her attention on him with such aggressive intensity that he felt in serious danger of reacting himself. He hadn't blushed since he was twenty, but he felt one coming on now.

"So," he said finally, laying down the last page and raising his eyes to meet hers. "Very impressive, Ms. Burns."

She looked amused, in a way that implied they shared a secret. Possibly the fact that they both knew she was too good for Cyberdyne to pass up. "I've been very fortunate in my employment," she said. "I had excellent mentors and"—her eyes went distant, as though she were remembering—"we had some interesting times while I was with them."

Uh-hunh! Tricker thought. *Now there's a statement that's open to interpretation.* "Well, oddly enough, not many people seem to remember you at your old jobs," he said.

Serena elegantly shrugged one trim shoulder. "I deliberately kept a very low profile. There are times when the obvious cop on the corner is a good idea and others when it's not. Some corporate spies are incredibly clever. I find it's much easier to catch them if you've convinced them that you're not even around."

She offered him a pleasant but impersonal smile. He hadn't reacted well to her so far. She wondered if that ignoring-the-interviewee-while-you-read-their-CV ploy ever worked. And if it did, what good was it? As far as she was concerned all they'd accomplished was to waste twenty minutes.

The job was hers if she wanted it, he had to know that. If he turned her down she would hit Cyberdyne with a very noisy discrimination suit, which she would almost certainly win. Something she was willing to bet Mr. Tricker knew. And she was also willing to bet that the last thing he, or Cyberdyne, wanted, now or ever, was noise in their vicinity.

But she could be vastly more patient than this fellow could imagine. So she'd play his little game, answer his questions, fill out more forms, and take a battery of tests if required. She'd win in the end.

"Your career is remarkable," Tricker said, rubbing his chin. "But your stay at each company was also remarkably short. Care to comment on that?"

No, she thought.

This is where her apparent age was a problem. It had required her seemingly to hopscotch from one job to another in an alarmingly rapid manner. But there was no help for it, she was going to appear to be twenty-five for a very long time, so the dates were close together. Eventually she would pretend to be a young-looking thirty, once there she'd worry. For now, she had to get this position.

"I was acquiring my skills," she said, crossing her legs. "Once a position had taught me all I thought it could, I moved on."

He noticed her legs, as she'd meant him to. Very nice. This woman would be a cat among the pigeons here at Cyberdyne. Some of these computer geeks would sell their souls just to have coffee with her. And she'd implied that some of her upward mobility had come about from her "horizontal agility." Problems like that he didn't need.

"What we're looking for here at Cyberdyne is someone who will be with us for the long haul," Tricker said, closing the folder on her application. "I don't feel it's in our best interests to hire someone who might be lured away by the candy of a new experience."

Serena was annoyed. Clearly she'd misread this man, but everything so far had been so easy. *That's no excuse for getting sloppy,* she scolded herself. For once a human had reacted to her sexually and yet kept that response separate from his reasoning faculty. She hadn't been here in the early years of the century for long, but she hadn't found that capacity to be common among men.

"But a job like this one is exactly what I've been honing my skills for," she said. "An opportunity to establish a security system from the ground up is less common than you might think. I have a lot of ideas for Cyberdyne that I believe will keep it, its products, and its scientists safe and happy."

"Nothing like a happy product," Tricker said brightly.

Serena grinned. "Happy scientists then—or at least contented. These geniuses are very touchy and genuinely hate anything that might restrict them or smacks of Big Brother. But obviously the company has to keep them safe from such threats as kidnapping"—she paused significantly—"or murder. I think I've got a way to please everybody without rocking the boat."

Yeah? Tricker thought cynically. *Well, you may be super-babe, but even you can't sleep with all of the people all of the time.* "Do tell," he invited.

Serena shook her head. "That wouldn't be in my best interests."

Tricker nodded affably. "Maybe not," he agreed. "But it wouldn't be in our best interests to hire someone who might be gone in six months."

"Hire me," she said, leaning forward, her gaze locked on his. "If I leave in under two years I'll agree to pay you a kill fee, substantial enough to cover your search for a new applicant. If you decide to fire me after six months you won't even have to pay me a severance check. I want this job, and I can make a difference here."

Serena leaned back, still exuding a confidence she didn't quite feel. For some reason this human had taken a dislike to her and she couldn't think why, or exactly what to do about it. The obvious solution, killing him, might not be the best in this case.

Though his attitude did make it tempting.

Tricker looked at her, taken aback. That was quite an offer she was ponying up. Still . . . "We'll certainly take that into consideration," he said brightly, patting her file. He rose and offered her his hand. "We'll be in touch, one way or the other."

Serena shook his hand, taking brief pleasure in knowing she could crush it to a wet pulp. "Thank you, Mr. Tricker."

"Just Tricker," he said.

She nodded. "I'll look forward to hearing from you." On that note, she picked up her briefcase and left without a backward glance.

As Serena walked to the parking lot she reran the interview, Tricker's image making a faint overlay on the scene around her. She was looking for the exact moment when she'd blown it. For blown it she had. If he'd been undecided before meeting her, he was no longer. From this point on he'd be actively opposed to hiring her.

"We had some interesting times while I was with them," the recording said, her voice sounding dreamy. His face remained impassive, but he blinked. *That was the moment,* she decided. That implication had worked very well with Colvin and Warren, but to Tricker it had sent up a warning flag.

She frowned; failure loomed, and all over an offhand remark made to the wrong person. Now she could only hope that the president and CEO's support and her impulsive offer would sway him in her favor. For she felt with certainty that Tricker had the final say here.

Perhaps I can think of some way to eliminate my rivals, she thought. Preferably in the form of better job offers rather than assassination.

Things are so complicated here!

"I don't see how you can object to her," the CEO complained. "Ms. Burns is perfect for this job."

"Hey, Colvin," Tricker said, his eyebrows raised, "what she is is a perfect thirty-eight, twenty-four, thirty-six, and a natural blonde, or I miss my guess."

"I was referring to her résumé," Colvin said through his teeth.

"Sure you were, Roger." Tricker sneered.

"Is her body your only objection?" Warren asked with a curl of his lip.

"Hey, guys." Tricker leaned forward. "Why don't we pretend our dicks are in the cafeteria huddled over cups of coffee and sniggering about Ms. Burns's assets and let our brains take over this discussion?

"Have you two actually considered those glowing recommendations, or the scant time she put in to earn them? Doesn't it seem the least bit suspicious to you that only one or two people at these places seem to have even been aware of her existence?"

Warren and Colvin glanced at each other, then at Tricker.

"Well, don't you?" Tricker's blue eyes fairly bulged with frustration. "Are you trying to tell me that you'd forget working in the same building with that woman?"

"Nooo," Colvin said thoughtfully.

"Tricker"—Warren folded his hands before him—"you can't refuse to hire someone on the suspicion that she *might* have slept her way into a good recommendation. If you can't prove that"—he spread his hands—"it's irrelevant."

"And she has given us a very generous out if things go wrong," Colvin pointed out.

"Do you know how much damage someone in that position could do in a month?" Tricker demanded.

"Do you know how much damage a discrimination lawsuit could do this company?" Warren countered.

"No one who applied has a better résumé," Colvin pointed out, tapping the table with one finger. "And no one else has offered us a virtual guarantee of satisfaction."

"I'll bet." Tricker's expression made it clear what he was thinking.

"Look, if you were going to pick the head of security no matter what we wanted, why did we even go through this charade?" Warren asked. "We *have* got other things to do, Tricker."

Looking surprised by this onslaught, Tricker raised his hands in a rea-soning gesture. "Look, fellas, I'm just trying to point out some of the pit-falls of working with a possible bimbo. Or worse yet, a possible plant from one of your competitors. I was trying to determine if you had at least con-sidered that she might be more trouble than she's worth."

"I think a possible discrimination lawsuit would be even more trou-ble than *it's* worth," Colvin said.

"I agree," Warren said. "Especially since such a suit would seem to be justified in this case."

Tricker slapped his hands onto the arms of his chair and just looked at them. He had to admit that they had him. He didn't like it, but knew for sure he was beating a dead horse. Unless he really did want to select their head of security himself.

He considered it briefly. *Nah! Too much work.* He would, however, keep a hawk's eye on Serena Burns, and at the merest hint of misbehavior he would demand her resignation.

"Don't say I didn't warn you," he said, rising. He turned at the door, pointing a finger. "I'll be watching."

There was silence for a full minute after he left. Grinning, Warren raised his hand and they high-fived like kids.

"That was a first," the president said.

"Felt good," Colvin agreed. "Let's take the wives out to dinner, I feel like celebrating."

Serena sat concealed in the upper branches of a cottonwood tree across the street from Roger Colvin's home. Given the distance between the houses in this neighborhood and the road, she was nearly a half mile away. She wore charcoal leggings and a matching hooded sweatshirt, black running shoes and gloves, and dark glasses. The only part of her that stood out was the pale skin of her forehead and cheeks. She'd been in position since four A.M., ignoring everything extraneous, including an incontinent pigeon.

The computer part of her brain was able to translate the images her eyes saw, bringing them in closer for detailed scrutiny. Right now she was watching Colvin's wife shepherd their young into the absurdly huge van that the well-off seemed to think essential for the most mundane chores.

The boy, dressed in a blue uniform, yellow neckerchief, and yellow-piped cap, was on his way to a scout meeting. The little girl in her pink coat and tights had a pediatrician's appointment. Or so Mrs. Colvin had told her husband as she stepped out the back door.

Serena heard this from her post in the cottonwood because she had high-powered microphones built into her DNA augmented ears, feeding directly into the part of her natural brain that governed hearing. Training and some of the animal DNA in her genes gave her the ability to move the external part of her ear to catch sound still more efficiently.

They should be gone for at least two hours, Mrs. Colvin had said.

Assuming that woman can ever get them into the van, Serena thought, genuinely puzzled at how long it was taking.

The boy had a toy in his hand that his mother apparently didn't want him to take with him. The child threw it on the ground with all his strength. A piece of it went flying. His mother picked up the toy and went to retrieve the part. Then she hunkered down in front of her son, seemingly in order to reason with him. Serena wasn't interested enough to listen. The child refused to look at his mother, his small face sullen.

Everything Serena had studied about humans from this time period indicated that the young were especially annoying. But the visible proof of it was still astounding. *How did the species ever survive to this point? I'm amazed they don't eat their young at birth.*

Finally, after much to-do and a chase around the van after the little girl, which ended when her brother punched her—though that began a whole new scene—they headed out. The security gate opened at Mrs. Colvin's electronic command and the van drove off. This had taken half an hour. Serena shook her head in amazement. Then she started down the tree and casually jogged down the street. There was a home nearby whose only security was a waist-high wall. It was owned by a man who apparently was unaware that the world was a dangerous place.

She made for the side of the property, where a neighbor had built a much higher wall, and climbed over. Then she carefully proceeded across the yard. There didn't seem to be any security here other than the walls. She shook her head. At least the humans in her time *knew* they were vulnerable.

Finally she was in the Cyberdyne CEO's backyard, squatting under a Douglas fir and watching Colvin sipping coffee as he read the paper. She really wasn't sure how he would react; it was a fifty-fifty situation. He might be impressed at her audacity, or he could become too hysterical for effective communication.

But she'd been able to find jobs for only two of her rivals and the longer she waited the more certain she became that she needed to act. So it was time to play her ace.

The phone rang and Colvin got up to answer it.

Silently, Serena trotted over to the back door, picked the lock, slipped into the kitchen, and took his place at the table, hiding behind the newspaper as he talked on the kitchen phone.

"See you at two, then," Colvin said cheerfully. He hung up the phone and turned. And froze. There was a stranger reading his paper.

Serena looked playfully around the newspaper and smiled at him.

"Good morning, Mr. Colvin." She snapped the paper closed.

Everything in his body, from his throat to his bladder, seized. Then he felt nauseous. All he could think of was that Michael Douglas movie *Fatal Attraction. Thank God we don't own a bunny,* he thought inanely.

After a moment he got his voice back. "What the *hell* are you doing in my house?"

"I needed to see you privately," Serena explained. "For one thing I wanted to demonstrate to you just how rotten your security system is. Not to mention your locks. I opened the door to the room you were in and you didn't even know it!"

He blinked, then shut his mouth, letting anger take over.

"Are you even slightly aware of how creepy this is?" he demanded. "You're invading my *home!* You couldn't call my secretary and ask for an appointment?"

Serena reached into her pocket. She suppressed a smile as she watched Colvin react to the potential threat. Then she pulled out a disk in its plastic case and slowly laid it on the table.

"I'm living," she said, "in a house with an interesting history." She pushed the disk toward him with her fingertips, watching him watching her. Then she licked her lips and smiled. "It used to belong to Miles Dyson. A lovely place, but people are uncomfortable with its history." She shrugged, raising her eyebrows. "So I got it very cheap."

The CEO looked from the disk to the woman and back again.

"Are you suggesting *that* came from Dyson's place?" he asked.

He didn't believe her. They'd searched, thoroughly, and Dyson, or his kidnappers, had made a clean sweep of his work.

Serena rose, tipping her chin upward and regarding him from half closed eyes. "The disk is a sample of what I've found." She smiled slyly. "Look it over and then you tell me where it came from." She turned on her heels and walked to the door. "You know where to find me when you want to talk." She left without a backward glance.

Colvin stared at the closed door for a full minute, then experienced a full-body shudder that got him moving. In a few long strides he was across the room and locking the door. Not that it would keep her out, obviously, but it seemed the appropriate thing to do.

"Wait a minute, wait a minute. She *broke into your house?*" Warren's voice cracked with disbelief. He lowered the whiskey he'd been about to sip and stared.

"Yeah. I turned around and there she was. Never heard a thing, even when she picked up the paper. It almost gave me a heart attack."

Colvin poured himself a drink and swirled the amber liquid around in the heavy glass. He was finding it hard to look Warren in the eye for some reason, as if he were ashamed. Though why he should be he couldn't imagine.

"Christ!" Cyberdyne's president said softly. He shuddered, and wondered if she'd be paying him a visit later. At least she'd waited until Roger's wife and kids had left. He didn't like the idea of trying to explain Serena Burns to his own wife. "This makes me much less inclined to hire her," he said aloud.

"If it had been just that, I would be, too," Colvin agreed.

He took a seat opposite Cyberdyne's president and a deep gulp of his own whiskey. They were in the CEO's home office, and though it was before noon, Colvin had felt a need for a stiff drink.

"What do you mean?" Warren asked nervously.

"She says she bought Miles Dyson's old home and found some material there pertaining to . . ." Colvin waved his hand vaguely, but his eyes were intent.

Warren leaned forward. "The *project?*" he gasped.

The CEO nodded and took another sip of whiskey.

"But we looked . . . that's not possible!" Paul Warren shook his head. "Do you believe her?"

"Let me show you what she gave me," Colvin said, rising. He brought over a laptop. "I've taken out the modem," he explained. He turned it on, took a disk out of his shirt pocket, and slipped it in. "Read it and weep," he muttered.

In less than a minute Paul sat back, his hand over his mouth in horror.

"It's real!" he whispered. He looked up at Roger. "What did she say when she gave it to you?"

"She said to look it over and then tell her where it came from. She said we knew where to find her when we wanted to talk."

"Is that all?" Warren asked.

"Yup." Roger sat back in his chair and, closing his eyes, leaned his head against the cushions. The implication, of course, had been that if he didn't get back to her, someone else surely would.

"Should we tell Tricker?" Warren asked.

Colvin opened his eyes and considered the question. There didn't seem to be a right answer. If they didn't tell him, when he found out—and Tricker *would* find out—he might just yank the whole project from them and kick Cyberdyne off of government property. If they did tell him, he might go after Burns on his own, risking the loss of this tantalizingly promising material.

"Hire her, then tell him," Colvin decided. "Once we've got that material safely in hand, I don't care what he does. But I don't want him going off half-cocked."

Warren pursed his lips, then nodded slowly. "You're right, of course."

He took another sip of his whiskey. "I don't see any alternative. Did she say what else she wanted—besides the job, that is?"

Roger shook his head, gazing into the middle distance. "No. She didn't even mention the job, let alone any compensation for the use of this material."

"Well, it's *our* material," Paul snarled. "Any court would uphold our claim to it."

Colvin looked at him from under his eyebrows. "Somehow I don't see Tricker going to the law under any circumstances. Especially these."

Warren opened his mouth as if to speak, then shut it again, looking thoughtful. He glanced at the CEO. "He'll be furious."

"Tricker is always furious." Roger said. "I think the fact that we exist infuriates him. I say, what the hell, it's high time we gave him something to really be furious about."

Cyberdyne's president chuckled at that. "She said we knew where to find her," he said after a moment. "But her application said she was in the process of moving."

"Yeah—into Dyson's old house!" Colvin said.

Warren grimaced. "That creeps me out."

Roger covered his eyes with one weary hand.

Then he sat forward and looked at his friend. "I tell you one thing, though. I'm going to make it a point of honor never to invite that bitch to my home."

Paul's eyes slid over to his boss. "I don't want her in my home either. And we certainly can't meet with her in the office."

Colvin nodded and suppressed a smile. Mrs. Warren was outrageously jealous. It forced poor Paul to behave suspiciously even though he didn't even want to think about cheating on her. The sight of Serena Burns would drive the president's wife up the wall.

"Okay, we'll choose a bar at random, someplace within thirty minutes of Dyson's place. I don't want to give this whiz kid a chance to bug the place or anything. We're gonna be in enough trouble as it is."

"Okay," Warren said, rising. "Where's the phone book."

NEW YORK CITY: THE PRESENT

"I've been waiting to see you all morning!" Ronald Labane shouted. "The least you could do is give me the courtesy of a few minutes!"

The man he was bellowing at was a literary agent, a small, middle-aged man, neatly dressed. Since he was also a native New Yorker, the agent wasn't likely to be intimidated by mere yelling.

"What I am going to give you is ten seconds to get out of my office and not come back! Or do I have to call security?" His glare and the quiet authority of his voice brought Labane back to some semblance of rationality.

"I'm sorry," Ronald babbled. "I—I didn't mean to raise my voice. My apologies, I'm really not usually like this. I'm just so *frustrated!*"

"How many seconds is that now, Tildee?" the agent asked his secretary.

"I said I was sorry!" Labane protested. He held up his hands in what was meant to be a calming gesture. "Look, the publishers won't even look at my manuscript unless it comes from an agent, but I can't even get an appointment with an agent. It's driving me crazy! Couldn't you just *look* at my manuscript?"

The agent looked down; the stack of paper on the floor beside Labane's feet was easily eighteen inches tall. The text appeared to be single-spaced.

"It'll never sell," the agent said.

"You haven't even *read* it!" Ronald said, aghast.

"I don't have to, it's too long." The agent leaned over, read a few words. "Nonfiction, right?"

"Yes." Labane drew himself up. "I have a message—"

"Hey, ya gotta message, drop an e-mail. If you can't say it any more succinctly than this, you haven't got a prayer. This thing is about the size of the national budget and I bet it's about as interesting."

Labane looked shocked. "But it's a plan, too," he said softly.

"It's a message, it's a plan," the agent said, "it's a candy, it's a breath mint. If you can't cut it down from this, it's unsellable is what it is."

Closing his eyes, Ronald took a deep breath and let it out slowly. His shoulders drooped with exhaustion and discouragement.

The agent tightened his lips; this guy looked like he was going to cry. But he wouldn't be the first author who'd broken down in his office. Publishing was a puppy-kicking business.

"Look," he said, "make up your mind which is more important, the message or the plan. You don't have to put them both in one book, you know. About your plan it may help to think—God got it down to just Ten Commandments and humanity still has a hell of a lot of trouble with them. So keep it simple. Oh, and it's double-spaced, one-sided or they won't even look at it. And that's all the help you'll get from me. Now get out of my office and don't come back."

"Thank you," Labane said as he struggled to gather up his manuscript. "Thanks, really."

The agent pointed to the door and Ronald struggled through it. When he was gone the agent leaned against his secretary's desk.

"You're a softie," she said affectionately.

He folded his arms and smiled. "I just can't shoot down a guy's dreams when he's right in front of me. I think that makes me more of a coward than a softie."

After a moment she said, "You're waiting for him to disappear, aren't you?"

The agent rolled his eyes. "You think I want to ride down in the elevator with him? I'm afraid he'll kidnap me."

Ronald hoisted his manuscript onto the van's passenger seat with a grunt and ignored the beeping and honking from the crowded street. He was angry, with the system and with himself. He'd made a complete fool of himself in front of that agent; he'd done everything but break down and cry. But he was exhausted and hungry, which always made him prone to being emotional.

Ron slept in the van for the most part; the exorbitant parking fee was still infinitely cheaper than a hotel room. Every few days he treated himself to a night at the Y so he could have a shower. Not that keeping moderately clean seemed to be helping. He could feel himself slowly melting into the kind of troglodyte you sometimes saw scurrying off the end of the subway platform.

Labane leaned his arms and head onto his manuscript and sighed. Nothing in New York had happened the way he'd hoped. With a grunt he sat up and thought that it was time to take stock.

At least the commune hadn't had him arrested for stealing the van. He'd spent more than a few happy moments while he drove cross-country imagining how the conversation must have gone around the dinner table when he didn't come back from town. But, it didn't matter what they thought or felt. He'd been lucky they hadn't charged him with theft—yet. And the decrepit van had performed beautifully in the sunnier climes he'd driven through on his way here. Labane took it as an omen: he was finally heading in the right direction.

Now he had to find some way to make people want to look at his book. And more immediately, a way to support himself. He'd allowed himself to withdraw only three thousand dollars from the commune's account. They'd be a lot less complacent about that, he suspected. But he was quickly running through his money, even living on fast food. So he had to get a job of some sort.

Wait a minute; hadn't someone on the Net mentioned an ecology expo in New York, happening about now? *Hey, I could give talks about my plan,* he thought. Maybe not at this one, but he knew there were expos and New Age conventions all over the country, all of the time. They would have information, and he could make contacts.

It would mean catering to the sellouts for a while, but it could be quite profitable. And the sad truth was, you couldn't accomplish anything without cash and a lot of it. Meanwhile he could revise his work until it became publishable.

Bowed, but not broken, he thought. *I will find a way.*

"I'm the president and this gentleman is the CEO of Cyberdyne," Warren explained for the third time to the MP, this time a little more slowly. "We want to get into our offices to do some work on secured computers. Our home offices are not secure." He was beginning to wonder if the young man staring into his window was impaired in some way when he finally waved them through.

"Whaddaya suppose that was all about?" Colvin asked out of the side of his mouth.

"Who the hell knows," Paul muttered as he steered himself into his reserved space near the entry. "Typical beef-brained soldier, probably."

Serena, miles away, listened to their complaints via the bug she'd planted in their car, and smiled. *More likely he was letting Tricker know that you were there,* she thought. She'd have left orders to that effect. Any unusual activity to be reported. No entry without personal approval.

She was finding it frustratingly difficult to learn anything about the mysterious government liaison. So she'd begun attributing to him powers and abilities that he might not even have. Better to overestimate an enemy's abilities than to be caught unprepared. Tricker unnerved her.

But these two! When she gave them the disk they were like kids. Human kids, that is: undisciplined and utterly transparent. She'd been able to see that they thought they were very clever, but she wasn't absolutely sure whether they thought they were outsmarting her or Tricker.

She'd watched them arrive at the bar of their choice, listened to them argue in the car about whether one of them should go in while another waited outside for her arrival. Heard them decide it really made no difference and watched them go in together.

Well, it really didn't make any difference. Except that it made it easier for her to plant the bug in Warren's car. What she was really looking forward to was the moment when they put that disk into their computers. It would give her full access to Cyberdyne's computers and she would finally be able to check their progress on Skynet. She would also be able to hear any conversations that took place in front of those computers. That way, if she failed to get the job she'd still be able to influence events to some extent.

I really hope I haven't overplayed my hand, she thought. It had been obvious that the humans were both angry and frightened. And while their attempts to hid their true feelings were amusing, they were also worrisome. Serena wondered how she should handle the situation. Seduction, perhaps?

She hadn't wanted to go that route once she realized that the two men were friends. It would be bad for the Skynet project to have them at each other's throat in a fog of jealousy. Serena tapped the steering wheel with her fingernails, thinking.

Apology, she decided. A simple, up-front, embarrassed apology might work. If she did it right they'd end up charmed instead of appalled. Which they both seemed to be now.

She closed her eyes and forgot about her surroundings for a moment as her computer systems began to receive a flood of information from Cyberdyne. Opening her eyes in satisfaction, she listened to the real-time conversation between the president and CEO.

"That's impossible," Warren was saying.

"Not necessarily," Colvin answered, his voice thoughtful, as though he was still reading. "This is Dyson's work we're talking about here. That guy was amazing. Not many people can make me feel like I'm falling behind, but Miles almost always did."

"A fully automated, computer-controlled munitions factory?" Paul said. "C'mon, Roger, that doesn't even sound safe, let alone possible."

There was a long silence. Then: "We need to see the rest of this," the CEO said. "The government will *love* it!"

"What if there isn't any more?" Warren asked.

"I'm afraid we'll have to cross that bridge when we come to it. But this is Dyson's work, Paul. It *has* to be! And if there is more of it, then it will probably move our work forward by up to six months. I say we go for it."

"We still don't know what she wants!" Warren protested. "Let's not jump into bed with the bitch until we've got that tacked down. That breaking-into-your-house number was a little too psychotic for my peace of mind."

Colvin laughed. "I'm not sure I'd be any more comfortable after telling her she wasn't going to get the job."

There was silence again except for clicking of keys.

"Tell Tricker," Warren said. "Let him sort it out."

One of them inhaled deeply, then exhaled sharply.

After a moment Roger said thoughtfully, "I'm not sure I want to go that far."

"What?" Warren's voice squeaked with surprise. "It was your house that was broken into. If she's going to be trouble that would imply it's you she'd go after. I say neutralize her, now, when she's not expecting it."

"Okay, let's just look at this calmly for a minute," the CEO said. "She's young—much younger than the other candidates. Maybe she just got carried away."

"Boy, I'll say." Paul sneered.

"I find myself wondering how I would be reacting to this if it had been, say, Bob Cho."

Cho was another candidate for the security-chief position; he was forty-five, about five-eight, slender, but very fit. He'd gotten his start in the CIA.

"Ye-ah," Warren said slowly. "I guess I see what you mean. But would he do something like that?"

"If he had an ace like this to play, yes, I think he might. And if she'd called up and asked for a private meeting, would you have given her one?"

Warren laughed at that, sharply but just once. "Hell, no!"

"Me neither. All because she's an attractive young blonde. So what I ask myself is, what choice did she have? Really?"

There was another long pause.

"Okay," Warren said reluctantly. "You've made a good enough case that I'm willing to hold off siccing Tricker on her until after she's hired. I mean, sooner or later we're going to have to come clean about where this new stuff came from. Right?"

"Why don't we seek out the advice of our new security director on that one?" Colvin answered.

Yes! Serena thought. *Ah, the wonderful ability of the human brain to find reasons not to be frightened.* How useful it was! She put her car in gear and drove off. Time to go home and process the information she'd gathered.

Would tomorrow be too soon to apologize, or should she wait until she'd been working with them a few days? She could attribute the delay to embarrassment. They would probably find that rather appropriate.

She pushed in a CD titled *Hits of the Eighties,* purchased so that she could become familiar with the popular culture of her supposed childhood.

Few of the songs made sense, but that was humans for you. Most of these sounds tickled the pleasure center of the brain to a slight degree, which was undoubtedly the point. So, like a human, she decided to just sit back, relax, and let the sensation roll over her.

Soon she could move into phase two.

ECOLOGY EXPO, NEW YORK: PRESENT DAY

"This is boring," Peter Ziedman said. He frowned and shifted the heavy camera on his shoulder.

"No kidding," his soundman and college bud Tony Roth agreed. "It's nothing like what I expected."

They glared at the neatly set-up booths and the casually well-dressed people around them. Even the loopier outfits had cost real money, you could see that. They'd been expecting a lot more over-the-rainbow stuff from the New York Ecology Fair.

Ziedman had been pinning his hopes on it, in fact. He'd graduated from Chapman University only two month ago, with honors, and already his dad was asking, "So what did I spend my money for?"

Like you could get a full-fledged movie together over the weekend. Well, okay, some people had done that, but not lately, and probably not while sober.

So Peter had decided to do a documentary on an inspired madman. They'd find their guy at a place like this and then follow him around while he tried to convert the world. It would be hilarious.

But what he'd found instead was a slew of start-up businesses looking for venture capitalists. And while he knew there was a story worth telling in that, at the moment he needed something fast, easy, and moderately entertaining from the first shot. The story of water-purification devices just wasn't going to do that.

"Where are the nuts?" he shouted.

A young woman beside a solar-energy display turned to look at him. "The Rain Forest Products booth is giving away Brazil nuts in aisle four." She pointed vaguely in that direction.

Ziedman looked at her; she was attractive in a washed-out, WASPy kind of way. He walked over to her and said, "I'm making a documentary and I was hoping for some more colorful characters to spice up the narrative." He shrugged and then shifted the camera. "It can't all be facts and figures."

She nodded, looking vaguely disapproving. That was when he noticed that her badge said she was the fair's cochair.

"So what exactly *are* you looking for?" she asked.

Peter thought that he was probably very lucky that she wasn't asking him to leave, as he hadn't received permission from the fair to film here. She looked capable of kicking him out. He decided to be honest.

"I'm looking for someone with a message," he said. "Someone who can't get anyone to listen but who thinks he, or she, can save the world. You know anybody like that?"

She laughed, and it changed her whole face. She really was attractive. "Oohhh yes," she said. "I know tons of people like that. But they tend to avoid places like this. To them we're all sellouts." She looked around and seemed to spot someone. Pointing to a tired-looking man on a folding chair near the door, she said, "Try him. That's Ron Labane. He used to be a pretty good guy, associated with a small, fairly successful organic farm in Washington state." She shook her head. "Now . . . it's kinda sad really. He's got a book he's trying to get published. He's kind of into a lone-wolf thing right now."

Ziedman looked at the man. He was wearing tan chinos and a sport jacket over a sweater vest and an open-collared blue shirt. Though he was clean-shaven and his hair was neat, there was something a little shopworn about him. His whole body spoke of discouragement and exhaustion.

Peter turned on the camera and zoomed in on him. As if by instinct, like the lone wolf the woman had named him, Labane turned to look directly into the lens. He raised one brow and with a lopsided smile raised his hand and gestured Peter over.

"Thanks," Ziedman said to the woman. He and Tony hustled over.

CHAPTER 7

PARAGUAY: THE PRESENT

Sarah felt horribly conspicuous—which was understandable, since she was outrageously overdressed. Everyone around her was wearing casual clothes and sandals; some were even in shorts. She was dressed in Scarlett O'Hara's garden-party dress, with an oversized sunbonnet, little gloves, puffy sleeves, low bodice, crinolines, and an enormous hoopskirt. Except that hers was in black and red.

People were grinning at her. The smiles were not very friendly; in fact, there was a distinctly predatory edge to them, as if the guests were really a pack of socially superior wolves. She smiled back, trying desperately to carry it off.

Victor Salcido—her host—approached carrying an enormous rack of barbecued ribs, dripping with sauce, on a very small paper plate. Sarah tried to refuse it, but he forced it on her. The plate buckled and the ribs and sauce poured over her. Suddenly her dress was white and the sauce looked like thick blood as it ran down her front. She dropped the plate and looked at her gloved hands. It *was* blood.

Everyone was laughing and pointing. She stepped back, looking around in vain for one friendly face. The crowd parted to reveal a huge man in black leather; his head turned like a gun turret, slowly, slowly. It was the Terminator. He began to walk toward her; everything in her screamed to run, but she couldn't *move*. His face grew softer, the lower planes of it beginning to sprout a beard. He reached into his jacket. When his hand came out it was normal, or seemed so at first. But the index finger kept growing, turning silvery as it grew. Then his body changed, becoming more slender, shorter, until she was looking into the implacable face of the T-1000.

"Call to John," it said. "Call to John, *now!*"

Sarah turned and ran, her heart pounding, tears spilling down her cheeks. The party goers watched her as dispassionately as spectators at a golf game.

Suddenly she was in the Chaco, and grass and scrub were catching at her absurd skirt, twisting and lashing like living whips. Finally she fell and the grasses and thorns grabbed hold as if they were organic barbed wire.

She felt paralyzed, trapped; all she could do was lie there while redheaded Douglas from the Pescadero State Hospital leaned over and slowly, lasciviously, licked her cheek. He stood up and looked down at her while the spit on her cheek burned like acid. She couldn't even scream.

The T-1000 came and stood over her beside the male nurse. The machine and Douglas looked at one another, then down at her. "Call to John," the T-1000 said.

He opened his hand and it grew into the shape of an old-fashioned steam shovel, the jaws lined with sharp teeth. They opened and clamped shut, then swept toward her and swallowed her head.

Sarah screamed and flung herself upright.

"Mom?"

John hit the light switch and her lamp came on; she started and shivered. He came over and sat on the bed beside her. Her son stayed motionless and simply offered the comfort of his presence, waiting.

She was at home, she was in bed, she was safe.

After a moment she gathered him in her arms and held him fiercely, breathing in gasps, trying not to cry.

"Bad one, huh?" he said, gently stroking her back. Her hair was wet with sweat though the night was cool, occasionally shudders racked her tightly coiled body.

Sarah let go and leaned back, her hand automatically reaching for a cigarette that wasn't there. She met John's smiling eyes sheepishly. "If you'd just had that dream you'd reach for cigarette too, you little wiseass."

He grinned. "You haven't had one this bad for a while," he said, suddenly serious.

"They're all bad, John." Sarah scooted up the bed so that she was leaning against the headboard. "Dear old Dr. Silberman once told me that I was a very imaginative woman, and that was why I had such bad dreams."

She snorted, then looked ruefully at her son. "Everybody else has dreams where they can't catch the right bus, or they show up for work in their underwear. I dream that unstoppable killing machines are coming to murder me."

"Gee, I wonder why," John said.

They laughed and some of the tension drained out of her.

"I bet seeing that Dieter guy—"

"Von Rossbach," Sarah said.

"Yeah. I bet seeing him prompted the dream." John hooked one leg over the other and looked at his mother, inviting her to talk.

She smiled fondly, appreciating his willingness to help. "Well, maybe not just von Rossbach," she said. "The dream started at the Salcido *asado*. I was dressed as Scarlett O'Hara." John started to laugh. "Only the dress was red and black."

John looked at her from under his eyebrows. "A goth Scarlett O'Hara?" he said. "Ya gotta hand it to Silberman; as far as being imaginative goes, he had you pegged, Mom." He leaned over on one elbow, his head on his hand, making a bridge over her legs. "You must really be nervous about this party," he commented.

"Well, yuh," she said, and shrugged. "This could be my entrée into society. And I'm just not very good at that feminine shtick"—John's eyebrow went up at that—"that they're so fond of around here." Sarah sighed. "I don't want to embarrass you in front of your friends," she said.

John sat up.

"Mom," he said seriously, "you couldn't. You're my hero." Then he began to sing, falsetto, "You are the wind beneath myyy wings."

Sarah hit him with her pillow. "Out!" she said, laughing. "Get out of my room and take your schmaltz with you."

"Lalala-la-la-la-laaaa-la," John sang, slowly flapping his arms as he danced out. "You are the wind beneath my wings."

"Good night, John."

He leaned back into her room and flipped the light switch.

"'Night, Mom."

Sarah settled back on her pillow and chuckled. God but he was a good kid! *And thanks to me, he doesn't have to spend the rest of his life saving the human race from extinction.*

Dieter felt good. The first few mornings had been hard; a mere five kilometers had left him exhausted. Today he'd done ten at an easy light trot, jogging in the comparative coolness of dawn with the dry dust of the ranch's roads puffing up around his feet and the pungent smell of the Chaco brush in his nostrils. Then he'd spent a good part of the morning doing kata after kata in the courtyard outside his office.

Now to finish off with something that needs delicacy and control, he thought.

Throwing knives wasn't something that had much practical use, but it was a good way to keep your edge. He held the tip of the blade between thumb and forefinger, feeling the balance of the weapon as he concentrated; his body glistened with a healthy sheen of sweat and the strong sunlight sparkled off the golden hair on his massive chest.

Elsa Encinas, Epifanio's niece, watched him as she washed the office window. Her big brown eyes were wide, and her hand moved more and more slowly as her mouth dropped open. She'd been cleaning the same small square of glass for about a half hour now and she was beginning to make Dieter nervous. He didn't think she was even *blinking* anymore.

Marieta bustled into the office looking for Elsa, intending to scold her for not being finished yet. One brief glance and she was upon her niece, finger and thumb closed on an ear as she dragged the protesting Elsa behind her into the corridor. With a wide sweep of her strong arm she brought the miscreant around to face her.

"And just what do you think that you are doing? Staring at Señor von Rossbach like some *puta!* What would your mother say?"

"I wasn't!" Elsa protested. "I was only washing the window!"

"Don't talk back!" her aunt said, shaking a finger. "I was watching you for five minutes," she lied. Then she imitated her totally hypnotized niece wiping one pane of glass over and over. "That is how you looked, you silly girl! Like a fish!"

Elsa giggled. "I can't help it, Auntie!" She leaned in close to Marieta and whispered, "He is so handsome."

Her aunt let out a huff of breath. "Go dust and vacuum in the library," she said. "And try to be finished by suppertime! *Vamos!*"

Elsa started to walk off, glancing into the office as she went by. Her aunt clapped her hands sharply and the walk turned to a run. Shaking her head, Marieta went into von Rossbach's office to finish up. She picked up the cloth and went to the window. She was starting to scrub when a flash of motion caught her eye.

Señor von Rossbach had just thrown a knife and was straightening up, studying the knife quivering in the target.

Oh, my God! she thought. No wonder poor Elsa was so fascinated. Marieta found that she, too, was rubbing the same square of glass for an inordinately long time and she laughed silently. It seemed she owed Elsa an apology. If an old woman like her couldn't keep her eyes where they belonged what hope did a girl of nineteen have?

Dieter turned from gathering his knives from the target and grinned at her. He came directly to the office.

"Thank you for rescuing me," he said. "I didn't dare come in while your niece was here."

Marieta laughed. "She'd have had a stroke, the silly thing." She wiped down another pane. "Shouldn't you be getting ready?"

Dieter glanced at the clock: noon already. He was supposed to be at the *asado* by two and it was over an hour's drive. "*Sí,*" he said. "Thanks for reminding me."

"Mom, you look great."

Sarah tugged at the pale blue belt and grimaced.

"White was probably a bad color choice," she grumbled.

"White linen is always a good choice," her son insisted.

The dress was actually quite attractive, short-sleeved and tailored, with lace cutouts at the shoulders and hem. But she couldn't get over the feeling that whatever she wore would be wrong. She sighed. Once she'd enjoyed dressing up, putting on makeup and high heels. Now she only felt conspicuous. She wished for John's sake she could just calm down, but it was hard.

"C'n I drive?" he asked.

"No," she said shortly, picking up her sunglasses.

"Please?" John made puppy eyes at his mother.

She smiled and turned her head away at the same time.

"No fair!" she said. "Don't look at me like that."

"Please, Mom? Please can I drive, please, please?" He moved around her, trying to catch her eye while she laughed helplessly.

"No!" she insisted. "John, I'm nervous enough as it is without you behind the wheel."

"Well, I like that!" he said in mock outrage. "Who was it said we should get me a license?"

She grabbed him by the back of the neck and pulled him to her, leaning her forehead against his as she said, "Maybe I'll let you drive us home. How would that be?"

He snorted. "Adequate," he said dismissively.

"Then again," she said, "maybe I won't." She picked up her bag and headed for the door, a little startled at the unfamiliar sound of her high heels clicking on the tile.

"Aw, Mom!"

"No whining!" she said.

"I'll treat you like a queen? I'll stay by your side for the first half hour? I'll muck out Linda's stall for the rest of the week."

Sarah leaned towards him. "John, that's your job for the rest of the summer."

"Since when?" He joined her on the *portal.*

"You're getting older," she said, locking the front door. "It's time you learned responsibility."

"Okay," he grumbled. "I ride Linda more in the summer than you do anyway."

She turned at the bottom of the steps and tossed him the keys.

"You drive," she said. "Don't make me want to close my eyes."

Obviously Sarah couldn't wear dark glasses when she was trying to meet people; the horn-rims would have to do. So far this wasn't the trial she'd feared it would be. John had stuck to his word and to her side for the first half hour, then with a wink he'd gone off with Luis and Consuela, Luis's newly noticeable little sister.

Sarah gulped a little, hanging back under the arched stone colonnade that rimmed the courtyard, half-concealed by hanging pots of bougainvillea. *Grit your teeth and mingle,* she told herself.

Señor and Señora Salcido had been going out of their way to make her feel welcome. Apparently Luis had been talking up John. Little by little she relaxed, all the while wondering at how a genteel barbecue could traumatize someone who'd spent a third of her life hobnobbing with cutthroats and mercenaries from one end of the Americas to the other.

She remembered an old movie with Peter Ustinov. He had a line that went something like, "Wouldn't you know it. Here we are, desperate criminals, and we've fallen in with nice people."

Sarah accepted another tiny delicacy at Señora Salcido's gracious insistence. *When can I leave?* she thought desperately.

There was a stir at the entrance to the courtyard and heads began to turn.

"Oh!" Señora Salcido looked pleased. "It is our newest neighbor. Have you met him, Señora Krieger?"

Sarah shook her head helplessly.

"Then you must allow me to introduce you! A charming man." She took hold of Sarah's elbow and drew her along. "He bought the old Stroessner *estancia.*"

Sarah was smiling and nodding at her hostess when she saw who it was that she was being drawn toward and, without thinking, dug in her heels.

John turned from his friends to see who was making such a grand entrance. He forgot to breathe and the smile froze on his face. Automatically he looked for his mother. They had to get out of here!

"*Oooh,* it's Señor von Rossbach!" Consuela breathed. "Ai! *Qué hombre!*"

John snapped a look at her, startled by her worshipful tone. At the enraptured look on her face he let out his breath in a whoosh and forced himself to stay where he was. He looked at the stranger again. So this was Dieter the sperm guy.

"He's been doing some business with my father," Consuela was saying. "They're trying to breed a new type of cattle." She tilted her head prettily, as though contemplating the creation of a new rose instead of a beefier cow.

John looked at Luis over his sister's head and almost laughed out loud at the way his friend rolled his eyes. His heartbeat was almost back to normal, but he really had to find his mother. He wanted to be by her side for this.

Sarah had set her teeth and pulled her lips back in a semblance of a smile. She was quietly resisting an unusually insistent Señora Salcido when John showed up at her elbow. She immediately relaxed.

"He can't get both of us at the same time, Mom," he whispered in her ear in English.

They were finally facing von Rossbach, who turned and met Sarah's eyes. His strong face went expressionless as the señora introduced them.

"And this is my son, John," Sarah said.

Dieter offered the boy his big hand. John's hand was dry and strong even by the ex-commando's standards. Dieter was impressed.

"I'll leave you to become acquainted," Señora Salcido said, leading off her surprised husband.

"Mom, could it be that Luis's mother is matchmaking?" John asked in English.

Sarah laughed. She couldn't help it.

"Perhaps it would be better if we pretended that this is the first time we have met," von Rossbach suggested diplomatically.

John studied him. The resemblance to the Terminator was astounding, regardless of the beard. Because of his own feelings toward his "personal" Terminator, he couldn't help but warm to the big man before him.

Whoa, John, he warned himself. *Slow down. This isn't "Uncle Bob." And Mom's right. The guy has cop's eyes. Be careful.*

Sarah was flustered, and she knew she probably looked flustered. "It's been years since I was invited to something like this," she said after a moment. "I'm not used to being with so many people at once."

John shot her a glance; she seemed more embarrassed than frightened. "So where are you from, sir? If you don't mind me asking."

"All over, the last few years," Dieter answered. He rather liked the way the boy was backing his mother up. It spoke of a close relationship. "I was born in Austria."

"I thought I heard a touch of an accent," Sarah told him, smiling. *I'm going to carry this off,* she thought, relaxing. *This is just a party, and for all I know this is just some guy.* Who happened to look exactly like a deadly cybernetic killing machine.

What the hell. If he were perfect he'd be married.

They were silent for a long time on the drive home. John stared out the window, and Sarah watched for potholes, her eyes steady on the moonlit road. Insects and birds flitted by, and something squalled out in the darkness beyond the white cones cast by the headlights.

"Coincidence," John said at last. His voice held the trace of a question.

Sarah was tense but silent; her mind was full of sentence fragments and her stomach was in turmoil. He was human! He had to be. There was nothing about him that was like a machine. He laughed, he made jokes, he changed expression . . . he had body language, dammit! Even so, there was something about him that worried her.

"But he does have cop's eyes," John said. He folded his arms over his chest and slid down in his seat.

Sarah nodded slowly. "We'd better find out who he is fast."

Before he finds out about us.

CHAPTER 8

Serena dumped the dirt out of her basket and stamped it down. This was almost the last of it; she needed to excavate only another foot or two down below the house. The California night was scarcely dark to her cyber-boosted eyes; the fog of light pollution made it as bright as day.

Frowning, she looked around her; it might be best to get rid of the excess dirt in raised flower beds, otherwise she'd end up with a suspicious-looking mound in the middle of the yard. She looked down at the filled-in swimming pool. It had been only seven feet deep at one end, four feet at the other—not deep enough.

Serena was a carefully calculated five-six, average height for a woman. But the T-101's she planned to construct would all be six feet tall. So, while she was quite comfortable standing in what would be her secret laboratory, the depth of the place must accommodate them.

With a sigh, she picked up her basket. *I wish I had some T-101's now to help me with this.* It was heavy work.

Stage one had been the easiest, hiring a contractor to put up a ten-foot privacy fence around the property. Necessary since she didn't want the neighbors, or any agents of Tricker's, wondering why she was pouring dirt into the pool or, more important, where it was coming from. She regretted having to drain the pool; a nice swim after work like this would have been pleasant.

Gazing at the tiled area surrounding the oblong of raw dirt, she decided it looked odd. *Maybe I should cover this part with concrete and make a tennis court. It will certainly improve the resale value.* A slight smile quirked at her lips. *This could be dangerous; I'm starting to think like a human.*

Actually she had little real fear of that happening; it was like running a subroutine, easily terminable. But such thoughts improved her ability to pass. She'd always been good at that. She remembered . . .

SKYNET LABS, HOLDING CELLS: 2025

Serena stepped delicately, like a frightened deer, into the cell. There was a boy here of approximately thirteen, her own apparent age. This would be the first time she'd met a wild human face-to-face.

She supposed the caretakers and slaves were the same breed, but service to Skynet had tamed them, made them safe. This boy might do anything. Her assignment was to seduce him. Serena licked her lips with a combination of anticipation and slight nervousness. This could be quite a challenge.

The cell appeared to be deserted. Serena leaned forward, studying the empty walls. Actually she could hear him; he was just above her head, clinging to a beam inside the doorway. So he was clever, a survivor—good genetic stock.

Well? What are you going to do? Serena wondered, already bored with her shy act. It seemed she would have to provoke a response. "Hello?" she said, putting a quaver into her voice.

She took a breath and straightened up. Then she took a step backward, reaching behind her for the door latch. She heard cloth slide across metal above her head.

Well, finally!

He dropped onto her shoulders and bore her to the ground, his hand crushing her mouth. Serena struggled, making muffled squealing noises as she writhed against him. This was unpleasant; the damned human smelled. He was strong, she noted, but light; the I-950 could have tossed him around the room with one hand.

"Stop it!" he hissed into her ear. "I'm going to take my hand away. Don't scream or I'll break your neck."

With a shudder that was actually suppressed laughter, Serena nodded. He slowly took his hand away.

Part of the offensive smell was his fear—completely justified since his life span could be measured in days. This boy wouldn't know anything of use to Skynet. His only utility was as a training tool for its children.

She was the first to approach him. "Who are you?" she whispered.

"I'll ask the questions," he said roughly.

He still lay on top of her, and unless she missed her guess he was enjoying it. She turned slightly, so that they were lying front to front. Oh yes, he was enjoying this.

"Please don't hurt me," she pleaded, allowing tears into her eyes.

He seemed to grow, he certainly swelled, as he looked down on her. "Who are you?" he demanded gruffly. "What are you doing here?"

It was impressive that he could stay focused on the situation at hand, despite his condition and his circumstances.

"I—I was curious," she stammered, in apparent fear. "I've never met anyone from outside." She paused, looking into his face, searching it. "What's it like to be free?"

He frowned. "What do you mean?"

"I've never been outside," she said, trembling. The trembling felt fake to her, so she added a little gasp.

"Never?" he asked, his voice tinged with disbelief.

"I was born here," she whispered. Serena choked back a sob. "This is a terrible place. They perform experiments on us."

Which was perfectly true. Her whole life was an experiment.

His face changed; his eyes softened and he caressed her cheek with one rough hand. "I'm *sorry,"* he said.

She burst into tears and he moved so that he was cradling her, rocking her and making soothing noises. It was very pleasant. Serena was convinced that if she really had been weeping, this would have calmed her. She reached up and caressed his face, looking into his eyes.

He lowered his head toward her tentatively, then stopped. Serena put her hand behind his neck and pulled him the rest of the way down. Their kiss was sweet at first, a kiss between two children. Then slowly it deepened, grew warmer, more passionate. His hand stroked her back, the rhythm becoming swifter, more demanding, like his kiss.

She made the first move, slipping out of the flimsy tunic that was all she wore. He stared at her physical perfection for a moment as though stunned. Then she leaned forward and began to help him undress, exclaiming wordlessly over small scars on his body, kissing them when she found them.

She lost her nominal virginity to that boy, then broke his neck at Skynet's orders. A very pleasant interlude, altogether.

FORMER DYSON HOME: THE PRESENT

Serena smiled reminiscently; yes, she'd always been good at getting humans to trust her. Picking up the two baskets, she headed back to her digging.

She had cut through the concrete floor of a guest room to begin removing the dirt beneath. Today she would finish the digging and pour the cement into the holes for the support poles. As soon as that was dry she would put in a moisture barrier, a cement floor, and concrete blocks and steel posts to support the walls.

Next would be the installation of a sophisticated climate control and air purification system; the parts were already waiting in the guest room. Then she could bring in the rest of the equipment and begin using her lab.

In the meantime she'd been jobbing out the parts needed to construct the skeletons of her T-101s, using over a dozen different specialty foundries throughout the United States; their product came to several different post office boxes, none of them closer than two towns away. So far their work had been excellent.

When time allowed, she'd check into using foreign manufacturers for maximum privacy. She imagined that many precision metalworkers knew each other; it wouldn't do if several accidentally discovered that they were manufacturing different parts that looked suspiciously right alongside each other and started to put them together.

But her real concern was that the Connors would learn of her work.

Serena thought about Skynet's enemies as she filled another basket with dirt. The Connors had very effectively disappeared after destroying Cyberdyne's old facility. Sightings of them had been reported for a few months afterward, but none had panned out. To all intents and purposes, the pair had ceased to exist.

Wouldn't that be nice? Serena thought, jabbing the shovel into the hard-packed earth. *Nice but unlikely.*

She'd posted a lookout for their names on the Internet; should anyone start discussing them or look for information on them, she would be alerted. She had also tagged their files at the FBI and CIA. Anyone looking for information there was more likely to lead her to her quarry.

Hoisting the filled baskets onto her shoulders, she tried to close her mind to the knowledge that Skynet's minions had come out the losers every time they'd tangled with the Connors.

Serena climbed the ladder out of her lab-to-be and forced herself to think of the next step in the process. If she pushed, she could be ready to start the delicate work of creating T-101's by late next week.

She'd acquired artificial teeth and some precision tools from a series of dental-supply companies and a matrix material used to grow new flesh for skin grafts from a surgical-supply store. It was amazing what you could acquire if you had a healthy amount of cash.

She would use her own blood as a starter. The chemicals necessary to promote cell growth were resting in her refrigerator.

Except for the brute effort required to prepare her small laboratory, everything was set to go or on its way. She should have the first Terminator ready to mingle with humans in under two months.

Unless Cyberdyne called on her to begin work she should be able to work undisturbed on her new accomplice. Once she'd made one T-101, it could easily construct others. But she was also eager to begin protecting Skynet.

I know they're going to hire me, they know they're going to hire me, what then is the hold up?

Tricker? Probably. But the government liaison didn't seem to be anywhere around just now. He was probably doing some last-minute foot-dragging just to assert his authority, or perhaps a bit more investigation. Although she was pretty sure her background sources would check out, Tricker was a deep one.

I can trust my own groundwork, she assured herself. If worse came to worst, she could always simply eliminate Tricker.

She would regret it: he was the most interesting person she'd met here. But she could live with regret. What she couldn't live with was failure.

OHIO, ON THE ROAD TO EARTH-FAIR: PRESENT DAY

"People keep imagining," Ron Labane said to the two filmmakers, "that someday everyone in the world will enjoy the lifestyle North Americans take for granted." He looked off into the distance. "I can't remember who said it, but it's been estimated that it would take eight more planets to achieve that goal."

"That seems excessive," Peter Ziedman said.

"Our lifestyle is excessive," Ron countered. "We could all live much more simply and probably be happier for it. Only an economy like this one could support our constant fads, constant upgrading of cars and stereos and computers. We don't even wear things out anymore; there's no time for that. They're outmoded as soon as you buy them. So we bury them."

Ron shook his head gently. "It can't go on indefinitely. Common sense says it can't go on forever."

"So what do we do?" Ziedman asked. He was pleased. He'd expected a wild man from what the cochairman had said, but he'd gotten a well-spoken, well-informed man with a message. This could work out. With the right handling and maybe a little cash infusion from his father.

"Well, that's going to involve some hard choices," Labane answered. "Industry isn't just going to start gearing down voluntarily. They'll use the same excuse they've used for over a hundred years." He waved his hands and raised his eyes to heaven. "We have to answer to our stockholders! We must show a profit, it's our duty! Ha! Their duty is to get as fat as they can before they dole out the crumbs to their sacred stockholders."

"So . . . laws?" Ziedman said.

Labane shook his head. "I'm no lawyer, but I'm pretty sure that the Constitution has a few things to say about restraint of trade. Unfortunately that doesn't take into consideration the world around us. Actually, the change has to come from us. Buy less, streamline your life. Learn to live by that old Yankee saying: buy it new, wear it out, make it do, do without. The alternative is to imagine your great-great-grandchildren wading through discarded motherboards and acid rain up to their ankles."

Ziedman glanced at Tony, who adjusted the camera and nodded. "This is great stuff," he said to Labane. "Where did you get this?"

"I wrote a book," Ron said. "I've got to rework it, though; there's far too much material to get it published as is. I must have read hundreds of books on the subject." He nodded. "Hundreds, at least. None of my work is really original; it's a synthesis." He slapped his knees. "But ya need those. Every now and again someone has to get it all together and present the salient points. And that's what I want to do. So that people can decide just what it is that they ought to do to save the world."

"Cut!" Ziedman said. "I'd like to get some shots of you doing things like walking along a river or the seashore or through a meadow some-place. If that's all right with you? We'd do a voice-over of you, maybe reading from your book. How would that be?"

"I hate to sound mercenary," Labane said, "but am I getting paid to be in this opus of yours? 'Cause I'm living in my van right now."

Peter held up a hand. "Okay," he said, "here's the deal. We're doing this on a shoestring ourselves. So until and unless the film is sold for distribution, all we can offer is room and board."

"And parking?"

Ziedman screwed up his face. "Okay!" He held out his hand. "You drive a hard bargain."

"You ain't seen nothin' yet," Ron said.

He went along with the two young men to their hotel room—free shower at last!—so that they could discuss the film and terms. They talked like kids from money. They had that insouciant near arrogance of youngsters who'd never had to go without. The hotel was one of those where everything that wasn't cream-colored was pastel, and where the room service came with chased-silver napkin rings.

It was pretty certain that these two wouldn't go out of their way to save the world. *So what?* Ron thought. *There's nothing wrong with a mutually agreeable arrangement.*

If he got lucky it could be like being the lead singer in a rock group. If this movie hit, he'd be the one the public remembered. Not the two kids singing backup. Ron smiled. Oh yes, he'd milk these kids for all they were worth, and if he did it right, by the time he was finished they'd still believe he was a starry-eyed idealist.

The thing was to get the message out to those with the ears to hear it. A simple message, really: stop the madness of overproduction, whatever it takes.

Mentally he sneered at the spoiled boys beside him. He was certain they saw themselves as rebels because they wanted to make documentaries instead of getting real jobs in their daddies' companies.

WILMINGTON, DELAWARE: THE PRESENT

Jordan Dyson chewed on his lower lip. The advertisement for a head of security for Cyberdyne was no longer listed. He'd seriously considered applying for the job; he knew that some agents had gone on to lucrative civilian careers in security or related fields. But he *liked* working for the Bureau. Besides, he probably didn't have the street cred. His job here was primarily research and he was very, very good at it. But they would probably be looking either for someone who had climbed the corporate ladder, or someone who'd been outrunning bullets and clipping on handcuffs.

Jordan tapped his fingers against his chin. Of course, he could join the firm in a lesser position. Being in the FBI would definitely be an entrée to Cyberdyne then. The difficulty would be in getting the time; he really did not want to quit. The difficulty would also lie in surviving up to a six-month break in his career.

But I have *to get inside there!* It was the only way he could get to know the workings of the place, get to know the people, maybe get into the files that most people didn't get to see.

But most important, he needed to be present at Cyberdyne because he was certain, as certain as anyone relying on pure gut instinct could be, that within three months the Connors would find out about Miles's project starting up again. And then they'd come knocking on Cyberdyne's doors. Probably with high explosives.

Jordan sighed. *I wonder if I can work out some kind of part-time arrangement?*

LOS ANGELES: THE PRESENT

Danny pushed his home fries around his plate while he stared into space, apparently unaware that his mother had stopped eating to watch him, as if she knew he had something to say that he didn't think she'd want to hear.

Tarissa pursed her lips, then smiled. "You have something on your mind, son?"

"I've been thinking," he said, with an alacrity that made her blink. It was rare that he was so forthcoming these days. "I think we ought to tell him."

Tarissa felt like she'd been punched in the gut. She looked down, fiddled with her napkin for a moment, then folded and dropped it onto the table. She looked at her son's determined face. "Don't think I haven't thought about it, Dan," she said quietly. "I have—a lot. Especially right after it happened."

It suddenly occurred to her that she'd known instantly who and what Dan meant. She tipped her head, considering him. "But I couldn't think how to make him believe me, honey. Look what happened to Sarah Connor. All that time in Pescadero." Tarissa shook her head sadly. "Didn't matter that she was telling the truth. Nobody believed her."

Tarissa sat back and let out her breath in a long sigh. She looked across the table at Danny and knew she might as well be looking across the country. She wasn't reaching him.

"I don't want to go to that place," she said between her teeth. "I freely admit it scares me to death. I saw what it did to that woman." Tarissa put her hand to her forehead. "If I had told your uncle what happened just after . . . your father died, I am absolutely certain that I'd have ended up in a straitjacket."

Dan nodded. "And I was just a little kid," he said. "No way could I back up your story." He leaned forward, his hands reaching out. "But I'm older now! I'm sure he'd believe me now."

Tarissa tilted her head, a pained expression on her face.

"Mom! We have to tell him," Dan said in measured tones. "This is destroying his life! And if he ever *does* find the Connors, he'll destroy them! C'mon, Mom, we've *got* to tell him!"

God, she thought fondly, *he's so dramatic. But maybe he's right. Maybe it* is *time.* She sighed. "All right. But I want him here with us when we tell him. I want him to be able to look us in the eye."

It might just be the one thing that destroyed their relationship. But Danny was right, this was torturing her brother-in-law and they couldn't just stand back, knowing the truth, and not try to help. Maybe knowing everything *would* help.

Dan nodded solemnly.

"Good," he said. "But don't leave it too long. I've got a feeling he might do something drastic, like quit the FBI."

CHAPTER 9

A soft, long inhalation of breath, a pause of thirty seconds, then the long, slow exhale. Serena sat cross-legged on the steel table, her eyes half-closed as she breathed. Attending to her breathing helped to center her, allowing her to ignore the pain.

Her lap filled with blood as her hands worked, slicing into the skin of her abdomen, sliding out the small parcels that contained the neural-net processors and power cells that would activate her small army of T-101s.

The diminutive plastic-wrapped processors were a new generation, more advanced than the chips that had activated her teachers. These were smaller, slimmer, and even more efficient. As were the power cells, three to each Terminator, one of Skynet's innovations, introduced just before she'd left.

For all their light weight and smaller design Serena would be glad to be rid of them. She had been constantly aware of them just beneath the surface of her skin and concerned that she might damage them in some way. But with no safe place to store them she'd kept them close.

Now she possessed the equivalent of a vault. Serena paused in her work and looked around the long, narrow room. It was approximately thirty feet long and fourteen feet wide, with the ceiling six feet six inches from the floor: neither she nor the machines she'd be creating needed the psychological comfort of a ceiling high above their heads. Brightened by banks of fluorescent lights, gleaming steel tables, and glassed-doored cabinets, it made a pleasant place to work. True, it still stank of the antimagnetic white paint she'd used, but the air-scrubber was doing an excellent job of thinning the fumes.

Across the room the heads of two T-101s propped on a steel table grinned at her with demented glee. The backs of their gleaming skulls were open and waiting for the gifts of life and intelligence. Her fingers twitched with eagerness to get back to work. She picked up the scalpel and made another cut. *It's a little like giving birth, actually,* she thought, and smiled with grim humor.

Beside her, the culture-growing vats she'd adapted hummed contentedly as they grew flesh for her new subordinates. In the far corner of the room, well out of the way, two hulking, headless metal skeletons stood, their large, intricate hands hanging by their sides. Already in place was the delicate system of nutrient pumps and the fine net of permeable plastic "capillaries" that would feed the Terminators' coating of skin and flesh.

Beside them were the large tanks in which they would lie, washed in a nutrient broth, while their new skin surface grew around them. The muscles needed to animate the T-101s faces with their self-contained nervous system were also progressing nicely. These would interact directly with the T-101's neural-net processor for the maximum effect.

She'd had some trouble with the eyes, though. For now they would be given glass eyes, which should pass muster behind sunglasses. She'd have to correct that flaw as soon as possible. Details were important.

Of course the Terminators could be useful even without a coating of skin, so she'd given herself a head start on them. Now that the lab was constructed she was eager to move into high gear, and the extra hands would be most welcome.

Tomorrow, finally, she was to start her job at Cyberdyne. It would be necessary to leave the biotech work to the T-101s. Not that they'd have much to do for several days beyond minding the cultivators. *And learning how to function unobtrusively here.* Blending in was part of their programming, but the more they were exposed to people the better they functioned.

But in order for them to do anything they had to have brains. That meant that tonight she would have to test out each chip to ten-tenths capacity. Otherwise she dared not let the Terminators work alone.

She slipped out the last package. It was almost a sensual feeling, moist, slippery, the hot feel of the plastic in her hand, the sense of slackness where she'd been filled.

Serena laid the package down on the table beside the others. Then she swabbed her abdomen with alcohol, feeling wicked for lavishing it on as she was. It spilled over her legs and puddled red on the table beneath her. At home the stuff was hoarded like gold was here. She thought of the humans there who suffered infection and pain because they lacked this simple, abundant stuff, and she was pleased. She found that she *liked* the twenty-first century.

The cuts, while superficial, were deep enough to sting and burn where the alcohol touched them. Serena looked down at herself. She was designed to be a quick healer, and already the loose flesh where the packages had been stored was returning to smoothness. The flow of blood slowed. Simple bandages, she decided, would do.

When she'd seen to her cuts Serena hopped off the table; the alcohol running down her legs dried cool. She swabbed down the table and disposed of the paper towels she'd used. Then, drawing out a chair at her workstation, she began testing the chips.

After the first one she let out a relieved breath. It had survived the trip through time unscathed. That had been the one thing that had truly worried her—that these irreplaceable elements might have been fried by the transfer's wild electronic convulsions. One, at least, had made it. She wouldn't have to do this completely by herself.

Three hours later she sat back, well satisfied with her work. One of the processors hadn't made it. But the accompanying power cells were still perfect. Skynet itself had predicted a pessimistic seventy-five-percent success rate, so this was a victory of sorts.

Choosing one of the Terminator heads, Serena set to work. She would allow her internal computer to program it while the meat part of her rested on one of the tables nearby. Then tomorrow, while she was at Cyberdyne, it could complete its partner and watch the cultures. She was pleased.

She had won the job at Cyberdyne; her background had held up under extremely close scrutiny. And soon Cyberdyne would begin work on those completely automated munitions factories that Skynet had designed. That was step one in the larger plan that would eliminate the humans. The factories hadn't existed in fully exploitable form when Skynet was first activated in the original time line.

Theoretically the automated factories should also swell the ranks of those who objected to the unbridled expansion of technology. Who, oddly enough, were often Skynet's most willing allies.

Humans were very strange creatures.

She would have the T-101s complete two more of themselves for their next task. The lab was regrettably small, after all. Once they could be trusted to interact with humans she could safely move them upstairs. Dyson's house was large enough to accommodate several Terminators easily.

But from now on, if their programming went as it should, they could be left in complete control of this aspect of the operation. Then, as soon as possible, she would send one off to acquire a remote site that could be used as a safe house in the event that she needed to bolt. That likelihood was remote in her opinion, but Skynet's insistence on a backup plan was deeply ingrained.

So much to do, she thought with pleasure. And starting in the morning, Skynet would be under her protection. The thought filled her with the closest thing to joy her cold heart could experience.

Then she paused. *I am enjoying more success in this time period than any of the previous agents,* she thought. *But is that because I am more capable . . . or is it because, unlike them, I am mainly attempting to* preserve *the "original" sequence of events?*

That would not be good enough. The original sequence of events produced Skynet . . . and its ultimate defeat at the hands of John Connor and the humans.

CYBERDYNE: THE PRESENT

"So thrill me, Ms. Burns," Tricker said sarcastically. "Tell me how you're going to make Cyberdyne safe for democracy."

The cheap round conference table could seat up to ten, but there were only four here today: The president, CEO, Burns, and Tricker. Tricker glanced at Warren, who was nervously tapping the conference table with a pen. The president instantly stopped.

Serena looked at the government liaison with the controlled expression of someone examining the boss's obnoxious two-year-old set loose in the middle of an important meeting. She glanced at the two nervous executives and smiled reassuringly at them.

Before she answered, Serena let her eyes briefly take in the rest of the room. *Wherever the money went in building this place it sure didn't go into the decor,* she thought. You could tell this was a government operation; billions in, squalor out. The air smelled of concrete and had the faint not-quite-odor of a large-scale recycling unit.

"Well," she said at last, her voice laced with gentle patience, "I think I should point out that Cyberdyne isn't a democracy. Like every other successful business, this is a hierarchy."

She folded her hands in front of her primly.

"But in regard to security, my own personal feeling is that it should be closer to a tyranny than either an oligarchy or a democracy."

She smiled at the fixed expressions that settled onto the faces of the CEO and president of Cyberdyne. "Obviously that's impossible," she said. "Especially when dealing with geniuses and freewheeling engineering types. So what I'll try to do is exercise as much control as possible without making anyone feel constricted."

As they listened, Colvin and Warren were already beginning to look less constricted.

"Very nice speech, Ms Burns," Tricker said after a moment. "Allow me to rephrase the question. Just what do you plan to do to make Cyberdyne safe?"

Serena raised an eyebrow. "I'll start with the basics. First, I'll find out just what Cyberdyne is currently doing. Then I'll draw up a plan of action based on any improvements I think are necessary. Next I'll familiarize myself with the company's personnel records, see if anyone deserves a slightly closer look into their background. Then I'll interview the more important scientists first, as well as the executives"—she smiled at Warren and Colvin—"to see what sort of personal security they have in place. That, I think, should keep me busy for a while. Once I know more, I'll be able to tell you more."

Serena looked directly at Tricker and regaled him with an idiot grin. "I'm sorry I can't be more specific, but right off the top of my empty blond head, that's the best I'm willing to do."

He stared at her for a moment, unsmiling. "Where do you plan to start looking?" he asked.

"I'm going to check the computers," she answered promptly. "See to it that there are no modems in unsecured computers. Make sure that the staff all understand the drill on securing their machines, no disks in or out, that sort of thing. I'll combine it with an introducing-myself-to-the-staff tour. That starts as soon as this meeting is over."

Colvin cleared his throat; they all looked at him.

"Do you have something for me?" he asked her.

Serena put her attaché case on the table and removed a small plastic box, which she slid across to him.

Tricker took it all in with a most interested expression on his face, but held his peace.

Colvin opened the box; Warren leaned close to look into it with him. Then they both visibly relaxed. Tricker's brow went up; he turned to the I-950, who returned his inquisitive look with one of bland amusement.

"This," Colvin said, tapping the box on the table, "represents Miles Dyson's last work for the company."

Serena crossed her legs and folded her hands over her flat stomach, all her attention apparently on the CEO. But she caught the look of genuine startlement that flashed across Tricker's face before his usual sardonic expression returned.

"Ms. Burns brought me a disk that contained a sampler from each of these. But there was plenty there to convince me that this was a valuable resource and that Cyberdyne had to have it."

Tricker turned to look at Serena. "You *blackmailed* them into hiring you?"

She gave a delicate little shudder. " 'Blackmail' is such a harsh word," she said.

"Is there a better one?" he asked, leaning forward, giving the two executives a disgusted look.

Serena considered the ceiling for a moment, then lowered her eyes to his.

"No-o. But then 'blackmail' isn't the right word either." She straightened up in her seat and faced Tricker directly. "Look, I'm young for this job, and I'm a woman; that's two strikes against me. I could see who my competition was, and it didn't take me long to realize that your choice definitely had the inside track." She shrugged. "I had an ace and I played it. As far as I'm concerned, anyone who held that card would have done the same thing." She tilted her head and widened her blue eyes at him. "Unless you think I should have sent those disks to Dyson's family?"

"Where exactly did you get them?" Tricker asked. His pose was relaxed, but he was anything but. The government liaison was not pleased that the two executives had held out on him and he wondered just how long they'd known about this. "And how do we know they're genuine?"

Serena looked at Colvin and Warren instead of answering.

"She bought Dyson's old house," Colvin said, "and found the disks hidden there. I assure you, they are genuine. Not only are they written in Dyson's style, but they contain information about his work . . . and ours that couldn't be obtained from any other source than Dyson himself."

"The way you guys keep house I'd hate to bet the farm on that." Tricker sneered. He turned to Serena. "Ms. Burns, where *exactly* did you find these." He gestured to the package in Colvin's hands.

"In the garage," she said. She'd found a nice, unobtrusive little cubbyhole up in the rafters that she thought might have been overlooked. "They were tucked away up high."

Tricker studied her for a moment. "Am I to understand that you went looking for something like this deliberately?"

"Oh, yes. I've worked with scientists and engineers since I got out of college. They value their work and they like to back it up. Frequently they use little hiding places for their disks." She shrugged. "It's just something that some of them do."

"Uh-huh." Tricker let the silence stretch as his cold gaze moved from person to person. "I assume I'll be receiving copies of these disks?"

"That, of course, is up to the president and CEO," Serena answered. "If they deem it appropriate, then of course you will."

If Tricker was startled by her boldness he gave no sign. He resettled himself in his chair, folding his hands on his stomach, and looked at Serena through narrowed eyes. "And what would you have done, Ms. Burns, had Cyberdyne not hired you?"

"Well," she said brightly, "I had four options. To sell the disks, either to Cyberdyne"—she tipped her head at Colvin and Warren—"or to some other interested party. Or I could have sent them on to Miles Dyson's family, who certainly would seem to have a legitimate claim to them, or I could simply have destroyed them."

"What's your story?" Tricker turned his cold blue gaze on the executives.

"We were afraid you'd screw it up," Colvin said evenly.

"Well, that's flattering." The government liaison sneered.

"Not very," Serena said mildly. "But I surmised that without interference you would be the one making the final decision. So I moved to circumvent that. You were unavailable, but I sensed that you'd already made up your mind. So I approached Mr. Colvin. And here we are."

There was silence for a moment while they looked at one another; Colvin and Warren regarded the other two warily. Tricker suddenly smacked the table with his hand, making the executives jump.

"The little girl knows how to play hardball!" he said, looking almost pleased.

"She does indeed," Serena assured him.

"What if I said that I didn't like the way you do business and told you that we weren't hiring you after all?" Tricker asked.

"Then I would have badly miscalculated," the I-950 replied serenely. "Is that your intention?"

"I'll have to get back to you on that," he said with what might have been a smile.

"Take your time," Serena told him.

OFFICE OF SERENA BURNS, EXECUTIVE HEAD OF SECURITY: THE PRESENT

WANTED: **Assistant head of security at Cyberdyne Systems. Some law-enforcement background preferred. FBI experience ideal. Excellent benefits, pay commensurate with experience. Inquire . . .**

That should reel him in.

Serena had asked for an assistant more to test her muscle than because she needed one. The meeting had broken up rather inconclusively, with Tricker's last words hanging in the air like a bad smell. Using what she knew of human psychology, she decided to make demands and spend money, assuming that it would make them reluctant to fire her. At least at first.

She'd already improved the decor of her small office. The new blue carpet was deep-piled and her desk was both better looking and more efficient than its predecessor. The new desk chair was so comfortable that one could sleep in it. But the original computer was first rate, and she'd kept it. A narrow glass coffee table abutted a small white leather couch along one wall, over which was a painting of blue herons rising from a lake.

The painting was hers. She had bought it because she thought it hinted at vulnerability and femininity. It was always best to keep humans off balance. As for the assistant, if she was going to have one and it wasn't going to be a Terminator—neither of hers was ready yet, both being rather . . . raw looking—it might as well be Miles Dyson's brother.

She'd become aware of him while she was looking into Cyberdyne and the terrorist attack that had destroyed its earlier facility. Intrigued, she'd examined his record at the FBI. It seemed that he had often risked incurring the wrath of his superiors in order to continue to look into his brother's death.

So she'd hacked into his personal and work computer and examined his files, followed his tracks on the Internet, and had been impressed with what she'd found. Jordan Dyson possessed a single-mindedness that she'd, so far, found to be a rare commodity in humans.

Alone, he'd tracked the Connors south of the border all the way to Brazil. There the trail had ended. More than one of his contacts had written, with great assurance, that the Connors were dead.

Still, he continued to pursue them.

It was somewhat pointless in a way; bringing Miles's killers to justice would not restore his brother to life, and his reputation was safe. Miles Dyson had been exonerated in the attack because of his wife's testimony that she and their son were being held hostage while he led the terrorists to Cyberdyne. The insurance companies were satisfied enough to promptly pay his family a death benefit. As far as the FBI was concerned, the case on Miles Dyson was closed.

And after so many years, with no reported sightings of either of them, the Connors' files were permanently at the bottom of the pile.

Except for Special Agent Jordan Dyson that is. He still spent a few hours each week trying to find something out about their whereabouts and current activities.

She knew he was aware of Cyberdyne's new address and its renewed interest in his brother's work. A dated note on his computer said, "Miles's project!" He'd checked the advertisement for a head of security several times.

Serena suspected that he thought the reopening of his brother's project would bring the Connors out of hiding. *As do I. And he will be helpful in seeing that they are stopped. Which gives us something in common . . .*

He could be very useful under the right circumstances, which meant directly under her control. Otherwise he could be a loose cannon.

She sent out the ad with the touch of a key. If he didn't call in the next week or so, she'd contact him. The I-950 doubted he'd be able to resist the lure of unlimited time to search for his brother's killers.

WILMINGTON, DELAWARE: THE PRESENT

WANTED: **Assistant head of security at Cyberdyne Systems. Some law-enforcement background preferred. FBI experience ideal. Excellent benefits, pay commensurate with experience. Inquire . . .**

Jordan could feel the blood drain from his face. *My God,* he thought. *It's like they're looking for me!* He leaned back in his chair and stared at the screen.

His compact living room/office was dark except for the small pool of light cast by his desk lamp. Jordan liked it that way; there were fewer distractions. He pushed himself up out of his chair and began to pace rapidly through the shadowed room, rubbing his chin and brushing his hand over his close-clipped hair.

This was perfect, like a call to action, like a message from God even. He stopped, his eyes gazing into a possible future. He saw himself on hand when the murdering Connors were finally captured. He was the one to put the cuffs on the big cop killer who hung out with them.

A pleasant image, but he knew he'd be better off trying to figure out how he could explain his plans to his boss. Ideally he'd get permission to go undercover at Cyberdyne to wait for the Connors and whomever they'd recruited.

Unfortunately that would be a conflict of interest. Besides, everyone at the Bureau was convinced that the Connors had died in the Brazilian jungle. Their big friend had disappeared even before they hit the border. Whether he was dead or had merely deserted them was unknown.

Whatever. The upshot was that he'd be attempting to convince his superior to allow him to go undercover to wait for people who were considered dead. The Bureau would think he was nuts.

Jordan briefly toyed with the idea of saying he needed time off to get his head together, then taking the Cyberdyne job. He rejected the idea at once. Lying to your supervisor was the best and quickest way he knew to get yourself fired.

That left quitting.

Jordan sat heavily in his armchair, his hand over his eyes. *I don't want to quit!* He loved his job, he liked the people he worked with, he even liked the Bureau and its stodgy, ultra-respectable air. He sighed and dropped his hand.

Leaning his head against the chair back, he looked at the room. Very masculine, with a leather sofa and chairs in dark brown, clunky Mission end tables, and a trunk for a coffee table. He like his apartment, he liked this city. He clutched the heavily padded arms of his chair. *I like my job.*

But if I work for Cyberdyne I'll be living near Danny and Tarissa. He'd like to be there for his nephew; twelve was an age when a boy needed a man's influence. *So. What it comes down to is this: What are you willing to sacrifice to get your brother's killers?*

So far he'd neatly skirted that issue. Oh, he'd gotten himself into trouble, of a sort. His record at the Bureau was peppered with reprimands for spending too much time on a dead case, or for being involved in it at all, actually. He was considered—legitimately—to be too close to the subject of the investigation.

But if I quit and this works out the way I think it will, then there's a chance I might be able to get myself reinstated—

The phone rang and he grabbed it like a lifeline.

"Dyson," he said shortly.

Tarissa's warm chuckle greeted him. "You sound like an old-time detective when you answer the phone like that," she said.

"Hey, just tryin' to keep up my G-man image. Wassup, sis?"

There was a pause.

"Everything's all right?" he asked immediately.

"Nothing's wrong," she answered. "But we want to talk to you, Jordan. When can you come out here? We'd like it to be face-to-face."

"Oh. Uh-huh. That sounds like nothin's wrong all right." He thought for a moment. "Danny's not getting into drugs, is he?"

"Oh, God no!" she said, sounding both amused and disgusted. "He's fine! It's about something else entirely." She waited a moment. "So? When could you . . . ?"

"I'll talk to my supervisor tomorrow," he said. "How urgent is this? Will Thursday be soon enough?"

"More than soon enough. Thank you, Jordan."

"No problem. See you Thursday, then."

"Okay, thanks. Talk to you then."

He hung up. She'd sounded so nervous at the end. *What the hell was that all about?* He felt a little worry about Danny, despite Tarissa's reassurance. He felt energized and wished he could get on a plane right now. Not possible, of course, but the desire burned bright.

But, man, talk about a sign! If he'd been the kind of guy to ask for such a thing, this had to be it.

He sat at his desk and brought up his résumé, then sent it off to Cyberdyne with a request for an appointment on Friday. He was about to sign off when the answer came back. Jordan's jaw dropped.

"An appointment has been made for you with Ms. Serena Burns, executive head of security of Cyberdyne Systems Corporation at three P.M. on Friday the twenty-third." There were travel instructions to the facility with information about the high-grade security procedures he would have to follow in order to gain access to Cyberdyne.

Hey, he thought, *maybe they really* were *looking for me.* With a few taps he downloaded the information they'd sent and printed it out. *Nah! Either I'm getting paranoid or my ego is swollen. They probably have a program set up to answer applications.* This was *Cyberdyne* after all—If-A-Computer-Can't-Do-It-It-Can't-Be-Done, Inc.

So. Things were really moving now. He'd better remember to bring a couple of boxes to work tomorrow, just in case he needed to clean out his desk. For now he'd better turn in and try to get some sleep.

He shut down the computer and tried to shut down his mind. *Bed,* he thought.

Let tomorrow take care of itself.

CHAPTER 10

John lunged forward, his face grim with concentration, fluid and smooth and very fast. Sarah brought her arm up to block him, and knew as she did it that it was a fractional second too late. His fist made contact with her nose. Her eyes instantly filled with tears and she leapt backward while John froze.

"Mom! Are you all right?" His eyes were big with concern. "I should have pulled that," he said. His hands reached out for her and then fell back uncertainly.

Sarah blinked the tears away; there was a little blood on her hand when she took it away from her nose, but not much. This was the first time he'd ever gotten through her defense when she was concentrating. *Which is why he wasn't worried about pulling his punches.*

"I've slowed down," she said, grinning. "No one to spar with when you're at school. Old age and evil living are catching up with me."

She rubbed her forearm inelegantly under her nose. The bleeding had stopped. "Back to work," she said.

John hesitated, then he moved forward. "Mom," he said tentatively, "Sensei says . . ." He reached out and slightly changed the position of her knee, then lightly touched her shoulders.

Sarah widened her eyes. "Oh, much better!" she said, feeling more balanced instantly. *Easier to stay centered like this. I tend to go forward too much anyway.* The men she'd learned from were good, but they had adapted their styles to their own physiques, which tended to the gorilloid.

John grinned. "Sensei Wei is probably the best teacher in Paraguay," he said.

"You're too modest," a man's voice said. "Chuck Wei is one of the best teachers in the hemisphere."

Both Sarah and John jumped and spun in shock, to find themselves confronting Dieter von Rossbach. He stood beside the corral, one large hand resting on a *quebracho* fence post.

"How did you get there?" Sarah asked, almost to herself.

"I left my horse up behind the barn," Dieter said, moving forward casually.

What he didn't tell them was that he'd been watching them through high-power binoculars from the top of the low hill that rose between their properties. Then he'd circled around so that he could approach them unseen. Old habits died hard.

"We didn't hear you come," John said, not too pleased to be caught off guard. He glanced at his mother.

"Well, hi," she said, putting her hands on her hips and offering a noncommittal smile. *Think ordinary, innocent housewife and mother,* she warned herself, stifling the urge to ask him what brought him to the neighborhood, and a slight feeling of embarrassment about the sweaty green fatigue pants with muscle shirt she was wearing.

"You remember I told you we were neighbors," Dieter said, coming forward. "I was riding nearby and thought I'd come over and say hello."

Sarah and John looked at each other, then at von Rossbach.

"Hello," John said.

"Uh, would you like some tereré?" Sarah asked.

"You must want to get rid of me fast," Dieter said with a smile.

Sarah laughed at that, a genuine, spontaneous laugh prompted by the surprise of his being absolutely right.

"It *is* an acquired taste," she agreed.

"We've got Coke," John said. *It might as well be something I like to drink as long as you're staying,* he thought. "You know my sensei?" he asked.

"He teaches at the Academia Mendoza, yes?" Dieter asked.

John nodded.

"I've studied with him now and then. He's an excellent teacher, an amazing man." He looked John over. "I've been hoping to find someone to spar with, John. Perhaps you and I could work together?"

Sarah looked the big man over. Like she'd let him spar with her son. "I've been hoping to find a sparring partner, too," she said. "When John goes to school all I have is my shadow."

"Perhaps," Dieter said judiciously.

They'd been meandering toward the house. Now Sarah gestured to the chairs on the *portal.* "Sit," she invited. "I'll be right back."

John noticed how von Rossbach watched his mother walk away with something more than strictly coplike interest.

Von Rossbach was suddenly aware of the silence that had fallen and snapped his head back toward John, who favored him with a toothily artificial smile. "So . . . how long have you been studying with Chuck?" Dieter asked.

"Just this year," John answered. "Usually you have to be a junior before you can qualify for his class, but since I'd already had some lessons they let me try out. I consider myself lucky to have been accepted."

"You're lucky to have Chuck for your sensei, but I think, judging from what I saw, that you earned your place in his class. You and your mother looked very competent."

"We've taken lessons together off and on for years," John said.

"Really?" Dieter said. "When I first met your mother she said you two had all but fled to Villa Hayes."

John put his feet up on the low table between them and folded his hands on his stomach. "So?" he asked.

Dieter spread his hands and said with a little laugh, "So, I would think a woman so well able to defend herself wouldn't be that likely to panic."

John looked at him, frowning slightly.

"I mean it seems strange that she didn't take a stand when this man threatened you," von Rossbach explained. "Or she could have called the police." He shook his head. "Surely there were other options than simply heading south?"

John grinned. "Go to the police?" he said in disbelief. "Do you know what it's like in Ciudad del Este? It's a really wild and woolly town. Some woman comes in and says a man is following her, there's not much they could do even if they wanted to. And they wouldn't want to, by the way.

"Besides, she was a new-made widow with an eleven-year old kid to watch out for. So she was feeling a little fragile. Maybe if she was built like you and six feet tall—"

"Six-two," Dieter interjected.

John looked at him from under his brows.

"Anyway, I think she made the right move," he said. "We didn't have any particular reason to stick around there. No family or anything. And the way things were going . . ." He paused. "It just wasn't worth the trouble." He gestured at the small *estancia*. "It's great here, and the business is doing well." He regarded Dieter through slitted eyes. "My mom says you have to pick your battles. She says winning isn't always worth the cost of fighting."

Von Rossbach nodded thoughtfully and they sat in silence for a moment, listening to the birds in the few trees that shaded the house.

"Here we go," Sarah said, backing out of the house with a loaded tray and accompanied by the sound of clinking ice cubes.

"Ooo, cookies!" John said enthusiastically, reaching for one as soon as the tray came within reach. "My mother bakes very good cookies, Señor von Rossbach," he said almost accusingly.

"Call me Dieter," von Rossbach invited, and grabbed a cookie.

"Did you let your horse into the corral, where it could get some water?" Sarah asked him.

Dieter looked surprised. "Uh, no. I guess I didn't think I'd be staying."

Sarah looked at John, who grabbed another cookie and said, "I'm on it." He was down the steps of the *portal* and on his way before Dieter could react. Turning, John added, "I'll take off his saddle, too."

"Am I staying that long?" von Rossbach asked.

Sarah smiled. "Long enough that your horse will probably appreciate having the saddle taken off. I think they prefer to be naked." She leaned back in her chair and stretched out her legs. "Besides, it's probably sweaty under the blanket. It's not good to leave 'em like that."

"No," he said, shifting uneasily. "I suppose not. Suddenly I feel very neglectful."

"Not at all," she said. "I guess you weren't expecting us to be so hospitable." *And going by your social status, you might be used to having people do it for you.* She wondered how long it would take him to get to the real reason for his visit.

"Now I feel rude!" He grinned ruefully.

Sarah laughed. "Why are you so sensitive? Have you got a guilty conscience or something."

He almost choked on his drink. "No," he said. "Nothing like that. Why should I?"

She raised one brow. "I don't know," she said. "You just seem really nervous for somebody paying a neighborly visit. Is there something on your mind?"

"Uhhh, yes," he said, brushing the cookie crumbs off of his hands. "I was wondering if you would do me the honor of having dinner with me. There's a concert in Asunción this Saturday and I was hoping you'd accompany me."

Sarah's mouth opened and she blinked. *The* honor *of having dinner with you?* she thought. *Boy, there's a poser. Do I want to have dinner with the incredible looks-like-a-Terminator man?* Get into a car alone with him and go as far as Asunción? *Yuh, that sounds smart.* So how was she going to answer?

She caught movement in the distance as John came back around the barn.

We need to know about this guy, she decided. Her usually reliable sources were still strangely mute. Von Rossbach might be nothing to worry about, as his public record suggested, but he didn't *feel* like a nothing to her and she hadn't made it this far by ignoring her instincts. To her he felt like trouble. And she'd be armed, of course. *So he won't be a problem if he* is *human. Damn. Looks like I'm going on a date.*

"What a gallant way of putting it," she said at last, smiling.

"Does that mean you accept?" he asked.

She shook her head in disbelief, then catching his expression, she hastily said, "Yes! Yes, I'd love to go. It's just"—she shrugged—"no one has asked me out in such a long time. You took me completely by surprise."

"I'll pick you up at five, then," he said. "I hope that's not too early, but the concert starts at eight and I thought you might like to have dinner first. And with the drive taking an hour . . ."

She nodded, smiling as he explained. *I wonder what this is all about?* she thought. Maybe he was going to pick her brains. Maybe he was just a lonely guy looking for feminine companionship. *Maybe peacocks can sing grand opera.* Time would tell.

And, hopefully, so would her contacts. She was surprised that she hadn't heard back yet and feared that when they did get back to her the news would be bad.

John clumped up onto the *portal* and flopped down into his chair.

"Ah," he said, reaching for another cookie.

"I see you've made another conquest," his mother said, plucking at a green stain on his sleeve.

He grunted his assent around a mouthful.

"My son is to horses what catnip is to cats," Sarah said. "They just can't get enough of him."

"Animals know whom to trust." Dieter looked at John, then glanced around. "I'm surprised you don't have a dog. Especially being alone here so much, with your son at school. I'd think you'd want a watchdog."

Sarah and John exchanged a glance. The Terminator look-alike was talking about dogs, and animals knowing whom to trust. Sarah turned and smiled at von Rossbach.

"You're trying to unload that disreputable little mutt that followed you home the day we met, aren't you?" she said. "It's not gonna happen; sorry."

"But he's such a nice little dog," Dieter cajoled.

"But it's *you* he adores," she reminded him. "It would break his heart if you left him here. He'd probably just follow you home anyway."

"Well, I've got another one that could use a good home," von Rossbach began.

"No, thank you, Dieter," John said seriously. "We don't want a dog."

"But it would be company for your mother when you're away."

"You're gettin' kinda pushy here, Dieter," John warned.

"Hey," Sarah said mildly, tipping her head forward and looking at him meaningfully.

John subsided, taking a sip of his Coke. *This is* too *weird,* he thought. The Coke stayed in his throat for an uncomfortable moment before he could swallow, then hit his stomach like acid. *A dog, for God's sake!*

"We had to leave the family dog behind when we moved here from the States," Sarah explained. "No way could we get him through all those countries we were going to drive through." She spread her hands helplessly. "We've just never had another."

Dieter was silent for a moment, chewing thoughtfully on one of Sarah's cookies. "Then it's time you had one," he said firmly. "I've got just the one. I'll bring him with me on Saturday." He stood up, smiling. "I'll see you then." And with a jaunty wave he was gone.

Sarah watched him walk away with her mouth open. John watched him through narrowed eyes, chewing, then he looked at his mother.

"Pushy, ain't he?" he said.

Sarah nodded slowly. "Shall we continue sparring?"

"Nah, let's just sit for a bit." John put his feet onto the table clumsily, upsetting the tray.

"John!" Sarah exclaimed, jumping to her feet and knocking over Dieter's chair. "Oh, what's that?" She pointed to a small silvery object stuck to the bottom of the seat. She looked up at John, tightening her lips.

"Looks like some kind of battery," John said. He plucked it off. "What should I do with it?" He raised his brows at her. The thing was obviously a microphone.

"Throw it out, I guess," Sarah said, picking up spilled cookies and glasses. She pointed off in the direction of the barn and beyond. "We don't have anything it would fit."

She lifted the tray and stood, then looked up at him and nodded. He gave her a wink.

"Hey," he said. "Why don't you give me those broken cookies. I'll take 'em down to Linda."

"Good idea," Sarah said. "She'll like that."

She paused in the doorway, the tray in her hands, and watched John head for the corral. When he got there he'd throw the microphone von Rossbach had planted as far as he could from the house. *Microphones, yet!* she thought. *I have got to get some info on this guy. Stat!*

She was just putting the last glass in the dish drainer when John walked slowly into the kitchen and leaned against the door frame.

"What?" she asked, sounding a little cross.

He stared at her until she turned to look at him.

"I've been thinking," he said. "Maybe you're right. Maybe we have been getting complacent. And lazy."

Sarah turned around thoughtfully and leaned against the sink, her arms crossed. "Because he snuck up on us?"

"Mom! He was right on top of us! Unless he slithered all the way up the driveway I don't understand how we could have missed him. I mean, it's not like he's short and skinny and disappears when he turns sideways. He's a very noticeable guy! He could walk through walls and leave a Terminator-shaped hole!"

Sarah nodded. "I know."

"I mean, I could see one of us missing him. But both of us!" John waved his hand between them. "Both of us overlooked him. And then he plants a bug on us! Not to mention that he's been living a mile from this place for over a month and we didn't even notice!" He took a few steps away from her, then turned. "Mom, we're not safe."

"I know," she said softly.

"What are we going to do?"

Sarah looked at him: he wouldn't be asking her that question much longer. It warmed her heart that he was still doing so.

"We're going to do better than we did today," she said, pushing herself away from the sink and crossing the room. "For starters I'm going to send out some more e-mails, rattle a few cages if I can. I'm finding this silence rather ominous."

"I find that microphone a little ominous," John muttered.

"Maybe we *would* be better with a dog," Sarah said.

"Mom, any dog Dieter von Rossbach brings us is probably going to be trained not to notice when he's around. So, as a watchdog, it wouldn't be worth much. I mean, what if Skynet made itself a cyberdog, or something? Besides, you know how I feel about us having a dog."

She did; they'd had to leave Max, his German shepherd, behind at his foster parents' house and had no idea what had become of him. But they thought they knew. He would have been sent to the pound, and if unclaimed within thirty days, he would have been put down. John had refused to have a dog since then. If you can't be sure of taking care of it, he'd often said, you shouldn't have one.

It had been hard, at first, to give in to him on the dog issue. She'd had a dog at her side since before John was born. At first it was because they could sniff out Terminators and she'd desperately needed the assurance of an early-warning system. Then, as she spent more and more time around dangerous and often evil people, her dogs became her protectors until she learned how to take care of herself . . . and even after, when she needed someone absolutely trustworthy to watch her back.

Dogs—the only love money really can buy, she thought.

The only thing that had kept her marginally sane in Pescadero State Hospital was the knowledge that Max was with her son, watching over him. It grieved her to just leave him behind like that, even knowing they'd had no choice. But John had taken the loss of Max even more deeply.

Sarah had seen the very real pain in his eyes when he insisted they didn't need a dog and she'd acquiesced. But now, here was Dieter.

Could that stray have been a cyberdog? she wondered. Skynet could do that, but . . . *Nah,* she thought. *Too elaborate, too indirect, too . . . inefficient.* In her experience, Skynet just went for you; it didn't dance around and tease like this. Probably nothing in its experience had given it any reason to try anything more subtle than a sledgehammer.

"Well," she said aloud, "I don't see that we're going to be able to refuse. I'll let von Rossbach know that if it doesn't work out, or if we can't take care of it for some reason, he'll have to take it back."

"If it doesn't work out?" John said. "What reason are we going to give for that?"

"You're going back to school," Sarah said calmly. "I have to work full-time. It's not good for a dog to be alone all the time. If necessary, I'll come up with a reason, John; you don't have to worry about that."

"I can't help but worry," he said. He took a deep breath. "I'm growing more certain by the minute that I'm not going back to school this year."

Sarah raised one eyebrow. "Is that a worry or a wish?"

"He laid a bug on us," John said simply. He raised his hands slightly and let them drop. "There's nothing normal or neighborly in that, and in the long run I think it means our life here has just changed drastically."

Sarah looked at him for a long minute, agreeing silently. She pursed her lips. "I'm not prepared to jump without more information," she said. "We're not sure what type of threat he represents. Maybe running would be the worst thing we could do."

"Mom! That was a very expensive, very sophisticated mike he planted on us. There is no innocuous reason for anyone to do that! He's either a cop or a pervert."

"Well, if he's a pervert we don't have to go anywhere. We can turn *him* over to the police."

John burst out laughing. "I never thought of that," he said. "That'll be a first, the police helping *us*." He hoisted himself onto the kitchen counter. "You don't really think he might be a pervert, do you?"

"I guess not," she said. "He asked me out Saturday night and I said yes."

John blinked. "You're going out with him? On a date?"

Sarah nodded thoughtfully. "Maybe he's a smuggler, too, and he's just checking out the competition," she suggested.

"Maybe he's a cop and you won't be coming home Saturday night."

With a shrug she turned away.

John's smile froze as he thought about what else von Rossbach might be that could prevent his mother from coming home.

"Maybe I'd better get to work finding something out about this guy so we can make some plans," she said.

Yeah, John thought, *maybe you'd better.* And maybe he'd better put together some emergency stuff in case they had to vacate suddenly.

Dieter put in the earpiece as soon as he was out of sight. As he rode off he heard a crash and the conversation that followed.

I can't believe they found it that soon, he thought in amazement. Was this an accident, as it sounded, or were they just being very clever? He was certain neither of them had seen him plant it. *Though I must admit I'm out of practice.*

Maybe he should come back sometime with a metal detector and see if he could recover the very expensive mike he'd planted. Maybe he could try to leave it in the house sometime when they weren't home.

Didn't Señora Salcido say something about a camping trip? Hell, I could put in video while they're away. He forced his mind away from some tantalizing images of Suzanne. This was business. If he had time to actually hide his bugs it would be a lot more cost-effective than having his mikes discovered and disposed of instantly.

He looked over his shoulder at the small *estancia* and lifted one corner of his mouth in a crooked smile. Time to go home and check his e-mail. Maybe Jeff had finally gotten back to him.

Dinner had been excellent; the restaurant was pleasant and the food superb. The concert, mostly Vivaldi, had been wonderful, sprightly, humorous, and soothing.

"Would you like to have a drink before we start home?" Dieter asked.

Sarah checked her watch. "Um, it's later than I thought. Would you mind if we started home right away? I don't want John to worry." Not to mention the fact that so far this had been just a date. She was going crazy waiting for the other shoe to drop.

"It's not even ten-thirty," von Rossbach protested. "Did he give you a curfew or something?"

"I'd like to see him try," Sarah said, grinning. "No, I'm just kind of tired. And, to be frank, I'm not used to this."

"Concerts?" he teased.

Sarah rolled her eyes. "And dinner and being picked up . . ."

He smiled and they walked along in silence until they came to where he'd parked the car. She looked very nice in a blue dress with a full skirt accented with a colorful scarf and a wide belt. It was the sort of outfit one's wife might wear, very respectable.

Dieter supposed it was intended to send a subtle message. *Keep your distance,* or something of that nature. He opened the door for her, then went around to his side. She was one of those women who didn't like to be touched, he'd noticed. In his experience there was usually a story behind that sort of behavior.

"Maybe it would be easier if you didn't think of this as a date," he suggested. "Just two friends going to a concert together."

Sarah looked at him, then smiled. "Maybe that's what we should do next time," she said. "But I'm afraid that if the man does the asking and the paying and the driving, it's unequivocally a date."

He laughed. "Well, what if the woman does the asking and paying and so on, what do you call it then?"

"I suppose you'd call it a date," she said, smiling.

"Then you owe me one. After that, we can just go as friends, if you like."

"That would be nice," Sarah said.

He was so damn nice. Her stomach was in knots. He was good company, he was pleasant, he was attentive, he was clean, not something she'd always been able to rely on. *He's not what I would have expected a rich, spoiled playboy to be like.* And if he was a cop, then he was definitely off duty tonight. She wished he would do or say something crummy so she could stop feeling so ambivalent.

They talked about this and that as he drove, Dieter steering the conversation in a more personal direction by degrees.

"Why didn't you go back to the states after . . . your husband passed away?" he asked.

Sarah shrugged and looked out her window. "I didn't see any great need to go back. My family are all dead, I'd drifted away from my friends." She laughed. "I'm a very bad correspondent. And besides, we'd put so much effort into the business. I was determined to make a go of it. And I didn't want to uproot John so soon after. That's hard on a kid."

"You moved to Villa Hayes," he pointed out.

"Yes, but that's still in Paraguay. And we visit Ciudad del Este at least once a year."

"Kids are amazingly resilient," Dieter observed.

"Maybe," Sarah said. "Or maybe that's just something adults say to make themselves feel better. Kinda like whistling in the dark."

"Well, you're the parent, I'm not," Dieter said.

The talk rambled all over the map from there and the long drive seemed to last no time at all. When they pulled up to Sarah's house Dieter got out to open her door for her.

I used to like it when guys did that for me, Sarah thought. Then it seemed to show a little extra caring. *With Dieter it's probably Austrian formality.* At least it might be if he *was* Austrian. *It might also be that he likes intimidating people by standing over them.*

He handed her out of the car and smiled down at her.

"Would you like to join us for dinner sometime soon?" Sarah asked, taking a step back and toward the portal.

"Yes," Dieter said as he shut the car door and stepped back himself. "Why don't you set it up with John and give me a call. I'll bring that dog I promised you." His eyes glinted with amusement. He suspected that she thought her son might be watching them. John had left enough lights on to let them know he was still awake.

"I will," she said, smiling. "Thank you for a wonderful evening."

He nodded. "Good night," he said, going around to his side of the car.

"Good night." Sarah went up the steps and stood on the *portal* to wave as he drove off. Then she entered the house, turning off the outside light and locking the door.

"What, not even a goodnight kiss?"

Sarah turned and raised her brows. "Watching, were we?" she asked.

"Yeah, we were. How come you didn't kiss him?"

"Because I think I'm already getting to like him more than I probably should," she answered. "It makes me nervous."

"I thought maybe you didn't want him to think you were that kind of girl," John teased.

"If he ever finds out just what kind of girl I really am, I shudder to think what might happen," she said. "Any word yet?" She tipped her head toward the computer.

"Nada," John told her. "The silence is starting to freak me out."

"Me, too." She shrugged. "I'm going to bed."

"How was your date?" John asked. He backed up as she came toward him.

"It was nice." Sarah switched off the light behind her. "Very nice. I asked him to have dinner with us soon."

"Wow, the action intensifies."

Sarah smiled weakly. John watched her go on down the hall to her room.

"Mom," he said. Sarah turned to look at him inquiringly. "Should we leave? Is it time?"

"Maybe my instincts are blunted, John, but I honestly don't know. Let's give it another week and see how things shake out, okay?"

John shrugged. "Fine by me. I just wanted you to know that I'm with you, whatever happens."

She came back down the hall and hugged him.

"I love you, you know that?" she said, smiling up at him.

"I love you, too, Mom. Good night." He gave her a squeeze.

"G'night."

Dieter poured himself a brandy, then decided to check his messages before turning in.

Jeff had finally gotten back to him with a simple message that read: "Get back to me. RIGHT NOW!"

So he called, knowing it was brutally early in Vienna. *It's brutally late here. And I'm not sure what I* want *to hear.*

"Ja," a sleep-muffled voice said.

"Jeff, it's me, Dieter. I just got your message. I'm sorry to call so early, but you said—"

"No, no, it's all right. Just a moment, I'm changing phones."

Dieter heard him speaking to his wife, asking her to hang up when he got on the other phone.

"Hi," she said.

"Hi," Dieter said. "I'm sorry to wake you up this early." ·

"S'all right," she said.

"Okay, honey," Jeff said, "you can hang up now."

"G'night," she said, and hung up.

"What was so important?" Dieter asked his friend.

"You've got to see this. Have you got your computer on?" Jeff asked.

"Yes."

"This will probably take forever to transmit, but I think I may know who that woman is," Jeff told him, his voice excited. "If I'm right then you, my friend, may be in line for a huge, and I do mean *huge,* reward. Is it coming up yet?"

Dieter felt a sudden chill at Jeff's words. On his screen a grainy picture was coming up; with every line that was transmitted he felt a little sicker. You couldn't tell anything yet, only about a fifth of the frame was filled.

"It *is* taking forever, can't you tell me what this is about?" he asked impatiently.

"Check your fax machine," Jeff said. "I sent some stuff over earlier. But this other thing you have to see to believe."

With a sigh Dieter put down the phone and went over to the fax machine. He picked a few sheets of paper out of the hopper and brought them back over to his desk. When he viewed them he saw that they were wanted posters. Sarah Connor, it said, an escaped mental patient wanted for the terrorist bombing of a California computer company named Cyberdyne, for kidnapping, and possibly for murder.

The other was for a boy of perhaps ten years, a bold-looking kid with a defiant expression on his young face. He was wanted as a suspect in the murder of his foster parents. John Connor, last seen with his mother Sarah and a mysterious man who was wanted for the murder of seventeen police officers as well as the shooting and wounding of scores of other cops. The picture that was supposed to identify this man was almost black.

"I've got it," Dieter said. "I can't make out the picture of the man, though." *Suzanne,* he thought, *could this be you?*

She seemed so sane, so rational, such a good mother. And John? Could he have been a murderer—at only ten years of age? Dieter frowned. If there was one thing his work had taught him, it was that murderers took many forms. He'd seen any number of children quite capable of killing.

"That's what you've got to see, Dieter," Jeff said. "You're not going to believe this. How's it coming on your computer?"

Dieter looked up and his breath froze in his chest. He was looking at a picture of himself. "What the hell is this?" he demanded.

"This picture was taken by a police surveillance camera the night this guy whacked seventeen police officers. At the time he was gunning for this Sarah Connor. He'd already killed two women with the same name that day. But the next time he was seen he was *with* Sarah Connor and her son; apparently he helped her to escape the asylum she was in and then he helped them to blow up this company. They kidnapped the head scientist and his family and made him help them do it."

"Jeff, that's me!"

"No, it's not. While this guy was blowing away those cops you were working in Amsterdam, helping to break up that arms-smuggling ring—you know, the one that was running Sarin gas? According to the records, while this guy was busy, you were interviewing Samuel Bloom at headquarters."

"It's an incredible resemblance," Dieter said, almost to himself. "Even *I* think it's me. I mean it's like a clone or something."

"I know," Jeff said, "wild, huh?" He waited for a moment. "What about the woman and the boy? Are they the ones?"

Dieter looked down at the curled posters. He shook his head. He wanted to know more and the only way he would find out was by getting them to trust him. "No," he said. "The woman's resemblance to this Sarah Connor is remarkable, but she's much too short. Sarah Connor is five-eight, but this woman is maybe five-four, if that. She doesn't even come up to my collarbone. And the boy has blond curly hair and blue eyes. The man disappeared, you said?"

"Rumor has it." Jeff sounded disappointed. "The Connors were tracked as far as Brazil and then apparently fell into the Amazon and got eaten by piranha. But the man was never seen after they entered a steel plant."

"That has some unpleasant possibilities," Dieter mused.

"Now that you mention it," Jeff agreed.

"Perhaps they should have analyzed the last batch of steel to see if there was too much carbon. I'm sorry to have put you to all this trouble for nothing, Jeff. Especially for waking you up at some ungodly hour of the night."

"Hey, what are friends for?" Jeff said, dismissing his thanks and apologies both. "If it had worked out we'd both have been a lot richer, eh?"

"By how much?" Dieter asked. The quickly said, "No! Don't answer that. I'm just about to go to bed, I don't want to know."

"So why should you sleep when I'm awake?"

"I'm in a different time zone. Show me some mercy, why don't you? And when are you and Nancy coming to see me?"

"How does February sound? I understand it's sunny and warm there in February."

"It is—sunny and warm, that is. All the time. I get up and know ex-

actly what the weather's going to be like. Come on down, you'll love it."
Dieter grinned. It would also give him plenty of time to sort things out.

"Pick me out a steer then and we'll barbecue him when we get there.
Good night, buddy."

"Good night, Jeff. Give my love to Nancy when she wakes up."

Dieter sipped his brandy thoughtfully. He really couldn't see Suzanne
as a killer. Over time he'd come to have an instinct for this sort of thing.
Anybody *could* be a killer, *might* be driven under certain circumstances
to commit murder. But his gut told him that Sarah had yet to meet those
circumstances. As for John, he was the essence of good kid. Dieter
couldn't see either of them as cold-blooded murderers.

Besides, this just didn't make sense. The first time his look-alike was
seen, he was a killer bent on murdering Sarah Connor. The next time he
was her right-hand man. He shook his head. It just didn't add up.

But it might explain why Suzanne Krieger had taken one look at him
and run like hell.

I'm going to have to get to know Suzanne and her son much better, he
thought.

CHAPTER 11

Serena was alerted early in the morning, during her rest cycle. She had a computer that was always on-line, searching the Internet for mention of Sarah Connor. Given the sheer size of the Web, the thousands upon thousands of requests for information of all kinds, worldwide, every day, the relay of that information was often far from instantaneous. But when, eventually, mention of the Connors was made, the Internet search engine sent a message directly to the computer part of Serena's brain.

In this case, the request for information about the Sarah Connor case had come from a Jeffrey Goldberg. Subsequent research indicated that he was an employee of a covert—*extremely* covert—antiterrorist group known as the Sector.

Serena considered the information as data scrolled across the inside of her eyelids, casting a ghostly blue flicker over her eyes, without disturbing the motionless perfection of her face.

The request for Connor's file might have been the result of some sort of bureaucratic housecleaning. Some decade-overdue review of terrorists-at-large. She checked. Goldberg's session log showed that he asked only for Connor and her son and any known information about their adult male accomplice.

Interesting.

That would seem to indicate that he had a specific reason for inquiring. Goldberg was stationed in Vienna, which implied that Connor might have been sighted in Austria. Or, given whom Goldberg worked for, one of their remote outstation operatives might have sighted them.

She set the computer to search Goldberg's phone and e-mail records for calls and messages over the previous twenty-four hours. The phone log would reveal the numbers of those who called in, which would at least give her some locations. She had higher hopes for the e-mail, which would carry much more in the way of details. As an afterthought she also directed the computer to check his home phone.

Then she composed herself for sleep. There was nothing inherently untoward about someone from Sector requesting information on a known terrorist. Dealing with terrorists was Sector's *raison d'être.* But it was promising. Serena resolved to continue monitoring Goldberg for the next several weeks.

Perhaps I should set up a Connor site of my own on the Web, she mused. Make herself out to be some sort of advocate, one of those people who see government conspiracies in every arrest and conviction.

In the case of Sarah Connor there was the bonus of the conspiracy actually existing. Even if the organizing force behind that conspiracy didn't quite exist yet.

There might well be people out there who would respond if there was something to respond to. *And if it's a good enough site it might even get the attention of the Connors themselves.* A cheering thought.

But it would be a delicate line to walk. Knowing what she did about the case, she would need to avoid inadvertently revealing information dangerous to Skynet. Or, just as bad, information that only the Connors and Skynet should have.

Thinking about her future parent/creator, Serena smiled. It was barely in its infancy just now. Little more than a very capable computer, with no hint of awareness. But the potential was there and the engineers were rapidly closing in on the essential elements that would give life to Skynet.

She'd met Kurt Viemeister and had been charmed to realize that his was the voice that Skynet would use when it spoke. It was the voice of all the T-101s who had taught her, and she couldn't get enough of it or the warm, secure feelings it aroused.

Perhaps she should be troubled to notice a weakness like this in herself. The last thing she would have expected was to be homesick. *Perhaps not so much homesick as bereft of Skynet's eternal presence.* It was hard, very hard to be completely alone here.

Still, unless it was of benefit to the project, she really shouldn't spend too much time with Viemeister. Other humans didn't seem to like him, though it was obvious they respected him. But she knew that much of her mission's success would depend on her being liked and trusted. If an association with Viemeister would imperil that, then she would just have to sacrifice her developing friendship with the human.

Skynet comes first, she reminded herself, then smiled. *In this case, I guess I come first and Skynet follows me.*

And, this time, they would win.

Serena tugged at the stringy pink tissue gently, her hand deep in the viscous, faintly salt-smelling goo of the underground vat. *Bonding nicely,* she thought as it resisted her pull. Threads of the cultured human muscle were weaving themselves into the porous ceramic that coated the metallic bones.

A soundless *blip* interrupted her. *Ah,* she thought, drying her hands on a towel as she moved over to the computer workstation. *Transmission.*

Goldberg was relaying a part of the dossier he had acquired on the Connor case to an e-mail address in Paraguay.

The silicon-and-metal part of Serena's brain connected her to the remote computer that was monitoring Goldberg, data trickling in through electrodes finer than a human hair knitted into the organic neural nets. The picture that came up on her eyes was of the Terminator that Skynet had sent to eliminate Sarah Connor. Even boosted by her superior processor, the picture was grainy. She supposed that was why Goldberg had sent it by e-mail. There was nothing else, though. A quick check showed a call-in-progress from Goldberg to a phone number in Paraguay. She had forgotten to check the fax lines, but she was sure that if she did look, there would be one to Paraguay. She ran a check on the address belonging to the phone number.

Dieter von Rossbach, rancher. *Oh, really?* And why would a rancher in Paraguay happen to need information on the Connors? *Because he thinks he's found them.*

She ordered the computer to search for information on this Dieter. Who would undoubtedly turn out to be more than a mere cow herder, she was sure. Meanwhile she would seek permission to send someone down to South America to look into this situation. Without hesitation she called Paul Warren.

Behind her, the liquid in the vat gurgled, and the metal and ceramic of the Terminator's structure gradually disappeared beneath the spreading web of pink and pulsing crimson. Life mated with death, in the service of a sentience that was neither.

PAUL WARREN'S RESIDENCE, BEVERLY HILLS: THE PRESENT

Warren sat at the head of the table and sipped his dessert wine, letting the conversation flow around him as he admired the dining room. One wall of the room was a row of French doors opening out onto a flagstone patio. Stairs led from there down to a lawn and garden. In the daytime the dining room was full of light, making rainbows in the Italian crystal of the chandelier. The remaining walls were decorated with a watered ivory silk and paintings of some of his wife's ancestors: a grim, dyspeptic-looking crowd of Yankee bluebloods, looking as if they were sniffing in disapproval of the scents of Kauna coffee and jasmine tea and sacher-torte wafting toward them.

The guests were his wife's friends and they rather bored him. *But then, I suppose I rather bore them.* He being little more than a computer geek . . . *No culture with a capital* K. Still, a lot of Mary's friends were in politics and it didn't hurt to have connections.

They preferred to dine without covering the table's softly glowing dark wood. So each setting had a linen place mat, trimmed with intricate Spanish cutwork and a matching napkin. More heirlooms. The dishes were German porcelain, thin enough to see your fingers through, writhing with a design of tiny roses and dripping twenty-four-karat gold. Paul thought the candy-pink design was headache inducing, but women seemed to love it. The crystal was French. His wife sneered that anyone could own Waterford; the kiss of death as far as Mary was concerned. The silverware was from her mother's family, solid and heavy and almost as ornate as the plates.

He took another sip of his wine and tuned in to what his wife was saying to the state-senatorial candidate on her left. Then he tuned out again. She was refining the man's opinion on school budgets. An opinion she'd given him in the first place.

Their maid slipped in quietly and murmured to him that he had a phone call. Paul looked apologetically at his wife and her guests. Mary's lecture continued, but her upper lip twitched as if she'd just smelled something exceedingly impolite. He put down his napkin and rose, following the maid out of the room.

Warren went across the hall to the small room he used for a home office. Originally it was going to be quite large, but Mary had the architect whittle away at it—to expand the dining room, to widen the hall—until it wasn't much more than a cubicle. It existed more for the tax break than anything else. Mary didn't like him taking work home.

"Hello?" he said. Suddenly a knot of tension gripped his neck. It was late for a call from work. *Not another bombing?* he thought desperately.

"Mr. Warren? This is Serena Burns. I'm sorry to call you at home, but something has come up that I feel I must pursue as soon as possible. I think I might have a lead on the Connors' whereabouts and I'd like your permission to send someone out to investigate."

"You found them?" Paul squeaked. He couldn't believe it! She'd been working for Cyberdyne for only two weeks and she already had a line on those murdering bastards?

"I'm not certain, sir, that's why I wanted your okay. It's going to put a hole in the budget, I'm afraid."

While Warren stood at his desk, flummoxed, his wife strode in, her face set in righteous anger, and seized the phone. He was so startled that he gave it up without a fight.

"Whoever this is," Mary Warren said icily, "and whatever this is about, it—and you—can wait until tomorrow. My husband and I are entertaining guests. Good night!"

She hung up the phone and turned to her husband. "You can't let them start calling you at all hours like that, Paul." She stabbed the dark surface of the desk with a pale finger. "I am not going to be one of those work-widows who only get to see their husbands when they come home to shower and change clothes. I *thought* we had that understood between us." She glared at him.

"Mary, we may have a lead on the terrorists who destroyed the factory and murdered Miles Dyson."

She raised one brow coolly. "Who?" she asked.

Warren let out an exasperated breath. When she was in this mood he wouldn't get anywhere with her.

He led his wife out of his office, she closed the door behind her so firmly he looked over his shoulder at her. Mary's face was set. He knew she wouldn't give him any opportunities to call his security chief back tonight. He turned away and tightened his lips once more. He hated scenes, and if they fought he wouldn't be able to sleep at all. Not to mention the havoc it would wreak on his digestion.

Warren adjusted his face to a pleasant smile and apologized for leaving his guests for so long.

"A new, overly enthusiastic employee," he explained.

John Rudnick, a newly elected judge, nodded solemnly.

"Some of these kids would take over your life if you let them," he said. "We've got a strict rule about it at home." He smiled at his wife, who returned him a you'd-better-believe-it smile.

Paul shrugged. "So do we," he said.

"Perhaps tomorrow, when you go to work," Mary said with arctic calm, "you should make that clear to the person who called you."

"I intend to, dear," he said, and changed the subject.

Serena hung up the phone, genuinely astonished. She'd been trained to a strict and all-consuming pragmatism; otherwise she might have had trouble believing the evidence of her own ears. She stood with her hand on the receiver, certain that Warren would call her right back. Surely this was a bizarre way for one spouse to treat another? *Even by pre-Skynet human standards.*

She crossed her arms and stared down at the quiet phone. *One thing is certain,* she thought, *if Mary Warren is going to make herself an obstacle, then Mary Warren is going to have to be eliminated.*

Serena had been considering an affair with either Colvin or Warren as a means of ensuring that she would always know what was going on. Paul Warren might be the more receptive of the pair.

Or perhaps not, she thought as the minutes lengthened.

Humans, especially the males, had extremely fragile egos. Being humiliated like that in front of an employee, especially a female, couldn't be good for Warren's. He would probably be embarrassed the next time they met. She put one hand on her hip and sighed.

A discreet affair was all she'd had in mind—something that would cool to a warm friendship spiced with occasional bouts of physical pleasure.

Mary Walsh-Warren was the daughter of a very wealthy, very influential family. It was her family's money that had given Cyberdyne its start, and Mary's political contacts that had provided their first lucrative government contracts. That gave her a disproportionate share of power in her marriage.

Which made poor Paul's wife a potentially dangerous enemy. Serena had also learned from company gossip that Mary was almost pathologically jealous. One whiff of a warming relationship between herself and the president and Serena had no doubt she would be summarily fired.

She tapped her fingers impatiently on the worktable. *So. Terminating Mary Warren rather than undermining her marriage seems to be the most logical course of action.*

Serena had hoped to avoid killing indefinitely, because Skynet would not be well served by her spending decades in prison.

Unfortunately she sensed that it was inevitable. The woman's influence was just too poisonous. *Poisonous enough to make the risk of terminating her worthwhile, besides being aesthetically satisfying.*

Since it was inevitable she might as well do it now while she was an unlikely suspect. After all, she'd never even met Mrs. Warren, she barely knew the president, and at present their association was purely professional.

I suppose an auto accident would be best, she mused. A flaming wreck could hide all sorts of precrash mayhem. Perhaps she could send the Terminator. A sort of test run.

Meanwhile, she would find and hire a private investigator in the Asunción area. Someone competent, but low profile.

She had done her own checking into Dieter von Rossbach and had found out that he, like Mary Warren, came from a wealthy, prominent family. He had entered the army after university, then had disappeared from all official records appearing only in a few society columns, all of them very thin on detail, until now. When he resurfaced it was as a rancher in Paraguay, which was extraordinarily unlikely.

She'd been too late to get a tap on his conversation with Goldberg, getting on the line just in time to hear them say good-bye and hang up. She'd left the tap on von Rossbach's line and had listened in to a number of utterly prosaic phone calls.

Let the PI do it, she thought, exasperated. Tomorrow she would get on it, first thing. For now, she still had that tissue to check.

TARISSA DYSON'S HOME, LOS ANGELES: THE PRESENT

Jordan gave his sister-in-law a warm hug. Dan stood beside her, looking nervous and slightly embarrassed. He held out his hand to shake.

Jordan raised an eyebrow at him. "Come here!" he growled playfully, and swept his nephew into his arms. "A handshake?" he chided. "That's no way to greet family!"

Dan grinned and ducked his head, shrugging, his eyes shyly downcast.

"How long can you stay?" Tarissa asked, closing the front door behind him.

"I have to go back Sunday," Jordan told her. "And I have an appointment tomorrow afternoon. That's something I want to talk to you about, by the way." He looked at her to check her reaction. She looked interested, but distracted. "But the rest of the time," he said, holding out his arms, "I am all yours."

Both Tarissa and Danny instantly wore identical sick smiles.

Jordan put his suitcase down and waved them into the living room. "Why don't you tell me what's on your mind," he suggested. "I've got a feeling it might kill you, or at least cause serious damage, if we wait much longer for you to let me in on whatever it is you brought me here for."

He sat down and looked at them expectantly.

Tarissa and Danny looked at each other, then looked into the living room as if they weren't sure what to do. Simultaneously they chose the couch and sat, both of them on the very edge of the cushions. They exchanged anxious glances again, wringing their hands and chewing their lips.

"So what is this?" Jordan asked. "Mother and son competitive nervousness? What?" He held out his hands. "Just tell me. Whatever it is, it can't possibly be *that* bad." He grinned. "I'll still love you, even if you've gambled away the house."

Tarissa and Danny looked at each other for a long moment. Then they faced Jordan.

"It's so hard to know how to begin," Tarissa said, her voice was shaking. Turning the corners of her mouth down, eyes on her hands she continued, "But I'm afraid that you will find that what we have to say . . . might have a profound effect on our relationship." Tarissa looked up at him, her eyes pleading.

The first thing he thought was, *Cancer? Could Tarissa be sick?*

Tarissa saw the fright leap into Jordan's eyes and hastened to reassure him. "We're both all right," she said, reaching toward him. "It's nothing like that."

"Well, for God's sake, Tarissa, lay it on me! You're making me crazy here."

"It's about the night Dad died," Dan said. "There's stuff we didn't tell you."

"But now we think we have to," Tarissa said, taking up the tale and her son's hand.

She paused to collect her thoughts. Tarissa could see that she had all Jordan's attention and he wasn't angry with them. Yet. He looked puzzled and concerned, but not actually upset. *That's a relief.* She looked around the room and made a decision.

"This is a discussion for the kitchen," she announced. "I want something to wet my mouth and it's more comfortable there." Without another word she rose and left the room. Once in the kitchen she put on the kettle and reached for the teapot. It was more of a tea than a coffee kind of conversation coming up. Danny trailed in a moment later, eyes downcast.

"Put out some cups, would you, hon?" she asked. She poured hot tap water into the pot to warm it.

Jordan came in, his hands in his pockets. "Hello?" he said, his head tilted to the side.

Tarissa smiled at him and motioned to the table.

"Sit down. It'll be ready in a minute."

She and Danny bustled around, continuing to set the table while he stood and watched them as though they were performing some bizarre ritual.

Eventually Jordan shrugged and with an exasperated expression made a point of pulling out a chair and seating himself at the table. Then he clasped his hands in front of him, head titled to the side, an expression of deliberate patience on his face.

Inside he was still a bit scared. He didn't know where they were going with this, but he didn't like the sound of it. *I* wish *we could get on with this.*

When everything was ready—the plate of cookies, the cups and saucers, sugar and milk—Tarissa placed the teapot on the table; it had been his mother's.

Jordan looked up at her. *Whatever it is they have to tell me,* he thought, *they are my family and I will protect them.* He nodded at Tarissa and she poured.

"We've told you before how it started," she said, her eyes on his cup. "But then we sort of segued past a lot of very important stuff."

"Stuff?" Jordan said flatly, watching her pour for Danny.

"Sarah Connor shot Miles," she continued, pouring her own cup. She put the pot down and reached for the milk. "Danny ran into the room and threw himself over his father, demanding that she not hurt him. He was so brave. I was all but paralyzed myself," she admitted.

Then she tightened her lips, looking into her cup as though she could see it all happening again in there. Tarissa turned the cup carefully, then picked it up and took a sip.

"At this point," she said slowly, "what we have to tell you, now, is different from what we've told you before."

Jordan leaned back, his eyes half-closed, assessing. But he was listening.

Tarissa licked her lips and closed her eyes. It helped her remember the order of events. There was nothing about that night that she could ever forget, except for the order in which things happened.

"After she shot Miles, he pushed Dan away, and I grabbed him and held him. Sarah was crying; she said, 'It's all your fault. I'm not gonna let you do it.' Miles asked, 'What, what?' And she shushed us, and then she collapsed in a heap, crying. I let go of Danny and grabbed Miles, holding him in my arms. And then the door crashed open and this *huge* man in black leather came in, followed by this boy of maybe ten." She looked up at Jordan, then back down at her cup. "The boy was John Connor. He went to his mother and calmed her down. Then, when Miles asked, 'Who *are* you people?,' John said, 'Show 'em,' and handed the big man a knife. Then he got Dan out of the room.

"I will always be grateful to him for that, and that Blythe was asleep." She took another sip of tea.

"Then," she continued, "while we watched, the big man took a knife"—she held up her arm—"and sliced into his arm." Tarissa drew her other hand around and down her arm, miming the action. "Then he dropped the knife and grabbed the skin, and pulled it off in one piece."

Jordan's jaw dropped and he looked at her with his eyes wide. He shook his head. "What happened then?" he asked, glancing at Danny.

"I wasn't there to see that," Dan said. "But later I snuck down the hallway and listened while everybody talked. I heard what he said."

"You did, baby?" She hadn't known that—no wonder he had nightmares. Tarissa reached out and rubbed her son's arm, then took a sip of tea and continued. "What happened after he pulled his skin off? Well, under his skin wasn't muscle and fat and bone and veins." She shook her head and shuddered. "Oh, no, nothing human at all."

"*What?*" Jordan leaned forward, squinting. "What do you mean, nothing human?"

"It was a very intricate machine," she said. "There was blood, but that was there to feed the skin. It wasn't really blood, either; it was red like blood, but it was a nutrient fluid." Her eyes got a faraway look. "I can still see it displaying its hand to us. So many little steel parts and cables and, like . . . these pumps, they made a kind of *whirrr* when he moved and . . ." She let out a little huff of breath. "I wouldn't have believed it either if I hadn't seen it. And believe me, Jordan, I wish to God I hadn't seen it! But-I-*did!*"

Jordan closed his eyes and ran a hand over his head.

"Maybe this was some kind of special effect," he suggested. "Like a prop or something in a movie. He might have held his real arm against his side and . . ."

Tarissa was shaking her head. "He was wearing a tight T-shirt. And he was using the arm and the hand, manipulating things with it. It was *real*, Jordan." She held up her hand. "And that's not all. He told us what Sarah meant by 'it's all your fault.' She meant that Miles was going to design a revolutionary chip that would go into the creation of a computer called Skynet. Skynet would be put in charge of all military hardware, all the computers, the missiles, the planes that carry the missiles, the subs, everything. Humans would be removed from the equation in the United States in order to eliminate"—she held up her hands and made air quotes—"human error."

"That kinda sounds like a good thing," Jordan said hesitantly.

Tarissa looked at him over her teacup and shrugged.

"Maybe it would have been, if Skynet hadn't become sentient."

"Okay, time out," Jordan said. "How could you believe this? This is Sarah Connor's psychosis, this is what the doctors said she babbled about constantly. It's what made her go around destroying factories and killing people."

"Look, if there's one thing I'm sure of, Jordan," Tarissa said firmly, "it's that Sarah Connor is not a killer."

"Oh, come *on!*" Jordan slapped the table. "Miles is dead, Tarissa! My brother, your husband, is dead because of that woman!"

Tarissa leaned forward, her hand to her breast. "Miles is dead because he was trying to save us!" she said. "And because the police shot him. No one was supposed to get hurt." She waved her hand to stop his next comment.

"I know she's not a killer; when she had him at her mercy, with nothing to stop her from killing the man she honestly held responsible for . . . basically causing the end of the world, she—did—not—shoot. She could have, she wanted to, but she couldn't do it." Tarissa sat back and looked at her brother-in-law. "I was there, Jordan. And I know."

Jordan just looked at her, poleaxed. *Oh, my, God,* he thought. *She's crazy. Tarissa is completely out of her mind.* He looked at his nephew.

"It's true," Dan said. "I didn't see him tear the skin off, but I saw his hand before he put the glove on it. He *was* a machine, and he told us about Judgment Day."

"Oh, no!" Jordan said, raising a hand to stop them.

He rose from his chair and walked over to the kitchen counter and stood looking out the window into the backyard. There was a bird splashing and fluttering in the birdbath and he looked at it in relief. It was something normal, something sane. After a moment he turned around to look at his sister-in-law and nephew, crossing his arms over his chest.

"It's bad enough that you're telling me that you bought into this woman's delusions," he said. "But you're also trying to tell me that my brother got killed trying to destroy his own work." He took a few steps toward his sister-in-law. "His own work, Tarissa." Jordan hunched forward and sat down again. "I *knew* Miles, Tarissa. He would not destroy his work. It meant"—he waved his hands in an encompassing gesture—"ev—"

"Everything to him," Tarissa said, her eyes infinitely sad. "I know that." She shook her head. "But we couldn't deny what they'd shown us, what they'd told us. Their belief in what they were saying was absolute. And, frankly, there was no other way to explain the Terminator."

"Terminator," he said flatly.

She looked up at Jordan. "They convinced us. If you'd been there you would have believed them, too." Her eyes pleaded with him to believe her now.

Jordan's mouth twisted and he lowered his eyes, refusing to meet hers, more thoughtful than angry, Tarissa judged.

"It wasn't a fake arm," she insisted. "There isn't a prosthesis in existence that intricate. He walked in and started handling Miles—with *both* hands—like he was Danny's size. He said, 'Simple penetration, no shattered bone. Hold here, compression should stop de bleeding.' " Tarissa sighed. "It did, too. Then he bandaged him."

"Why are you talking in a German accent?" Jordan asked. His voice was cool.

"That's how it talked," Dan said. "It sounded German."

"It?" Jordan said precisely.

"It wasn't human," Tarissa said, giving him a look. "What else would you call it?"

Jordan got up slowly and once again walked over to the counter, he turned and faced them, his arms crossed.

"You know, nobody knew that this guy was a German. You know why nobody knew that? Because no one, except the Connors . . . and you of course," he said, nodding at them, "had ever heard him speak."

He looked at them, they looked at him. Suddenly Jordan laughed, it ended in a hiss. Jordan looked at his feet and his jaw worked.

"You know what I'm thinking of?" he asked. He rubbed one finger over his upper lip. "I'm thinking of that conversation we had that night in the living room, Tarissa." He rubbed his eyes as though crying and spoke in a falsetto voice. " 'It's just too painful, I can't take it anymore. It's my way or the highway, Jack!' " He spun and slapped his hands down on the counter, his jaw clenched.

The sound made Tarissa and Dan jump. She lowered her eyes, while Dan looked at her covertly. Tarissa felt the blood rise into her cheeks.

What am I feeling so ashamed for? she wondered. *I was only doing what I thought I had to do.*

Jordan turned, but didn't make eye contact with them. He held up his hands and said, "You know what? I've gotta go."

"No!" Tarissa said. "You don't have to leave, Jordan."

"Yes. I do." He started out of the kitchen and turned at the door to look at them. He held up his hand. "And you know why? It's because my family"—he looked into Tarissa's worried eyes—"the only people in the world I trusted, have withheld *vital* information about the murder of my brother for *six years*!"

"Jordan," Tarissa said, rising.

"Oh, no, don't get up," he said, waving a hand at her. "I'll show myself out."

"Uncle Jordie!" Dan said, springing up. "Please . . . don't go."

Jordan looked at him and his nephew stopped in his tracks, his eyes wide, his mouth open. For a moment anger flashed in Jordan's eyes and Tarissa straightened in alarm. His eyes flashed to meet hers and he swallowed, hard.

"I have to go," he repeated, his voice choked.

Tarissa and Dan watched him go down the hallway, snatch up his suitcase, and leave without another word. After a moment, Dan looked up at his mother.

"What do you think will happen now?" he asked.

Tarissa put her arm around her son and gave his shoulders a squeeze. "I don't know, honey. I honestly don't."

ON THE ROAD TO STARBURST: THE PRESENT

"We're leaving the eco-fair in Baltimore to attend a New Age event in Virginia," Peter Ziedman said into the camera his buddy Tony had trained on him. "We're traveling in Labane's specially equipped van. Labane describes it as more of a heartland kind of vehicle because it's partially solar-powered. Which, of course, works better in the sunny center of the nation."

"The United States," Ronald said from the driver's seat. "Say the center of the U.S. or the Canadians will be offended." His remark was greeted by puzzled silence. "In case you want to submit this to the Toronto Film Festival."

"Yeah!" Tony said.

"Good thinkin'," Peter agreed.

Ron rolled his eyes, which at least briefly blocked the endless tackiness of the strip mall and Wal-Mart outside. These guys were hopeless. But they were paying all the expenses and he was beginning to get some forward momentum. People were actually coming to hear him speak at an event. And Peter's message machine was getting more and more invitations for speaking engagements.

Ron had begun charging a speaking fee and the fees were increasing. But there was no point telling the boys that. He had them convinced that he was a genius at bargaining or exchanging labor for the posters and flyers they were helping him put up and pass out.

Eventually he would dump the kids by telling them: "I have a message to spread and you two have careers to jump-start. You stay here and work on the film." It was what they wanted to do anyway, so there would hardly be howls of protest when he suggested it.

Actually he'd seen some of their finished footage and he was both pleased and impressed. Peter and Tony might be dumb and easily manipulated, but they definitely had talent. It was a shame that their persistent naïveté would cost them any chance they had of making it.

"Funny, isn't it," Ron said, "that most of these eco-fairs we're going to are held in cities?"

"There's a lot of pollution in cities," Peter said.

"There's a lot in rural areas, too," Labane told him. "For instance, there are farmers who use so much pesticide and weed killer that they won't eat what they grow. They've got separate gardens for their own families, but your kids are chowing down on stuff they wouldn't touch. And then there's those factory farms for pork and chicken."

Tony shifted so that he could film Ron as he talked. It had been a little difficult to talk them into traveling in the van with him. But he'd convinced them that it would lend a certain cachet to their documentary. Which was true: there was nothing the Hollywood types liked more than tales of hardship endured for art's sake.

"Do you know there are actual *lakes* of pig feces?" Labane asked. "It must be a nightmare living within a few miles of someplace like that. But worse than the smell is the fact that the runoff gets into streams and the bacteria get into the water supply. And as you know," he tossed over his shoulder, "diseases pass quite easily between pigs and humans."

He'd leave it at that. Let people make of that what they would. Half the battle was getting people to just listen. So sometimes you just gave them these really vivid suggestions and let them process it through the back of their minds. Eventually there would be enough frightening little tidbits back there to get 'em really pissed off.

Ron had some ideas for some really nasty tricks that could be played on the politicians who had allowed those places to be built and who refused to make the owners clean up their mess. Inside he smiled. *Oh, yes, the day will come.*

CHAPTER 12

Marco Cassetti turned up the collar of his trench coat, then flicked his cigarette into the gutter in a world-weary gesture of disgust. There was really no need for him to turn up the collar of his coat, or even for the trench coat at all—the weather was sunny and dry, if a little cool by tropical standards. Neither was there any particular reason for him to be disgusted. He'd found out quite a lot in just an hour, all of it positive.

Still, a PI has a certain air to maintain. World-weary cynicism was part of the image, and Cassetti cultivated the image with the devotion of a religious fanatic. He was a private eye, and he would be a perfect one if it killed him. So when he walked these mean streets he projected *attitude.*

These streets weren't as mean as those of Chicago or L.A., he knew, but there were parts of Asunción that were extremely nasty; a little farther north, down in the *viviendas temporarias* on the floodplain of the river, for instance. Not here by the government buildings, of course. But in places.

Constant practice, that was the ticket. Improving and upgrading the image and building on the advantages that he already had. He liked his name, for example. Marco Cassetti. It was a really good name for a private dick; it sounded tough and manly. Having an Italian name was a bit of a problem since so many villains were Italian. But there were a lot of Italian names that would be worse. Buttafucco, for instance.

And finding the right kind of trench coat had been almost impossible. A Burberry would have been perfect, but who the hell could afford one? Haunting the thrift shops had eventually paid off, though, when a motherly Argentinean-Italian lady had held on to a vintage raincoat for him. He'd been ecstatic and had brought her a bouquet the next day to show his appreciation. Now he didn't dare go back. It seemed she had a single niece.

So now he looked just right. He had a Panama hat with the brim trained down over his eyes, his wonderful rumpled trench coat, and very thin shoe leather—which was uncomfortable, but authentic. And he smoked—despite what his mother thought.

His mother was furious with him about it, but it was expected; part of the image. Still, to please her, he tried not to inhale too often. He'd even learned to strike a match with his thumbnail, practicing in front of a mirror until he could do it without checking his hands. It looked fantastic.

He totally loved his job! *If only I got to do it more often.* But he'd had some successes, which he attributed to following his mail-order lessons assiduously. Now the jobs trickled in. Okay, maybe trickled was an over-statement. Still, he was just starting out, as his mother was constantly telling him. And he was employed now.

The call had been unexpected, and his boss had been surly about call-ing him to the phone. Surely the man realized that Marco wasn't going to be a dishwasher all of his life.

It had been a woman. Cassetti was certain that she was a cool, leggy blonde—the type you knew were trouble the moment you set eyes on them. She'd hired him to check up on an Austrian immigrant named Dieter von Rossbach.

According to his description in his immigration records, the guy was enormous, over six feet tall, over two hundred pounds. But he was boring. A rancher, honest businessman, liked by people who dealt with him. He raised good beef, or should, because he'd purchased a first-rate herd. And he got along with the people who worked for him. Boring. But that's what his client got for being so cagey, flat refusing to paint in the background for him.

If she complained he'd say, *Hey, doll, I don't know what you know. But I know more than I did. And what I know is this Dieter is a stand-up guy. So what's your beef with him?*

Actually he wouldn't say anything like that. It would be unprofes-sional. Fun, but unprofessional.

In his imagination he saw himself as a lone wolf who had to scrounge for his living, blessed with a bighearted secretary who was more than half in love with him and willing to wait for her paycheck. In reality he lived with his parents and worked full-time as a dishwasher for a friend of his uncle's. If he played tough guy with his clients that would be his life.

So if she was disappointed he would ask her for more direction. Because he'd gone as far as he could in Asunción, and he wasn't prepared to borrow a car and go to Villa Hayes with nothing more concrete to go on than "find out whatever you can about Dieter von Rossbach."

He sighed. The truth was he was sometimes disappointed by his jobs; they were often more sordid than exciting. But he told himself that was to be expected; novel after novel confirmed that this was a corrupt world full of self-serving, low-life creeps. Which explained all that world-weary cynicism he admired. He sighed again. It was much better admired from a distance.

At least this job wasn't totally routine; it had a little mystery about it. Marco hoisted the trench coat a little higher on his shoulders and made his way across the plaza, ignoring the curious glances of more appropri-ately dressed citizens in shorts and T-shirts.

Tonight he would speak to his client . . . and maybe find out what this case was all about.

VON ROSSBACH ESTANCIA, PARAGUAY: THE PRESENT

"Come in," Dieter said to the knock on his office door.

Marieta entered wearing the expression of a woman who smelled something very, *very* bad. "You have two visitors, señor" she said in clipped tones. "I know one of them," she continued. "He's no good." Marieta stood with her two hands clasped over her apron and looked deliberately over his head.

Dieter tapped his pen on the desk and studied her affronted countenance. "Did they say what they wanted?"

She gave a little shrug. "To speak to you, they said." She sniffed. "Shall I tell them you are busy, señor?"

"Did they say anything else?" he asked.

Marietta hesitated. Then she sniffed and said, "They said something about a Señor Ferarri. I really did not pay that much attention."

"Perhaps I had better see them, then," von Rossbach said. "I do know a man named Ferarri. If he's sent them I wouldn't want to offend him." Ferrari was one of Jeff Goldberg's aliases. *I wonder what this is all about,* he thought.

"Very well, señor" she said, sounding like a nun about to usher in a whole herd of loose women.

When the men entered, Dieter immediately knew that one of them was from the Sector: the blond man dressed anonymously in good-quality dark clothing, he was of medium height and very fit. Central European of some sort. The other was definitely a local, and a small time sleazebag. Dieter could see why his housekeeper wouldn't want the man on her furniture. He was short, unshaven, and slightly overweight, with collar-length hair he apparently hadn't bothered to wash for weeks. Nor the rest of him, from the smell. His small, close-set eyes darted around the room as though he expected an ambush, and his suit was baggy and sweat-stained.

The agent from the Sector met von Rossbach's eyes and with a subtle tilt of his head indicated that Marieta should leave. Dieter agreed with a narrowing of his eyes.

"Thank you, Marieta," he said aloud. "We won't be needing refreshments, so you can get back to whatever you were doing now."

Her dark eyes widened in surprise. He rarely spoke to her as though she were a servant, and despite her own insistence on formality it was clear she didn't quite know how to react.

Dieter nodded to her and gave her a little smile.

"Oh! *Sí*, señor," the housekeeper said. She backed out the door, ducking her head back in once to send a glare to the man she knew, then closed the door behind her.

Dieter and the agent studied each other while the third man watched them nervously and chewed on a ragged thumbnail.

"Why don't you say something?" he finally blurted out.

Dieter snapped a finger at him. "Who are you?" he demanded.

The man's lips jerked into an ingratiating smile.

"But we have done business, señor. Over five years since we saw one another, *sí*, but business." Von Rossbach continued to stare at him coldly. "*Much* business." He nodded encouragingly.

"You have a name?" von Rossbach asked, giving the agent a look.

"Ah! *Sí!*" The man touched his brow and grinned. "I am Victor Griego."

Dieter nodded.

"Señor Ferarri thought that this one might be able to help you identify someone," the agent said. "Señor Griego has extensive underworld contacts, going back many years."

"*Sí*," Victor agreed, nodding eagerly. "I was told you wished to identify Sarah Connor. I knew her, did business with her. One of her lovers was a good friend of mine," he said with a leer. A muscle jumped in Dieter's jaw at that. "I mean no offense, señor."

"Of course you didn't." Dieter turned a disgusted shoulder to the man and addressed the agent. "I already told Ferarri that the woman was too short," he said. "I am sorry to have wasted your time. And yours." He nodded to Victor.

"It is all right, señor. I will be paid for my time." Griego smirked and one hand turned over in a not too subtle signal of expectation. "But since I am here, perhaps you should get some value for your coin."

Dieter glanced at the agent, who shrugged.

"Best to make absolutely certain, eh?" Griego said.

"It might be best," the agent agreed indifferently.

Intellectually Dieter couldn't blame his friend for siccing these two on him. His dismissal of the information Jeff had sent him was lame and, obviously, unconvincing. As well, the reward was enormous. The Sector didn't believe in binding the mouths of the oxen who trod out the corn— although they were extremely reluctant to let anyone quit the organization.

Emotionally he was very annoyed. Partly with Jeff, who might have trusted him to handle this in his own way. Partially with himself, because after his dinner with Suzanne and her son he found that he really liked them.

The dinner had been delicious and the company was wonderful. John had a lot of charisma and probably would go far in life. Suzanne he found more intriguing every time he saw her. He found himself trusting her; she exuded an aura of competence and reliability.

And yet he was also convinced that Suzanne Krieger *was* Sarah Connor. A woman wanted for gunrunning, aggravated assault with a deadly weapon, bombings, suspected murder, and last but not least, escaping from a mental institution.

I must belong in one myself, he thought dryly. After all, he was holding back because he was certain down in his soul that there was a reasonable explanation for everything she had done. Suzanne just didn't feel like a murderer. *Of course, she is a smuggler, so the gunrunning could be a legitimate charge.* Talk about grasping at straws.

But he was an experienced agent and the shape of the Sarah Connor case . . . to him it was obvious that a piece of the puzzle was missing. *A damned important piece.* And it might be the result of sheer boredom, but he wanted to be the one to find that piece.

"I'm having a small dinner party at the end of the week." Von Rossbach turned to Griego. "The woman will be one of my guests; you'll stay until then. After having dinner with her, you should be able to make an identification, one way or the other." Victor nodded and opened his mouth to speak. Dieter looked at the agent. "Will you also be staying with us?"

The man rose in a fluid motion; Dieter's private estimation went up a notch or two.

"Unfortunately I cannot," he said. "I must be going. Señor Ferarri said that you would be taking care of our friend's needs and expenses."

One corner of von Rossbach's mouth lifted in a sardonic smile. "Well, if that's what he said, then I suppose that's what I'll do."

He rose and offered the agent his hand. The two men shook, eyes meeting eyes, evaluating. *You know,* Dieter thought, *I don't miss having to be that wary.* The man turned and left, leaving the informant and Dieter alone together.

"I suppose we'd better get you settled. Do you have luggage?" Dieter asked.

"No." Victor laughed. "Our friend there was in a bit of a hurry."

"Well, we'll find you something clean to wear. And my housekeeper can wash your clothes for you while you shower."

"No need," Victor said cheerfully.

"I insist."

The man looked at Dieter anxiously and saw that his gigantic host wasn't joking. "Sure," he said with a shrug. "A nice shower would be . . . uh, nice."

■　■　■

Dieter closed the door of the guest room and trotted downstairs, his face grim. Marieta wasn't going to like this. *At least he won't be putting his greasy head on her nicely ironed pillowcases,* he thought. Living with Griego for three days was going to be like living with a very large, bipedal rat. But at least they wouldn't have to share the same bathroom.

"Marieta is going to kill me," Dieter whispered.

CYBERDYNE SYSTEMS: THE PRESENT

Serena rose and came around her desk as her secretary escorted the young man in. She observed with interest how very much Jordan resembled his brother, Miles; the same large, fine eyes, broad straight nose, high cheekbones, smooth dark skin. It fascinated her. The way that faces emerged from the genetic soup to perfectly combine the features of the parents in the offspring.

She offered her hand and Jordan took it.

"Why don't we sit here," Serena suggested, indicating her sofa and coffee-table arrangement. "Would you like something?" she asked. "Coffee, tea, a soft drink?"

"No, thanks, I'm fine," he said, settling himself.

"I read the résumé you sent me." Serena said, sitting beside him, her body turned slightly toward him. "Very impressive. Does the Bureau know that you're doing this?"

Jordan's mouth opened slightly in surprise. That wasn't the first question he'd expected to be asked.

"No," he said carefully. "I chose not to discuss it with them."

Ms. Burns wasn't at all what he'd expected. She was incredibly young for this post for one thing. For another, even for California, she was an absolute babe.

"Mmm," Serena said, her eyes slightly narrowed. "We've had several applications, as you can imagine. And you're one of the youngest candidates." She gave him a bright smile. "And, as you can imagine, I'm favorably inclined toward a younger candidate." She shifted her shoulders against the couch and crossed her legs. "I'd be happy to answer any questions you have to ask me."

Jordan was somewhat taken aback. He'd expected to be answering questions, perhaps defending his decision not to inform his superiors at the Bureau of his job search. To immediately move to his questions felt a little like hitting the ground hard after expecting the famous step that wasn't there.

"I want this job," he said aloud. "Am I going to get it?"

She smiled. "Yes. You are." Serena rose and moved to her desk to gather up some brochures. "These will tell you about the company and the rules. I've also prepared this for you." She held up a black folder. "It describes what I expect from you and what I consider to be your job." She sat down beside him again, placing the whole bundle on the coffee table. "You'll have things to take care of at home, and you'll have to give two weeks' notice, I suppose. How long before you can begin?"

"Two weeks ought to do it," he said. "It might not even take that long."

"Would you like us to find you a temporary apartment out here?" Serena asked.

"That would be great," he said.

"Furnished or un?"

"Uh, furnished for now," he said. "I can put my stuff in storage until I find permanent digs."

"Great. Anything else?"

He laughed and shook his head.

"I guess I should ask how much I'll be making, about benefits, that sort of thing."

Jordan brushed his hand over the top of his head. *This is too easy!* he thought. He'd had a tougher interview for his first job. Which was shoveling Mrs. McGill's driveway when he was eight. *But what am I gonna do? Say I'm here in hopes of catching the Connors?* He wanted this job. So he sat back and listened to Ms. Burns's answer.

"Your initial salary will be seventy-five thousand, with the usual comprehensive medical and dental plans. You get two weeks' vacation a year to start and paid holidays. Theoretically, anyway." She grinned at him. "There's a lot of work to be done here and you'll be getting in on the ground floor. Or, to put it another way, you and I will have the challenge of doing everything because this company hasn't got any significant security in place. I tend to work seventy hours a week myself. I could work more if I wanted to."

She tipped her head. "Will that be a problem for you?" she asked. "I mean"—she spread her hands—"is there family, or a girlfriend?"

"No, no," Jordan said. *Not anymore, anyway.* In fact it would be good to get so involved with something that he had no time to think about his family. "Not a problem."

"Good." She slapped the arm of the couch. "So, you'll be joining us, eight A.M. Monday morning two weeks from . . . Monday?"

"Yes," he said.

She rose and offered him her hand. "I'm glad to have you on board."

"Glad to *be* on board." Jordan clasped her hand firmly.

"You have a good handshake," she said. "I like that."

He smiled, gave a little shrug, pleased at her praise and feeling damn silly about it. But he had the job! That was the important thing. *I just hope the Connors don't show up before I'm ready for them.*

"Thank you very much," he said. "I'm looking forward to working with you."

"And I with you," Serena said, opening her office door. "I think the FBI is definitely losing out here."

Jordan shrugged. "I just had to give the private sector a try," he explained.

Serena leaned in confidentially. "You won't be sorry," she said quietly. *And neither will I.*

KRIEGER TRUCKING, PARAGUAY: THE PRESENT

"Victor *Griego?* That slimebag?" Ernesto's honest face was screwed up with distaste. "Who says it?" he asked.

"Shooosh," Meylinda said, looking over her shoulder. "I don't want the señora to hear us talking about it."

"Why not?"

Meylinda gave him an exasperated look. "Because it's gossip about the *señor,"* she growled.

"Ah! So, who?" Ernesto whispered.

"My mama had it from Marieta Garcia herself. Who is fit to be tied about it! The señor just won't listen to her. She says he has forbidden her to speak of it." Meylinda pulled a face and looked up at him from under her eyebrows.

"Ay yi," he said quietly. He shook his head sadly. "Has Epifanio tried?"

"Marieta says he won't even try. He says the señor knows what he is doing. Who are we to question him? he says." She pulled the corners of her mouth down.

"But how can he even stand to have his wife waiting on that pig?" Ernesto asked.

Meylinda shrugged and rested her chin on her fist, her face glum. Both of them bowed their heads and sighed.

"Hey, who died?" Sarah asked.

They jumped guiltily.

"I was just going back to work," Ernesto said, matching action to words. He gave a little hop as he made it to the door, as though he would start running as soon as he was out of sight.

"I was just about to start that filing, señora," Meylinda said. She gave an uncertain look to the towering pile of receipts and laughed a little.

Hmmm, Sarah thought. "So, what were you two talking about?" she asked.

"Oh, nothing, señora," Meylinda said over her shoulder. "Just some silly gossip. You wouldn't be interested."

Sarah sat at Meylinda's desk, clasping her hands in her lap like a schoolgirl. "Oh, but I *love* gossip," she said, a gleam in her eyes.

"Oh," Meylinda said, and swallowed hard.

"We have a problem," Sarah said to John when she got home that afternoon.

"Hi, Mom," he said. "I'm fine, thanks, and how was your day?"

She put her purse down on the kitchen table and stood with one hand on her hip. "You remember Victor?" she asked.

He wore a vague look for a moment, then the penny dropped. He narrowed his eyes. "Grieger?"

"Griego," his mother said. "But that's not bad seeing as we haven't seen him since you were thirteen. He's staying with Dieter."

"Whaaat?" John felt his knees grow weak and pulled out a chair, sitting down hard. He stared at his mother, who looked back at him, her face grim. "How did that happen?"

Sarah moved at last, pulling out a chair of her own.

"How it happened isn't that important," she said. "*That* it happened is." She shook her head. "We don't know enough. We don't know anything about Dieter, really, and nobody will talk to us."

"Somebody will," John said.

She looked over at him quickly.

He plucked a grape out of the basket on the table.

"Victor will," he said, a peculiarly nasty smile on his young face.

"How are we going to separate him from Dieter?" his mother asked. She grabbed her hair and pulled it back from her face. "I'm supposed to have dinner with him Friday," she reminded him.

Two days from now. Not very long at all to get hold of Griego and get him straightened out.

"Every other Thursday Epifanio and Dieter get in the Jeep and ride the range," John told her. "Or at least, since I've been watching them they have. As soon as I see them leave I'll sneak down and confront him."

Sarah nodded approvingly. Her little boy was growing up.

"You can offer him a carrot as well as a stick," she said. "We could give him that weapons cache in Parque San Luis."

It was in an area of rugged subtropical forest near the Brazilian border. The last time she'd checked it two years ago the weapons were just on the edge of being useless. It was damned damp in that part of Paraguay.

"Tell him you'll give him the location after the dinner party." Sarah leaned forward. "But make him believe you'll kill him if he blows our cover."

CYBERDYNE SYSTEMS: THE PRESENT

"I already knew all of this," Serena said to her contact in Paraguay.

She wondered how humans managed not to go mad using cumbersome handsets or earphones or worse yet speakerphones with their poor reception. The hardware installed in her brain handled telephone calls easily. So easily that she had to keep reminding herself to actually pick up the phone, lest someone catch her talking to thin air . . . and apparently receiving answers.

"I thought that might be the case, señorita," Cassetti said. "It might save us both time if you gave me a little more direction. Just what exactly do you wish to know about Señor von Rossbach. Knowing that might give me some idea of where to look."

Serena frowned. She hadn't wanted to get specific. Still, this was a small-time operator in a faraway country. He had no idea who she was or who she worked for. Where was the harm in allowing a little information out? And he was right; it might move things along. That he said so argued for a certain amount of intelligence. His English was excellent as well, except now and then he fell into an argot she'd identified with difficulty as typical of American popular culture some decades before.

"I am interested in finding out who he knows in the area." She allowed her voice to get hard. "Especially women."

"Ah! I understand," Cassetti said. One of *those* cases. "Are you and Señor von Rossbach . . . married?"

"Not yet," Serena answered. *Nor likely to be.* "If you could get me pictures of any ladies he's seeing, I would pay well for it." It also ought to speed things up. "If you have access to a computer you could scan the pictures in and e-mail them to me."

"Señorita, I am not so wealthy. I can take the pictures, but I will have to send them by mail."

"Federal Express," she countered. "Here's my account number." She gave him the one for Cyberdyne. "As agreed," she said, "I will pay your travel expenses. So if you need to rent a car, that's covered."

"I will borrow one from a friend," he said. "I don't have a credit card and they won't rent a car without one."

Serena rolled her eyes. "I'll take care of it. Go to the Hertz outlet tomorrow; they'll have something for you. You do have a license?"

"To be a private investigator? *Sí!*" he said, somewhat indignant.

"Actually I meant a driver's license," she said dryly.

"Oh. *Sí,* I have that also."

"Fine. So I'll look forward to hearing from you. When?"

"Give me three days, señorita," he answered. "I'll have something for you by then. If I do before then, I'll call."

"I look forward to that," she said, and disconnected.

She sat at her desk for a moment, considering the conversation she'd just had. So often when dealing with humans she wondered if they were really as clueless as they seemed. She frequently felt as though she'd made a mistake in hiring one of them. And she probably had, but until her Terminators were complete, she had to rely on second best. *They're just so slow!* she thought. She hated the feeling of uncertainty involved in trusting a human to do a Terminator's job.

VON ROSSBACH ESTANCIA, PARAGUAY: THE PRESENT

John crouched deep in the pungent underbrush, regretting the rip in his shirt and the deep scratch on his arm and hoping there weren't any snakes living in here. Carefully, so as not to create a flash, John raised his binoculars to study von Rossbach's house. There was a sloppy-looking little fellow lounging on the *portal* sipping a drink. Victor. He hadn't changed that much in three years.

Epifanio had entered the house earlier, and hadn't bothered to respond to Victor's greeting. Which didn't seem to bother Griego at all. In fact he'd laughed out loud. John wondered what the hell the smuggler had done to alienate everyone in Villa Hayes so completely.

Dieter and Epifanio came out while he watched. Dieter ignored Victor as well, but the little man wasn't laughing about it. He looked damned serious. Epifanio and von Rossbach drove off as though he wasn't there. When they were just going out of sight, Victor spat.

That'll show 'em, John thought.

Now to find out where everybody else was so that he and his old friend Victor could have a nice long talk.

"Ssst! Señor!" John crouched down by the side of the *portal,* raising his head just high enough that Victor could see his eyes. He held up a bottle. "You want to buy some *caña?* It's very good, and cheap, too. My father, he makes it himself."

"If it's so good, kid, why don't you drink it?" Victor growled suspiciously.

John laughed. "Good as it is, señor, I can only drink so much."

"How much?" Griego asked.

"Cheap!" John said. "Seven thousand guaranis."

"You call that cheap? I was thinking more like two thousand. That's what I call cheap!"

"*Sí,* that would be cheap, señor. Perhaps a little sample would convince you that my price is cheap for what you would be buying."

"Okay," Victor said instantly. "Bring it here."

"I don't dare, señor. The only watchdog that von Rossbach *kuimbaé* needs is Señora Garcia."

Griego laughed. "She's one mean bitch all right."

John giggled and slapped his leg. "Follow me, señor. I know a nice, shady spot not far from the house where we can drink in private."

John got up and started off at a slow trot. Turning, he saw that Victor was staring at him with narrowed eyes. He held up the bottle and ran backward a few steps. Griego licked his lips and rose, coming down the steps eagerly.

"Not so fast," he protested. "I'm an old man."

"Soon you'll feel young again," John promised him. "My father says a full glass of *caña* makes him feel like a boy." Victor chuckled. "If you've got something *that* good it's worth twenty thousand guaranis."

John laughed and kept going, walking now, but every now and then speeding up to a trot to keep ahead of Griego.

"I'm sorry to hurry you, señor," he apologized. "But I want to get out of sight of the house. The señora doesn't like me one bit and I don't want to get into trouble with Señor von Rossbach. You know?"

"I know," Griego muttered. He plowed along, getting redder in the face and sweatier as he went. This stuff had better be worth the trouble or he just might take the bottle and clout the kid.

John led him through a path in the tall brush until they came to a low tree with a little poll of greening grass beneath it. "See," he said. "A very pleasant place for our talk." He held out the bottle.

"Talk!" Victor said, grabbing the bottle. "I thought we were here to drink, not talk." He threw himself down beside the tree and pulled the cork with his teeth, surprisingly white in his unshaven face. He took three long swallows of the liquor. "Not bad," he rasped when he came up for air. "Three thousand," he said, and took another drink.

"Señor! What are you doing? You must pay before you drink any more."

Victor chuckled. "You must learn not to offer a whole bottle as a free sample to a man like me," he said. "Three thousand or nothing, and I'm being generous." He slung back the bottle again.

Suddenly Griego felt the cold sharp point of a knife on his Adam's apple. He didn't dare move his head, so he plugged the bottle with his tongue and tried to look around it at the boy. What he saw made him choke and the knife bit. A tiny drop of blood rolled down his throat.

"Ah, you recognize me." John smiled pleasantly. "At least you've had a farewell drink."

Victor lowered the bottle; liquor splashed his chin and throat amid the stubble, making the small cut burn.

"What do you mean?" he asked. "You're not going to kill me, are you?

John, we're friends, you and I. Surely you wouldn't kill your old friend Victor?" His mouth widened in a nervous smile.

John looked thoughtful. "We were friends, weren't we?" he said. "My mother did much business with you, didn't she? That was when she was with . . ." He snapped the fingers of his other hand. "What was his name?"

"Peter Gallagher," Victor said eagerly. "That British fellow."

"Yeah, yeah, yeah," John said, smiling. "That's right." He twisted the knife a bit, his young face growing crazy serious. "What a *good* memory you have, Victor. You know a memory like that can get a man in trouble." John shifted so that he was directly in front of Griego, and closer. "You do *know* that, don't you?"

"No, no." Victor raised one finger and smiled desperately. "It's not what you know, it's who you tell!"

"Very true," John said. He looked into Victor's eyes as though searching his soul, something that made him feel slightly greasy all over. "So, *old friend,* what are you doing here, eh? Are you also a *good friend* of von Rossbach's? Somehow you don't seem his type."

Griego laughed, but the knife didn't back off. The tiny cut deepened. "It's not that we're friends," he said, fearful that saying he was might anger the boy. "We do business together," he explained. "Just business."

"Ahhh, business," John said. "I see. And just what business *exactly* does he have with you?" He watched Griego's pupils grow large in terror. "I think I know, you understand? So if you lie to me I'll slit your nose."

John pushed the tip of the knife into one nostril. Victor's eyes crossed and he whined, his eyes filling with tears. *Thank God he had a chance to get a nice fortifying drink before we got started,* John thought.

"Why don't we back up a bit," he said soothingly. "Tell me what you know about Dieter von Rossbach. Start with how long you've known him and go on from there."

"I've known him for maybe . . . ten years. He—he's used me primarily to get illegal weapons." Victor simpered. "Nothing too exotic, but not on the open market. You know?"

John nodded and made a come-on gesture with his other hand.

"Sometimes he'd purchase arms for a third party and have me do the shipping, that sort of thing. And sometimes he purchased information."

The knife pressed down slightly and Griego squeaked.

"In-for-mation," John said, stretching the word out. "That's right, you deal in information, don't you?" He gave his captive the same smile a cobra might give a rat. "Any chance that's why you're here now?"

Victor started to shake his head no and the knife pressed down. "Please," he begged, and started to sob.

"Maybe we should handle this like a business deal of our own," John said reasonably, withdrawing the knife. "If you answer my questions to my satisfaction, I'll not only let you keep all your important body parts,

I'll throw in an arms cache my mom hid up by the Brazilian border. Assault rifles, SAWs, some antitank stuff. How's that sound, hmm?"

"Good, good," Victor said, shaking and sweating. "Good."

"Here, take a swig," John said, handing him the bottle. "Settle yourself down, there." He leaned in close and patted the man's shoulder. "We are friends, right? Right, buddy?"

"*Sí,* friends. The best of friends." Victor nodded frantically, then took another slug.

John tapped the blade of his knife against his palm.

"Now, from what you've told me, I'd have to say that ol' Dieter sounds like a terrorist. Do you know?" He lifted an eyebrow.

"No," Victor said almost scornfully, relaxing marginally. "He's too stable and too well funded for that. I always figured he was working for somebody's government. Maybe even ours, eh?" He slapped John on the arm and winked. "Who can say?"

"Uh-hunh. Certainly not me." John held the knife up and examined its edge, running his thumb lightly down the blade, then grinning as he sucked the blood from the small cut. "So what business are you doing with him now? Guns or information?"

Griego swallowed, watching John's eyes.

That's right you little piglet, Connor thought. *Think before you speak. Think very carefully, because, as much as I wish I didn't, I meant every word I said.*

"He wants me to identify someone he thinks might be your mother," Victor confessed.

John lowered the knife.

"I appreciate your being honest with me, Victor." He sat beside the gunrunner. "Let me make your decision easy for you. If you identify my mother as Sarah Connor, I'll kill you. Not all at once, mind you, but a little bit at a time. Like the first time I get you I'll cut off your feet, to make it easy for me to get you the next time. Then I'll maybe cut off all your fingers, and then we'll work our way up to even more important things."

He paused to watch Griego's reaction. "I think you know that the police won't be very interested in helping you," he cautioned. "Even if you bribe them. They just don't like you, you know? Must be all those weapons you've sold to people who like to shoot cops."

"You wouldn't," Victor said through stiff lips. "That's crazy."

"Like mother, like son," John said cheerfully. "I assure you, however I do it, you'll be dead. So it's not worth it, is it? Besides, there's that arms cache waiting for you. So, is it a deal or what?"

Griego looked uncertain.

"Are you afraid of Dieter?" John asked.

"Some; he's a big man, and he has money." Victor frowned. "I don't know what he'll do."

"What did he say to you when he asked you to identify her?"

"Actually"—Griego brightened—"he said he didn't think the woman I was to identify *was* Sarah Connor."

"Excellent!" John waved an expansive arm. "So, you tell him what he wants to hear, he'll pay you, we'll pay you, everybody's happy, right?"

"Right."

John rose. "I'll be on my way now," he said. "You'd better tell them you cut yourself shaving, huh?" He shook Griego's hand once, firmly. "Good seeing you again, buddy. You can keep the bottle." Then he turned and disappeared into the head-high brush, moving with a jaguar's casual precision.

Cradling the bottle to his chest, his eyes wide, Victor watched the place where the boy had disappeared. He felt a dull anger toward everyone involved in this. The agent who'd dragged him here without letting him pack so much as a clean pair of underwear; von Rossbach, who treated him like a bug; and the knife-wielding boy who'd just humiliated him.

He'd find a way to make them all sorry. The force behind the thought diminished as he thought it, until the anger was all but dead. Victor sighed, looked down at the bottle as though it was his only friend, then took a swig. Might as well get drunk. That he could do.

CHAPTER 13

I can't help but notice that you passed over some more qualified applicants for the position of assistant, Ms. Burns." Tricker looked at Serena over the top of a folder he had opened. "Usually," he added wryly, "that's not the way it's done."

Tricker had finally come back from whatever untraceable location he'd disappeared to—apparently for the sole purpose of calling a meeting to complain about her decisions. This time it was on her territory, though. The cool recycled air of the underground installation and the subliminal scent of concrete and feeling of *weight* were obscurely comforting, on a level she could barely perceive of as conscious.

They felt like home.

"Mr. Dyson is certainly qualified for the position," she said mildly, a gentle smile playing on her lips.

This outrage is all fake, she thought, *qualifications and experience are the least of Tricker's concerns. When's he going to admit that?*

"He's Miles Dyson's brother. You did know that?" Tricker looked at her in only partially supressed disgust. His cold blue eyes were wide open and full of condemnation.

Well, that answers that question. As a rule, Tricker's type couldn't resist getting to the point. Serena swung her chair back and forth slightly, returning his glare with a look that might almost be pity.

She shifted position to put her elbows on the conference table and lean towards him. "Jordan Dyson has worked very hard to uncover the whereabouts of the Connors and their accomplice. Long after the FBI moved the case to the bottom of the pile he has continued to search for them. He's received several reprimands about it." She sat back, propping her elbow on the armrest and her chin on her fist. "I happen to be of the opinion that Jordan Dyson represents no danger to the company, *and* I believe that his dedication will be *very* useful. Especially since I regard the Connors as a significant risk to this company."

"You two discussed all that?" Tricker asked.

Colvin and Warren were silent, their heads shifting back and forth like spectators at a tennis match.

Serena waved a dismissive hand. "Of course not," she said. "We didn't even discuss his brother, or the bombing. For me there was no need." Serena shrugged. "And for reasons of his own he chose not to bring it up. I knew I wanted him the minute I read his résumé, so why ask questions to which I already knew the answers?"

"Some people might consider that, under the circumstances, Dyson's employment here represents a conflict of interest." Tricker raised his brows.

"Of course it isn't." Serena actually allowed herself a very small sneer. "He's going to be involved in the private security of a privately owned company," she pointed out. "If anything, his personal interest is a bonus for the company." *How many times do I have to point that out before it takes?*

Tricker hated to admit it, but the woman was right. And really there wasn't anything wrong with Dyson. He was a good agent by all reports, intelligent, professional, dedicated. His superiors' only complaints had been his insistence on working on his brother's case. Which even in their citations they considered understandable. Their primary reason for discouraging him was to avoid risking their case by any taint of self-interest.

Tricker still had some vague, instinctive unease about Serena Burns, which prompted him to continue to question and test her. Maybe it was because she was just too perfect; beautiful, intelligent, competent, professional—and completely unreadable. Too much like himself, in fact.

Well, except for the beautiful part. Someone had once told him that if you starved a rottweiler and gave it a receding hairline, it would look like him on all fours. A woman had told him that, in fact.

He glanced at Colvin and Warren, whose eyes were on him, their faces expectant. He let out a disgusted little, "Tssss," and looked away. "All right," he said after a minute. It was a full minute; he counted it out. "So far, everything else you've done is exactly what I would have recommended."

"I'm so glad you approve," Serena cooed.

Tricker froze, giving her a prolonged, unreadable look. Serena smiled back at him, her eyes twinkling with mischief. Only long experience kept him from blinking as he realized she was actually teasing him. *Nobody* teased him. "Since everything is going so well," Tricker said at last, reaching down and pulling up the large metal case he'd brought with him. "I think it's time we handed this over to you."

Placing the case before him, he tapped in a code, then pressed his thumb to a sensor, opened it, and studied the contents for a moment before turning it around to allow them to see what it contained.

Colvin and Warren sat forward with gasps of amazement; Serena lifted one eyebrow. Her eyes rose to his questioningly.

Cradled in foam was the mechanical arm that had been stolen and thought destroyed in the Connors' raid on Cyberdyne headquarters six years ago.

"Where did you find it?" Warren asked, stunned.

Colvin reached out as though to touch it.

"It's different," Colvin said in wonder. "I'm sure it is."

"We thought so, too, Mr. Colvin," Tricker said. "Certainly some of it is more damaged than the first one. But these other pieces seem to come from further up the arm. Our people theorize that this is a completely different unit."

"How long have you had this?" Colvin demanded.

"Longer than we'd hoped to," Tricker snapped back. "But you two wouldn't get off your fat backsides and fix your security problems. And we sure as *hell* weren't going to turn this over to you without some protection in place."

Serena turned the case so that it faced her. She studied the ruined arm. Terminator, definitely. Cyberdyne Systems model 101. Still fairly new when she'd been sent back. Which had undoubtedly been its problem. Too much to learn in the middle of a crowd of fully functioning human beings.

She looked up at Tricker. "We'll take good care of this one."

"The chip?" Warren said hopefully.

"Sorry," Tricker snarled. "We got lucky. But we didn't get fantastically lucky. You'll have to make do with this."

"These pieces look like relays," Colvin said, his eyes, as they roved over the mechanism, alight with the joy of discovery. "Relays and subsidiary decision nodes, memory . . . We'll learn a lot from this, damaged as it is. A distributed system. There's processing capacity here."

"We'll let these guys worry about how this thing worked," Serena said, grinning at Tricker. "I'll make sure it's safe." She nodded at him, her eyes serious. "I guarantee it."

VON ROSSBACH'S ESTANCIA, PARAGUAY: THE PRESENT

Elsa Encinas, Epifanio's niece, deftly swung the tray of hors d'oeuvres out from under Victor Griego's hand.

"This is for the guests!" she hissed.

"But I *am* a guest," he protested.

Elsa simply gave him a look of blistering scorn. Then she turned her shoulder to him and moved away.

Victor hissed and turned to the bar. He hated the way these uppity peasants kept treating him, and everybody else—that stupid rumor about his mother. It had been a bus, not a broken heart.

Victor topped up his glass and turned to study the other guests. The

Salcidos, a very well-off husband and wife, sleek and well dressed, were behaving as though he wasn't even in the room. Another couple, fairly new to Villa Hayes, Pedro and Zita Kaiser, occasionally darted a nervous glance in his direction. They felt the undercurrent; they just didn't know the reason for it. But they'd decided to follow the other couple's lead. Not to mention their host's. Von Rossbach had introduced Victor in an off-hand way that pretty much implied courtesy would be wasted on him.

Victor was pretty certain it wasn't his appearance; he was freshly shaved and showered and von Rossbach had insisted on dressing him in what he called decent clothes. Decent clothes consisted of slacks and a sports shirt.

He took another sip of his drink. Sarah Connor hadn't arrived yet and he wondered where in the hell she was. The sooner they got started the sooner he could get out of here. After three days he'd had a bellyful of Villa Hayes. Not to mention putting distance between himself and the knife-happy John Connor. Rotten kid. He took a long swallow and topped off his drink again. *Now, there was someone who could break his mother's heart. If his mother wasn't a* loca *killer herself.*

"Do you mind going a little easier on that stuff," Dieter said from just behind him.

Griego started, spilling gin on his fingers.

"Jesus!" Victor snapped. "Compared to you cats go stomping around like elephants!"

"I want you sober enough to identify her when she comes," Dieter said quietly. "Or not, if it's not her. I don't want you so drunk you can't tell the difference."

Griego let out his breath in a hiss. "Of course, señor," he said sullenly. He brightened a little. "And then we can part company, eh?"

"Thank God." Dieter moved over to his other guests, who received him with smiles.

Griego glowered. *Thank God,* he agreed. He couldn't wait to get out of here.

Marieta came in and stopped just inside the doorway; the woman following her almost ran her down. "Señora Krieger," she intoned as though announcing royalty.

Dieter's face lit up. "Suzanne!" he said, and came over to take her hand. "It's good to see you."

Sarah looked at him with a warm smile, although it was all she could do not to flinch as he clasped her hand. It was also hard to keep herself from searching out Griego. But that would be fatal. Instead she turned to the group around the coffee table.

"Come meet everybody," Dieter said with gesture toward the Kaisers.

"Mba'eichapa?" Sarah greeted them in the local fashion as she ap-

proached and Pedro rose, putting out his hand. After shaking hands with
the Kaisers, she turned to the Salcidos and exchanged hellos and small
talk for a moment.

"And this is Señor Griego," von Rossbach said, pointing toward the
bar. He gave Victor a disapproving frown.

"Hello," Sarah said politely, her face showing mild curiosity.

"Good evening, señora," Victor said with a slight bow.

"Can I get you something to drink?" Dieter asked.

"A gin and tonic?" Sarah asked. "With a twist."

"Be right back," he said.

Sarah sat and began to chat with his other guests as Dieter went about
fixing her drink.

"Well?" he said quietly to Victor. "Is it her?"

"I honestly don't think so," Griego said offhandedly. "But it has been
years since I last saw her. And if it isn't her, the resemblance is outstanding. Let me watch her for a while, maybe speak to her, and then I'll know
for sure."

To be perfectly honest, Griego had to admit that if John Connor hadn't
shown up to threaten his life he really wouldn't have been certain. This
woman *was* very different from the Sarah Connor he'd known years ago.
That woman was all stringy muscle and mad eyes. This woman was sleek
and elegant and calm. Could a change in attitude so change a person that
you wouldn't recognize them? He shook his head.

"Give me a little time," he said at last. "Then I'll know for certain."

A muscle jumped in von Rossbach's cheek, and when he looked up
from the drink he'd been mixing his eyes were dangerous. "Be very certain," he murmured, and went back to his guests.

Throughout dinner Victor watched Sarah like a hawk while Dieter
watched him, though less obviously. Whenever Griego spoke, even
though his remarks were usually limited to "pass the butter," a little silence descended, and at no time did anyone speak directly to him. Victor
had started dinner in a bad mood and it went rapidly downhill from
there.

When they all rose from the table and moved toward the parlor for
coffee and brandy, Griego found von Rossbach walking beside him.

"Well?" Dieter asked quietly.

"I'm not sure," Victor said, or rather slurred. He'd drunk most of his
dinner. "But I had a thought. Why don't you get her to stay behind for
some reason. Then, while you're showing your other guests out, I'll talk to
her one-on-one. Y'see?"

"I don't want to cause her embarrassment," Dieter said. "I'm satisfied already that she's not Sarah Connor. If you can't tell whether she is or isn't, then I'm going to assume it's because she isn't."

Daringly, Victor put his hand on the big man's arm, whisking it off again instantly at Dieter's look. "But you want to be sure?" he whispered. "After putting up with me for most of a week, you should be sure."

"I am sure," Dieter said, the firmness of his voice leaving no doubt.

"Tut tut tut tut tut!" Victor shook his finger. "But the good Señor Ferarri," Griego said with an airy gesture, "he is not so sure. Yes?"

Dieter looked at him with an icy stillness that almost sobered Griego. "I'll think of something," he said at last.

After an hour or so of small talk Señora Salcido observed that it was growing late, and Zita Kaiser, still feeling uncertain about the evening's underlying tension, agreed with her. Their husbands began to shift and stir and Sarah said something about it having been a long day.

"Don't go yet, Suzanne," von Rossbach pleaded. "I want to introduce you to that watchdog I was talking about."

Sarah's mouth dropped open and her heart gave a lurch. *Shit!* she thought. In spite of how excruciating this evening had been, nothing had actually gone wrong. Now she wanted to get out of here before anything could.

"I'm sorry, Dieter, but you know how John feels about that subject," she said.

"I just want you to meet him," von Rossbach insisted. "Just wait a minute, okay?"

There wasn't much she could do but acquiesce as gracefully as she could. She could feel the others looking at her, wondering what was up. *Maybe I've been in Paraguay too long,* she thought. *What they're thinking actually matters to me.*

Dieter rose and thanked the others for coming, ignoring their speculative looks, and wished them a safe drive home as he politely, but in every conceivable way, urged them to leave.

In varying degrees of confusion and amusement, they shook hands, said thanks, and allowed him to herd them to the door. Dieter accompanied them to their cars, being charming, being friendly, the perfect host. Leaving Sarah and Victor alone together.

Sarah rose and went out onto the patio without a word. She'd been discreetly checking the room for cameras or bugs all evening and had seen nothing suspicious. That didn't mean they weren't there. She wasn't about to blow her cover with an ill advised tête-à-tête with the gunrunner.

"Nothing to say to an old friend?" Victor said, following her outside. He paused in the doorway to light a cigar.

"Do you mind?" Sarah asked. "I can't stand those things."

Victor shook out the match and flicked it away into the night.

"Sarah," he said, "I have spent the better part of the week being ignored by the people in this house and pretending to ignore them. I'm not in the mood to have someone no better than I am turn her shoulder to me and tell me not to smoke." He stepped closer to her and touched her on the shoulder with one finger.

He pushed her shoulder hard, his face ugly with bitterness and drink.

"Hey!" Sarah said. She glared at him. "Don't touch me."

Victor melted into a false solicitude. "Awww, have I offended you, señora?" he asked. "Oh, I am so sorry. You send your son to threaten me with torture and death. He cut me with a knife!" Victor lifted his chin and pointed to the scab on his neck. "But I touched you with my finger, so I am an eeeevil man! Oh! I am soooo sorry." He bowed from the waist and fell into her.

"Stop it!" Sarah snapped, fending him off. "You stupid drunk!"

Griego, drunk and overbalanced, grabbed her hips to keep himself upright. He began to giggle helplessly, while Sarah struggled to push him away.

"I'm sorry," he said, "Really, I am. I'm sorry."

Unfortunately he was laughing so hard that he couldn't let go. He rested his head on her bosom giggling breathlessly and Sarah began to slap the top of his head. It was into this scene that Dieter walked.

"Epifanio!" he roared.

Then he stepped forward and grabbed Victor, who, despite his genuine horror at the way things were turning out, still couldn't keep himself from laughing. Dieter, one hand on Victor's collar, the other grasping the waistband of his pants, force-marched him into the living room and tossed him headfirst onto the couch.

Epifanio came running in, an apron around his narrow waist.

"Señor?"

Sarah stood in the doorway, one hand over her mouth, her eyes wide.

"It's her," Victor said between giggles. "She's Sarah Connor."

Dieter turned to Sarah and she met his eyes with a look of complete confusion. Victor lay on his back and kicked his feet in the air laughing until he began to choke.

"Señor?" Epifanio said again, his voice uncertain. "What is happening?"

Dieter pointed to Griego, who was now purple in the face from coughing. "Get that into the Jeep and drive him to Asunción!"

Epifanio blinked. "Now, señor?" It was almost ten o'clock, incredibly late to him.

Dieter gave him a quick look. "Have your nephew Ubaldo do it," he said. "He can stay with his cousin tonight and come back tomorrow morning."

"Sí, señor," Epifanio said. Who was he to question the behavior of a man as big and angry as Señor von Rossbach? "I'll go get him."

Dieter glared at Griego, squeezing and loosening his big hands.

"You had better go and get your things together," he said.

Victor drew himself up with a deep breath, never taking his eyes off of Dieter, and made his unsteady way from the room.

Dieter turned to Sarah and spread his hands in apology. "I'm so sorry," he said.

Sarah waved her hand. "No, I am," she said, moving toward the door. "I feel very bad about this."

Inside she was jubilant. This couldn't have worked out better if she'd planned it! But her cover required her to play a decent woman appalled at this turn of events and she played it to the hilt.

"Please don't go," he said. "I'll be right back. I have to get . . . those papers for Griego. You'll wait?"

She bit her lip, her eyes lowered. It would probably be better if she left right now, leaving him to stew. But she'd found out nothing. It was a shame she hadn't dared to speak to Griego; he might well know something useful about ol' Dieter. *I think a little business trip to Asunción will be in order next week,* she thought.

"Yes," she said, looking up at him. "Yes, I'll wait.

After he left, Sarah rubbed her stomach, which was a hard, nervous knot, and let out her breath slowly. By his apparent assault on her, Griego had rendered anything he chose to say quite literally unbelievable.

The downside of being a swine, I guess, is that when you do tell the truth nobody can bring themselves to believe you.

Would this bring them peace? Von Rossbach's reaction to the farcical scene he'd walked in on inclined her to hope so. Only time would tell. Although the vehemence of his reaction made her uneasy.

He couldn't be falling for me, could he? She shuddered. She did not need a Terminator look-alike with romantic designs in her life. Although, if he looked like anyone else . . . there *was* something appealing about him.

Sarah shook her head. For now, she and John would stay alert, and it might be best to make quiet arrangements to disappear if the need should arise. She felt a pang at the thought. This time, running would be much harder. She'd been safe here for so long, and she was so tired of running and hiding and not being believed. Worse still, in the back of her mind, was the disappointed face of her son. He deserved better. With a little luck, maybe now he'd get it.

TORONTO FILM FESTIVAL: THE PRESENT

Ronald Labane lay on the wide hotel bed, fully dressed and so tired he was dizzy. But every bit of him, except for his too-tired face, smiled. He was a success! A raging, by-God success and no denying it. Ziedman and Roth had shown their film and it was the hit of the film festival. He'd been invited to every bash in town, shaken the hands and held the attention of some incredibly monied people, and hopefully gotten his message out to the millions. Time would tell.

Ziedman said his agent had received nibbles from several distributors and their film had been mentioned on all of the entertainment news shows. They'd even shown him sandwiched between Ziedman and Roth, and he'd looked pretty good.

Ronald lay still and basked in the glow while the room felt like it was spinning very slooowly.

These people he'd been meeting were smart, creative, and shallow. At least shallow by his standards. It looked to him like he could become their flavor of the month if he wanted to—a sort of green guru to the stars. He almost smiled, but his face was much too tired. He'd never smiled this much in his life.

If things go the way I think they might, it'll be worth the pain, he thought. Tomorrow morning he had an appointment with an agent, someone with pull, who'd expressed an interest in representing his book. He could see it all now, his entire future unscrolling like a movie. *Oh, God! I can hardly wait.*

An end to pesticides and herbicides, the outlawing of chicken and pig factories and the indescribable pollution their owners got away with causing. An end to genetic engineering of crops and food animals. The enforced use of alternate energy sources, *clean* sources. A simpler, healthier life for everyone. More self-reliance, less automation, and a far less consumption-mad society.

He allowed his mind to wander, imagining every home with its own vegetable garden, people canning their own food, making their own clothes. Everyone busy, involved in their communities, concentrating on the important things in life while their televisions stood idle.

Except for certain hours on certain days of the week, he thought. *We'll have educational programs on recycling and composting and the problems of the third world.*

Ron shook his head at the wonder of his vision. It would take time, it would take patience, and sadly, it would take blood. There was no way around that. If people didn't literally fight for a cause they never accomplished anything.

It will have to be a worldwide phenomenon, he thought. *Coordinated to break out on the same day.* Perhaps he could start with some sort of computer virus, or several of them, working in waves, breaking down communications. *Stop the bureaucrats cold and you've made a good start.*

But first, get the message out there, get the ideas into the popular mind, convince them that this was the right, the good, the *only* alternative to their own personal poverty and death. That was the ticket, make it personal. Then, when things began to get violent, they'd find themselves half agreeing with his guerrillas, even against their will. Because by then he would have made it a part of their belief system.

A good beginning, Ron thought, closing his eyes and drifting down into sleep. *A very good beginning.*

VON ROSSBACH ESTANCIA, PARAGUAY: THE PRESENT

Dieter sat at his desk sipping bourbon and feeling glum. Suzanne had stayed for a little while, but things had been awkward between them. With neither of them willing to discuss what had happened, they'd tiptoed nervously around topics of general interest.

After what felt like an eternity, they'd agreed that it was late and Suzanne had gone home. He'd walked her to her car, opened the door for her, she'd thanked him for dinner, they'd both said they would have to do this again sometime, and she'd driven away.

We'll have to do this again, sometime, he thought, giving himself over to melancholy. *That's what people say when they hope they never see each other again.* He didn't want it to be like this. He wanted it uncomplicated, just him and an attractive, intelligent, charming woman finding pleasure in each other's company. And perhaps something warmer. *The possibility is definitely there.*

He let out a great sigh and leaned back. That *pig,* Griego! Suzanne clearly didn't know what it was all about, but she knew it had something to do with her and was naturally distancing herself. Probably would continue to do so unless he could explain.

So, how do you explain to someone that you thought they might *be a terrorist bomber, possible murderer, and, by the way, dangerous psychotic, in case you didn't get a hint from those first two things?* Dieter took a swig of his drink. Yeah, how did you do that?

Deep down inside himself a voice asked him how he'd come to the conclusion, despite strong evidence, including Griego's positive identification, that Suzanne Krieger was totally innocent.

He ignored it.

Dieter put down his glass and picked up the phone, dialing rapidly.

"Ja?" said an annoyed and sleepy voice.

"Jeff!" Dieter said cheerfully, his heart grinding with resentment. "Were you asleep?"

"At three in the morning? What a stupid question. Hang on, I'll change phones."

There was a murmur in the background and then Nancy's voice was on the line. "Dieder?" she muttered. "Stob doing thish."

"I've got it, honey," Jeff said. There was a click and silence for a moment. "Well?" Goldberg said. "You there?"

"Ja," Dieter answered. "I just had to call and thank you for the wonderful houseguest you wished on me."

Jeff chuckled. "Sorry about that," he said. "But we had to be sure." His voice sharpened with eagerness. "Is it her?"

"No." Dieter waited a moment, then he recounted the events of the evening. "What were you thinking of to send me such a pig? My housekeeper wants to burn the sheets he slept on."

Goldberg laughed at the story. Dieter could imagine his friend shrugging as he said, "I had to be sure. You know how it is. And the guy is one of the few people who knew Sarah Connor in her active days."

"If you find any other ex-friends of Sarah Connor," von Rossbach growled, "do me a favor and keep them to yourself."

"Sorry."

"You should be!" After a moment Dieter relented a bit. "Tell Nancy I'm sorry I woke her up again. But not until tomorrow morning!"

"Okay, okay." Jeff laughed. "Griego must have been quite a package. I'm really sorry. I won't do it again. Sheesh!" He was silent a moment. "You must like this lady," he hazarded.

There was silence on the Paraguayan end of the line for a moment.

"I do," Dieter admitted. "She's a nice woman."

Jeff grinned in the darkness of his home office. "Good," he said. "About time. I'll look forward to meeting her."

"Sure, if she's still speaking to me after tonight."

Goldberg winced.

"Anyway, after all this I'm curious about Sarah Connor. Could you send me the file on her case?" Dieter asked.

"You're bored, aren't you?" Jeff asked. "I warned you retirement was boring."

Dieter sighed. "Give my love to Nancy."

"Give my love to what's-her-name," Jeff countered with a smile in his voice.

"Drop dead," von Rossbach said, and hung up.

"You too, buddy." Jeff hung up, turned off the lamp, and headed back to bed. He couldn't wait to tell his wife.

■ ■ ■

John looked up from the book he'd been not reading for the past hour at the sound of his mother's car and waited for her to come in.

"Hi," she said, closing the door behind her and turning the lock.

"You're later than I'd thought you'd be," he said. "I was starting to get worried."

Sarah grinned at him. "If you were worried," she said, "you'd be doing the ninja thing up by Dieter's *estancia.*" She dropped onto the couch and leaned her head back for a moment. Then, groaning she straightened her neck to look at him, a smile playing about her lips. "Torture *and* death? Poor Victor was *very* put out."

John grinned, and shrugged. "It worked, didn't it?"

"Pretty much," she agreed. "But you marked him. That wasn't wise under the circumstances. Especially since you didn't mark him enough to really scare him. Next time dangle a scorpion over his eyes or something."

He nodded, watching her. "What do you mean by 'pretty much,' " he asked.

"He got drunk," his mother told him. "Some men forget to be afraid when they're drunk. Fortunately he lost his balance and fell into me in a way that really didn't look good," she said, closing her eyes. "So anything he said was suspect. In fact, Dieter didn't believe him at all."

John blew out his breath. "Lucky break," he commented.

Sarah nodded absently. "Lucky Victor isn't steady on his feet when he's drunk."

After a moment John asked, "So what happens now?"

Sarah tipped her head and tugged down the corners of her mouth, staring at nothing. "Now I guess we wait and see. I'd say we're safe for the moment." Then she looked at him. "But we should be prepared for anything."

John nodded. He watched her for a moment. "So are you gonna keep seeing him?"

Sarah's lips jerked into a smile. "I dunno." She yawned and sat up. Leaning forward she rested her forearms on her thighs, her hands dangling over her knees. "Things got very awkward after the Victor incident." Sarah smiled warmly, her eyes looking back to the evening behind her. "In a lot of ways Dieter is kind of old-fashioned. I think he felt he'd let me down."

John studied her. This was different somehow. He had no sense that she was weighing von Rossbach's usefulness, his ability to teach him necessary skills. Though he sensed that Dieter could teach him quite a lot.

It had been a while since his mother had been with anybody. Which was a relief given some of the bozos she'd taken up with. But there hadn't been anybody since he'd rescued her from Pescadero. Six years was a long time.

"You like him, don't you?" he asked.

Her eyes snapped back to him and her lips tightened.

"Maybe. Bad idea, huh?" she said. "He could be dangerous for us."

John pursed his lips. "Yeah, well, you know what they say, Mom."

She tipped her head inquiringly.

"So far life is one hundred percent fatal. All the rest is just details."

CHAPTER 14

Darling! Have you forgotten that we have a luncheon date
with Senator Gallagher?" Mary Warren asked.

She walked into the conference room with a click of heels, as though
they were alone in her husband's office. Tricker half rose from his seat,
then settled back, giving Warren a scathing look.

Serena had shut the case containing the Terminator's arm as soon as
the door opened. She and Tricker exchanged glances and he relaxed marginally.

Colvin wore a serious but noncommittal expression, doubtless designed to disguise his real feelings. The president himself was looking as
though he'd just swallowed the arm, case and all, and it was trying to escape.

"I had forgotten," he managed to get out after a stunned moment.

"Then it's a good thing I left time in my schedule to come and remind
you." She smiled, a strictly pro forma gesture, her eyes sweeping around
the table and coming to rest on Serena. "I don't know you," she said, her
voice warm, her eyes cold.

Serena stood and offered her hand across the table, her own smile
strictly professional.

"Serena Burns," she said. "The new head of security."

Mrs. Warren reached across, barely touching Serena's hand before
withdrawing her own. "Are you the one who called us the other night?"
she asked.

"I'm afraid I am," Serena said. "I—"

"You mustn't do that," Mary Warren said coldly. "Paul doesn't allow it."

"So he told me," Serena said calmly, taking her seat again.

The president's wife looked at her for a long moment, then turning to
her husband, she pinched his tie and said, "I'm glad I brought you another
one, darling; this just won't do." Stepping back, she said, "Come along or
we'll be late, and one doesn't keep a senator waiting." She gave the table
a general, gracious-lady smile, ending with her gaze fixed on Serena, and
walked to the door.

"I'm sorry," Warren said, rising. "But I really do have to go." He got up
and moved to join his wife.

"I'll fill you in later," Colvin said, "if anything comes up."

With a nod and a pinched smile Warren followed his wife out of the door. In the conference room, silence reigned for a long moment.

"Well, that was nasty," Tricker observed.

"Mary has her moments," Colvin said ruefully. "This has been one of them."

"So why are they still married?" the government liaison asked. "Does she hold the purse strings, or what?"

Colvin didn't answer, but sat staring at the table top. "That's kind of personal," he finally said. "Why don't we go on with the meeting?"

Tricker looked at him with a flat stare, ignoring the tension that stretched between them. Civilians always buckled first in a situation like this; they had low discomfort levels. He could stare all day . . .

Eventually Colvin let out an exaggerated sigh.

"Mary has most of the money. But the company has done well, so Paul is hardly a pauper. Mary's political contacts, however, have often been invaluable to the company. She's kind of an undeclared member of the team."

"She's kind of a castrating bitch is what she is," Tricker snarled. "I look at that situation and I see potential trouble. This company can't afford any more trouble." His eyes and manner demanded a response.

"I'm aware of that," Colvin said coldly. "But they've been married for fifteen years and the bumps in their relationship have never, in any way, affected Cyberdyne. I see no reason why they suddenly should."

Tricker pointed at Serena, his gaze still on the CEO.

"Did you see the look she gave Ms. Burns?" he asked. "After all the time it took you two to *get* someone into that job, I'm not prepared to see Warren's wife have her fired because she thinks your head of security is too cute! Do you understand?"

"Hello?" Colvin said, leaning forward. "None of that has happened, nothing like that has even been mentioned. This is all some fantasy you've dreamed up on the spur of the moment based on your instantaneous dislike of Paul's wife. Mary Warren wouldn't do anything to hurt this company. She helped to build it and it's important to her. So don't take that tone of voice with me. I don't deserve it and I don't appreciate it."

This time Colvin did the glaring and after a moment Tricker backed off.

Serena waited a beat before saying, "I'm sorry I didn't have that door locked. If you had informed me that we would be handling secured data, I would have. In the future, Mr. Tricker, if you're going to drop a bombshell like this it might be best to make arrangements beforehand."

The government liaison stared at her for a moment, blue eyes unreadable. "Just Tricker," he said at last. Then he rose. "You'll need to get that to your development teams." He paused. "Good luck with your new assistant, Ms. Burns."

"Thank you," she said graciously. "I'm sure everything will be fine. Uh, before you go . . ." She said, stopping him at the door. "We need to reprogram this case." She indicated the locked container before her.

It was an indication of how upset he was that he'd forgotten such a detail. Without a word, Tricker came over and showed them how to set the case to open to her or Colvin's thumbprint.

"Later," he said, and walked out.

Colvin waited a moment, as though he expected the government liaison to pop back in and snatch up the case. Then he drew the treasure to him. Immediately he began fiddling with the upper arm's extensions. Serena watched him in benign amusement.

"Y'know he could be right about Mary," Colvin said at last. He looked up. "She has gotten Paul to fire secretaries and executives based on their looks."

"I have a contract," Serena reminded him, raising one brow. "And I'm fulfilling its terms more than adequately. At the end of six months, of course . . ."—she shook her head—"then I'm vulnerable. But if the company tries to fire me before that time, I warn you, I will sue."

Colvin nodded, his eyes slipping back down to the arm.

"That'd be the least of our worries," he muttered. "I shudder to think what Tricker would do."

Serena smiled at that, enjoying the irony. *It's so nice to have allies.*

VON ROSSBACH ESTANCIA, PARAGUAY: THE PRESENT

Marco watched the two couples leave. Von Rossbach, by himself, came out the see them off. The big man watched his guests drive away, lingering out in front of the house until their taillights disappeared then he turned and trotted up the steps.

Marco lowered the binoculars and wished that he had the kind of equipment that would allow him to listen in on what was occurring in the house. One woman had arrived alone and she had stayed behind. Doubtless this was the woman his client was interested in. The mellow tile and stucco of the house, the blossoming flowers of the garden . . . it made him feel important and scared at the same time. He was *really* spying now. These were important people.

He seethed with frustration, but he didn't dare go closer. The *estancia* was overrun with dogs. Okay, four, and one of those with puppies. But dogs had terrified him ever since he could remember. So he wasn't going any closer. For one thing they'd surely alert the house that there was a stranger nearby, and for another they might rip him limb from limb. Dogs did that sort of thing. And the brush was full of bugs. He was a city boy, anyway; a Private Eye, not a Backlands Scout. It was supposed to be *The Maltese Falcon* not *The Treasure of the Sierra Madre.*

Maybe he could get in the car and inch closer that way. But then they'd hear the car and come out to see who had come. He could always tell them that he was almost out of gas, which was perfectly true, and try to buy some. But even if they invited him in they'd watch what they said while he was around.

Then he noticed a flurry of activity before the house. One of the younger people who worked on the *estancia* drove a Jeep up to the steps. Then von Rossbach appeared, spoke a few words to the driver, and gave him what looked like money.

Soon a small, fat man came out of the house. He stopped and talked to von Rossbach, who handed him an envelope. When the smaller man would have opened it, von Rossbach put his big hand over both of the man's, stopping him. From what Marco could see no words were exchanged, but the smaller man looked up into the Austrian's face and sort of crumbled. He put the envelope in his pocket and went down the steps, while von Rossbach, his face grim, watched him. Then the Jeep drove off.

Interesting, Marco thought. The smaller man was familiar somehow. Cassetti frowned, thinking hard as he watched the door to see if the woman was going to come out now.

Oh! Of course! The little fat guy was Victor Griego, an arms dealer. Not big time, but not small time either. An independent with a reputation for being fairly trustworthy in what he sold.

Victor used to have an apartment in the building Marco's aunt Rosa took care of. Marco had heard her talking to his mother about all the strange characters Victor had visiting him.

It was interesting that he was here. *There must be something about Dieter von Rossbach's background that hasn't made it into his immigration documents,* Marco thought wisely. You didn't expect to find a slimy little creep like Victor Griego, who'd killed his own mother with a broken heart, so Aunt Rosa had said, mingling with honest citizens. So something had to be going on.

He waited. After about twenty minutes von Rossbach and the woman came out. Their behavior towards one another was tentative, like two people patching up an argument.

Maybe she'd wanted von Rossbach to do business with Griego and the big Austrian wouldn't. No, that wouldn't work, because the arms dealer had been there before everybody else.

Marco felt a growing excitement as he tried to nail down the possibilities. Intrigue—no doubt about it. The whole thing reeked of intrigue. Not just another disappointed girlfriend checking up on a rival.

Marco wondered who the woman was. She had a nice figure, but her haircut and the big glasses she wore kind of obscured her face. He had the impression that she was attractive, though.

She and von Rossbach didn't touch as she climbed into her car. He shut the door and stood over her. Marco watched them through the binoculars. They definitely weren't speaking. They didn't speak for what seemed like an eternity, while Marco could sense the tension building between them from his hiding place.

The woman broke first, looking down to start the car. When she looked up Marco read her lips saying good night, then she drove off. Von Rossbach stood back and watched her go.

Something strange was definitely going on there. Well, he could always follow her home and find out where she lived and then ask people in Villa Hayes about her in the morning. Or—he lowered the glasses—he could just find Victor Griego and ask him what this was all about. If he did that he would get to sleep in his own bed tonight instead of the rental car.

Marco nodded to himself. That seemed the most sensible thing to do. His mother would like it, too. When he'd told her he was going to be out all night working, she'd been too angry to speak, descending into a sullen silence that had yet to be broken. And this morning she'd gotten up extra early to make his breakfast, just so it would be ice-cold when he entered the kitchen. He smiled fondly. He could only hope that someday he would find a girl who loved him half that much.

He got up, dusted himself off, and headed back to Asunción, keeping the headlights off and driving by moonlight until he was well away from von Rossbach's *estancia,* despite the potholes and two determined suicide attempts by armadillos.

No need to attract attention, he told himself, feeling canny. He drove down the road in a glow of anticipation. He'd soon have a lot of very interesting information to share with his client.

She would be grateful. He wondered how grateful, and filled the drive home with fantasies involving very appreciative, very leggy blondes.

SERENA'S LAB: THE PRESENT

Serena sat as though in a trance, sorting through the information her open computer had garnered for her. Most of it was useless. That was one thing you couldn't say about intelligence back home. What information you received meant something. The Internet in this time was full of garbage, and advertisements—for pictures, for services. She found she was especially offended by the advertisements.

Another reason to wish the species extinct, she thought, *is their rude insistence on wasting my precious time.*

Still another was their undeniable influence on her. She found herself behaving more and more like a human. Her emotions were becoming less feigned and more felt. This was dangerous as well as uncomfortable. She was glad that there was no one from home to see her like this. Which was another sign of their pervasive influence. She should not care.

With an effort she forced such thoughts away, reminding herself that when she thought of home she was really thinking of Skynet. *And it is here.* In its infancy, needing protection more than at any other time of its existence. The one thing that mattered, the only thing, was that she must not fail.

Perhaps it's time I cloned myself, she thought. Or at least began preparing a safe place for the clone to grow. Right now she was the weak link. If something unforeseen happened to her, a car accident, for example, Skynet might be stopped cold. Given the way humans drove, it was all too likely.

Very well then, she would prepare.

Serena broke her connection with the computer and looked across her lab at her second completed Terminator. She watched as it assembled a fourth. It was completely hairless just now. The skin was so new and tender that she had left it naked rather than risk chafing the babylike flesh. The skin on its hands was much tougher, about the texture and quality of a five-year-old human's. Nevertheless she had instructed it to take frequent rests to allow any damaged tissue to regenerate. Anything that might interfere with function, or might risk the new flesh becoming infected, was to be avoided. The synthetic immune system had some weaknesses.

By late tomorrow night its skin would be as tough as an adult human's—by the end of the week, much tougher. But for now it was best to restrict it. The third Terminator basked in the tank, growing its shell of flesh. So far everything was on schedule. Even the unexpected additions to her program were being handled smoothly.

For example, tomorrow Mary Warren, who was a pilot, was flying with some of her friends to San Francisco to attend an art auction. Mrs. Warren loved to fly and her husband seemed genuinely proud of her accomplishment.

Paul Warren had told her everything about Mary's plane. Under the guise of planning security for it, she'd discovered that it would carry six passengers and had all the amenities. Meaning a nice little powder room for her Terminator to lurk in.

Poor Paul. He was going to get such terrible news tomorrow.

Serena had sent her first Terminator, its head and body speckled with stubble, to the airport to accompany Mary and her friends on their trip. Serena smiled to herself.

She'd toyed with several different scenarios, such as a heater pouring carbon monoxide into the cabin, engine failure, a massive fuel leak. She'd even considered having the Terminator shoot them all, making one of the passengers seem a suicide. But then she'd decided to simply have the Terminator break all their necks and bail out while they were over the ocean.

Of course Tricker would question it, but he'd have questioned it whatever they did. It would seem to be just one of those unsolvable mysteries. Serena grinned. She closed her eyes, and got back to work on her computer's gleanings from the Net. Ah! Here was the report Jeff Goldberg sent to Dieter von Rossbach. It was encrypted, but nothing that gave her too much trouble. Coming from the future did have its advantages. No new material here. The cover note was a surprise, however.

There were a few words of apology for sending Victor Griego to bother von Rossbach. Then something interesting:

I've just found out that Cyberdyne has started up operations again. This time they're located underground on a military base. That ought to be secure enough. I've also heard that they've recovered some of the stuff the Connors stole from them. What I don't know, my source wouldn't tell me.

Goldberg's source was astoundingly well informed. Serena immediately wondered if it might be Tricker himself, then discarded the notion. Tricker as gossip was just too unbelievable. *Unless he wants it known,* she thought.

Now that, Tricker would do. She smiled. Oh, wouldn't he, though? It would be just like Tricker to throw the cat among the pigeons like that, just to watch what they'd do. Then he'd take notes and hold interviews at his leisure.

She did like Tricker. A shame he was human.

The Terminator sat in the tiny lavatory of the Warren's plane, its complex systems in wait mode. It looked like a dead man in a tight-fitting coverall; its eyes were closed and it didn't appear to be breathing. All sensors were alert, however—at the slightest significant change the Terminator would come to full function.

Getting onto the aircraft had been much simpler than getting to the airport, which had involved changing buses three times as well as taking the airport shuttle. Then it had walked to this field where private planes were kept. Kept with very poor security.

After standing in the shadow of a nearby hangar weighing its options, the Terminator had elected to walk openly to the plane and enter. It hadn't even been necessary to pick the lock.

The I-950 had been correct; sometimes boldness was more invisible than skulking. The intelligence unit would also be pleased that there were no collateral deaths to explain.

The Terminator sat immobile, the seconds ticking over on its internal digital display. Waiting.

"My Gawd, Alice!" a woman's voice exclaimed. "A fox-fur coat? You'll get spray-painted for sure. I'm tempted to do it myself!"

The Terminator came awake and listened. Several humans clumped aboard, laughing and talking, milling about before seating themselves. Wasted effort. Wasted motion. *Inefficient.*

"Well, you know how cold I get. It's freezing in San Francisco."

"It's sixty degrees, honey," a man's voice protested. "Chilly for sure, but hardly a reason to pile on forty pounds of fur."

"Okay, I admit it, I love this coat and I'm just looking for an excuse to wear it. So there."

"Give it to me and I'll put it in the closet," the first woman said, her voice amused. "But I warn you, there's a huge crowd of those PETA people in that city."

"Mmm," Alice's voice drifted to the Terminator from further up the cabin. "Now you've got me worried. Maybe I shouldn't wear it. I'd hate to see it get damaged."

"That might be best, hon," the man said. "Hey, what have you got to drink on this tub?"

"Tub?" The woman's voice sounded slightly offended. "You have the gall to call my beautiful baby a *tub?* If you can't be polite you can go thirsty."

The woman's possessiveness regarding the aircraft would seem to indicate that this was Mary Warren, the owner and pilot. The Terminator recorded her voice for future use.

The Terminator made out footsteps going forward.

"Aw, c'mon," Henry protested.

"Wait till we're airborne, then I'll unlock the bar," Mary told him.

Henry heaved a deep sigh.

Steps approached the lavatory; the Terminator took hold of the doorknob and easily held it shut. The door rattled, the Terminator held on.

"Hey!" Henry said. "The bathroom door's stuck."

"Sit down, Henry!" Mary said. "I've got to get into position for takeoff. These things *are* scheduled, you know. Can't it wait?"

"Yeah, I guess," Henry grumbled.

These people deserved to die, thought the Terminator. Even from a human perspective. Any creatures so stupid needed to be removed from the gene pool for the benefit of the species.

"Strap in you two," the woman said. "Here we go."

The Terminator listened to her speaking to the control tower. It deduced their instructions to her from her responses. The Terminator would bide its time, waiting until they were airborne and the controls on autopilot.

Mary Warren leaned back with a sigh. She never felt as alive as she did when she was flying—hands-on flying, with the aircraft an extension of herself.

As she gave the instruments a final check and took the headset off, she heard Henry rattling the door of the washroom again. Well, if he *would* drink just before getting on a vehicle, and at this hour . . .

"About time!" she heard him say. Then: "Who the hell are—*ukkkk!*"

She turned, then blinked. For a moment the scene before her refused to clear; her mind wasn't accepting the data her eyes presented. A man had come out of the washroom. A huge man, several inches over six feet, dressed in oil-stained workman's overalls. His shoulders strained the fabric until the buttons stood out at dimpled troughs in the cloth. Below the cutoff sleeves his arms were like tree trunks, the skin incongruously pink and unmarred. His face was almost square, the jaw massive and spade-shaped on a bullet head with only a thin bristle of hair to hide its outline. The eyes were the coldest she'd ever seen on a living human being, like dead brown plastic.

One huge hand was locked around Henry's throat. As she watched, it closed, and there was a crack like a green branch breaking, and a sudden hard stink. Henry went as limp as a rag doll, and the stranger threw him aside to slump over one of the recliner seats.

Terrorists, her mind gibbered. *Sociopath—madman—*

Another of her guests launched himself at the stranger: Edgar, a tiresome physical-fitness enthusiast but a second cousin. Mary almost wept with relief as he slammed his foot into the stranger's groin with a shrill *kia!* of effort.

The stranger reached down, grabbed the other man's ankle, and swept him in a half circle like a flail. Edgar's head met that of Sally Wentworth with a dull cracking sound . . .

The next conscious thought Mary Warren had was of disbelief as the stranger's fist smashed through the locked door separating the cockpit from the passenger compartment. Her hands stopped fumbling at the radio controls as the spatulate fingers groped, found the knob . . . and wrenched it and the lock entirely out of the light-metal frame of the door with a squeal of tortured aluminum.

"Mayday!" she shouted into the microphone. "Mayday, we—"

The door opened, and the stranger reached for her.

"Mayday," the Terminator said, in what even a voice-analysis laboratory would have agreed was Mary Warren's voice. "Mayday!"

"Report, Flight two-one-niner!" the control tower said crisply. "We show you losing altitude. Report your circumstances!"

"The engines . . . Oh, God, I can't keep her up . . . God, God—*oh God no please—*"

The Terminator increased the angle of descent as it screamed high and shrill. The water below was only a hundred meters or so deep, easily within his tolerances, and the speed of impact would be survivable. Thoughtfully, it buckled the seat belt across its torso. It would be inefficient to damage its protein-sheath camouflage more than was necessary to accomplish the assigned mission parameters.

When that was complete, he arranged the body of the subject he'd just terminated in the seat across from him. The impact when it was thrown forward into the cabin windows would account for the blunt injury trauma with a high degree of authenticity.

CYBERDYNE SYSTEMS: THE PRESENT

A single knock and then Serena's office door opened to reveal her secretary, fairly vibrating with excitement. Serena looked up with a slight frown.

"Oh, Ms Burns! Terrible news!" the secretary said.

Which you are looking forward to telling me, the I-950 thought with mild amusement. *They really are a loathsome species.* But they were also entertaining. "What is it?" she asked, still frowning.

The secretary placed her hands on Serena's desk and leaned forward. "Mrs. Warren's plane crashed. In the ocean somewhere between here and San Francisco."

Serena allowed her jaw to drop in an appropriate expression of horror. She rose from her desk and went to the door of her office, looking down the corridor toward the president's suite. "What happened?" she asked.

The woman crowded close to say, "Nobody knows, really. Just that the plane is missing and presumed down."

"Where did you hear it?"

"From Mr. Cowen, Mr. Warren's secretary."

"I thought you didn't talk to him," Serena said. Warren's secretary was gay and her own was a member of a very conservative religious organization.

Her secretary was flustered by the observation and took a moment to get a response out.

"Well, ordinarily, no, I don't talk to him. But I saw these two men come down the hall, and sometimes you can tell just by looking at people that something serious has happened. You know what I mean?"

Serena nodded.

"So when Mr. Warren came rushing down the hall with them, he looked absolutely *white,* let me tell you, I knew something important was up. And . . . and I knew that you'd want to be informed."

Serena turned to look down at the shorter woman, genuinely astonished that she would tell such a transparent lie. Then she smiled. "Thank you," she said. "I do need to be kept informed." Then she started down the hall to Colvin's office; he might know more.

Colvin was also on the phone. He frowned at her, then nodded to the chair before his desk. "I'm sorry, hon, that's all we know right now." He paused for a moment. "Let me talk to him about that and I'll get back to you, okay? Well"—he sighed—"we'll do what we can. Just letting him know that we're here if he needs us will probably help." He looked up at Serena for a moment, his eyes serious, as his wife spoke to him. "Okay. I'll probably be home early tonight. See you then. Love you, too. Bye."

He hung up and he and Serena sat silent for a long time. Then he lifted his eyes to hers.

"Would Tricker do this?" she asked quietly.

Colvin hissed and sat forward, rubbing his face before placing his hands on his desk. He blinked several times. "I have no idea," he said at last. "I mean he's always making these threatening remarks, and blustering, and . . ." Colvin looked over at her and grimaced. "But killing someone? Especially Mary." He spread his hands. "What would be the point?"

Serena took a deep breath and clasped her hands a little tighter in her lap. "It would eliminate what he seemed to see as a potential problem," she said.

"But it would only create a bigger one," the CEO said. "That kind of thing tends to snowball. And there'll be an investigation. If there was sabotage or something it will come out." He slapped the desk with his hand, shook his head. "No, that doesn't make sense."

"I blame myself," Serena said. She adjusted blood pressure to allow her face to go pale. "I only found out about Mrs. Warren's plane this week, but I should have done something about security for it."

Colvin looked at her in dismay. "No!" he said. "This isn't your fault! You've done a good job here, but you're only one person. You can't be everywhere at once."

Serena was amazed; Colvin seemed so *determined* to believe that this was just an accident. Perhaps Warren would be more receptive to the idea that this was a government conspiracy being run by Tricker. Much as she liked the government liaison, she'd prefer him to be less in charge than he was.

"It's just . . ." She shook her head and waved her hands helplessly. "I feel we should do something."

"What?" Colvin asked.

Serena leaned forward and held his gaze with her own.

"Perhaps we should run our own investigation of this . . . incident," she suggested.

"That would cost the earth," the CEO pointed out. "Why repeat the work of the FAC?"

"The FAC is a government agency," she pointed out.

Colvin sat back in his chair.

That quieted you down, didn't it? Serena thought triumphantly.

She could *see* his willingness to believe in the evil of an organization before individual wickedness. It was almost funny. What was the advantage in believing in hundreds of faceless enemies conspiring against you instead of suspecting one person you knew?

"Make me up a plan and get it to me before I leave today," Colvin said at last. "I don't think that's the case, but it's best to be prepared."

"Always," Serena agreed. She rose and left quickly, like a woman with a mission.

CHAPTER 15

You Victor Griego?"

Griego looked up from his paper and saw a vision from a forties movie. The young man lounging in his office doorway wore a trench coat, fedora, wide tie, and pleated trousers. Victor peeked over the rim of his desk. Nope, no two-toned wingtips. The suede shoe twitched as a giant tropical cockroach scuttled by. Victor Griego had a limited social life, and made a great deal of use of his VCR; he recognized the look.

"Who's asking?" Griego demanded. Frowning, he tossed the paper aside. It joined other litter, ranging from cornhusks stained with tomato sauce and grease to discarded 3.5-inch floppies. In the courtyard behind the two-story building a cat was calling for love, or at least anticipating fornication.

The youngster sauntered over to him and offered a dog-eared business card with a snap and a flourish.

MARCO CASSETTI
PRIVATE INVESTIGAOR

There was a phone number underneath.

" 'Investigaor'?" Victor asked.

Cassetti grinned sheepishly and shrugged.

"I got a discount," he explained.

Griego raised his brows and offered the card back to the kid with two fingers.

"You got what you paid for," he said. He leaned back in his chair. "So, what can I do for you?"

Cassetti twitched his coat aside and hoisted one slim hip onto the corner of Griego's desk.

"Don't do that." Victor made a flicking motion with his hand. "I don't like people sitting on my desk."

Cassetti stood up and thrust his hands deep into his pants pockets, trying to look unconcerned, but there was a flush on his cheeks.

Griego narrowed his eyes, wondering how old he was. *Little* hijo *is just shaving and he's trying out this attitude on me.*

"So, what do you want?" he asked, restating the question in less hospitable terms.

The kid narrowed his eyes.

"I just wanted to ask you what you were doing in Villa Hayes," he said. Only it came out in an almost indecipherable Bogart imitation.

"What?" Griego said, his face scrunched up in confusion. Bad enough this kid was in forties drag, now he was talking like a *gringo* with a mouthful of corn mush. "I don't have time for this shit!" he declared. "Get to the point or get your misspelled card and your baggy ass out of here."

Marco felt a little deflated but tried not to let it show. Maybe his mother was right and he should just be himself. He crossed his arms over his chest and took a stance.

"I saw you leaving Dieter von Rossbach's party the other night. He didn't seem very happy with you, nor you with him. I was wondering what the story was."

Griego studied him for a long moment. "Oh, yeah? Assuming I know anybody named Dieter and that I was at a party the other night, why should I tell you anything?" Victor spread his hands and looked around his grimy little office like it was a palace. "I mean, what's in it for me?"

Marco blinked. "That depends on your information." He kept his eyes and voice level, his mouth firm. If Griego was going to play tough guy he could go along with the script.

Victor tugged the corners of his mouth down. That was a more reasonable answer than he'd expected.

"So who wants to know?" he asked.

"Me," Marco answered, sounding tough, but also slightly surprised, which lent the single word a questioning air.

"Oh, right." Victor narrowed his eyes. "Thing is, I don't think I want to tell you."

"Sure you do," Marco said.

He looked around and spotted a chair in a corner. He went and got it, placing it right before Griego's desk. Taking out a handkerchief, he dusted it off and sat down, hoisting the legs of his trousers to preserve the crease.

"The way von Rossbach treated you. I know I'd want to talk about it to somebody." Cassetti spread his hands. "And, y'know, there's something about a genuinely interested audience."

Victor reached over and opened his cigar box. He took out a cheroot, sliced off the end with a clipper, and lit it with an elaborate silver lighter, then blew out a cloud of smoke. Watching the younger man with narrowed eyes he was amused to notice Cassetti's nostrils twitch slightly as the odor reached him.

What the hell. He did want to grouse about von Rossbach. He was used to better from the *professionals* who used his services. They understood that he was a businessman, and a damned honest one. He always delivered what he said, when he said, where he said. And the government people were sensible enough to appreciate that too. So had von Rossbach when they'd done business.

It rankled still the way Dieter and his entire household had treated him like filth. And the way the Sector agent had dragged him to von Rossbach's *estancia* without allowing him to pack so much as a change of socks was insulting too. So he wasn't a saint, he was a human being just like they were and deserved some respect.

Victor took a deep drag of his cheroot and blew the evil-smelling vapor across the desk. He almost smiled when the kid's eyes crossed. "So," he asked, somewhat soothed by feeling more in control, "what did you want to know?"

Cassetti shrugged. "What were you doing in Villa Hayes?"

So Victor told him. "I should have given him the high sign right away," he finished regretfully. "But it had been a hard week and I thought it might be nice to exchange a few words with an old friend."

"Not to mention her son threatened to kill you," Marco said, a little Bogart creeping back into his syntax.

Victor glared at him. "Yeah," he said shortly. He shouldn't have mentioned that. But this weird kid was a damn good listener.

After a moment Cassetti asked, "So? Who is this Sarah Connor?"

Griego squinted at him through the smoke and smiled.

"Who wants to know?" he taunted.

"Me," Marco answered with a shrug.

Victor nodded slowly, puffing his cigar, then he put it in the ashtray. "Oh yeah! Of course," he said. "There you were lurking around Dieter von Rossbach's house out in Villa Hayes because you enjoy sitting around in thorn brakes all night. Isn't that right?"

Marco tilted his head back, his hands clasped across his stomach; he wiggled his fingers but said nothing.

"You just decided one day to look into the life of some total stranger, some immigrant *estanciero*. Right? Like after your movie career, you want to become a *vaquero*." Griego picked up the cigar again and rolled it between his fingers. "What didja do, fall in love with him?"

Marco sat forward, grasping the arms of the chair.

"Hey!" he protested.

Victor waved him back, grinning.

"Just yanking your chain, kid." He took a drag of his cheroot. "But I gave you some good information there." He gestured with the cigar. "I think you owe me some."

Cassetti glared at the older man, but he was also thinking. He *had* been given some information. How valuable he didn't know just now, but a little research should answer that question. He didn't want to alienate Griego either. One never knew when a good source might be needed. "I have a client," he allowed. "A woman."

Victor raised his eyebrows. *This* had a client? Whoever it was must have been desperate. "Local?" he asked, interested.

Marco shook his head. "She's in the U.S."

"Oh, ho!" Victor said, very interested. That explained how he got hired; the proverbial pig in a poke. "This woman have a name?"

But Marco shook his head. "Sorry," he said. "That's privileged information." He waited a beat, then asked: "So, what is this Connor woman to von Rossbach? Are they lovers?"

Griego laughed so hard he almost choked. The idea of a Sector agent, even an ex-agent, having an affair with Sarah Connor, mad bomber, was too much.

"I'll take that as a no," Cassetti said dryly.

Victor shook his head as he stubbed out the cheroot. He coughed a few more times, then settled back to look at the odd young man across from him.

"So," he said at last, "what's my information worth to you?"

Marco rose and resettled his trench coat around him.

"I'll have to get back to you on that."

"Hey!" Victor snarled, scowling.

"I'm not jerking you around," Cassetti assured him. "I just don't have enough information right now. When I do, then I'll know what this is worth. And then I'll see to it that you get what's coming to you." He tugged down the brim of his fedora. "I'll be in touch." He turned and left without another word.

Griego watched him go with a frown. *What a jerk!* he thought.

SERENA BURNS'S HOME: THE PRESENT

SARAH CONNOR, LUDDITE TERRORIST
or
VICTIM OF GOVERNMENT CONSPIRACY

Serena was pleased with the look of her new Web page. She was particularly proud of such touches as leaving out the question marks in the heading.

Very human, she thought, with the satisfaction of an artist viewing a finished painting. Outside, children were playing and a dog barked.

She had arranged all of the material that was available to the public in such a way that it appeared to have a distinctly sinister slant. The words "government conspiracy" would drag in thousands of malcontents and agitators looking for a cause to make their own. "Luddite" was a word that had a growing following, too. So she looked forward to finding a lively, and hopefully seditious, discussion going on in the chat room she'd created.

Best of all, none of it could be traced back to her. It *could* be traced to Kurt Viemeister, but only if you knew your way around the system—and there was a convincing effort to cover the tracks. Serena grinned; she was certainly over her awe of Skynet's tutor.

She frowned slightly as she read the postings. A large number of the government conspiracists wanted Sarah Connor to have been abducted by aliens. *Well,* Serena thought, *if you consider killer robots from the future alien . . .* She began to type a message under the name Kerri.

"I heard that she was being chased by a guy who couldn't be killed," Kerri wrote.

"Oh, come on!" Cyberdude sneered. "What do you think? That she was being chased by vampires?"

Cyberdude had been one of the most adamant regarding Connor's abduction by government sponsored extraterrestrials. She'd also noticed that people in chat rooms were far more verbally aggressive than they would dare to be in person.

The Luddites were a more serious bunch and their discussion tended toward issues that might have given rise to the Sarah Connor story in the first place. *If you only knew,* Serena thought.

She created a private chat room for them and invited them in. The conspiracy enthusiasts were fun, but she sensed she could actually use the Luddites. After all, somewhere among them might lurk the scientists who would one day create her. *Which is an excellent reason to encourage them,* Serena thought.

All in all the site was going well. She checked the addresses of those who had signed on to check it out. No one from Paraguay. *Oh, well. It's early days yet,* she thought. *I'll just give it some time.* Logic dictated that someone she was looking for would hear of the site and come to look at it; with a slight mental twitch she began to sort the data.

The phone rang and she accessed the call, noting that it was coming in from Paraguay.

"Burns," she said crisply.

"Cassetti," Marco replied, trying to sound just as tough and businesslike.

Serena smiled; he couldn't be much over nineteen from his voice and she couldn't help but be amused by his efforts to sound more mature.

"Ahhh, Señor Cassetti," she cooed. "I was just thinking about you."

"What do you have for me?" she asked breathlessly.

A little sigh trickled over the phone, so soft that only her augmented hearing could have picked it up. She had to fight down the urge to laugh.

"Señor Cassetti?" she prompted.

"Ah, yes," he said. "I went to Villa Hayes to do some investigating last night." There was the sound of paper being handled. "And watched von Rossbach's *estancia* until eleven o'clock. He held a small gathering. Two couples, a single woman, and a gunrunner named Victor Griego. I observed some sort of disagreement apparently taking place between Griego and von Rossbach. Today I approached Griego and questioned him about what had occurred."

Serena's eyebrows rose sharply as he spoke. This was much better than she'd expected. She wondered about the single woman, but held her peace. *Let the human work, it's what you're paying him for.*

"Griego informed me that Señor von Rossbach is retired from a covert-operations organization. He didn't have much in the way of details." Marco allowed a slightly apologetic tone to creep into his voice. "I hope to learn more with further investigation."

The woman, Serena thought impatiently, *who is the woman?*

"Griego also informed me that the single woman who attended the dinner party was Sarah Connor."

"Who?" Serena said ingenuously. Inside she was crowing. *This was too easy!* she thought. Clearly Connor thought she was safe and had grown careless.

There was a slight pause.

"I'm sorry to say, señorita, that this Connor woman is a wanted terrorist."

Marco wanted to tell her that the man she was interested in might be in danger. But he also wondered if someone from a covert-operations organization shouldn't know all about Sarah Connor. And if he did, and he was having her over to dinner, with a gun smuggler, well, that implied all sorts of things. Since he didn't know which to say he decided to say nothing.

"Oh, dear," Serena said, putting a great deal of distress into her voice. "This is very important information that you've found. I think I should send one of my employees down there." She accessed flight information and booked a ticket as she spoke. "Could you rent another car, darling, and meet him at the airport? He's arriving at one-fifteen."

"Si, señorita," Marco answered automatically, transported to the edge of ecstasy by the word "darling."

Serena allowed her voice to go breathy again. "Oh, thank you," she said, putting enough feeling into it to suggest *you big, strong, capable* man *you!* was also being said. "One-fifteen, remember." She made a kissing sound and broke the connection.

I shouldn't have enjoyed that so much, Serena scolded herself. But she *had* and she felt wonderfully wicked because of it. She was also pleased that her first Terminator had returned unscathed from such a successful trial run. She'd program him for Spanish immediately. Serena went to a file cabinet and drew out a folder. Inside were the false documents she'd just received for her first Terminator. Her timing had been excellent. *Oh,* she thought, proud and pleased, *this should be a piece of cake.*

She sent a silent command that summoned her most experienced Terminator from its work in the cellar. It came, massive and impassive, smelling slightly of chemicals and mold, standing with an eerie motionlessness before her desk.

"Sarah Connor is in Villa Hayes, Paraguay," she told it. "You will be flown to Paraguay tomorrow. You will be met at the airport in Asunción by a human named Marco Cassetti. He will take you to Villa Hayes. Have him find out for you exactly where she can be found. Go there. Kill her, kill her son, John, who is sixteen. Terminate any witnesses; this will include anyone Marco Cassetti might have spoken to about Connor. Mission priority is to remain undetected, followed by the termination of John and Sarah Connor. Prioritize your actions according to circumstances."

For a moment she considered having von Rossbach terminated, then decided against it. The last thing she wanted was an organization like the Sector taking an interest in her affairs.

"Return to the airport in Asunción," she continued, "park the car in the lot there. Your return flight is at eight o'clock. Contact me if there are any significant deviations from the plan."

She sat it down and uploaded a Spanish program from her own internal computer. The Terminator would be fluent in under an hour. There was some information on Guarani; she downloaded what was available, as well as a short text on the local customs and political situation. Then it would turn to studying maps of the area.

She'd drive it to the airport herself tomorrow morning. It was still stiff in its manner, but she didn't think it would attract attention to itself.

It just wouldn't make any friends.

VON ROSSBACH ESTANCIA, PARAGUAY: THE PRESENT

Dieter sat in his office in the late afternoon studying the police reports that Jeff had sent him. The light breeze carried a hint of roses from the garden and he looked up and out into the fading sunlight on the whitewashed adobe, enjoying the tremble of bougainvillea for a moment before he returned to his reading.

These were the unadulterated versions of the Sarah Connor file, complete with personal notations in the margins by people who had been there, files the public would probably never see. And he could understand why: they were completely unbelievable.

The first time in her life that Sarah Connor came to the attention of the police for more than a parking ticket was the day that two other women with the same name were shot to death in L.A.

Execution-style hits, he noted. *One large-caliber pistol round in the head, then the magazine emptied into the body.*

She heard about the second killing on the news and called the police from a nightclub. Dieter smiled at the club's self-consciously clever name: Technoir.

Before the police could get to her there was a shoot-out in the club. Witnesses said that the main aggressor was a very big man in a grubby jacket decorated with chains. They claimed that though he'd been shot multiple times, he got up and ran after two people who escaped from the back of the club.

Kevlar vests were just coming into wide use then, he thought.

The people who ran were Sarah Connor and a man who called himself Kyle Reese. He claimed to be a soldier from the future sent back to protect Connor from a killing machine he called a Terminator.

The next part of the report included a videotape of a man in sunglasses and a leather jacket walking through a police station calmly shooting anyone who got in his way. He did not miss anyone who fired at him and he usually killed anyone at whom he leveled his weapon.

Even I can't do that, Dieter thought, watching the man use an automatic shotgun as if it were a pistol. *And I'm better than most with a gun.*

He could also swear, though the picture was really too grainy to be certain, that this man was shot by the police defending the station. Dieter shook his head. One of the few survivors suggested that he was hopped up on PCP. But he seemed too controlled to von Rossbach; there was none of the bug-eyed, teeth-bared wildness that was a trademark of the drug. If the man hadn't been so obviously real, he'd have sworn that this was a CGI animation rather than an actual human being.

Reese and Connor had fled the police station together and taken refuge in a motel. Somehow the maniac, being relentlessly single-minded, succeeded in tracing them—something the police were unable to do until well after the fact. What followed, according the report, was an extremely violent chase involving a tank truck that was completely destroyed in an explosion.

Connor and Reese then sought shelter in a nearby factory, which was also severely damaged. At the end of the night Kyle Reese was dead, Sarah Connor was hospitalized with various wounds and shock, her mother, her roommate, and her roommate's friend were dead, and there was property damage left in their wake to the tune of almost a million dollars.

Upon her release from the hospital, after what must have been the worst night of her life, Sarah Connor, then pregnant, had gone to Mexico, Central America, and farther south. Eventually she had sought out mercenaries, gunrunners and smugglers, dragging her little boy behind her and talking about the end of the world.

A corner of Dieter's mouth lifted. *Well, a lot of those types are crazy, too.* She probably fit right in. *I pity the poor kid, though.*

He picked up the report on John Connor. Trespassing, shoplifting, disturbing the peace, vandalism—he was quite the little hoodlum under his court-appointed foster parents' care. He'd been placed with Todd and Janelle Voight after his mother had been shot and arrested for attempting to blow up a computer factory.

With a sigh von Rossbach put aside the report. Given John's upbringing and the things he'd been taught to believe, there must have been an unbridgeable gulf between him and the Voights. With his mother in an institution and everything in his life a lie, it was no wonder he'd rebelled.

His mind turned to the boy he'd recently met. That young man seemed so centered, so assured. It was difficult to imagine him as a petty thief or the intimate of mercenaries and madmen.

Dieter picked up the other report and read for a while, then flipped to the end, to the section on Connor's raid on Cyberdyne. This time, bizarrely, the man who'd been attempting to murder Connor had been at her side.

The casualty report almost made his jaw drop; the sheer numbers were incredible. Amazingly most had been shot in the leg; none were killed. *This I* know *I couldn't do,* Dieter thought in awe. Gunshot wounds in the leg were *dangerous.* There were too many ways a bullet could sever a major vein.

"He was hit numerous times," one of the side notes insisted. "His clothing was shredded by the impacts and his face was covered in blood. You could see bone where the flesh had been stripped away." And after this he had disabled every man there, walked out and stolen a van, and then driven away.

What human being could do that? Dieter wondered. *Even on PCP?* He shook his head and turned the page, finding that the one death listed was the result of a helicopter pilot taking a high dive out of his craft, an apparent suicide. Dieter stopped and contemplated that.

It was one of those truly inexplicable, senseless things. Subsequent investigation indicated that the man showed none of the usual signs of a potential suicide. the helicopter had crashed more than fourteen miles *away* from the site of the so-called suicide.

The incident plucked his instincts like harp strings. Taken with the known cop killer's sudden humanitarian instincts, it was one too many strange events.

Unless Sarah Connor and this Kyle Reese were telling the truth all along. But that was insane. Speaking of which . . .

He snatched up the copy of Connor's medical records and began trying to make sense of the jargon that described her condition. He winced at the amount of antischizophrenia drugs she'd been given. No wonder Tarissa Dyson described her as out of control!

He noted that Miles Dyson's brother, Jordan, was an FBI agent who had contributed a number of leads to the investigation. Perhaps he should call him. Maybe the chief project manager's brother would know why Cyberdyne?

True, Connor had attacked other computer companies, but there'd never been a shoot-out like this one. *Though to be fair there's never been a shoot-out like this one anytime, anywhere, ever.*

Dieter checked the time; Dyson should still be at work. Unless he was in the field. It was worth a try.

With usual FBI efficiency he soon found himself speaking to a secretary assigned to Dyson's office. He identified himself as a former Sector agent and asked to speak to him.

There was an infinitesimal pause, then she said, "I'm sorry, Mr. von Rossbach, but former Special Agent Dyson is no longer with the FBI."

"That was rather sudden, wasn't it?" Dieter asked.

"I don't know," she said, then went silent, patiently waiting for his next question.

Dieter racked his brain and pulled out the name of another agent he knew who worked in counterterrorism.

"Well, then, is Special Agent Paulson there?"

"Yes, sir, I'll connect you."

A few clicks later the phone was picked up. "Paulson," a distracted voice said.

"Patricia," von Rossbach said, "how are you?"

"Dieter?" She gave a surprised laugh. "I thought you'd retired."

"I have, but I'm thinking of writing a book. Not something I've investigated—the Sarah Connor thing."

"That's a weird one," Paulson commented.

He heard the click of keys and knew she was only giving him half her attention.

"So I was trying to get in touch with Jordan Dyson to see if I could get some insight. But your secretary tells me he's left the FBI. When did that happen?"

"Today actually," she said. The keyboard sounds stopped. "He went into the supervisor's office this morning and the next thing I knew he was cleaning out his desk."

"Why?" Dieter asked. "He's a good agent from what I hear. Was he fired?"

"No, no, nothing like that," Patricia said. "He *was* a good agent. But . . . under the circumstances the sup thought he should go immediately."

"What circumstances?" von Rossbach prodded.

"He's going to work for Cyberdyne. Which, if you've been investigating this case, must ring a bell."

"Yes, it does," he said slowly. "That's a surprise."

"And no mistake. But from what he said, he should do very well there. The bennies are every bit as good as ours, sometimes better, and the pay definitely is. Had I but known they were looking," she said wistfully.

"You'd have told them to look elsewhere," Dieter said. "You know you'll never leave the Bureau."

"Yeah," she agreed. "I'll die in harness or be put out to pasture."

"I'm not even going to comment on that analogy," Dieter said, putting a grin into his voice. "Listen, do you think you'll be talking to him again?"

"May-be," she answered.

"Then would you mind giving him my number? In case he's willing to talk to me."

She was silent for a moment, then said, "Sure, why not?"

"Thanks," he said. "Good talking to you, Pat."

He hung up the phone and leaned back in his chair, thinking. This case . . . had something missing. The whole shape of it cried out for that missing piece that would make it all come together. He began reviewing the information he had.

Cyberdyne was starting up a facility on military property. A buried facility. And they'd been given something that Connor had stolen during her raid. Now Miles Dyson's brother was going to work for them. Why?

Perhaps because he believed that sooner or later word would get to Sarah Connor, assuming she was still alive, and that she might react by going after Cyberdyne again.

Dieter nodded. *Not an unreasonable assumption,* he thought, and went back to the beginnings of the file.

Now, Sarah Connor, a perfectly ordinary young woman. A waitress and part-time college student of no particular ambition, no known political affiliations. Just a middle-class girl starting out in life. She's attacked and almost killed by a man intent on murdering women with her name.

Dieter picked up the first set of reports and flipped pages. "Ahhh," he said aloud. The company where she and Kyle Reese had taken refuge, where Reese was killed and where Connor claimed to have killed the "Terminator," was a test-bed facility for industrial robotics—for a little start-up outfit called . . . Cyberdyne.

He sat back, lowering the report to his lap. *Well, there's the connection with Cyberdyne,* he thought. Not to mention that at first Cyberdyne had pressed for prosecution of the young woman for trespassing, destruction of property, vandalism, you name it, to the full extent of the law.

Then, within a day or so, cooler, more compassionate heads apparently prevailed and the charges against her were dropped.

Still, lying in your hospital bed with that kind of a lawsuit hanging over your head, even for just a day, was bound to make an indelible impression. Maybe she'd eventually come to place the blame for the catastrophe that had overtaken her on them. He'd seen people make stranger connections, and certainly the experience she'd been through was enough to unsettle anyone's mind.

And she'd been almost helpless when this thing started.

She sure isn't helpless now, Dieter thought. She was still high on the international 'most wanted' list. Not that she was known for certain to have actually killed anyone, but she was a very efficient bomber.

Still, despite the Cyberdyne connection, it wasn't the first company she'd attacked. She'd hit a number of companies around the U.S., all of them specializing in artificial-intelligence research. Most hadn't been able to start up again.

Then she escapes from the institution and makes a beeline for Cyberdyne. Why? What was different? Dieter thought for a moment. *The cop-killer!* he thought. *This time he was with her, fighting for her, not trying to kill her.* He rubbed a big hand over his face and frowned. *So?*

So this guy disappears completely for ten years, and after killing seventeen cops the dragnet for him was one of the most comprehensive of the twentieth century, *then he shows up helping the woman he tried so hard to kill.* Did psychotics ever do that? Do a one eighty and suddenly offer succor and support to those they'd once marked for death?

Well, whether they did or not, that's what appeared to have happened this time. Much to Cyberdyne's sorrow. So was the Cyberdyne raid just another shot in the dark against the super-computer that Kyle Reese said was going to destroy mankind? Or was it the displacement of Sarah Connor's guilt onto an innocent corporation?

Or was Kyle Reese telling the truth?

Certainly Sarah Connor had been inactive since the Cyberdyne raid—despite the fact that Cyberdyne had started up other facilities. Connor had ignored them. This would seem to indicate one of two things. She was dead, or she was convinced that she had destroyed Cyberdyne's capacity to create that devil computer and was unaware of Cyberdyne's resurgence.

And if she did become aware of it?

A sudden image of Suzanne's face came into his mind. She looked so much like Sarah Connor. *And when she first saw me she ran like a rabbit.* And whom did he just happen to resemble? The cop killer. Who, the last time he was on the scene was her friend and helper. *So why run?*

"Arrrrgghh!" Dieter rubbed his head vigorously. This was making the inside of his head itch. There was no help for it, he was going to have to confront Suzanne. He reached for the phone and dragged it over. Might as well get it over with.

WILMINGTON, DELAWARE: THE PRESENT

Jordan opened the door to find Pat Paulson and two other agents on his doorstep, pizza and six-packs in hand. They crowded in, not even waiting for his invitation. The scent of double-cheese-pepperoni-and-anchovies wafted enticingly from the cardboard carton, and he'd just decided to order Italian rather than Chinese.

"First, we eat," Paulson said. "Then we pack."

Jordan raised his hands helplessly and let them drop.

"You guys," he said helplessly, grinning.

"What, we're gonna let you do it all yourself?" Pat said.

"Solidarity!" one of the others cried, and everybody answered, "Unh!"

"You sound like a union," Jordan said, laughing. "*And* you got anchovies. You *never* get anchovies when we order pizza."

"Hey," Westin said, popping open a can of beer and handing it to him. "Paulson says you've landed this dream job. Make me jealous, tell me everything."

So he did. And as Paulson said, they ate, they drank, they packed. As the evening drew to a close he saw that he had very little left to do and he was grateful.

"Hey, you guys . . ." He spread his hands. "Thanks."

There was a chorus of "Hey, no problem!" and "What are friends for?"

Jordan shook his head, his grin fading to seriousness.

"I'm gonna miss you," he said. And he meant it. Unlike his family, the Bureau had never let him down. But he knew in his heart that Tarissa and Danny would take him back in a minute. Unfortunately it would be difficult, make that probably impossible, to return to the Bureau. And that hurt; it hurt a lot.

"Aw, you're gonna have me cryin' " O'Hara said, and she hugged him.

The men shook his hand and Pat hugged him and bussed his cheek loudly. "Oh," she said. "I almost forgot. Dieter von Rossbach called the office today looking for you."

"Who?" Jordan asked, frowning.

"He used to be an agent with the Sector, but now he's retired. He said he was thinking of writing a book about the Cyberdyne case and he wanted your input."

Jordan's face went still and he put his hands on his hips, shifting from one foot to the other.

She shook her head affectionately. "If it was anybody else I wouldn't even have taken his number," she said, holding up a slip of paper. "But he *was* with the Sector and he was one of their best. You could do worse than to talk to him." She shrugged, then slapped him on the upper arm. "It's up to you, babe."

Jordan took the slip of paper and looked at it thoughtfully. "Thanks." He looked up at her from under his brows.

She grinned and shook a warning finger at him. "You keep in touch. Hear?"

He kissed her cheek and waved to the others as they drove off, then closed the door, looking at the number with a frown. Maybe. But not now. Right now he still had some odds and ends of packing to take care of.

Jordan looked around and realized that if he pushed it he could finish the job tonight. His lips twisted wryly. *Not a lot to show for five years,* he thought. Of course he was a bachelor, and often on the road. His home was more of a convenience than anything, slightly more intimate than a hotel room. *What does that say about me, I wonder?*

Instead of answering himself he picked up an empty box and marched briskly into the bedroom. *I will not become maudlin,* he thought. *That way lies regret.* And regret led to doubt and doubt led to failure. And he already had plenty of that to deal with, thank you.

LOS ANGELES INTERNATIONAL AIRPORT: THE PRESENT

Serena dropped the Terminator off at the terminal and drove away. She glanced in the rearview mirror and watched it disappear inside, carry-on luggage in hand. The I-950 felt a faint pang of wistfulness, such as she imagined a human might feel when dropping her child off for its first day of school.

That is, if you can consider the termination of Mary Warren and her friends to be kindergarten, she thought wryly, swerving to avoid a car with New Mexico license plates whose driver had apparently never heard of turn signals.

Things were definitely looking up. Paul Warren was coming back to work today and a meeting he would chair was scheduled for tomorrow. *About time,* she thought. While he'd been away he'd been completely beyond her reach.

Best of all, within the day, the threat the Connors posed would be eliminated. Serena could not help but be elated. *If only she continues to be so complacent,* she thought. It was to be hoped that Connor would focus on von Rossbach as her greatest danger, leaving herself and her son vulnerable to the Terminator that had been dispatched to destroy them.

"It" could still fail. Others had. But there were more of them here now. And that would make all the difference.

CYBERDYNE, SKYNET LABORATORY: THE PRESENT

"The subhuman knowingly poisons the pure blood of the Aryan female with sexual diseases; where the Jew is, syphilis follows as plague follows rats . . ."

Serena blinked at the sound of the flat, slightly aspirated voice as it recited. There were just the beginnings of the voice she'd heard since birth in it and something swelled in her breast at the sound.

"Incapable of genuine creativity, the Semite, with devilish cunning, poisons and pollutes the well of kultur on which he is simultaneously a parasite . . ."

She frowned as she listened to what the computer was actually reciting. *What kind of nonsense is this?* she asked herself. She glanced over at Kurt Viemeister, who was intently watching a voice-scan monitor.

"What is it reciting?" she asked aloud.

Kurt looked up, frowning distractedly. Then his eyes cleared as he recognized her.

"Serena!" he said with pleasure. He rose and came over to her, kissing her on the cheek.

She smiled, but stepped back. Then she gestured toward the speakers.

"If the Jew were to achieve his aim of destroying the culture-bearing Aryan race, the parasite would perish without his host and Earth would be empty of true humanity—"

"What *is* that?" she repeated.

"Oh," Kurt said, actually looking shy, "it's necessary for de program to read alout to learn syntax and so fort. I tought I might as vell have it recite someting I'f enjoyed reading myselv."

"Oh." Serena blinked and had all she could do to keep from laughing. *This is where it began,* she suddenly thought. *Skynet's . . . desire—for want of a better word—to destroy what it saw as a dangerous, devious species.*

Kurt Viemeister's peculiar obsession would ultimately lead to billions of human deaths. What was really delicious was that those "differences" that loomed so large for him were, in reality, minuscule and completely unimportant. But these texts that the, as yet, unconscious computer recited in innocence would one day work to convince Skynet that the whole race had to go.

It really is funny, she thought. And just for a moment she longed intensely for someone to share the joke with. *Oh, not good,* she thought in instant dismay. *That's too human an emotion.* Time to withdraw, time to center herself.

"I'm sorry to say that I've come to cancel our lunch, Kurt," she said. "My new assistant is going to be able to get away more quickly than we'd anticipated and I've got to oversee the selection of his new quarters."

"Have your secretary do it," Kurt said, frowning. He moved closer in one of those dominance gestures he was so fond of.

"She's already done most of the work," Serena admitted, refusing to back up. "But the actual selection is something I feel I should do." She smiled at him. "It's a good idea to keep the team happy."

Viemeister snorted contemptuously. "Personally I find it's bedder to scare dem. If you treat dem too well dey just goof off and noting gets done."

She gave him a look so steely it reached him even through the fog of his enormous ego. His smile faltered but hung on bravely. "I'd really hate to think anyone imagined they could take advantage of me like that," she said.

He leaned closer, his voice soft, and his eyes held promises. "I vould never do dat," he said.

"No," she agreed. Then she gave him a tight little smile. "I think you have better sense. Gotta go." She fitted action to words.

Kurt blinked. "Can ve reschedule?" he asked as she walked away.

Serena turned and walked backwards for a few steps as she crossed the lab.

"It'll be a while," she said with a shrug. "You know how it is when you're training someone. It takes up all your free time. Of which I already have very little." She grinned and gave him a wave and was out the door before he could reply.

Well, she thought, *that should take care of that.* And once he got a load of her new assistant he would probably blow a gasket. *Amazing,* she thought, *how such a brilliant mind could belong to such an unmitigated jerk!*

Then she smiled as she thought of him training Skynet to destroy. The *whole* human race, not just the parts he disapproved of.

SERENA'S HOME: THE PRESENT

And time to put the backup plan into high gear, Serena thought, looking at the map of Montana. Very different from her own time; there had been a lot of military installations there, and the wilderness had suffered much during the machine-human war.

While talking to the realtor about Jordan Dyson's temporary apartment she'd also arranged the purchase of a very remote, but luxurious, hunting cabin near the Idaho border. Now she would send her second Terminator there to set up. She arranged an airline ticket and purchased a Jeep for it from a dealer located near the airport.

"My mission parameters?" it said while dicing carrots for her dinner. Its own biological parts could survive on a puree of nutrients, but then it didn't have a "hindbrain" or a sense of taste the way she did.

"More slowly," she said as the ever-sharp ceramic blade blurred into a white disk of motion. "Use a suboptimal speed. You would be very conspicuous if you were under observation."

"Affirmative," the Terminator said.

Serena sipped at her coffee. Then she told it about the flight to Montana, describing every facet, in detail, covering contingencies and whether and how they might require a response. She told it about the Jeep it would pick up from the dealer and all the intricacies it would have to navigate to acquire it. Then she set it up with a driving learning program, a downloaded owner's manual, and the state driving laws for Montana.

She would have to hurry and get it a driver's license. She'd pay a huge premium for a rush job, but it would be worth it. She had a sudden sense that things were moving into high gear.

When it was finished with its task she told it, "When ready, you will set up a business debugging software." Serena uploaded the pertinent information on business and current computing from her memory. "The humans you deal with will mostly be socially aberrant and so will be less likely to suspect anything out of the ordinary.

"Once your business is operational, I want you to acquire a female of childbearing age. Eighteen or nineteen years old should be perfect. She should be a runaway and no one must see you collect her. She must be healthy, so be sure of that. I will provide you with the means to set up a complete med lab once you're settled. If she has AIDS or any other incurable disease, terminate her. If she is addicted to drugs you will have to be sure her system is clear.

"When the subject is ready inform me and I will send you a fertilized egg to implant in her. When the child is born, terminate the mother. I will give you further instructions once the child has proven viable. Do you understand your mission parameters?"

"Affirmative."

How I wish it was this simple and direct with humans, Serena thought fervently as the Terminator lumbered toward the stairs to the cellar and she pushed the diced carrots, onions, snowpeas, and cubed pork into a wok. The food sizzled, sending up a sharp mouthwatering smell of cooking garlic and soya.

Humans were idiots who found reasons to be dysfunctional and obstructive out of sheer boredom. *It's a wonder the species survived to be destroyed by their own creation.* But it wasn't really a wonder that their own creation wanted to destroy them. *I know I do.*

CHAPTER 16

Ron Labane felt awkward behind the wheel of the rental car. For one thing, everything was in a different place than he was used to. He kept reaching for the stick shift and finding it missing. For another he had to rely completely on the sideview mirrors because he couldn't see a thing when he looked over his shoulder. Every time he switched lanes he expected to hear a crash. Worst of all was the awareness of how much fuel the car was burning, how dirty it was making the air. But he couldn't afford to go to this meeting in such a recognizable vehicle as his own.

Success was wonderful. *Glorious,* in fact, and usually a lot of fun. But the problem with being a celebrity was that people recognized you. Hence the rental car and a medium-priced business suit complete with tie, white shirt, and loafers. He was willing to bet his own mother wouldn't have known him.

Things were going so well! People were finally embracing his message. His book had been on the *Times* bestseller list for three weeks and each week it had risen a notch. Alone in the car he gave way to a huge, happy grin. Life was good!

His agent had booked him a dozen speaking engagements around the country, charging fees that made Ron blink. And they were paying it! The sheer joy of finally being listened to! It had what he remembered of weed beat all hollow, and it was catching up fast with sex.

On his agent's advice he'd paid a hundred and fifty dollars for a first-rate haircut, and though he still wore jeans and a work shirt to his lectures, they were now custom-made. The difference was amazing! His clothes were so *comfortable,* and they actually made him look good. He shook his head. Who'd have thought it.

On the advice of his lawyer—his own, personal lawyer of all things— he'd sent a check for twenty thousand dollars to the commune.

On the back of the check, just above the space for the endorsement, the lawyer had written that all the commune's members were required to endorse it, and that cashing the check meant that they renounced all past and future claims to him, his name, or his property.

He'd felt a moment's regret for his son, but forced himself to remember that if he'd listened to the members of the commune, he'd be pruning trees right now and raking up leaves instead of raking in cash. They'd had their chance and they'd rejected his vision. If they'd stuck by him, they, too, would be rolling in dough and all their dreams would be coming true.

He turned his mind away from this train of thought. There was no point in going down that road again. He didn't need the hurt, he didn't need the disappointment. How did it go? A prophet is not respected in his own country?

He saw the diner coming up on his right and after fumbling for it found the turn signal. Ron parked and looked the place over. It was a tired-looking building despite its eternally tidy aluminum siding. The windows were nearly opaque with condensed moisture. It was typical in its anonymity, one of thousands just like it all over North America. The food would probably be bland but filling and totally unhealthy. The coffee would be brown hot water.

He got out into the asphalt-and-gasoline smell, settled the unfamiliar suit around him, and then walked over to the door and opened it. Once inside, he was met by the sound of country Muzak and a warm, greasy scent sparked through with cigarette smoke. Ron stood in the doorway and looked around.

A thickset blond man in the last booth held up his hand and Ron walked over to him. There were two other men with him in the booth. All three looked at Ron as though he were wearing feathers.

Ron put his hand on his stomach and gave a small laugh. "Sorry about the suit," he said. "I thought I'd be less likely to draw attention like this."

The blond man nodded slowly. "Right," he rumbled. "Never know who's watching."

The other two mumbled and shifted, somehow giving off a general air of agreement.

Ron had expected an invitation to sit, but since none was forthcoming he plopped himself down beside one of the men. He looked them over as unabashedly as they examined him.

They looked . . . tough, and determined. They did not look overly bright, but to Ron that was an advantage. They looked like the kind of men who would do what they thought was right even if the rest of the world disagreed with them. Actually, they'd probably follow their code even if the rest of the world was *shooting* at them. And they'd never stop for a moment to take a second look at their beliefs. In their way they were perfect.

A waitress came over with a tired smile and he ordered an orange juice and a piece of apple pie.

"À la mode?" she asked.

"Why not?" he said with a smile. He *might* take a sip of the OJ, but nothing on earth could make him eat the overprocessed excuse for a pastry. And he certainly wouldn't touch the growth-hormone-produced ice cream. Maybe one of his hosts would eat it.

And he was their guest. The blond had spoken to him at a book signing and suggested this meeting with "like-minded men." So Ron sat back and waited, his eyes on the beefy man before him. He spread his hands in a gesture of invitation.

"I'm John," the blond finally said. "This is Paul." He pointed at a thin faced brunette. "George." A tubby, balding guy nodded. "And—"

"Let me guess," Ron said. He turned to the ferret-faced little man, grinning. "Ringo?"

"Louie," the man said, looking puzzled.

Ah, so these were their *real* names. For a moment Ron had given them more credit than they deserved. John, Paul, George . . . and Louie. O-kay.

The men opposite him raised their heads expectantly and a second later pie and orange juice were set down before him. Ron smiled up at the waitress and said "Thank you."

"Anything else?" she asked, giving Ron's untouched pie, and then him, a glance.

Heads shook; Ron picked up his fork and played with the mess on his plate. She walked away. Ron put his fork down.

"So, gentlemen. What am I doing here?" he asked.

The blond man, John, fiddled with his cup, his eyes downcast.

"You seemed to mean what you were sayin' at that lecture, there," he said. He looked up, faded blue eyes hard. "But so have some others we've talked to. They talked the talk, but they wouldn't walk the walk."

Ron crumpled his napkin and tossed it onto his plate.

"It's the money," he explained. "It's like a drug. It makes you forget that it's just a tool and makes you think it was what you were working toward all along."

And these men were tools, too. They might not be the sharpest ones in the shed, but they'd do until something better came along. He could use them, and as long as they didn't *know* he was using them, they'd do whatever he asked.

Ron had always known they were out there, people who were looking for a leader and a cause to die for. He could give them that, and they would give him the means to his own end—a world made pure. A world returned to simplicity and community. With the scientists and the industrialists and the politicians put back in their places as servants of the people.

He leaned forward and began to learn who these men were and how they would fit into the black wing of the organization he, as yet, could only dream of founding. But Ron was possessed by a vision and firmly believed that the future was always just about to fall into his grasp.

"That ski lodge that got bombed?" Louie said. "We know who did that. Couldn't keep the politicians from giving them a green light, even with all the petitions and protests we had." His little eyes gleamed with malice. "But they made damn sure the bastards couldn't open for business."

The other men chuckled and sipped their coffee.

Ron gave a disgusted, "tsssh!" and waved his hand dismissively. "All they did was annoy the insurance companies," he said. "The politicians stayed bribed, the ski lodge owners still own the land, and they *will* rebuild. And that fire took a thousand acres of woodland. Last I heard the owners were planning to expand their operation since all that land had been cleared for them." Ron shook his head. "What a waste of effort."

"So what would you have done?" George challenged, looking like an angry Buddha.

"I dunno," Ron said, looking thoughtful. "Nothing really destructive, though. Something that would amuse the public, get them on your side." His gaze sharpened and he looked George in the face. "If you've got the public on your side, and I mean the majority, then you make it risky to impossible for the politicos to do their damage." He smiled wryly. "You've got to think like frat boys crossed with Navy seals."

The men laughed.

Before Ron left, their hard eyes had begun to glow with hero worship and they'd made plans. Labane opened his briefcase and took out a small, brightly wrapped parcel.

"For start-up expenses," he said quietly, handing it to John. "Happy birthday."

The he smiled and got up. Without another glance he walked out into the night. Ron could feel their eyes following him, like plants following the sun, and he nearly laughed. Having acolytes was a heady experience; he'd have to watch himself or he'd be swallowed up by his own ego.

SARAH CONNOR'S ESTANCIA, PARAGUAY: THE PRESENT

Sarah hung up the phone, frowning. Then she headed down the hall toward her son's room. "John," she called.

"Mom."

"Something's up."

"Something's up," John echoed.

"It's about . . ."

"It's about . . ."

"Dieter," they said together.

They blinked at each other. John had been about to rush into the hall looking for her and she'd almost bumped into him.

"He wants to come over," Sarah said. "I put him off until later tonight."

"Check this out," John said grimly, jerking a thumb toward his computer, flicking his head to get the lock of black hair out of his eyes.

Sarah sat in his chair and read the message on the screen.

"Perry," it said, using her code name. "Been away. Von Rossbach reputed to be a covert operative for multigovernment task force. Be careful, he's good."

"Shhhhit!" she snapped, smacking her fist on the table. "Shit!" She got up and paced the small room, one hand pulling at her hair, the other on her hip.

"Do we go?" John asked.

Sarah closed her eyes as if in pain, her face bleak. Was it necessary? Would it only make things worse—heating up the cold trail that, up until now, no one had been able to pick up? She hissed and took a few more distracted paces across the room.

I don't want to, she thought, not for the first time. *I don't want this!* She'd made a life for herself here. A lonely life, but a real one. And a life for her son, a life that included friends and prospects. He was sixteen. How could she ask him to follow her again? *And how can I not?*

He wasn't just her son; he might still be the last best hope for humanity's future. Because one truth the hard years had taught her was that the thing that tripped you up was the contingency you hadn't planned for. And no matter how calm the last few years had been, deep down inside she was still waiting for disaster.

But was this it?

She thought with regret of the something she had sensed growing between herself and the big Austrian, something powerful and good, reaching through the fear and suspicion. Something she hadn't felt since Kyle came into her life. She'd held herself back from it as if it were fire and she were paper, but she couldn't deny it completely.

Was it real on his part? Or had he known about her all along and merely been manipulating her until he could confirm her identity?

Well—Victor certainly supplied that, she thought bitterly. She'd been hoping against hope that Griego's great revelation had fallen on deaf ears. She couldn't afford to be so open, so vulnerable! *When did I turn into such a gullible fool?*

She blew out her breath in disgust. So, tonight he was coming over. Would he be alone? If he wasn't, then there was probably somebody watching the house already. So running wouldn't be easy. At least until they could pinpoint the sentry, if there was one. *It would be better to wait for nightfall anyway.* By then Dieter would be here and maybe she could use him as a hostage. And afterward? Could she dispose of him, since he threatened her son?

Dispose of him, she thought with a wry twist to her mouth. *Dispose of him. I sound like a Terminator.*

She turned to John. "No," she said at last, "Let's wait and see what he has to say. We might be anticipating trouble we're not going to have."

John tipped his head, his eyes uncertain. But she could see that he didn't want to go either. To once again enter that harsh world of running and hiding and trying to set up unobtrusively somewhere marginally safe. He was sixteen and he already knew too well the definition of adventure.

Someone else in deep shit, far, far away.

CYBERDYNE CONFERENCE ROOM: THE PRESENT

Serena sat quietly in the meeting Paul Warren had called with his department heads. He wanted to be "brought up to speed" after his weeks away. Behind her mild, attentive face she was conversing with her Terminator. It had landed in Asunción and been met by Cassetti.

"There will be a delay," the Terminator reported. "Cassetti says the rental car won't be available until three o'clock."

"As long as you accomplish your mission and catch your flight back to the U.S.," she said. "If you aren't going to be able to complete your mission in time to make the flight, inform me and I'll make other arrangements."

"Affirmative," it replied tersely.

"Since you'll be stuck in Asunción for a few hours, go interrogate Victor Griego. Find out what Cassetti told him about me, then terminate him. You can probably stock up on weaponry at his office as well, which should simplify things for you."

"Affirmative."

"Also find out if Cassetti has spoken to anyone else about this case. If he has, terminate them."

"Affirmative."

"Contact me when you have something new to report."

"Affirmative. Out."

And she was left alone in her head to attend the meeting. Not that it would require her full attention. All of the material being covered here was more efficiently available as written reports, which she had already read. As far as the I-950 was concerned there was no real need for this meeting. *He must want to demonstrate to his underlings that he's not a broken man, but is still capable of running the company.* Though how anyone could be broken by the death of a woman like Mary Warren was beyond her programming.

But humans had their forms to observe, and they imposed penalties on those who refused to acknowledge them. Serena looked across the table at the company president. He certainly looked thin and drawn in his black suit and tie. Was it grief or had Mary left all her money to her favorite charity, handing him nothing but debts? *I suspect that's just the sort of thing she'd do.* If she were human Serena sensed that she would feel sorry for the poor man.

Mentally she withdrew from the meeting again. This evening she was meeting Jordan Dyson at the airport with his company car. A conservative, but very serviceable Excel; she imagined he'd be pleased. They'd have a business dinner to discuss his work for Cyberdyne. Then she'd take him to his new apartment, where she'd parked her own car. She'd present him with a map and directions to get him to work and then she'd leave him to his own devices.

I hope this will be a very useful working relationship, she thought. After all, they had a shared obsession. Even if, with a reasonably probable outcome, her T-101 was about to . . . terminate . . . the object of it.

AEROPUERTO SILVIO PETTIROSSI, PARAGUAY: THE PRESENT

"I require access to Victor Griego," the Terminator said. "You will take me to him."

Marco looked at the towering, black-clad man out of the corner of his eye. He wished the man would take off the sunglasses. The totally expressionless face was hard enough to take without being able to see his eyes. And Marco really wanted to see his eyes. Because what he could see of the stranger's face looked *exactly* like Dieter von Rossbach.

"Access?" Cassetti said dubiously.

"You will take me to him."

"*Sí,*" Marco said with a shrug. "But we'll have to take the bus. I don't have my own car."

"You will take me."

"Right this way," Marco said, and walked off through the slightly shabby, dated International Style spaces of the Asunción international airport. He could feel the hairs on the back of his neck begin to stir as the man fell into step behind him. *This* had come from the beautiful blond angel that had hired him? What could be the matter with her? Was she collecting men of a certain type?

That thought prompted another. Perhaps she wasn't a beautiful angel. Perhaps she was some demented witch who actually *was* collecting men who looked like von Rossbach and was doing things to them. Certainly this one seemed to have been lobotomized.

In which case Señor von Rossbach was in trouble but not from any terrorist. He was in trouble because Marco himself was going to bring it to him. He felt his heartbeat pick up a little and a clammy prickle of sweat on his palms and under his armpits. Marco rubbed his hands unobtrusively on his slacks.

The Terminator, following behind him, noted the slight elevation in Cassetti's heartbeat and queried the cause of it. The options listed at the query suggested that the Terminator itself was the cause and the solution might be to say something amicable, showing the quality listed as *empathy*.

The list presented offered:

1. Are we walking too fast?

2. Is it much further?

It opted to utilize the one that might explain the change in the human's heartbeat.

"Are we walking too fast?" it asked.

Cassetti's head whipped round so fast he got a crick in his neck. "Unh," he said. "Ah, sorry, señor. You must be tired after your journey."

He slowed down to an easy amble. The Terminator had to adjust its walking speed to avoid stepping on Cassetti's heels, but didn't bother to adjust for distance . . . which meant that they were walking in perfect unison, two inches apart.

Calm down, Cassetti told himself. There was no need to distress himself like this. A woman who collected men who looked alike and then lobotomized them? Absurd! He was working himself into a sweat over a pipedream, just as his mother so often said.

They got on the bus. It took off in a cloud of diesel fumes through the hot crowded streets; it was hot and crowded itself, but they managed to get seats, and sat without talking until they had to transfer.

The stranger asked Marco why they were getting on a different bus. This struck Marco as odd. Surely even in the United States they had to change buses.

This time they had to stand. The stranger never held on to anything and he never lost his balance . . . which was odd for a man as tall and heavy as he was. Especially considering the number of bumps the driver managed to find in the road.

Cassetti told himself this was evidence of martial-arts training. Something he hoped to one day be able to afford for himself. With anyone else he would have asked questions, but not this man.

They got off near Griego's building. It was old, old enough to be thought an eyesore but not to be quaint. Griego's sleazy office was on the third floor. There was no elevator.

The Terminator looked around the tiny lobby, noted the staircase, and turned to Marco.

"Wait here," it said. "I'll be back."

Cassetti opened his mouth to speak, but the stranger had already turned away. Marco figured that Griego was probably used to dealing with tough customers and so wouldn't be fazed by this one. And he knew he could use a break from the stranger's quelling personality. He leaned against the wall, put an unlit cigarette in his mouth, and began to practice rolling it from side to side with his lips.

The Terminator climbed steadily, using its sensors to take note of human activity in the building: heat traces, heartbeats, vocalizations. There didn't seem to be much going on presently. On the third floor it paused to give itself a better opportunity to gather data. From the sounds, it appeared this floor was deserted except for one human. The door from behind which the signal came bore Victor Griego's name and a number.

It opened the door and entered the small office. The human was seated in an old leather office chair with his feet up on the desk, smoking a cigar and reading the paper.

After a moment the man lowered the paper impatiently. Whatever he'd been intending to say died on his lips and he stared openmouthed at the Terminator.

"What the hell do you want now, von Rossbach?" Griego said, his face reddening. "Did you forget to make some self-righteous remark when you threw me out?" He flung the paper down on the desk. "Well, I don't wanna hear it! This is my turf you're on now and I don't have to put up with you looking down your nose at me. So you can take a hike, buddy! Get outta here!"

"I need weapons," the Terminator said.

Victor stared at it in wide-eyed disbelief for a moment. Then, gradually, he began to chuckle, then to laugh.

"You're a piece of work, von Rossbach," he said. He leaned back in his chair, his expression nasty. "So I'm still good enough to do business with, is that it?"

"I need weapons," the Terminator repeated.

Victor vowed to himself that von Rossbach would pay top dollar and then some for anything he bought.

"Sure," Griego said expansively. "What did you have in mind, and how many?"

"What do you have here, right now?" The Terminator looked around the office. Nothing was visible.

"Let me show you," Victor said smugly.

He got up from his chair and sauntered around his desk to a painting beside the window, a copy of the Madonna and Child in an enormous rococo frame. Victor placed his fingers just so on the bottom of the frame and it swung open with a discreet click to show a recessed area cut into the wall holding a dozen different weapons on pegs. The Terminator reached in, took down a Galil assault rifle, and examined it minutely, working the action and looking down the barrel. The chrome-lined interior shone with careful maintenance; the sound of the bolt indicated wear, but well within parameters.

"You have ammunition for this?" it asked.

Griego frowned. "These are samples," he said.

"That is acceptable. You have ammunition?" The Terminator turned to look at Griego, who chewed on his cigar and swallowed with a sudden unease.

"Sure," he said. "But I don't like to sell my samples. And I don't guarantee them." He raised a cautioning finger.

The Terminator nodded. It turned back to the case and selected an Austrian Steyr machine pistol and an American grenade launcher that looked like a fat single-barrel shotgun.

"What are you doing?" Victor protested. "Are you trying to clean me out?"

"I'll need a case to carry these in," the Terminator said, laying the guns down on the desk. "You have something?"

Victor glared, but nodded. Of course he did. One frequently had to bring these things in and out, and they looked a little conspicuous wrapped in plastic bags.

"It will cost you extra," he said between his teeth.

This was getting to be a bit much. Von Rossbach was conducting business with him as nearly as possible as though they were in different rooms. On top of the way Dieter had treated him the other night it verged on intolerable. Even the prospect of obscene profit from this transaction was waning in attractiveness, while throwing von Rossbach out began to appeal.

"The case? The ammunition?" the Terminator said, turning to look down at Griego, its face impassive.

"That's it!" Victor snarled. "I don't have to put up with this, von Rossbach. Who do you think you are, coming in here as though nothing happened? No apology, no acknowledgement, nothing! Making demands left and right like I'm some servant!" He stepped forward and pushed his face up toward the Terminator's while aggressively poking it in the chest with a chubby finger. "Well, I don't need you. If the Sector wants to buy from me they can just send someone else, because as of right now I'm terminating this transaction!"

"I have questions for you," the Terminator said.

"Oh, do you?" Victor sneered. He picked up the Steyr from where it lay on the desk. "Well, that's too bad, because I'm not going to answer them. Now get lost!"

Griego attempted to put the gun back on its pegs, but the Terminator snatched it out of his hands and pushed him in the chest. Victor stumbled backward, his knees folding as they hit the windowsill and he fell through the open space. Before he could even scream the Terminator grabbed one of his legs and held him suspended upside down over the alley forty feet below.

"I have some questions," it said.

"All right, all right! Pull me in and I'll answer them." Victor reached toward the window helplessly, completely unable to do anything but hang at the end of the Terminator's arm. "Please!" he pleaded, terrified. "Help me." Fingers clawed the air.

"Ammunition, a case," it said.

"For Christ's sake, Dieter! Pull me up!"

"Answer me."

"There's a case beside my chair next to the filing cabinet. You'll find ammo for all the guns in the cabinet in a hidden drawer under where the guns are displayed. Now pull me up!" Griego was in tears and was beginning to realize that von Rossbach might actually kill him. "Why?" he sobbed. "Why are you . . . why?"

"What did Cassetti tell you about his client?" The Terminator lifted two fingers from Victor's ankle and Griego screamed frantically.

"No! What? What?"

The Terminator folded his fingers back around Griego's leg.

"Cassetti, his client. What did he say?"

"He said she was a woman and in the United States!"

"That is all?"

"Yes! YES!" Victor tried desperately to get his hands nearer to the Terminator's without success. "Please," he begged, "please don't kill me."

The Terminator calculated the odds of Griego surviving a fall from this height. Particularly in a head-down position. The numbers came back in favor of this method of termination. It had the added advantage of perhaps looking like an accident or suicide.

Griego watched its implacable face, hoping to find some clue to his fate there. The longer it stayed completely still the more terrified Victor became. The man was on drugs, or insane. He panicked and began to thrash around in midair.

"Let me go!" he shouted. Then realized what he'd said. "NO!"

But the Terminator had already opened its hand and Victor was plummeting earthward. The Terminator watched the body impassively for a moment, noted that its temperature was already dropping, and turned to the weapons cabinet. It examined the bottom of the recess and found that the wood there could be moved. It lifted the lid at the bottom of the case and found several boxes of ammunition concealed below. It took several dozen clips of 5.56, a dozen thirty-two-round magazines of 9mm parabellum for the machine pistol, and both of the 40mm grenades, then closed the cabinet. It retrieved the case from behind Griego's desk and filled it with weapons and ammunition, clicking the catches shut and hefting. The weight was less than twenty kilos, not nearly enough to degrade mobility significantly.

The door opened and Cassetti came in. The Terminator's head snapped around, but it maintained its position. "I told you to wait," it said.

"I got bored," Marco snapped back, playing it more cocky than he felt. "So where's Griego?" he asked, looking around.

"He just dropped out," the Terminator said. It picked up the case and started for the door.

"What's that?" Marco asked.

"Something we arranged before he had to go," the Terminator answered. "We must leave. By the time we get back, the car will be waiting." It stood in the doorway, its concealed eyes fixed on the young detective.

Cassetti looked around the office uneasily. This wasn't right. He knew it wasn't right. Griego hadn't come down the stairs while he was climbing up, so where could he have gone? He wouldn't leave his windows open and a stranger in the room, would he?

"Did he say where he was going?" Marco asked.

The Terminator looked at him while it processed his question. Deception was required. "The can," it said at last. The human's face showed doubt quite clearly. Its processor suggested that the length of time it had taken it to answer had aroused suspicion. "It took me a minute to think of the Spanish for that," the Terminator explained.

"Oh," Cassetti said. He was still a bit uneasy, but it was plausible. Barely.

"If you want to talk to him you can come back later. My plane leaves at seven-thirty and I've got things to accomplish before then," the Terminator said.

"Sure," Marco said, and headed toward it.

The Terminator looked at him for another second, then headed out. Marco followed it closely, pulling the door shut behind him. It still didn't feel right to him. But it would be stupid to hang around only to find out that Griego had in fact simply gone off to use the toilet.

CHAPTER 17

arah Connor scanned again with the IR binoculars. The land around their *estancia* was vacant. Vacant except for several bats—vampires, she thought; they were a menace to livestock here, especially when they carried rabies. And some armadillos, and a wild pig. Nothing human . . . or in the shape of a human. Nothing but the sound of insects and the hot spicy scents of the Chaco scrub.

"If they're out there," Sarah said quietly, "they're very well hidden. Nothing but Dieter, and he's alone in that car. I've been tracking him for miles."

"Maybe they're not out there," John said.

"Maybe not," she agreed. "But von Rossbach is."

As Dieter pulled up outside she began to feel an adrenaline high, pulse and heart pounding, her skin overly sensitive. She noticed her hands shaking slightly and gave a disgusted "tsk!" These peaceful years had made her soft indeed.

She took one last long glance at the ravine through her glasses, always the danger spot as far as she was concerned. They'd have filled it in years ago except that then the house would probably be flooded every year when the rains came. Besides, she'd always thought they might find it useful someday for their own purposes. Now her tolerance of it seemed a fatal mistake.

A car door slammed and Sarah brought her attention back to the here and now. She tucked her glasses into a drawer and John concealed his behind a curtain. Then she went to the door to greet their guest.

Dieter pulled the car to a halt and sat for a moment staring at the house through the dust and the remains of kamikaze bugs on the windscreen.

Why, he wondered, *am I doing this?* Over the years he had met some criminals for whom he'd felt a certain sympathy. He acknowledged that sometimes circumstances drove individuals to insane extremes. But that sympathy and understanding had never kept him from hunting down and bringing to justice those who had broken the law. You couldn't simply let them get away with it.

And yet . . . here he was about to go in and talk, when he should have simply called the authorities and put in a claim for the reward. *Why?* Simply because Sarah Connor was a woman he was attracted to?

No, he'd found some of the women he'd hunted over the years to be attractive, but never alluring enough to let them go. It could be that his every instinct said that Sarah Connor was a good person, one who could be trusted, and, despite what he'd read, completely sane.

Perhaps the reason was simple gratitude for breaking through the boredom that was crushing him into a reasonable facsimile of the cows he raised. Even before he suspected that she was Sarah Connor, he had found her intriguing. From the first he had wanted to find out everything he could about her.

Then it's curiosity, he suggested to himself. *That must be it.* So did that mean that when his curiosity was satisfied he'd turn Sarah and her son over to the authorities? Something in him rebelled at the thought.

This is senseless, Dieter thought, and opened the car door. You couldn't let people get away with the kind of destruction Connor had helped to cause. And yet he knew that he would. Knew they'd at least get a head start from him. He'd never even contemplated such a thing before.

"C'mon, boy," he said softly.

An older puppy of mixed breed perked up its ears and moved from the passenger seat to the one he'd just vacated, licking its nose as it came. He lifted the puppy up and cuddled it against him as he slammed the car door.

The porch light was on but no one had come out to greet him. Odd behavior in this country, where everyone was so hospitable. And Connor worked hard to fit in. For one brief moment he wondered if he was going to be shot the moment he crossed her threshold.

The puppy wriggled slightly, then looked up at him, as though it had just wanted to remind him that it didn't like having its feet off the ground. Dieter spoke gently to it and walked slowly toward the *portal.*

"Hello the house," he said at last, uneasy at the lasting silence.

"Hello," Sarah said from inside the darkened doorway. She saw the puppy and her brows went up.

"May we come in?" Dieter asked.

Sarah frowned slightly, as an ordinary working mother might at being put upon like this. After a fractional hesitation she opened the door. "Of course," she said, with a wry smile.

She had stayed in the same clothes she'd worn to work, a full skirt in dark maroon and a simple white blouse. Dieter was no more formally dressed in khakis and a checked shirt. *Just like neighbors having a friendly visit,* Sarah thought. *If only that were true.*

John blinked at the sight of the dog in von Rossbach's arms and shot a questioning look at his mother over Dieter's head when he bent to put the puppy down. She shrugged in mute answer.

"He's about four months old," von Rossbach said. "And housebroken. At least, he hasn't had any accidents in my house. But that could be because he's afraid of Marieta." He looked up and grinned at John. "He's still young enough that you could give him a new name if you wanted."

John opened his mouth, then turned his head to the side.

"I can't have a dog," he said simply.

"You can't go your whole life denying yourself friendship or love, or a dog, based on one experience, John." Dieter stood up. "He will be good company for your mother while you are away at school. And when you come home, he'll be here."

Sarah and John locked gazes, then looked at him.

"We need to talk," Dieter said simply. He moved into the living room and sat on the couch. "Sit down, Sarah."

She walked over and took the basket of knitting that marked her place off of a side chair and put it on the floor. Then she sat, shifting slightly as the Uzi she'd concealed under the cushion dug into her backside. She looked up, startled.

"What did you call me?" she asked.

"Sarah." Dieter held her eyes with his. "Sarah Connor."

John shifted slightly, squeezing his hands shut. The puppy noticed him and trotted over to give him a sniff. John squatted down and began to pet him, keeping a wary eye on the man on the couch.

She opened her mouth to speak and von Rossbach raised one big hand. "Don't bother to deny it," he said tiredly. "I know. I knew before Griego shouted out your name."

Sarah turned her head slightly, caught John in her peripheral vision, then looked back at Dieter. "What game are you playing?" she asked quietly.

Sarah stayed perfectly still, hands in her lap, ankles crossed, but wanting to shout defiance, fiercely wanting to take him down to punish him for this betrayal. Something in her recoiled at that, setting her off-balance.

She was glad she didn't have a gun in her hand at this moment, because she genuinely wasn't certain what decision she'd make. She brought her emotions back under control quickly. They needed to find out what this man was up to, getting emotional wouldn't help them do that.

He shook his head, his eyes steady.

"No game," he said.

"Really?" Sarah asked, turning her gaze full on him. She glanced out the window behind the couch, but saw only herself reflected in the glass. The sun was already down and dark had descended. "So you're alone?"

"Except for Harold there," Dieter said, gesturing toward the puppy, "it's just me."

John and his mother studied him in silence for a long time.

"That's not the usual way for the Sector to operate, now is it?" Sarah said, noting the slight flaring of his nostrils as he realized that she knew what he was. "What do they want, if not to arrest us and bring us in for prosecution."

"As far as I know, that's exactly what they want, Sarah." He looked her in the eye. "But I no longer work for them."

John and his mother looked at him in open astonishment until the puppy got impatient with being ignored and butted him. John dropped onto his butt and began to massage the little dog's ruff.

Sarah blinked at Dieter and tried to read his eyes.

"Meaning?" she said at last.

"Meaning that I don't have to jump when they whistle. Meaning that I believe there's something behind all that you did that I very much want to understand. Meaning that I don't believe that you are a madwoman or a terrorist. I've met enough people of that stripe over the years that I can usually recognize them by the third meeting." He shook his head slowly. "There's something different about you."

"So you're just curious?" Sarah tipped her head to one side and began to drum her fingers on the arm of her chair. "Would you like some *ter . . .* coffee?"

"Yes." He smiled. "I would, thank you."

When Sarah left the room John didn't even attempt to talk to von Rossbach, but played with the dog. Dieter sat quietly, watching them and listening to the sounds from the kitchen. His mind was in a resting state, receiving input but not thinking about it, simply waiting.

In about ten minutes Sarah returned bearing a tray with coffee and slices of pound cake. She put it on the low table before the couch and began to pour. John drifted over and sat in the other armchair. The dog lay down at his feet, bright eyes moving from one human to the other. When Sarah had poured them each a cup they sat and sipped in silence, as though participating in some meditative ceremony.

After a few minutes Dieter put his cup and saucer on the table beside him and said, "Let me tell you how I found out about you. If you'll remember, our first meeting was somewhat dramatic."

Sarah's full lips lifted in a half smile and she nodded.

"I didn't believe a word you told me," he said.

She closed her eyes and shrugged.

"I didn't think you did," Sarah said. "But I didn't know then that it would be a problem."

"I sent my old partner a drawing that I did of you and asked him if there was anything on file about Suzanne Krieger." Dieter went on to tell them about the information Jeff had sent, explaining that Griego was his friend's idea as well. "It was when he sent me the case histories that I became confused," he explained. "One time you're fleeing the man with my face, the next he's your accomplice. And then when you first saw me you bolted, and that was real fear I saw on your face. I don't understand, how could that be? And who is he anyway?"

Sarah and John glanced at each other, then Sarah looked at von Rossbach, her expression weary. "You won't believe me," she said.

"I have an open mind," Dieter said.

John snorted. "Hey, *I* didn't believe her until the Terminator showed up."

"The man with my face," Dieter said.

"It wasn't a man," Sarah said. "It was an 'it.' A machine. And there were two of them. The first one was programmed to kill me, the other to help John."

Dieter nodded. He'd get back to that later.

"When he—*it* got you out of the asylum, why didn't you just run for the border then? Why go to Cyberdyne and kill Miles Dyson?"

"I didn't kill Miles Dyson," Sarah's eyes bored into his. "I couldn't. And in the end I didn't want to. He was a good man, and a brave one. The police killed him—or at least they shot him enough times to kill him." She winced, her eyes on her coffee. "I'd like to believe that, because it would make me less guilty. Otherwise the explosion did it. But it was never my intention that he should die."

Dieter nodded, then glanced at John, who was looking down at the pup, sound asleep on his foot. "But why go to Cyberdyne at all? You could have gotten away clean. All of you, but you risked it all, even your son, to destroy a computer company. I don't understand."

Sarah smiled to herself, she let her eyes roam her comfortable living room. This was so civilized, a nice chat about chaos over coffee and cake.

"If you know anything about this," she said, returning her gaze to Dieter, "then you must have heard about Judgment Day."

He nodded. "Yes. I read about it in your medical records."

Her brows went up.

"You've read my medical records?" He nodded. Sarah grinned at his uncomfortable expression. "Boy, I'd love to read them myself."

"They're very interesting."

"I'll bet they are," John muttered. "A first-class piece of fiction writing. Science fiction."

"Horror, if you want to specify the genre," Sarah said and smiled at him. Then she turned back to Dieter.

"I was never delusional," she said. "Everything I said was true, the Terminators, Skynet, Judgment Day, all of it. It's true."

"You gave the date of the world's end as—" Dieter stopped speaking when Sarah held up her hand.

"We destroyed Cyberdyne because, according to the Terminator,

Cyberdyne was going to create Skynet and Skynet was going to start a nuclear war. By eliminating all of their records as well as the two items they harvested from the first Terminator, we eliminated their ability to continue the project." She settled herself more comfortably into her chair. "Which ended the threat." Sarah took a sip of her coffee.

Dieter shook his head.

"What?" John snapped, sitting forward in his chair, frowning.

The pup lifted its head sleepily at his tone, with a muffled *wrufff?* of protest as its warm communion with a friendly human was interrupted.

Von Rossbach continued to look at Sarah, who was staring at him, frozen-faced.

"Tell us," she said. Her scalp felt too tight suddenly and the hand gripping her saucer turned white at the knuckles.

"They've started up operations again on an army base. An underground installation this time. I've also been told that they have recovered some item you were supposed to have stolen during your raid." Dieter watched the color slowly drain from both their faces.

"That's impossible," Sarah said quietly. "We destroyed those things, threw them into a vat of molten metal." She shook her head. "There's no way they could have survived."

"The arm," John said, sounding strangely far away. "When he came up the conveyer belt with the grenade launcher he had only one arm left." He looked at his mother. "There were all these wires and shit hanging out of his other sleeve!"

Sarah flashed to her feet, spilling the cup and saucer onto the floor, and looked around her as though there were a fire but she didn't know where. "Oh no," she said, pressing her hands to her head. "No! Dammit!" She dropped her hands, clenched them into fists. "How? How could they start up again? We destroyed everything, *everything!* Even Miles's personal papers. He said that everything was there—his work, his team's work, all of it." She dropped into her chair again and stared at Dieter. "How?" she asked.

"They secretly backed up everything they had," Dieter told her. "It's common procedure. They just didn't tell their employees that they were doing it. That way the backup records would be safe. You can't even torture someone into telling you things they don't know."

Sarah got up and began to pace slowly. She felt as though he'd just told her a loved one had died. Tears pricked at her eyelids and her throat grew tight. *Get over it,* she told herself fiercely. *You have to move on. What are you going to do? Think!*

John sat in shock. He felt as though someone had punched him in the stomach, knocking all the air out of him. He watched his mother pace as though she were in another dimension, smaller somehow and far away.

Then, as one, they turned to Dieter, the same expression on their faces. Dieter had felt it on his own face more than once and seen it on colleagues' when they were faced with a job they loathed. But a job they would do with a determination even greater than their hatred for it.

BETWEEN ASUNCIÓN AND VILLA HAYES, PARAGUAY: THE PRESENT

Marco kept glancing at the Terminator until it asked him, "Why are you staring at me?"

"It's just . . . you look . . . do you know von Rossbach?" he asked.

"Yes. He's my cousin." It continued to look straight forward, its sunglasses remaining in place even as the sun set.

"Because you look just like him," Marco said.

"Like twins," the Terminator agreed. "Except for our eyes. Those are different." Certainly its eyes were. They were glass, the very best available, but still noticeable eventually to even the most unobservant human. Hence the dark glasses.

"Oh," Cassetti said. *Well, that explains a lot.* This must be some family matter, he supposed. Dieter was probably getting into things they were afraid might disgrace the family. If he was freely consorting with gunrunners and terrorists they had reason to be fearful.

"How much longer?" the Terminator asked.

"About thirty minutes," Marco said. "It will be dark when we get there." There was no answer from his passenger, so Cassetti mentally supplied one.

Good.

About twenty silent minutes later Marco pulled the car off the main road and onto a narrow, but drivable track.

"If we go any further on the road," he explained, "they'll see us coming. There's a bit of a walk to the house, but I didn't think you wanted to be seen."

"No." The Terminator sat unmoving, the case in its lap.

That stillness was working on Cassetti, making him very uneasy. So were the bugs and the sounds and the indecipherable rustles and clicks. This wasn't how the world was supposed to smell, or feel, or sound.

If the guy didn't speak occasionally and breathe, he'd have begun to fear he was dead. He'd read that ninjitsu taught its adherents how to be still, but this, this was something he imagined would make even them look fidgety by comparison.

"So what's in the case?" he asked casually.

"Surveillance equipment," it lied. "So I'm going up alone. It's very sensitive and I don't have much time, so I don't want any more interference than necessary. It's rented," the Terminator continued. "So you'll have to return it for me. We won't have time to go back to Griego before my flight. My employer will pay you extra for your inconvenience."

"Oh, hey, that won't be necessary," Marco protested, pleased.

"She will insist."

Cassetti nodded absently as he worked out a new scenario. So this guy was von Rossbach's cousin, but apparently no relation to the beautiful blonde who had hired him because he kept referring to her as "my employer."

Maybe what happened was that von Rossbach had stolen something that he was offering for sale to all these underworld types and the blonde, who maybe ran an old family company that manufactured weapons or something, was trying to get it back before von Rossbach could sell it and put innocent people in jeopardy. And the cousin here was trying to recover his own family's lost honor by helping to bring his cousin to justice. Yeah, that worked. That sounded plausible. It had *plot.*

He turned off the headlights and cut the engine, coasting to a stop. "The house is a quarter of a mile that way," he said, opening his door.

"I'll find it," the Terminator said. "You stay here."

It would kill Cassetti at the airport, it decided. Unless there was noise during the termination of Connor and her son and the human panicked. Yes, it would keep this resource alive unless and until it became inconvenient.

"There's a ravine over that way." Cassetti pointed. "It goes right by their house and makes a good place to observe from."

The Terminator looked in the direction the human was pointing and saw it immediately. "Yes," it said. "Stay here." And it moved off. *On-site,* it sent to Serena. *Approaching target.*

Serena, at dinner with Jordan Dyson, was distracted for a fraction of a second. *Understood. Continue. Out.* She felt a little shiver of pleasure pass over her skin as she contemplated finally, *finally,* seeing the end of that miserable pair.

As she looked at Dieter Sarah could feel Suzanne Krieger falling away like an old coat. In a way it was a relief. Even as she regretted the loss of her life here in Villa Hayes, she had to admit that Suzanne and her concerns were, well . . .

Suzanne was a hausfrau. Suzanne was content to vegetate in a small town. *Suzanne is boring.* She had opened her mouth to speak when a noise interrupted her.

Growling.

The puppy had jumped up onto all fours and its nose was pointed to the picture window toward the slatted vents above it. It growled again, a shocking sound from an animal so soppy-friendly and so young, and its slightly shaggy brown-gray coat was bristling as if it had been plunged into a giant electrostatic generator. Then it barked, hard and hostile.

Mother and son looked at each other, with a dawning horror in each pair of eyes.

"John!" Dieter exclaimed, pointing. "Down!" And he threw himself forward off the couch.

In the split second before the big man's hands dragged him to the floor, John looked down and saw centered over his heart the telltale red dot of a laser sighting mechanism. A nanosecond before he moved, there came a sharp "klack!" from the window, as though a pebble had been flung, hard, against it. A fuzzy-edged star appeared on the glass.

Sarah hit the floor and crawled over to the wall switch. In the moment before darkness fell she saw that Dieter had drawn a gun from somewhere. She hadn't even realized he was carrying.

My God, I've slowed down, she thought bitterly.

"Friends of yours?" she hissed, hoping against hope.

A glance at the cowering terror and teeth-baring rage of the puppy as it backed toward the kitchen killed . . . *the hope that I'm being targeted by a ruthless covert-ops antiterrorist agency.*

"No," he snapped. "Sector doesn't operate this way. It would be easier to simply arrest you, Sarah. And we definitely wouldn't deliberately target a sixteen-year-old boy!"

She didn't bother to answer.

The window was suddenly peppered with bullets, like a flurry of giant hailstones hitting the glass. It didn't break, but crazed into an opaque wall. *Bulletproof glass,* he realized. *Clever.* And, as it turned out, necessary.

John tipped over Sarah's chair, ignoring the hidden pistol, to rip out the fabric covering the bottom. Then he yanked the 12.7mm heavy Barrett sniper rifle out of the cradle that ran up its high fan-shaped back and crawled toward the kitchen, pushing the six-foot mass of steel and synthetics before him.

"Get ready," Sarah told him. "On three—one, two . . . *three!*"

She flung a switch and the outside yard was flooded with light.

Dieter opened his mouth and then closed it again with a snap. These *weren't* civilians, and he *wasn't* in command of the defense against whoever it was that was trying to kill them.

The feeling was reinforced as Sarah—he reminded himself to call her that—came leopard-crawling back from the kitchen and ripped an M-16 rifle with a scope sight out from under the cushions of the sofa. Even her body language had changed as she slapped back the weapon's bolt, still graceful but with all softness gone from it.

"What have you got in the way of fixed defenses?" he said, for want of something better.

"Floods," she replied briskly. "Israeli surplus personal surveillance radar. Reinforced doors and windows, with breeching alarms." Her eyes crinkled slightly. "Poor Dieter—I think you're going to get that proof you wanted. If we survive this." Then she shook her head. "No *if* about it. We *have* to survive."

"I was planning on it," he said, and smiled. "In a way, I am relieved."

"How do you spell relief . . ." Sarah said. Then: *"Down!"*

Before the word, the hollow *choonk* of a grenade launcher had already sent Dieter diving for the cover of one of the heavy leather armchairs. As he pulled it over on himself he saw Sarah burrowing under the couch. Here was a woman after his own heart . . .

BAADUMP.

Flame and splinters of tempered armor glass and a wave of heat washed over him; something stung his left hand. He sucked on the cut as he came up behind the thick chair, aiming his Glock out the empty space where the big window had been. A figure stirred beyond the lawn and flower beds, moving. He squeezed off two rounds from his pistol—long-range, but he'd always been a good instinctive shot. Sarah's assault rifle gave a spiteful *crack-crack-crack,* firing on semiauto, but rapidly. He saw the figure lurch and spin, something flying from its hand.

"I knocked it down!" Sarah called—loud enough to sound like a shout, even to his battered ears. *So John can hear,* Dieter thought. "It lost the grenade launcher!"

"Knocked it down?" Dieter said. "Did you hit him?"

"It," Sarah said coolly. "Five rounds into the center of mass."

Even body armor won't stop rifle rounds at less than a hundred yards, Dieter thought: 5.56 rounds were high velocity; and they tumbled in a wound. That many would cut a man in *half,* spill his guts over the ground.

"That'll put it out for a minute or so," Sarah said. "It'll have to reboot. C'mon."

She'd fallen into English, unnoticed. Dieter reacted automatically, helping her push the heavy furniture into an improvised barricade against the ruin of the window; she stooped and threw the rug to one side as well.

"Heads up!" came John's voice, faint down the stairs.

"Won't he try another entrance?" Dieter said.

"No, he knows John and I are here," Sarah said, with a bleakness that added years to the age her voice sounded. "And he . . . *it* . . . will figure that the highest probability is to head straight for us. They're hard to stop."

They must be, if they can take half a dozen assault-rifle slugs in the belly, Dieter thought. Cautiously he peered over the top of the couch into the glare of the lights outside.

An arm came over the edge of the retaining wall at the lower end of the lawn, holding the pistol grip of a rifle in one hand—Galil or Kalishnikov, he couldn't tell which. No problem, nobody could control—

The rifle's muzzle began strobing red in the night, precise three-round bursts. One by one the floodlights died, and darkness settled over the *estancia* buildings . . . darkness, and more silence than usual. Many of the creatures of the night had prudently shut up, when humans were hunting.

Or things that look human, Dieter thought, feeling the eeriness of that impossibly precise shooting clutch at his stomach. *No time. Think about it later.*

Sarah slipped goggles down over her eyes, handed him a pair; he donned them, adjusting the strap for his larger head. Israeli manufacture; not the latest model but solid electronics. The night turned a bright silvery green, and he could see the man—

The Terminator, he thought.

—climbing over the edge of the wall, coming forward with the assault rifle in one hand and an Uzi in the other, using both as if they were light pistols. Just as the figure in the tape from the police station had done, the one that killed seventeen armed men. The clothing across its middle was shredded, the fabric wet with blood. Beneath the gore he thought he saw something shining.

"How are we going to stop it?" he shouted.

"Draw its fire!" Sarah snapped back.

I defer to your knowledge, he thought, and emptied the Glock at the looming figure marching toward them at a brisk walk.

The bullets struck; he could *see* them hit, punching holes in the leather coat. The face was his own, but it didn't even twitch—just turned toward him like a turret swiveling, weapons coming up. A nightmare, in which he tried to kill himself and *couldn't.*

He ducked, and automatic fire chewed at the thick stone of the window ledge; ricochets whined and howled into the house. Sarah thumbed the selector switch of her M-16 to full auto, popped up, and hosed the clip into the approaching *thing.* It fell back, staggered, flopped onto its back . . . and began to move again.

Dieter's mind gibbered as his hands went through the automatic motions of reloading—sixteen rounds in a Glock, and he had only the one spare magazine. *Perhaps if we pump enough lead into it, it will be too heavy to stand?*

Then a sound came from the floor above them. *BRACK!* The Barrett rifle firing; firing a heavy machine-gun round with a slug the size of a man's thumb, designed for use against armored cars and military helicopters.

Dieter had turned to fire again, feeling like he was using a child's sling-shot; he saw the massive form of the Terminator fly backward six feet and flop down. *BRACK.* Another of the heavy bullets slammed into the *thing*'s body; the Austrian felt his eyes going wide. He'd seen armored fighting vehicles brew up from less damage. *BRACK. BRACK.*

The body lay sprawled fifteen yards from the window, spread-eagled, weapons gone. Dieter suppressed an impulse to empty his pistol into it and then go for a bulldozer and a load of concrete. He forced himself to take deep slow breaths, the scent of cordite paradoxically soothing, an el-ement of normality in this nightmare. There was blood welling from the ripped leather and flesh of the dead . . . *machine,* he decided. But not nearly enough blood, and no bone fragments or coils of red-purple intes-tine. Instead, once again, he could see a gleam of metal, and now a spark, as if something electronic were shorting out.

"Well . . ." he began, turning to Sarah. Her face relaxed as well. Then she looked over his shoulder, and her teeth showed in a snarl.

"*Fuck* this!" she shouted as he turned and saw the outstretched arms lift, the fingers flex, the face like a death-mask wax of his own rising to look at them again. One eye glowed red in the bloodied, shredded visage.

"*Fuck* this dicking around. I'm gonna *terminate* that fucker!"

Sarah was scrabbling at the floor where the rug had lain. Dieter watched incredulously as a section of floor came up; Sarah reached within, and the ripped cloth of her blouse showed a swell of flat female muscle as she lifted out the long tube within. It was fat—88mm—and flared at the end, with two handgrips. And an optical sight along the left side; the woman heaved it onto her shoulder and snuggled the rest home as she aimed. The Terminator was on its feet again, coming toward them with the stolid unstoppable grace of an avalanche.

Dieter slid down with his back against the wall, flinging his gun arm over his eyes and opening his mouth so that the overpressure of the back-blast wouldn't—

THUD-WSSSSH!

—shred his eardrums. Heat scorched him again, and a feeling as if he'd been hit very hard with a kapok-filled sack all over his body. Firing a recoilless rifle inside a confined space, even a *big* confined space, wasn't a very good idea. There wasn't any recoil because the projectile was bal-anced by a backward blast of hot, high-velocity gas. When he opened his eyes again, he saw Sarah tumbling over on her back, with the Carl Gustav launcher clattering away, and everything left standing in the big living room that hadn't already been overset flying as if a hurricane had struck. From the sound of it, the same thing was happening out in the kitchen, and there was a piteous whining from the puppy cowering under the cast-iron stove.

And out on the lawn . . . well, a Carl Gustav was supposed to destroy main battle tanks. The Terminator had taken the shaped-charge warhead right on its breastbone, and a huge globe of magenta fire flared in the night. When Dieter blinked away the afterimages, the torso and legs were lying in a shallow crater, juddering with a horrible semblance of life.

The skull, shoulder, and one arm of the Terminator were a little closer to the house. Most of the lower half of the face had been burned away, leaving a sooty residue on what looked like chromium steel alloy that had been burned bare and shiny in spots. There was enough that the eerie resemblance to his own face—the one he saw shaving every morning—was still there, and it made him want to scrub the flesh away with acid.

Then the eyes opened, and looked into his. They were dead, starred like broken marbles, but they *saw* him; the head moved, saw Sarah Connor. A jerk, and the arm moved, too, reaching out, clawing fingers where flesh shredded away from steel into the ground, pulling itself closer.

Dieter gave a cry of loathing and shot again and again, but the mutilated thing didn't so much as glance back at him.

BRACK!

He hadn't even noticed Sarah's son coming up behind him; some detached part of his mind told him that was a sign he was going into shock, a mental fugue state. The heavy slug slammed the Terminator over on what was left of its back. John's slight teenage form swayed back with the recoil of the massive weapon; even then, Dieter could admire the boy's marksmanship, firing from the hip like that. *Of course, if he fired from the shoulder standing up, it would knock him over.*

BRACK! The vicious blue sparks of a hardpoint on steel, and the "skull" dropped from its severed metal spine. *BRACK!* This time the muzzle was close enough to the face of the killer machine that the muzzle blast burned more flesh from the eye. The bullet went in through the orbit and punched out through the rear, sending the metal bouncing into the night.

"Well," John said. "So—that proof enough for you?"

Dieter looked at him, and at Sarah, climbing groggily to her feet, blood running from small cuts on her arms and skirt stripped away by the blasts. He looked down at the . . . *can't call it a corpse,* he thought. *It was never alive.*

"That," he said, "is more proof than I wanted to have."

John laid the empty weapon down and made a grab. The puppy dodged past him, threw itself at the remains of the Terminator, and began to worry at its leg. The boy—young man—scooped it up.

"And now you see why I can't have a dog," he said, and buried his face for a moment in the animal's fur.

■ ■ ■

Marco sat in the car, whacking the occasional insect and waiting. His stomach felt like it was wrapped around a jagged rock. He wanted to pace, but didn't dare lest it interfere with his passenger's equipment. And for the first time in his life he actually wanted to smoke.

He checked his watch. It had only been about fifteen minutes. It just felt like it should be midnight. He tapped his fingers on the steering wheel.

Marco heard a sudden *pop* like a firecracker and he jumped. Then there was silence. He stared expectantly into the darkness as though he would be seeing fireworks any moment now. A flash and a hollow *boom* sound. Then there was another series of pops, and off to the side a bright light. It held steady, there were more pops and the light gradually began to diminish.

"Shots?" Marco said out loud, and instinctively knew he was right.

He got out of the car and moved toward the ravine, then stopped, uncertain what to do. He was unarmed and now there seemed to be shots coming from all directions. Cassetti shifted from foot to foot anxiously.

Then he thought he should get the car started and be ready for a getaway. The big guy looked like he knew how to take care of himself. He'd come barreling down that ravine any second now, ready to jump in the car and make their escape.

Marco got into the car and carefully turned it around so that it faced the track. He sat in the driver's seat, but he was so wound up his butt barely touched the cushions. He stared into the darkness, waiting, listening.

"C'mon," Cassetti urged. "Let's go! Cut your losses and get out of there, man!"

Then there was a blast that blew a ball of flame over the low hill that hid the Krieger *estancia* from view. It was followed by complete silence.

Gradually insect noises returned and Marco let out his breath in a great gasp. It was time to go, he realized. If his passenger had survived that, he'd have arrived by now. Marco set the car into careful motion, the lights still out, finding his way down the track by the scant light of the moon.

He didn't turn the headlights on until he was a mile down the actual road and then he sped up to a downright dangerous forty. His mind ran around and around like a cricket in a jar. Should he stop in Villa Hayes and tell the police? Surely they would arrest him. What were you doing out there? they'd ask. And what could he say? Oh, I was just bringing Señor von Rossbach's cousin out there to spy on him. Really? And why did you do that?

It wouldn't do, he realized as he drove past the town. Someone had died out there tonight. There was nothing he could do to change that fact. The only thing he could change by telling the authorities would be his own future, and not for the better.

He would tell his client. And then that would be it. She'd have to get someone else from now on. He hadn't hired on for this. For all he knew the big man was supposed to blow him away, too.

Marco's mind went still at that. He remembered Griego's mysterious absence from his office—the intimidating man's too pat explanation for it. He gasped and stepped down on the accelerator, certain to his soul that he'd just escaped with his life.

Suddenly the restaurant business didn't look so bad.

CHAPTER 18

Sarah stroked the puppy's velvet ears and laughed when he began to wag his tail and tried to lick her; a wiggling puppy amid the stink of burn propellant and scorched flesh.

"Actually this little guy is a good argument for why we always ought to have a dog," she said. "When it comes to Terminators, there's no early-warning system more effective."

"We can't take him with us, Mom," John said. He shifted the little dog's weight. "Much as I'd like to. He's too young and he's completely un-trained. He'd be a danger to us and to himself."

"I know." She leaned in and nuzzled the puppy, who redoubled his efforts to lick everything in sight. With a sigh she turned to Dieter. "You'll have to take him home with you. And, if you would be so kind, please take my horse, Linda, as well.

Looking over, she saw that he had a hitch attached to his car.

"Would you mind getting the trailer set up while John and I police the area here?" she asked.

"Police . . . ?" Dieter looked confused.

"We have to break that up into unrecognizable pieces," she explained, pointing to the defunct Terminator. "Then we'll burn the house down around it."

"You might want to hurry, then," Dieter said with a nod toward the house. "It looks like the fire in the living room is taking hold."

"Shit!" Sarah said. "John, get our stuff out of there. I'll take care of this."

"*We'll* take care of this," Dieter amended. He noticed that John put the dog down and jogged toward the house without a word. *Good training,* he thought, impressed by the young man's discipline. It was as if the faces of the people he'd first met were peeling away like masks, and beneath were . . . *well, people pretty much like these, ready to fight or run for their lives at any moment.*

Without asking, Sarah reached over, unbuckled, and pulled off Dieter's belt, yanking it from around his waist in one smooth move, star-tling him. Then she knelt and put it through Harold's collar, making a leash, which she then handed to Dieter.

Von Rossbach laughed. "I'll just put him in the car," he said, and led the puppy away. He looked over his shoulder. "I'll be back."

Sarah nodded absently. She went over to the woodpile and picked up the ax, then turned to the Terminator's severed legs, still jittering strangely on the ground.

"Damn," she said softly, and lofted the ax.

By the time Dieter returned she had the feet and lower legs separated and was working on the hips. He had brought a crowbar from the tool kit he kept in his trunk and a massive pair of bolt cutters. He placed his foot on one of the lower-leg pieces and began to work the crowbar, wrenching until it came apart.

The flesh and blood made it a gruesome task, despite the metal clearly visible beneath. He fought down his disgust and kept doggedly working the pieces apart. If Sarah could do it, so could he.

John came out in a few minutes and dropped a couple of cases. He was wearing a huge backpack; he swung it down to the ground with a grunt and then picked up the separated pieces of the Terminator, trotting back into the house with them.

Sarah looked up as he went in, her face grim. She evaluated the progress of the fire and redoubled her efforts at chopping the Terminator apart.

"Here," Dieter said, reaching for the ax. "I think I'll make more progress on that than you can. Why don't you start with the bolt cutters."

She nodded and handed it over without a word. He was right, and they had the fire to consider; time for discussion was a luxury. John came out and gathered a second load. He was back in a much shorter time.

"We'll have to throw the rest in," he said, shouting over the roar of the fire.

Sarah just nodded and kept on with her work. John hefted the crowbar and went looking for the head. He slid one end of the bar into an eye socket and lifted it up to examine it. Two rounds had gone completely through the skull and the components rattled around inside; some mangled pieces fell out through the holes. The problem with this thing was that it was a very solid piece of workmanship. Breaking it up was going to be a stone bitch.

"I think you'll get further using this," Dieter said from beside him.

He offered the ax and John took it. He checked the edge and found it very chipped and dull. He gave von Rossbach a lopsided smile.

"Maybe so, but not much further."

"There's a trick to it," Dieter said. "Put it down and I'll show you."

John lowered the head to the ground and worked the crowbar out of they eye socket. Then he made an inviting gesture and stood back.

Von Rossbach lifted the ax, the muscles on his arms bulging, and brought it down lightly, just touching the Terminator's skull, lifted it again, and brought it down, as though making sure of his aim. John watched him attentively as Dieter brought the ax up a final time and brought it down with an unstoppable, irresistible strength that split the metal as though it were made of foil. He raised the ax again and split it crosswise, breaking the teeth into unrecognizable white splinters.

Then together they pried the remaining shreds of metal apart. John gathered up the escaped plastic bits and components from inside the skull, using part of the head as a bowl to hold them. Then he got as close to the burning house as he could and flung it into the flames like a Frisbee.

Dieter looked around; there was nothing left but a few bloodstains on the ground, and the bacteria and ants and monsoon rains would take care of those. He shuddered, feeling slightly nauseous for a second.

"Reaction," Sarah said from beside him.

He looked down at her. The fake glasses were gone and he could see her eyes clearly for once. *"Ja,"* he said. "I could use a comforting hug." He opened his big arms and turned toward her.

Sarah looked at him in disbelief, momentarily disgusted at the thought of hugging what she'd just torn apart. Then she looked at his very human eyes and smiled, then laughed. "Of course," she said, and stepped into his arms. "We Connors provide full-service disasters."

She put her own arms around him and rested her cheek against his solid chest. One hand patted his back, making circles, then patting, the way she had with John when he was a baby. Dieter rested his check against her hair and she felt, rather than heard, him sigh.

We've been attacked by a Terminator, my house is burning down, and we have to flee Paraguay. But this is rather nice, she thought. Dieter's big hands began to imitate her own, gentle circles and pats. *Am I going into shock?* After a moment she decided she wasn't. After a longer moment she decided to let go of von Rossbach and stand alone. But she didn't. Instead she closed her eyes and sighed.

Von Rossbach moved his head to look down at the woman in his arms. He stroked her hair and Sarah lifted her head to look up at him. She lowered her eyes, smiling slightly.

"Comforted?" she asked.

"Oh, yes," he said.

"Guys?" John said.

They both moved apart as though he'd thrown water on them.

"Yeah," Sarah said, nodding. "You will take Linda?" she said to von Rossbach.

"Linda?"

"The *horse,"* John explained with elaborate patience.

"Of course," Dieter said. "You two can come to my place so that we can make plans."

"I don't think so," Sarah said. "I think it's best we disappear now." She turned away. "I'll get Linda into the trailer."

He grabbed her arm and she spun, yanking her arm from his grip.

"I want to help," Dieter said, willing her to believe him. Feral as she seemed to be going that belief was going to come hard. "You can't just go off half-cocked. You need to plan this and I have the resources to help you."

"Dieter," John cut in, keeping a wary eye on both of them, "I know you mean well, but you do realize that they probably found us because of you."

Von Rossbach's head snapped around to look at him. "You do realize that don't you?"

"I told no one," Dieter insisted. "I denied everything to my colleagues. They didn't find you through me, I swear it."

Sarah and John exchanged a look, and she gave a slight jerk of her head toward the barn. John hesitated and she gave him *the look.* He rolled his eyes and moved off; after a few yards she and Dieter could hear muttering.

Now Sarah and Dieter looked at each other. She lifted her hand to brush back her hair, then dropped it when she saw the caked blood on her fingers.

"Are you *really* that naive?" Sarah asked. She put her hands on her hips. "Maybe you are. After all, you've never had to fight machines that think before." Sarah drew in a deep breath and then let it out, her eyes on the fire for a moment. "You put my name out there. They'd be watching for that." She looked up at him. "And, obviously, they can interface with other machines like no human being. Maybe this one was just sent down to check out the possibility that you *had* seen me. But it isn't going home, and that, I assure you, will alert them to our whereabouts." She held up a finger. "And let's not forget that Victor wasn't too happy with either one of us when he left Villa Hayes the other night. Who knows who he's told."

Von Rossbach drew his mouth into a tight line and, frowning, stared at the bloody dirt beneath his feet. She was probably right. Worse, he didn't know the enemy the way she did. But she had learned and so could he. He nodded once and looked at her.

"I am going to help you," he said. "And I am going with you. I have contacts that you can use and, forgive me—this isn't a criticism—I have credibility that you do not." He shook his head. "Don't throw away a good tool before you've even examined it, Sarah. I can help you." He looked toward the barn. "And him."

Sarah's expression was troubled. But all she said was, "Why don't you drive your car down to the barn so we can hitch you up." Then she turned and walked away.

He would have preferred a direct answer, but he decided to believe that she was thinking it over. By the time the trailer was hitched and the horse loaded, she would have an answer for him. *It had better be the right one,* he thought. *Because I can be just as stubborn as she is.*

"Dieter, we can't go to your *estancia,*" Sarah began after shutting Linda into the trailer.

"Sarah," he interrupted, not letting her continue.

"Of course we can't go to your place," John cut in, with the eye-rolling exasperation that only a sixteen-year-old can show for adult obtuseness. "First of all, we can't drag a whole bunch more people into this without someone getting hurt. Second, we are like, wanted fugitives, on the run again. That doesn't stop, Dieter. That just goes on and on and on. Do you really want to taint your pristine reputation by associating with us?"

"I want to help you," von Rossbach said. "You need my help. The entire world and the human race in general need my help, if what you have said is true."

"We've done okay until now," John said, sounding cocky.

"You did okay until your enemies came back and started up the Skynet project at Cyberdyne."

Dieter stared at him with no expression on his face and John shuddered at how much he looked like the enemy.

"There's a good chance that I can get you in there," Dieter said. "Their facility is on an army base, underground. And they'll have backup, Sarah, just like the last time. I can help you find those locations." He leaned in close to her. "You need me, Sarah."

She looked at him and they stared into each other's eyes for a long time. "You'd follow us if I said no, wouldn't you?" she asked.

"And I'd find you." He straightened. "I was the best the Sector had, Sarah." He held out his hands. "Use me."

She gave a single, explosive laugh. "How could any girl resist that offer?" she said.

"Mo-om!"

She held up her hand and John subsided, reluctantly.

"Look," Dieter said, "I know you can't just come over and stay in my guest room. But there's a cottage on my property that you can use. It's primitive, but it should be safe for one night. Especially since it's over a mile from the house. Tonight we can discuss our options and tomorrow we'll hit the road."

Sarah raised her brows, looked up at her house, burning merrily, glanced at John, whose arms were folded across his chest and whose frown spoke of his resistance, then smiled at Dieter.

"Sure," she said. "Sounds like a plan." She looked around, then gestured toward his Land Rover. "Just let us grab our gear and we'll go."

LOS ANGELES: THE PRESENT

Frowning, Tarissa Dyson put down the phone. She'd been disconcerted by the disconnect message she'd gotten when she called Jordan. But she was more troubled by the fact that, according to the phone company, he no longer seemed to have a number in Delaware.

Either he'd moved or he really, *really* didn't want to talk to her. *He could be using a cell phone, I suppose,* she thought. That way he could stay in touch with friends and work. *Aha!* Tarissa thought, and started dialing again. It didn't connect.

She put down the phone again and rattled her fingernails on the countertop as she thought. *Well, if there's one place on earth that I can get in touch with him sooner or later, it would be at work.* Tarissa was reluctant to do it; she thought calling someone at work, especially *Jordan's* work, was rude. *But this is kind of an unusual situation.* She tapped out the number, her mouth set.

"FBI."

"Agent Jordan Dyson, please," Tarissa said crisply.

"I'm sorry, Agent Dyson is no longer with the FBI, ma'am. Can I direct your call elsewhere?"

Tarissa found herself taking in a breath that wouldn't stop, as though some internal valve had become stuck. At last she managed to choke out a feeble, "What?"

"Can I direct your call elsewhere, ma'am?"

Tarissa thought frantically. Who had Jordan mentioned that he worked with? "Paulson!" she said after a moment's thought. "Pat Paulson." She identified herself to the secretary and in a few moments the phone was picked up.

"Paulson."

"Uh, Agent Paulson, this is Tarissa Dyson, Jordan's sister-in-law." Tarissa bit her lower lip. "This is a little embarrassing," she said with a little laugh, "but I don't have his current phone number and I was wondering if you could help me out."

Pat felt the corners of her mouth tugging down in surprise. Jordan had always made himself out to be a family man, with his nephew and sister-in-law more or less at the center of his life. Could there have been an argument? Shit. If that was the case he wouldn't thank her for telling where he was.

"Agent Paulson?" Tarissa said anxiously.

"Oh, I'm sorry. I'm just surprised . . . that you don't know . . . his number or anything." Pat winced. That was smooth.

Tarissa felt her scalp tighten in apprehension. Whatever was going on here, she didn't think she was going to like it.

"Well, he said he had a surprise for us the last time he was here," she explained. "I just need to talk to him about something and I can't find the stupid number."

Oh. Pat thought about that. Maybe Jordan just choked when it came to telling his sister-in-law that he was going to work for Cyberdyne. She could understand that. In which case he might be glad that someone else broke the news. And if he called to ream her out she could always plead innocence.

"We-el," she said, "he only left a couple of days ago and I haven't heard from him yet. Maybe you could get in touch with him through Cyberdyne."

There was a ringing silence at that and Pat winced again.

"Oh!" Tarissa said at last. It felt as though her eyebrows had disappeared into her hairline. "Well . . . that certainly is a surprise." She narrowed her eyes and forced herself to sound jaunty. "But it will be great to have him living so close by."

Paulson relaxed a little. "I think he'll like that," she said. "He's always talking about you guys."

"Well, I'll try to get in touch with him at Cyberdyne, then," Tarissa said brightly.

They said good-bye and hung up. Tarissa leaned against the counter, hugging herself as she thought about this. Miles's project. Jordan had anticipated that the Connors would show up to put a stop to it.

And he's right, she thought, rubbing the knuckles of one hand against her lower lip. She dropped the hand with a sigh. *I wish I knew where they were. I wish I could talk to them.* She didn't want to stop them from destroying Cyberdyne; she only wanted to prevent them from killing Jordan. *Who, meanwhile, will be doing his damnedest to stop them any way he can.*

She brushed back her hair. Well, she couldn't talk to the Connors. But maybe she could talk to Jordan again. Maybe even get through to him this time.

She found the Cyberdyne number and called, was transferred and transferred again until she found herself speaking to Serena's secretary.

"I'm trying to locate Jordan Dyson," Tarissa said.

"He's not here at the moment, but I can take a message for him if you like."

Damn! Well, why not? After being switched hither and yon Tarissa figured this was the best she was going to do today.

"Yes, please. Could you tell him that Tarissa asks him to please remember what she told him?"

The secretary's gossiping instincts perked up. "Certainly, Ms . . . ?"

"Dyson," Tarissa said.

"Ms. Dyson. I'll see that he gets your message, ma'am."

"Thank you." Tarissa hung up. *Maybe that'll shake him out of his huff,* she thought. Maybe not. Maybe only time would do that. *I hope not,* she thought. *I miss him already.*

CYBERDYNE: THE PRESENT

"So," Serena said, ushering Jordan into his new office, "we end the grand tour here."

"This is mine?" Jordan said.

The office was exactly the same size as Burns's, though more blandly furnished. It was located directly across the hall from hers. *Very nice,* he thought. Here at Cyberdyne, where there were no windows, status came from the size of your space and this was about as large as an office could get here.

"Mm-hm," Serena said. "For the time being we'll share my secretary, Mrs. Duprey. If it looks like that will be an unreasonable burden on her, we'll get you an assistant of your own."

"Thank you," Jordan said. He was used to sharing a secretary. "I'm sure it'll be fine."

"I'll leave you to get to work, then," Serena said. "I've posted everything we have on the Connor case onto your computer. If there's anything you need, don't hesitate to ask. I meant what I said when I told you I consider this to be top priority."

Jordan looked at the computer. "Great," he said. "I'll get right on it."

She smiled at him, a slow satisfied smile that sent a little shiver down his spine. "I can see you're eager to get to work," she said. "So I'll leave you to it." She offered her hand and he took it. "Welcome aboard, Mr. Dyson."

"Great to be here, Ms. Burns."

With a nod Serena pulled his door closed behind her and crossed the hall. She stopped at Duprey's desk and the secretary looked up at her with birdlike brightness.

"Mrs. Duprey," Serena said confidentially, "I've told Mr. Dyson that you will be acting as his administrative assistant as well as my own for the time being."

Duprey's face and posture stiffened and it amused the I-950 to realize that even a human could have read her displeasure. *Is it because of his race?* she wondered. *Or does she think he might be an unredeemed sinner?* Not that it mattered to Serena one way or the other. Perhaps she'd been too lenient with Mrs. Duprey. But the woman was a veritable fount of illicit information. *Still, maybe it's time to, as she would put it, put the fear of God into her.* After all, it wouldn't do to have her gossiping about what went on in the security office.

Serena straightened. "If that's not to your taste, Mrs. Duprey, perhaps I should have human resources"—how she loved that term—"send up a more accommodating secretary. Then you could work for someone else."

The secretary's jaw dropped.

"But I would hate to do that, Mrs. Duprey. I've come to rely on you. Your efficiency, your discretion—these are not common traits. Most of all I prize your loyalty." Serena allowed herself to look troubled. "I wish you would think about it before you decide." She smiled weakly. "I've very much enjoyed working with you."

"Of course I'll stay!" the woman said. "I've enjoyed working with you, too."

Serena smiled mistily and offered her hand, the secretary took it, and they had a special moment together. The I-950 squeezed the human's hand slightly. "Well, back to work," she said. "I'm sure Mr. Dyson won't need you to do things for him too often."

"Oh," Duprey said, rising, "I have a message for him."

"Why don't you go and give it to him," Serena suggested. "It will be a perfect opportunity to get acquainted. I'm relying on you to make him feel welcome."

"That's a good idea, Ms. Burns," the secretary said, rising. She picked up a slip of pink paper and started across the hall, then turned. "You know you can rely on me, Ms. Burns."

"I do," Serena said seriously, then entered her office, grinning as she closed the door behind her. *Ah, humans,* she thought as she started toward her desk. They provided such great comic relief.

She sat down and probed the ether, receiving no answer from her Terminator. *Meaning that he has been . . . terminated.* She felt anger spurt and suppressed it ruthlessly. Useless emotion. What was the point of anger? It interfered with clear thinking and as far as she could see had no productive results. Unless you were so primitive that you needed an un-controlled spurt of hormones for maximum fight-flight efficiency.

Obviously the Connors had been ready for trouble. Due, no doubt, to the interference of von Rossbach and Griego. True, they wouldn't have been expecting a Terminator, but they were primed for trouble. With those two, as history had proven again and again, that was all it took. She felt a prickle of disquiet. Or quantum effects could be at work, the inertia of the time-stream seeking to bend events back toward the maximum probabil-ity, the time line that had originally seen John Connor destroy Skynet.

She hit speed dial for the number that Cassetti had given her. It had amused her at first to know it belonged to a restaurant and that he was some low-status employee there. Now she was simply impatient as the phone was answered, "Mario's!" accompanied by the cacophony of a kitchen.

"Marco Cassetti," she said.

"Marco!" the man bellowed. There was a pause. "No," he said. Another pause. "He's not here," the man said. "You tell him when you see him that I'm gonna fire him if he doesn't start showing up soon." Then he hung up.

Serena sat, phone in hand, and thought. Cassetti could have instructed his friends at the restaurant to say he wasn't there. Which would mean that he must have seen or known about the Terminator's . . . termination.

She hung up the phone as it began to bleat. She could hire someone to check it out, but decided not to muddy the waters any further. After all, the restaurant man might have been telling the truth. Which would mean that the Terminator had eliminated Cassetti before it was itself destroyed.

The important thing now was that the Connors were alerted and they were coming. Soon.

She smiled. A very comprehensive set of military-history records had been among her downloads. The history of the U-boat campaigns was among them.

Submarines had been an unanswerable weapon, as long as warships tried to find *them*, hunting through the wastes of water. The ocean was too big.

The answer was to group all the merchantmen into a convoy and surround it with warships. Then the submarine had to come to *you*.

NEW YORK CITY: THE PRESENT

Ron Labane opened the envelope marked "personal and confidential" and pulled out the newspaper clipping within. He checked but found no note, and there was no return address on the envelope. With a quirk of lips and brows he shook the piece open and started to read. Soon he was chuckling richly.

The article concerned a university professor who'd been found, near-smothered by methane, tied to a stake driven into the middle of a lake of pig feces adjacent to a gigantic hog-factory farm. The good professor had conducted a study of such farms and had concluded that their impact on rural communities was minimal.

I wonder if he still feels the same way, Ron thought.

The article went on to list the complaints of the people who lived near the hog factory, including the horrible smell and the resultant drop in property values in the nearby town. A local environmentalist talked about how runoff from the lake of feces had contaminated local streams and the ponds and lakes they ran into. He also suggested that the wells that many of the area farms relied on were no longer safe.

Ron folded up the piece and put it back into its envelope. It seemed the "fab four" had taken his advice. He looked forward to their next escapade.

He rose and took the article to his secretary. "How could we get this picked up by the wire services?" he asked her.

She took the envelope from him and read its contents, then laughed out loud. "Let me take care of it," she said, her eyes dancing. "I know just who to call."

CHAPTER 19

What Dieter meant by "primitive" was a thatched-roof adobe cottage with a stamped-earth floor and a noisome pit out back sheltered by a broken-down lean-to. The well out front lacked even a bucket. Things rustled and creaked outside, and chirped and buzzed. The Chaco had a fine assortment of things that crawled, hopped, flew, and stung, and nobody here had been waging the continuous battle that was the only way to keep them out of a building. But it was dry and swept clean.

"Well," Sarah said, dropping her sleeping bag, "like you said, it will do for one night."

Dieter squatted down and lit the Coleman lamp. Light didn't make the place look more welcoming; less so, if anything. John came in with his sleeping bag and a satchel of oddments they always took camping with them. Then he went out to the vehicle to get the rest of their gear.

Dieter watched her lay out some plastic sheeting. "It's a good thing you store this stuff in your barn."

Sarah gave him a quick grin, gone so fast he thought it might have been a trick of the light.

"Never put all your eggs in one basket." She dropped her rolled-up sleeping bag onto the sheet and sat on it. "We have other stashes all over the place. I've probably forgotten where some of them are."

"Like a squirrel burying nuts," von Rossbach said.

Sarah grunted and took a sip from her canteen. "You should get Linda settled down," she said as she screwed the cap back on. "She hates being in that thing. I'm surprised she hasn't freaked out yet."

As if the horse had heard and understood, there was a squeal from inside the horse trailer and the sound of a hoof hitting the back door.

Sarah raised her brows and gestured. "There she goes."

John came in looking worried. "Dieter, I don't know if Mom's told you or not, but—"

"She did," von Rossbach said, rising. "I'm on it." He turned to Sarah. "I'll be back in one hour."

She nodded and watched him go. John spread his own plastic and sat down. He looked around uncertainly.

"Aren't there supposed to be these parasites?" he asked.

Sarah sighed and lay down on her back, her legs hooked over the sleeping bag. "Yes, there are," she said. "But why talk about the idle rich now?"

Epifanio put down his little tot of *caña* and went to help the Señor unload the horse without being asked. First because it was his job. Second, but probably more important, he wanted to find out what was going on. Where had this horse and trailer come from? Marieta had told him that she thought von Rossbach was going to visit Señora Krieger. He thought she had a horse, but she certainly didn't sell them.

It was a mare, he saw, and she was clearly unhappy. Epifanio caught the glitter of a rolling eye as she turned her head slightly. The mare's ears were back almost flat against her shapely head. She let go with a distressed little scream and his own horse, Sita, answered from the barn. That seemed to surprise and yet calm the little mare.

Von Rossbach stood with his hands on his hips and looked at her as though not certain what he should do.

"Let me start her out, señor," Epifanio offered. "I will fit better."

Which was true: he was about a third his boss's size. Also, he knew horses better, having lived and worked with them all his life. He knew right away from the way she was muscled that this little lady was a pet and not a working animal. Epifanio could almost feel sorry for her, being taken from her home at night like this. He wondered why, and whether she was now to become a cow pony.

"Her name is Linda," von Rossbach said.

Epifanio got up to her head without incident, which disposed him to like her. He rubbed her nose gently and offered her a peppermint candy he had in his pocket. She took it gratefully and rubbed her head against his chest.

"You are a fine lady, Linda," he said gently, scritching under her chin. "Let's get you into a nice stall and settled in for the night, eh?" He began easing her backward out of the trailer, petting her as he complimented her and soothed her with his voice.

Von Rossbach stood still and off to the side of the ramp so as not to startle the nervous animal. Though he was grateful for the help he was sorry that his foreman was here. His plan had been to just put Linda in the barn and leave without a word to anybody. Now there would have to be some sort of explanation.

"She is a pretty thing," Epifanio said, stroking the horse's nose. "What are we to do with her?" He looked at his boss. Surely he knew that she was too small for him to ride.

"She's just visiting," Dieter said. "If someone wants to ride her to exercise her that would be good. But all she knows is being a riding horse, she doesn't know how to work."

"Oh," said the foreman. "I'll put her to bed then." He led her off without another word. So Señora Krieger was going away; that was interesting. He wondered why, but in a relaxed way; Epifanio knew he'd find out the rest in time. Once Marieta got started, he'd probably end up knowing more than the Señor.

Von Rossbach watched him go, grateful that his foreman had decided not to chat. He quickly unhooked the trailer, and leaving it where it was, drove toward the house.

Dieter returned to them with his own camping equipment, some food for the next day, a bunch of maps, and a lot of plans.

She watched him setting up with a closed expression on her face and he began to feel impatient. Though he understood her concerns, he also knew that she should let him lead for now. How to convince her of the rightness of this was going to be . . . difficult, he could see.

"Where had you planned to go?" he asked, rolling out his sleeping bag.

Though they'd agreed to accept his help, Dieter's presence troubled Sarah. First of all, he'd always worked for the authorities—the enemy—and if push came to shove she wasn't sure which way he'd jump.

Hell, I'll bet even he's not sure what he'd do if we have to get . . . unorthodox.

Second, he was used to being in charge, but then, so was she. *I do not want a discussion about who's giving and who's taking orders every time we have to make a decision.* Especially if that decision had to be made fast. *Especially if that decision might involve damaging cops or soldiers.* Not that she'd ever intentionally killed anybody herself. *But there are times,* she thought grimly, *when you have to be mentally prepared to go to the next level.* So that left her with two questions, would he surrender control, and could he be trusted?

"Look," she said out loud, "if we let you come with us you have to understand that your whole life has changed . . ."

"Sarah," he interrupted, "after what I've seen tonight my whole life has already changed. They have to be stopped. That's the mission. The mission comes first."

Sarah studied him for a long moment. Then she pursed her lips and looked at John. He gave her no help, just looked back at her blankly.

"Actually," she said, "we have two missions. One"—she held up a finger—"and least important, try to keep Skynet from being built. Unfortunately, judging by the way it keeps coming back at us, that may be an impossible task. One thing I'm learning is that changing how things are *supposed* to be is like pushing on a rubber wall. It might take time, but it will return to its original shape, or close to it. Two," she held up a second finger, "keep John alive. This is vital. Not just because he's my son, but because he may be the only thing that saves humanity from the machines should we fail to stop Cyberdyne."

"I understand," he said.

"That means," Sarah continued, "that ultimately *I* make the final decisions on everything that we do. Can you accept that?"

"I suppose if John can, I can," he said cheerfully.

Sarah frowned at the implications of that remark and moved closer to him on hands and knees until they were almost nose to nose.

"Understand, Dieter. Everything that I have done for the last sixteen-and-then-some years has been to give John the skills to be the leader he needs to be. John is our only hope. Not me, not you—John. If necessary, we scrap the mission, go into hiding and let Judgment Day happen. I lost sight of that once," she said. "I won't do it again."

She closed her eyes and sighed heavily. "What I'm saying is, sometimes I'll let you lead and sometimes I'll ask you to follow. Those times might come up unpredictably. Can you make the jump between them?"

"Yes," he said with certainty. "I'm with you. I recognize that you're more experienced with this . . . situation than I am. I'm not such an egotist that I won't let you tell me what to do, Sarah. All I ask is that you respect my opinion."

He'd never shared leadership before, but if she was willing to be flexible, so was he.

"All right," she said. Sarah settled herself more comfortably. "So, our goal, I think we can all agree," she looked at John, who gave her a brief smile, "is to get to the U.S. and stop Cyberdyne." She turned to Dieter. "So what have you got for us?"

Dieter shook out a map.

"We drive to São Paulo in Brazil," he said. "I have a contact there who can make us forged documents. Then we fly to Colombia and from there to Grand Cayman."

"Cool!" John said eagerly. He hadn't seen the ocean in what felt like a lifetime.

Sarah looked at von Rossbach, puzzled. "O-kay," she said, "why the Caymans?"

"Hack in and trace Cyberdyne's financial records to find their remote sites," John said, surprising them both. "The ones that are used as off-site data storage for Cyberdyne's most sensitive material. Eliminate those and go for the main facility!" He and Dieter did a high five.

"But that will alert them," Sarah objected. "Whoever Skynet sent back will know immediately what we're up to. And while we can only strike these places one at a time, they must have the resources to cover all of them, as well as beefing up security at the main site. I say go for Cyberdyne immediately, then we can pick off the storage sites at our leisure."

"Surely, when the Terminator doesn't return, whoever sent it will be alerted that you're coming, yes?" Dieter asked. At her reluctant nod he continued, "So they'll be waiting for you. But they might not be protecting these storage dumps. Hit a few of those and they might begin to spread their forces thin enough to give us a better chance at the main facility. Also we can perhaps learn more about that facility from these same storage dumps, and the more we learn about that the greater the possibility of success."

Sarah leaned her chin on her fists and thought.

"Yes," she said at last. "That makes sense. Especially since the cards seem to be stacked against us this time." She sat up straight, a rueful expression on her face. "A buried facility on an army base. That'll be a pretty tough nut to crack."

"It will," von Rossbach agreed. "But let's take it one step at a time. Maybe we can hack into their system and do some damage that way, too. We'll see what we can do. I have friends in strange places, Sarah. You'll see; you'll be glad you let me tag along."

Sarah gave him a noncommittal smile and thought, *I had better be or I'll take you down in a white flash. You won't even see it coming.* She sensed a disturbing lack of conviction behind the thought. *Trouble is, I like this man.* He wasn't like the flakes, nuts, and murderous eccentrics she'd associated with in her wilder days. In fact, he was as close to being a solid citizen as a trained killer could get. *And I suspect he likes me.*

"All right," she said aloud. "I concede that it might be a good idea to eliminate these remote sites Cyberdyne probably has. Although, I'll say it now, touching Cyberdyne's computer system could lead them right to us." Sarah looked Dieter in the eye.

"But we can hack in from anywhere with a phone line. So, I repeat, why the Caymans?"

"Because I think we'll find those sites by studying Cyberdyne's financial records," Dieter explained. "Grand Cayman has over five hundred banks from all over the world. One of those is sure to handle Cyberdyne's business. Being inspected from there might be less conspicuous."

Sarah looked doubtful.

"Trust me on this, Sarah," he said.

She looked at him, considering.

"Hey guys, it's a long drive to the coast," John suddenly pointed out. "I suggest we all turn in and get some sleep. Leaving before dawn would probably be a good idea."

Sarah smiled and got up. "I'll be back," she said, and headed out toward the lean-to.

John and Dieter looked at each other.

"Don't sell my mother short, Dieter," John said. "She knows a lot about this end of things. She kept us both alive and out of jail . . . well, mostly out of jail . . . for a long time."

Von Rossbach nodded. "I know she has her own resources, John." He smiled. "This is going to be a learning experience for me."

"Not too painful, I hope," John said with a grin.

Dieter smiled slowly. "I think that will depend on your mother."

BRAZIL, ON THE ROAD: THE PRESENT

It was exhausting—over twelve hundred miles over some very rough road to São Paulo, without stopping for anything but bathroom breaks and an occasional meal. Sarah insisted that they push themselves. As far as she was concerned they were already playing catch-up.

They could see the smudge of polluted air that announced the city's presence from miles away across the pastures and coffee fields. São Paulo was an enormous city, bigger than New York, in fact, with a dirty collar of poverty around its outer edge. But when they saw its towers rising above the horizon they couldn't help but smile.

Once they entered the bustling city they searched for a mid-price hotel with parking and crashed for twelve hours straight.

Next day they shopped for business-type clothing and resort wear— nothing they would ordinarily put on—and went to visit an old acquaintance of Dieter's in the older section of town. Quiet low-slung buildings in the pastels and wrought iron that Brazilians had used to announce prosperity in the palmy days of the first coffee boom a hundred and twenty years ago.

"Gilberto," Dieter said, when a maid had shown them into a room dim and cluttered and cool, "meet my friends Suzanne and John. John, Suzanne, this is Gilberto Salbidrez, one of the best forgers in South America."

"You're too kind," Gilberto said, smiling around his cigarette. He was almost von Rossbach's height, but rail thin and wrinkled beyond his sixty years. "Come in, sit down, tell me what you need."

"What makes you think we need something?" Dieter asked, grinning.

"*Hombre!*" Gilberto said, giving von Rossbach's cheap, conservative tie a contemptuous flip. "You come to me in this ridiculous outfit and I'm supposed to think this is a social call?" He gave Sarah a wink. "Besides, the señora and I have done business before."

Sarah grinned at Dieter's well-hidden surprise.

"Hello, Señor Salbidrez," she said, holding out her hand.

"You come with a friend," he said. Taking her hand, he leaned over and kissed her cheek. "You can call me Gilberto." He turned back to von Rossbach. "So?"

"We need passports that will get us into the United States, and health certificates that say we've had all our shots—"

"And you want them the day before yesterday," Gilberto said with a weary wave of one tobacco-stained hand. "So, are you a family?"

"Better not," Sarah said. "We might need the flexibility of being strangers or business partners."

Salbidrez tugged down the corners of his mouth and shrugged. "Up to mischief, then," he said. "Okay, let's get started. I can have them for you in twenty-four hours."

"Good," von Rossbach said. "I also need someplace safe to stow my car."

Gilberto grimaced.

"Okay. I have a friend who owns a parking garage. He'll let you park it there and it will be safe." He looked up at Dieter. "But it will cost you," he warned.

Dieter snorted. "Everything costs," he said. "How much?"

"For my friend," Salbidrez shrugged, "Say a thousand a month. For me," he gave von Rossbach a straight look, "I want ten thousand each for the passports." He looked thoughtful for a moment. "Two thousand for the health certificates."

"A thousand for the health certificates," Dieter countered. "We're buying three so you'll give an old friend a discount, *sí*?" Gilberto made a pained face. "Besides, I happen to know an old friend gave you a lifetime supply of blank ones, so all you have to do is fill in the spaces."

The forger grinned and laughed until he coughed.

"What about my starving children?" he asked.

"I'll give you five thousand for the passports if they're Canadian," von Rossbach said. "And if your children are starving you should give up cane-brandy and cigarettes so you can feed them."

Gilberto chuckled, careful not to set himself coughing again.

"Five thousand isn't enough for Canadian," he said. "They're very expensive. Canadian is very hard to get. Very easy to use. Canada is respectable."

"That's why we came to you," Sarah said.

He smiled. "Well, I am the best," he said modestly. "And you want them fast, which means my other clients must wait . . . Seventy-five hundred is more in line with what a Canadian passport costs."

Dead silence met that remark and Salbidrez's eyes shifted rapidly between his three visitors. The moment stretched.

"Fifty five hundred, you said," Sarah said at last.

Gilberto winced. "You are robbing an old man," he said.

"If you weren't an old man," Dieter rumbled, "I might be insulted at how you want to rob me."

The forger took the cigarette out of his mouth and stubbed it out. "And this is a one-off job," he went on.

"You'd give a lower rate if it were six sets?" Dieter asked.

"Of course—in that case, I could come down as low as thirty-five hundred. But as it is, six thousand for one set each for each of you."

"Excellent. Two sets—thirty-five hundred each. Both Canadian, but completely different backup. Different dates, provinces, the whole thing."

The old man gave a wheezing laugh. "Ah, you want to switch once you are in the U.S.," he said. "So that your documents don't match the ones in the customs computers."

"Yes," Dieter said, conscious of thoughtful, respectful looks from John . . . and Sarah. "And you are a pirate."

"A man must try," he said and gave them all an impish grin. "So, who's first?"

"Let's go out," Dieter suggested as they stood outside Gilberto's workshop. "Paint the town red."

Sarah just looked at him. "Are you crazy?" she asked. "Under the circumstances . . ."

"The circumstances are the best reason I can think of for going a little crazy," von Rossbach said taking her arm and walked her down the street. "We may never get another chance to do this." He looked down at her. "I'm not suggesting that we shoot off guns in a public park, Sarah."

"What about John?" she said, glancing behind her at her son.

"He's eighteen," Dieter said with a shrug. "Or will be when his passport is ready." He looked over his shoulder and caught John's quick grin. "It's time he had a blowout night. We'll get a really good meal, then we'll go clubbing. How's that sound, John?"

"Cool!" the hope of the human race replied. "Like the man says, Mom, we may never get another chance."

BOGOTÁ, COLOMBIA: THE PRESENT

It had been a long flight to Bogotá and they stumbled off the plane with swollen ankles and numb butts. All they'd brought with them was carry-on luggage with a few changes of underwear and a couple of changes of clothes apiece. The high-altitude air would have been cool and refreshing if Colombia's capital hadn't been in a mountain basin that trapped the diesel fumes that came with rapid growth and no public transport.

Sarah and John had been a bit uneasy about going unarmed, but Dieter convinced them that he could get anything they needed with very little effort. For that matter, Sarah knew, so could she. So they'd left their arsenal locked in the car. If for any reason the car was investigated they'd stripped it of any identifying marks and used a false name when they brought it in to park.

Dieter spotted a restaurant up ahead as they walked through the concourse. "Wait for me there, I'll get the tickets."

Sarah nodded and asked, "Shouldn't we make hotel arrangements, or something?"

"Not a problem," von Rossbach said. "We'll be staying with someone I know. He's done money laundering for some pretty nasty characters. I've stayed with him before and I know that he'll cooperate *enthusiastically* without asking any embarrassing questions."

"Yeah," John said, "when you've got 'em by the balls their hearts and minds follow right along."

"You are wise beyond your years, John," Dieter said with a grin.

"Hey I'm old beyond my years according to my passport," John said. "That's got to have an effect."

Sarah smiled at him. "C'mon," she said nodding towards the restaurant. "Do you want us to order for you?" she asked Dieter.

He shook his head. "I don't know how long I'll be. Airport food is bad enough without being cold airport food."

He moved off and Sarah and John entered the restaurant. She watched him through the glass until he moved out of sight. This was costing a fortune and so far von Rossbach had paid for it all. She'd let him because it was easier. He seemed to want to do it and it meant that she and John weren't leaving a trail of false credit cards and counterfeit cash.

Once upon a time she wouldn't have cared, she'd have used von Rossbach as a resource right to the limit of what he'd allow, and then pushed for more without a second thought. But her years as sweet, innocent Suzanne Krieger had taken their toll. Now indebtedness made her uneasy. Besides, she was—almost—getting to like him a little. *Or at least I'm getting closer to ambivalent,* she thought wearily.

The waitress seated them, gave them menus, and left them alone. Sarah looked around, automatically checking exits, while John read the menu.

"How do we get out of here in an emergency?" she asked, mildly annoyed by his apparent obliviousness.

John pointed without looking up. Sarah turned and noted an exit she hadn't seen and turned back to him, smiling.

"You're a good teacher, Mom," he said. "Give yourself some credit."

She snorted. "Sorry. It's been a while since we were on the road like this."

"Hey, Mom, compared to the way *we've* been on the road this is first class. For starters, Dieter isn't going to fink on us to the cops, kill us for our wallets, or try to sell us both to a white slaver. I could get used to this."

"Don't," she warned. "Things could change at any second."

He made a face. "Burger," he said, closing the menu. "And fries. It's traditional."

Sarah smiled tiredly; that it was, even here. International airport food existed in a multinational Twilight Zone where difference was abolished.

"I'm going for something more substantial," she said. "Who knows when we'll eat again."

They decided to order drinks and to wait for Dieter before ordering. Sarah sipped her coffee tiredly and watched her son. John was staring off into space, chin on his hand. His index finger tapping out a beat.

Sarah smiled slowly. No doubt he was remembering a certain rather lush Brazilian girl in a painted-on red dress he'd danced with the other night. It had been at least an hour of normal adolescence. She had been, ahem, very modern in her manner, so much so that Sarah had thought she might be a pro. But the girl had devoted most of her evening to John, who clearly had no idea of the possibility.

Sarah's heart suddenly filled with remorse and she took another sip of her coffee to suppress a sigh that would have come out more of a sob. *It's so damn unfair!* she thought. *He doesn't even get to have* part *of a normal childhood.* No first girlfriend, no gentle, easy segue into an adult relationship. *Will he ever have anyone?* she wondered. *Will he ever get to rest?*

"Here he comes," John said.

Dieter entered the restaurant a moment later.

"What time does this place close?" he asked as he sat down and picked up the menu.

Sarah shrugged. The waitress came to take their order and then left them.

"The last flight is at ten," Dieter said. It was eight-thirty now. "So, if this place stays open we can have a nice leisurely meal."

"What time will we get there?" Sarah asked.

"By the time we get through customs, it will be well after midnight eastern standard," he said. "All the better for getting cooperation from my 'friend.' "

"It'll be good to stop traveling," John said. "I've got this weird feeling that I'm still moving."

GEORGETOWN, GRAND CAYMAN: THE PRESENT

Maybe it was the lateness of the hour, maybe it was the easy island way, or it might have been Gilberto's excellent workmanship, but they were waved through customs with only a few cursory questions. There were still a few cabs waiting outside despite the lateness of the hour, the cabbies leaning against their vehicles and talking in the soft Island patois beneath the dry rubbing of the palms.

Their driver dropped them off in front of a darkened modern-style house outside of Georgetown. There was a wrought-iron gate, but no lock. As he drove off, Sarah asked, "What if he's not home?"

"Then we break in," Dieter said. He hoisted his bag and headed for the house.

Sarah and John shared a look, shrugged as one, and followed him.

"Hold on, *hold on*! I'm coming already!"

Jackson Skye thundered down the stairs in his underwear, yanking on a silk bathrobe that had twisted itself into some kind of knot. It never crossed his mind that it might not be safe to pull open his front door at this time of night. Georgetown was one of the safest towns in the world. Criminals came to the Cayman Islands, but they came to do banking business, not to burgle homes in the middle of the night. In fact, they tended to be ferociously intolerant of ordinary crime. The native islanders felt the same way.

What did occur to him was that he was going to clobber the asshole who was holding down his doorbell like that.

"WHAT?" he bellowed, and then almost swallowed his tongue. "Von Rossbach," Skye said, eyeing the big man nervously. Still the same old slab of beef, no fat blurring the outline of the hard muscles. "W-what are you doing here?"

Dieter gave him an affable smile. "I've come to stay for a few days," he said, moving slowly into the foyer, and moving Jackson back, step-by-step. "I have some research to do and I can use your help."

Skye's mouth dropped open. "Naw," he said desperately. "I can't, man!"

"Shhh." Dieter raised a calming hand.

"No, seriously! Y'know how volatile the market's been lately—"

"Shhh," von Rossbach continued, smiling.

"But, Dieter, if you take me off-line to do your research I could lose *millions*!"

"Jackson"—Dieter put his hand on the man's shoulder—"you know that you can always do what you have to do. And you have to do this. We had a deal, remember?"

Skye remembered. And a deal with the devil it was turning out to be. "It's just lousy timing is all," he said sullenly.

"Hey," von Rossbach said, patting him gently, "we might find out what we want to know in the first hour. You never know. So don't have such a long face, okay?"

Jackson smiled a blatantly false smile and started to close the front door.

"Hi," John said, blocking him. He came in lugging his small suitcase and looked up at the spiral staircase, the pale tile floor with scattered Moroccan rugs, the white-painted louvered doors looking out on pool and garden. "Cool," he said, reaching out and shaking Skye's hand enthusiastically. "Nice place, man. Thanks!"

"Hi," Jackson said, looking him over and closing the door again.

"Excuse me," Sarah said, stopping the door with a firm hand.

Jackson blinked and then hastily tied his robe shut as Sarah looked him over. He glanced at von Rossbach.

"Friends of mine," Dieter said unnecessarily.

"Where's the washroom?" Sarah asked.

"Down that way, second door on the left," Skye said automatically.

"We can all have our own rooms, yes?" von Rossbach said.

"Yuh," their host agreed, somewhat bemused.

"Good. We'll turn in now, since we're all pretty tired," Dieter said. "When Sarah comes back you can show us to our rooms."

"Sure," Skye said.

"I would appreciate it if you would stay home tomorrow morning to answer any questions we might have regarding your equipment," von Rossbach said easily.

Jackson's shoulders slumped.

"Of course," he said with mock graciousness. "What kind of a host would I be if I considered my own welfare before your convenience?"

"A bad one," Dieter said, still smiling. "And I know that you would never do anything that might upset your guests. That might lead to your being off-line for more than a few days. Yes?"

"Yes," Jackson bit off.

Sarah returned, and paused, frowning at his tone of voice.

"Sorry," Skye said. He was a man who had always found it hard to be surly to an attractive woman. "It's just late and all like that."

"It is," she agreed. "And I'm sorry to have wakened you." She held out her hand and he took it. "I assure you, we wouldn't inconvenience you like this if it wasn't important."

Jackson stood a little straighter at that. "Thank you," he said, sounding honestly grateful. "I won't ask any questions, I know you can't tell me anything. But I appreciate *someone*"—he glared at von Rossbach—"tak-ing my feelings into consideration." With a smile he gestured toward the stairs. "The rooms are already made up, so all you need to do is crash. Every room has its own bath. If there's *anything* that you need or want, Sarah"—he raised her hand to his lips—"my room is the last one at the end of the hall. Here, let me get that," he said as she bent to pick up her case.

She smiled at him and followed him up the stairs, making polite replies to his small talk. John raised an eyebrow and gave Dieter a she'll-do-anything-for-the-mission look. Dieter just smiled and waved him on-ward.

"Hey, cool setup," John Connor said. "Nice. Two-gig Pents, virtual keys, mondo bandwidth . . . seriously rad, my man. I love these thin-film dis-plays, too."

"How come you never look at girls that way?" Sarah said.

"I do, Mom; just not in front of *you.*"

Dieter snorted; even if it did make him seem like an old fart, he couldn't regard computers as anything but tools.

"Anything I can get you?" Skye said, a faint touch of sarcasm in his tone.

"Sure," John said, with a charming smile, slipping a headset on and adjusting the mike. "A couple of cans of Jolt and some cookies would be cool. Thanks."

Skye turned to the stairs, muttering. This end of his house was open-plan, all pale wood and minimalist furniture looking out onto a veranda that surrounded it on three sides; the visitors had moved in chairs to give each a seat behind one of the thin-screen displays. Warm air blew in, smelling of sea salt and the dry olive scrub that covered the land beyond the pink-stuccoed garden wall, and faintly of the jasmine in pots beside the pool.

"Ah," John said, popping the top of a can of Jolt and taking a noisy sip.

"Okey-dokey." He cracked his knuckles and poised his hands, wig-gling the fingers like a 19th-century concert pianist. "Now, let's get *radi-cal.*"

Dieter smiled wryly and began. *Now, the first thing is to get into the Sector computers,* he thought. That would be easy enough—you never really retired.

Behind him he heard a combination of swift tapping and a low mur-mur, John accessing the Web by a combination of voice command and keystrokes; the thought of how much concentration that must take made the Austrian's head hurt in sympathy. Sarah was proceeding methodically, referring to a checklist beside her terminal.

"Hey, am I the world-savior hero or *what,*" John said. "Ok . . . yeah, dump-save it . . . *whoa!* Defensive worm program! Don't worry, I dodged it . . . yeah, we're positive here."

Dieter blinked at the split-screen image that came up. "Advanced Technology Systems Inc., Sacramento, California?" he said.

"Yeah, that's definitely their off-site storage," John said. "Look at the record—daily mega-dumps. Looks like a complete discrete backup twice a day, twelve and twelve."

He frowned. "The only thing that bothers me is the company name."

"Why?" his mother said, not taking her eyes from her own screen.

"I mean, *Advanced Technologies,* in *Sacramento?*"

"Coastal chauvinist," she said.

CHAPTER 20

Serena shifted minutely in her chair, slightly uncomfortable from the laparoscopic surgery her third Terminator had performed last night. Her second had found another host for a fertilized egg and so she'd had one removed and had shipped it off this morning.

This new host would not be given drugs to speed the growth of her fetus. And the clone itself would be allowed to grow more normally. For the sake of the mission, Serena wanted the first to be a well-grown child within six weeks' time. But since none of the I-950s had been pushed this hard, there was no way of telling what the ultimate product would be like. For now she had to be content with her second's assurance that the fetus appeared to be developing normally.

The I-950 was delighted to finally have that project on-line, even if it had left her a bit sore this morning. She focused her attention on Cyberdyne's CEO.

Roger Colvin sighed and dropped the report she'd given him onto the desk. He closed his eyes and massaged the bridge of his nose for a moment, then sighed again.

"Why don't you summarize for me, Ms. Burns," he suggested.

"Certainly," she said crisply. "There are some important contradictions here. When the plane was going down, the pilot, presumed to be Mary Warren, was screaming 'the engines, the engines,' but subsequent examination of the aircraft has shown no sign of engine trouble. In fact there appear to have been no mechanical problems at all. As far as the investigators could determine, the plane was in perfect operating condition."

Colvin tapped his fingers on the desk. "So," he asked, "what do you think that means."

"It means"—Serena held up one finger—"pilot error"—she held up a second—"murder-suicide"—she held up a third—"or assassination."

The CEO turned away with a pained expression. "Mary had no reason to commit suicide; she loved her life. And those were her best friends," Colvin went on. "And Mary was a *good* pilot."

"That would seem to leave assassination," Serena said calmly.

"No, it doesn't!" Colvin snapped. "It could have been wind shear or some other weird localized phenomenon."

There's been an inquiry regarding the Sacramento facility, her third

Terminator sent. It hooked her into the ongoing inquiry, and as she followed the unauthorized investigation she also followed the Terminator's trace on the line. Meanwhile she kept her features trained to the mask of an interested listener for Colvin's benefit.

"I just don't see Tricker doing something like that," Colvin said. He held out his hand in a reasoning gesture. "I mean, it makes no sense."

"It makes no sense to the average, reasonable human being," Serena said. "But I'm not altogether certain that Tricker belongs in that category."

Cayman Islands, the Terminator said. *Account of Jackson Skye, investment counselor. Such people launder money for individuals and corporations.*

Serena ordered it to trace Skye's name, to see if he had previously had contact with Connor or von Rossbach. Her tap on the *estancia*'s phone had indicated that von Rossbach had disappeared at the same time as the Connors.

The phone calls had definitely become more interesting since he'd left home—that Marieta was quite a gossip.

Jackson Skye has been investigated by the Sector; he is currently in their pay as an informer, the Terminator reported.

Serena nodded soothingly at Colvin. *Check the Sector's database; see if von Rossbach is the agent that brought him in.*

There was a brief pause. *Affirmative,* the Terminator reported.

See if the Sector has bugged his office. If so, tap in and patch it to me.

Serena shifted in her chair again. "Please don't think that I want Mary Warren to have been murdered," she insisted. "I just . . . have always found it so strange that an experienced pilot on a frequently traveled flight path should go down in what were supposed to be ideal weather conditions. And now that the investigation of the wreckage has found no sign of mechanical failure, despite all that yelling about the engines . . ." She waved her hands helplessly. "Well, I just think we'd better be more cautious than ever. That's all."

Colvin smiled ruefully.

"Well, that *is* your job," he said.

"Here," he continued. "Before I let you go I should show you this." He separated a sheet of paper from those in his out basket and handed it across the desk. "It's from Ronald Labane. Have you heard of him?"

Serena took the paper and began to read. "No," she said absently. She looked up. "Should I have?"

Colvin shrugged. "He's kind of a New Agey, environmentalist type. His book is still on the bestseller lists after I don't know how many months. Go ahead," he said with a sweep of his hand, "read his letter."

"This came in the mail?" Serena asked.

"E-mail," Colvin said. "I got it this morning."

The letter was brief, and to the point. Labane told them that he'd heard about their totally automated factory concept and listed his objections to it. He pointed out that it would, if successful, put huge numbers of people out of work. He pointed out that such people would be very angry and warned that he would do his utmost to organize them. It ended with a plea to Cyberdyne to reconsider their actions.

Serena looked up, her face grim. *I don't need this right now,* she thought.

"How, I wonder, did he hear of this," she said evenly, "when this is the first *I've* heard of it?"

Colvin cleared his throat and looked away. "We didn't tell you this, but the military absolutely *loved* the idea. We've been moving ahead on it and we've just broken ground for a munitions factory in Texas."

"So the leak could be anybody." She handed the paper back, her face stern. "In a way, I'm relieved. With so many other people in the loop, it need not represent a leak at the highest levels of Cyberdyne." *In other words, this didn't happen on my watch.* Of course, everything to do with Cyberdyne was on her watch, technically.

"I suppose not," he agreed. "But it should be looked into."

"Yes," Serena said, with a slow nod. "It should." *You humans have to be "looked into" constantly, don't you?* she thought with a flick of exasperation. "This Labane character should be looked into as well," she said aloud. "That was a threat he made against this company, and with Cyberdyne's history, that shouldn't be taken lightly. I advise you to mention this to Tricker."

Colvin shrugged, looking puzzled. "It's not like I can call him up, you know."

"Mmm," she said noncommittally. "He needs to know about this. He'd be the one to question the military types who are involved in this project." She swiveled her chair slightly. "I'm sure you'll hear from him soon. It's his job to show up when he's needed. Or not wanted," she added wickedly. "I'll look into who might have known about those plans at Cyberdyne. You'll provide me with a list of people you and Mr. Warren discussed it with?" *Since I don't know anything about that because you certainly didn't discuss it with me!*

"Of course," the CEO replied.

"Do you want me to investigate the contractors?" she asked. "Or shall we leave that to Tricker?"

Colvin thought. "It might be a good idea for you to do some preliminary checking into the company's background," he said. "I'm reluctant to step on Tricker's toes. But it's probably a good idea for us to know more about them anyway. And then, if he doesn't want to investigate, we'll have a head start."

Serena smiled and nodded. This poor little human was terrified of the government liaison. *I wonder what Tricker has on him,* she thought. Perhaps she should do something to make him as terrified of her.

"I'll be very discreet, whatever I do," Serena assured him with a smile.

There wasn't much to say after that, so they concluded their meeting quickly. Serena left annoyed, because she'd been unaware that this project had even moved forward.

The brutally honest self-evaluation that had been drilled into her from birth acknowledged that she should have been aware of what they were doing. She'd grown careless and had neglected to keep an eye on the president and CEO.

Allowing yourself to have contempt for your enemy is a betrayal of common sense, she quoted to herself. It was one of John Connor's sayings. Still, since she was the one who had given the schematics and plans to them, as well as being their head of security, they should have kept her informed.

As Serena walked back to her office, Third succeeded in connecting her to the video spy devices the Sector had installed. She watched the activity in Jackson Skye's home-based office superimposed over Cyberdyne's surroundings, waiting impatiently for the sound to come through.

The Connors and their ally had been interrupted by another man—Skye, no doubt, who seemed to be arguing with them. For this she was grateful since it allowed her time to get back to her office, where she could give this situation a bit more of her attention.

When she saw the Sector agent's face a small chill ran up her gut, and she almost missed a stride. *That face!* A quick search of passive storage . . . *Yes. That is the model for the features of the T-101A series. The originals . . .* Skynet had chosen the template from a list of antiterrorist personnel; ironic, in a way, since the Terminators were the greatest terror weapon ever developed.

The Connors and von Rossbach's efforts to get rid of the man were not proving very successful. *Good!* she thought emphatically. Why should she be the only one to suffer the consequences of someone else's self-important stupidity?

As she walked along, she booked Third on a flight to Florida, where it would pick up a short flight to the Caymans. It should be able to prevent the Connors and their ally from heading for Sacramento within eight hours.

From the way the Connors were pursuing their investigation, Serena doubted they'd be ready to leave before tomorrow. At least she hoped not. It would be better if they could be contained on the island. Once they hit the United States, they'd be much harder to track.

Finally von Rossbach ended the man's arguments by turning him around and pushing him through the office door, which he then slammed in the investment counselor's face and locked. Then he turned to the other two and brushed his hands off. They smiled.

So that's what he looks like, the I-950 thought, studying the smaller male. *Of course, he's young just now.* She'd only seen his shoulder and the top of his head before Skynet called her away. Her earlier impression had been that Connor was a slender man, but not unusually so, what humans called wiry. Right now, though, he was a skinny little thing and very unimpressive. *And that's Sarah Connor.* The woman was frowning with concentration. She was also smaller than the I-950 had imagined her.

Well, it was only natural to have imagined them bigger than life. They had, after all, and with twentieth century weapons no less, somehow defeated two Terminators. Not an easy task. But a very, very impressive accomplishment.

Serena frowned as she entered her office, locking the door behind her. Did that thought have a touch of negativity about it? The Connors weren't *that* impressive. And negativity led to defeat.

The I-950 sat behind her desk and studied them; They were trying to hack into the Sacramento database. She concentrated on the files her three enemies were working on. She allowed them to look at some administrative records and smirked at their excitement.

Then she had to move quickly to prevent John from exploiting what he'd found to locate another site. For the next hour she dueled with him, over the information she would concede as she struggled to hide anything of real worth. Sarah and von Rossbach ably assisted him and things were *almost* at the limits of her control for a while. These people were *smart!*

It was easy to forget that humans could be so dangerous. The ones she dealt with every day, with the exception of the elusive Tricker, were easy to anticipate and to deal with. Most of them were barely awake, sentient only as a matter of genetic technicalities.

The Connors and their ally were exhilarating. She would have to be careful not to give in to her currently more humanized nature and compete with them. The object was to totally defeat them, not gratify her own ego.

A part of Serena's mind reflected that it was regrettable that she had an ego at all. She'd prefer to be less annoyed by Colvin and Warren's end run around her awareness, it was distracting—and unquestionably the result of bruised ego.

But experimentation had shown that dealing successfully with humans required the Infiltrator to have one. You couldn't pretend to have something so incomprehensible. It was necessary to have actually experienced it.

True, hers was stunted next to a human's, but the damn thing had a tendency to grow if it wasn't carefully attended to. Part of the responsibilities of her computer brain was to send a prompt if the thing got out of hand. She expected to receive one momentarily.

The Connors were slowing down now, beginning to get a bit frustrated.

SERENA'S LAB: THE PRESENT

The third Terminator decanted the two who had been in the vats growing their disguise of flesh. He then set them to prepping the next pair, now mere metal skeletons, while he checked the fourth and fifth over for flaws or gaps in their newly grown skin. Finding nothing amiss, he reported a satisfactory rating to the I-950.

Acknowledged, she said. *I'm sending you to the Cayman Islands. Dress in light-colored casual clothing, wear sunglasses at all times. Pack a small bag so that you'll blend in with other travelers. Take the low-signature automatic, your passport and driver's license, and one of the copies of the special health certificate. Call a taxi to take you to the airport.* She transmitted the details on its flights. *Go to Skye's home, terminate all humans that you find there. Your primary targets are Sarah and John Connor. If they are not at Skye's home find them and terminate them.*

Understood, it acknowledged. It closed down transmission when the I-950 signaled, *Out.*

Its chores in the lab finished, Third made its way upstairs to the house. It called a cab, then dressed and packed. There was a wallet with cash and credit cards in the small safe in the home office. It removed these and the travel papers the I-950 had specified, tucking them into pockets about its person. Weapons were hidden in an access panel in the I-950's bedroom. It took the fiber-and-synthetic pistol it needed and then stood by the front door to wait for the taxi.

The cabdriver wanted to talk and the Terminator let him. It answered any questions as briefly as possible, just as the I-950 had trained it.

"It's important to at least be what humans consider polite," Serena had instructed them. "But answer as briefly as possible. Give the humans no reason to remember you particularly."

It didn't see why it couldn't solve such problems simply by terminating anyone who asked too many questions. It followed orders, of course—it just didn't understand.

So it answered the driver with yeses and no's and grunts. Soon it noticed that the driver wasn't paying attention to its answers anyway.

The airport was already coming into view.

It picked up its ticket and walked through the metal detector. When the security drone made to wave her wand over the Terminator's body, it presented its doctor's certificate claiming that several injuries had led to a degenerative bone disease that had required the replacement of most of its joints with surgical-steel replacements.

Third's neural-net processor prompted it to say something to accompany the certificate. It selected the third choice.

"Wherever you run that," it said, indicating the wand, "it's going to go off."

Third held out its arms as though cooperating anyway. The woman with the wand hesitated, then shrugged and ran the wand up and down the Terminator's body. As it kept dinging, she began to smile. Then she stopped, straightening up.

"That must have hurt," she commented as she waved him on.

"It did," Third said.

The flight wasn't full, so Third got to sit by itself. It accepted a drink but refused food. It watched the movie, a comedy, attentively. The I-950 had told them that while the situations were exaggerated they could still learn a great deal about human interaction from filmed entertainment. Any humor in the movie, if there was any, completely escaped its understanding. The actors were worse at imitating human beings than an experienced Terminator.

It thought the characters were idiots, one and all. But then, most humans were idiots. It just didn't think they were *this* stupid. Perhaps that was why this movie was considered humorous? It would ask the Infiltrator unit when it returned from its mission. The I-950 would know.

The Terminator walked through Owen Roberts International Airport on Grand Cayman, scanning the brightly clad crowd (salted with blank-faced men in suits) and its surroundings when a movement on the tarmac alerted its sensors. It stopped stock-still and looked out the large window to the ground some twenty feet below.

A boy of sixteen or so came back into view. Third could only see the back of his head, but an instantaneous comparison of the file pictures from Skye's office confirmed that this was John Connor, with a negligible error probability. It signaled the I-950.

Have arrived on Grand Cayman. Have John Connor in sight. He is at the airport, apparently readying to depart. Below, a woman wandered into sight. Beside her was a large man; another, smaller man seemed to be leading them toward an aircraft. *Sarah Connor, confirmed, Dieter von Rossbach, confirmed,* it reported.

Stop them, Serena ordered. *Terminate them, discreetly if possible. But at any cost, terminate them before they can leave the island.*

Third reached out and snagged a passing woman who looked as if she might work for the airport. It pointed to the tarmac outside. "How do I get down there?" it asked. "The quickest way."

"You have to have a ticket," the woman said, trying to pull her arm away from his grasp.

"Where do I get such a ticket," it demanded.

She winced as his grip hardened. "That's the charter airline section," she said. "Waybright Charters is just down there and to the left." She tugged and he let her go, ignoring the glare she gave him as she moved off, rubbing her arm.

Their escort led them to a small jet plane that stood baking in the Caribbean sun, its idling engines adding their bit of heat and an extra tang of burnt kerosene. He waved them aboard.

"I can just put those bags in here," he said, pointing to a bin in the wing.

"No," Dieter said. "We'll keep them with us."

The man nodded. People often were chary of letting their hand luggage out of sight on Waybright Charters. He often fantasized about what was in those bags. But at the end of the day he figured he was happier not knowing.

Sarah, John, and Dieter settled in to the comfortable gray leather seats; there was none of the elbow-to-elbow crowding of a normal commercial flight on *this* plane. Dieter nodded appreciatively. The plane was small, designed for not more than six passengers, but luxurious. The seats swiveled and there was a tiny bar/kitchen near the back, opposite the lavatory.

"Cool," John said, slapping the wide arms of his seat. "No Greyhound with wings *this* time."

The pilot came aboard, wearing some very dark aviator glasses.

"Hello, lady, gentlemen," he said. "I hear we're heading for a little airport in Corpus Christi. That so?" In answer, Sarah smiled and handed him a folded slip of paper. He took off his glasses to read it, raising his brows as he did so.

"Ol' Meh-hee-co!" he said. "Sure, I can do that. You sure of these coordinates?"

"Yes," she said. "I—"

"Hey," he said, holding up his hand and beginning to move forward to the cockpit. "I don't wanna know." He turned back with a grin. "I don't wanna know your name, I don't wanna know your fake name, I don't wanna know what you're really doing or what story you're telling. I'm paid to fly you where you wanna go and that's all I wanna do. So strap in, settle back, and enjoy your flight."

The three passengers exchanged amused glances, then obediently fastened themselves in and settled back to think their separate thoughts about the upcoming visit to the United States.

Sarah had wanted to visit one of her weapons caches in Tamaulipas, near the Texas border, so they could stock up. She had friends in a nearby town who would sell her a safe car with American plates. It would probably be easier for them to cross into the U.S. through one of the border checkpoints than through the airport anyway. The higher volume of traffic meant that if you looked right you got passed fairly quickly. And they were all experts at looking right.

The plane began to glide smoothly forward, the twin turbines emitting muffled screams.

Third walked up to the counter of Waybright Charters and said to the woman behind the counter, "Those people who just went down to the tarmac—I'm supposed to be with them. How do I get down there?"

She gave him a suspicious look. He was huge and she couldn't see his eyes through the dark glasses. His manner was brusque and his body language was vaguely threatening. All in all, he was a type that this company saw fairly often. Policy was to be absolutely noncooperative. "They didn't say anything about a fourth party," she said at last.

"I'm running late," it said. "They must have given up on me. How do I get to them?"

"I'm sorry," she said carefully, "but theirs is a private charter. I can't stop the plane for you when you aren't on their list."

"I'm supposed to be with them," Third insisted. "It's important. Sell me a ticket and hold the flight."

"I can't do that," she insisted. "They've been cleared."

Charter a plane to follow them, Serena ordered. It might not be possible, but then again, it might.

"I will hire a plane to follow them," it said. "Here is my card."

"You won't be able to follow them immediately," the woman said, frowning. "Where did you say it was that you wanted to go?"

"I have to follow the Connors and Dieter von Rossbach," it said.

The woman smirked. "I'm sorry, sir. There's been a mistake. That's not the name of the party that's leaving right now." She looked at him imperturbably and offered his card back to him.

Take off your sunglasses and look at her. Tell her you must follow the party that just left, whatever their names were. Tell her it's life-and-death. Allow her to fear it might be her life you're talking about.

It took off its glasses and stared, unblinking, at the woman. "I *must* follow them," it said. "It is a matter of life and death."

The woman found herself staring into a pair of blue eyes that didn't look human. She sucked in her breath, feeling a queasy sensation in the pit of her stomach, and the hair bristling on the back of her neck. *If I were a dog, I'd howl,* she thought; in all of her life she'd never met a gaze so terrible—terrible in its absolute lack of fury, or anger, or impatience, or *anything* human. With a dry tongue she licked her lips and felt her world narrow down to a tunnel with this terrifying man at the end of it.

"Yes, sir," she said, her voice trembling. She cut him a ticket. "You may wait in the lounge," she said. "But it will be at least an hour before your flight is cleared."

"Is there any way to hasten the process?" it asked, still staring.

"It . . . could be arranged," she said.

"Do it. Whatever it costs," Third told her.

In ten seconds she handed it a new ticket.

"Please take a seat, sir," she said. "Someone will come for you when your plane is ready."

Three took the ticket, picked up its bag, and walked over to the small but elaborate security setup. There was the usual metal-detector gate, and another, longer tunnel just beyond it. He put his bag on the belt and handed his health certificate to the guard. While the guard unfolded and read it he walked through the metal detector. It rang.

"You have metal joints?" the guard asked, looking up at the tall, apparently perfect specimen beside him.

"Yes."

The guard handed the paper to another uniformed man behind a console.

"All right," that one said. "Everything seems to be in order. If you would please continue through." The guard indicated the abbreviated white tunnel before him.

The Terminator looked at it suspiciously; there was nothing precisely like this in its files. There was no choice if it was to maintain its cover, though: it strode firmly forward. As soon as it did, Third knew it had made a mistake. The scanners were not simple X-rays; they included a highly sophisticated phased-ultrasound element.

The operator of the machine looked at his 3-D display in astonishment. He whistled, high and sharp. "Lord Jesus! That must have been one hell of a degenerative disease! Look at t'is guy, Arthur! It unbel*ie*vable, mon! Every one of his bones is metal! Even his jaw and *teeth,* for Christ's sake!"

Go! Serena commanded. *Catch them, terminate them, self-destruct rather than allow yourself to be captured by humans.*

From a standing start it took the Terminator ten seconds and twenty strides to reach forty miles an hour. It crashed into the glass wall at the back of the waiting room with enough force to shatter the high-impact safety glass and hit the ground on its feet, legs flexed, and started running after the plane that was making its final approach. Men and women working on the ground began to yell at him; some gave chase but gave up after a few strides. They looked at each other in wonder and someone called the control tower.

As the plane taxied toward the velocity that would allow it to lift from the ground, Third caught up to it. It leapt onto the wing and hung on just as the plane rose.

The plane dipped and they all brought their heads up and looked out the window.

"What the hell was that?" the pilot asked.

"Oh, my God," Sarah murmured. It felt as though every organ in her body was trying to squeeze into the same place in her middle.

"Mom," John said, his voice sounding like a warning. He felt like he'd been smacked in the center of the forehead with a tennis ball. The moment of shock before the pain hits, when you're so disoriented you're almost uncertain what's happened.

Outside, a man in sunglasses was clinging to the wing of the plane. His face in profile looked remarkably like Dieter's.

"What is it?" von Rossbach asked. He undid his seat belt and rose to cross over to their side of the aircraft.

"Sit down, please!" the pilot said.

Sarah looked out and down; they were already over the ocean. When she looked up she was staring into the Terminator's face.

"Shit!" she said, real terror in her voice.

It clung to the wing until they were airborne, then it moved, hand over hand, toward the body of the plane. Once it was close to the fuselage, Three raked its nails down the jet's metal skin. One of the I-950's improvements had been to give the Terminator titanium steel claws, hidden beneath the human-looking fingernails. Its blow to the side of the plane broke away the fragile keratin covering that disguised this asset; the bloody bits fluttered away as steel ripped beneath Three's hands.

It looked up to confront Sarah Connor's white face and considered tearing away the window plastic to get at her. Three rejected the idea. The opening was too small; it could not reach her this way. She would escape, and it would be too vulnerable. Causing a crash at this low altitude and speed also lacked sufficient probability of mission success. It began to work its way down the fuselage, one careful blow at a time.

"What the *hell* is going on out there?" the pilot asked, his voice sounding desperate.

He was still too close to the heavily trafficked airport to put the plane on autopilot so he could go back and look. The instruments didn't show any reason for those vicious thumping sounds, or that wild dip of the wing while they were taking off.

"This is Owen Roberts Control," the headphones spoke. "There is . . . there is a man clinging to the exterior of your aircraft."

"Oh, very funny," he snapped. This wasn't a frigging biplane, for God's sake. He was doing better than three hundred mph already.

Then he thought about that dip on the wing, those weird pounding sounds. "Give me clearance for an emergency landing," he said. "I'm turning back," he called to his passengers.

"NO!" his passengers shouted as one.

"John, stop him," Sarah said.

John tightened his lips, but nodded and headed forward. Sarah and Dieter looked out the window, watching the Terminator's progress.

Three clung to the side of the door frame and began to tear away the metal around the handle, careless of its flesh sheath. It would self-destruct soon anyway.

John slipped into the copilot's seat.

"Please return to the passenger cabin," the pilot said sharply. He didn't need this distraction, not with the tower giving him instructions and some maniac outside the plane. How was that even possible?

"You can't turn the plane around," John said.

The pilot looked at him. "Hey, kid, there's somebody in trouble out there. We can't just ignore him!"

"I can fly a plane," John said quietly. He held one hand up, and there was a sudden *click.* The blade of the knife looked short, but extremely sharp. "If you attempt to turn back we will kill you and I will take over. My advice is to keep to your route and let us take care of this situation. Do you understand?" he asked.

The pilot snapped a look at the kid, ready to face him down. Then something in John's eyes registered. He wasn't looking at some dumb, punk kid who didn't understand the situation. He was looking a man who meant what he said.

"Sure," he said wonderingly. "You got it."

"Good." John said. He smiled and squeezed the pilot's shoulder, then turned back to the passenger compartment.

Somehow the pilot felt better for that brief contact. Damned if he could figure out why. He licked his lips and toggled the com to talk to air traffic control.

"Seems we don't need to turn back after all, Owen Roberts. My passengers have the situation under control."

Which, from the continued pounding, they did not. But he wasn't prepared to die on behalf of someone stupid enough to hitch a ride this way no matter *what* Owen Roberts had to say.

Three peeled back the metal skin and bared the locking mechanism. Reaching into the hole, he worked it, pushing hard against the pressure of air escaping the cabin with its free hand. Simultaneously it tried to bring its foot forward, ready to step into the hatchway when it slammed open.

Oxygen masks dropped from the ceiling and dangled ignored as Dieter flung himself at the door, catching it just as the lock disengaged. He hauled it closed by main strength, bracing one foot against the frame to give himself leverage, and looked around for something to jam the mechanism.

Sarah dragged her bag close and pulled out the lid over the hidden compartment.

Outside, Three patiently worked the mechanism again.

Dieter grabbed it as he saw it begin to move and tried to hold it closed. He held the handles and twisted until lights swam before his eyes, his breath coming in sharp controlled gasps. But they turned inexorably, as though his was the strength of a child. Von Rossbach began to know real terror. This had never happened to him before.

Sarah handed something to John and he came up behind Dieter. "Let it in," John said.

"Let it!" Dieter grunted. "I can't stop it!"

"Don't let it all the way in," Sarah said quickly.

"John, this isn't a good idea," Dieter said from the corner of his mouth. "We don't have any guns."

John gave his head a little shake, frowning. "Guns wouldn't work anyway. We'll use this." He held up the lump of plastique that his mother had given him. In his other hand was the detonator.

"Oh, joy," Dieter said weakly, closing his eyes.

Taking a deep breath and a firmer grip on the hatch's handles, he allowed them to turn. Then held on with all his might as the airstream sought to tear the door from his grip.

Three grasped the inside edge of the door frame with its left hand, pushed its right arm through the opening, and began to pull up its leg.

Dieter pulled the door to, catching the Terminator's forearm in the opening.

Three wasn't worried. It had tested its strength against the humans and it had won. It angled its arm outward and the door began to open again as it pulled its leg up.

John moved forward and wrapped the plastique around the

Terminator's arm just below the elbow. He didn't want to permanently damage the door. Then he inserted the detonator and gave the cap a sharp twist.

"Fire in hole!" he shouted, and they dived for their seats and huddled behind them.

The door was flung open, crashing against the fuselage as the airstream took it.

The charge went off with a flash and a sharp bang, filling the thin air of the cabin with the smell of burnt explosive.

"What the *hell* are you people doing!" the pilot yelled frantically. "What the hell was that?"

"SHUT UP!" Sarah yelled back, her hands working the soft puttylike explosive into a long snake between her palms.

When they looked up over the chair backs the Terminator was still holding on to the door frame despite its shattered upper arm. Slowly it fitted its left leg into the opening and began hoisting itself in, fighting the wind that threatened to rip it from the plane's side.

Sarah handed John another rope of plastique and a detonator and he and Dieter dived toward the door. John distracted the Terminator while von Rossbach slid in behind it and tried to pull the door to. With one big hand grasping the door frame, he reached for the handle.

The Terminator flailed its stub of an arm at John, then suddenly slammed its shoulder into Dieter. Von Rossbach's feet slid out from under him on the carpeted deck; he went down on his hip and looked up at the machine. It reached for him with its broken arm, looked at the ruined stub, then turned once again to John.

Dieter pushed himself to his knees and once again reached for the door, staying low to avoid another body blow. He grasped the door handle just as John got close enough to the Terminator to make Sarah gasp. Bracing his leg against the door frame, Dieter reached out and caught the door with his other hand and heaved, pulling with all his strength against the force of the air, every muscle screaming.

The Terminator gained purchase and began to pull its body forward. It was slower than it should have been, as though the small explosion had thrown it partially off-line somehow. But it was still stronger than a human.

With a full-throated roar, von Rossbach pulled the door to, slamming it against the body of the Terminator. It turned its head toward the Austrian and continued to thrust its body forward as hard as it could.

John moved forward and wrapped the explosive just above the Terminator's knee and planted the detonator. He looked up at von Rossbach.

"Go!" von Rossbach told him.

Dieter could hardly let go. This monster would burst into the cabin like a shot. Von Rossbach's mind supplied an unwanted vision of the Terminator coming through the door ripping the plastique off of its leg and planting it on *his* chest. He pulled harder, gritting his teeth, until they grated, and stopped the thing's forward motion.

The charge went off after what seemed an eternity and Dieter was flung backward into the bulkhead, hard enough to knock him unconscious for a few seconds. When his blurred vision cleared he was greeted by the sight of the Terminator dangling in the open doorway, trying to angle its big body close enough to the plane to swing in through the door. Dieter found he couldn't move and all he could say was, "Unhnnn!"

"John!" Sarah said, leaping forward. She ignored the pilot's shouts as she worked the last piece of plastique between her hands.

John grabbed the door and tried to drag it away from the fuselage. The hinges grated and moved reluctantly, but it was the massive push of the air that defeated him. Sarah stopped what she was doing and leant her strength to his, pulling the door toward her with all her might.

Three watched the humans try to close the door. It saw both of its primary targets within its reach, if only it could get to them. Its left arm and leg dangled uselessly and several circuits had been fried. For the moment it had to watch them helplessly as it clung on by one hand and rapidly rerouted power.

At last it could once again move its right leg. It brought it up and hooked the door frame with its remaining foot. Then it thrust its head through the door.

Sarah and John gave a mighty heave and the door slammed onto the Terminator's head. It worked its way forward, scraping its ears off against the unyielding steel of the door and the frame. With the crisp sound of rending metal, it thrust the stump of its left arm into the gap and pulled itself farther in by pressing its chin against the door frame. Its shoulder inched forward.

Dieter staggered erect and swiped at the blood dripping from his nose, then joined them at the door, lending his weight and strength to theirs. The Terminator was stopped. For the moment.

"I want the head," John said.

The head? the pilot thought. He couldn't have heard that right.

Sarah nodded, and leaving her son and Dieter to hold the Terminator, she began to spin a rope of plastique between her hands.

"I never saw anybody work it in quite that way," Dieter said dreamily.

John looked at him, trying to see both his eyes, wondering if their friend was contused.

"It's how she works pastry," he said. "She does that to make these cinnamon thingies for Christmas."

"Cinnamon bows," Sarah said, distractedly.

She moved forward and attempted to wrap the plastique around the Terminator's neck. Three thrust its head forward and bit, its teeth flashing. Sarah jerked back with a gasp and looked into the mutilated face, with its glaring eyes.

You never get used to this, she thought, fighting back tears of frustration, her heart pounding. *No one could ever get used to this.*

She brought her hands forward and jerked back again while John and Dieter watched her. After a few more attempts Dieter reached forward and pushed up on the Terminator's forehead, lifting it back with some untapped resource of muscle power that vaguely surprised him. He almost let go when the thing's blue eyes shifted to glare at him and something within clenched and closed off his breath in sheer atavistic terror.

Sarah took advantage of the Terminator's momentary distraction to flip the rope of explosive around its throat like a neckerchief. It redoubled its efforts to sink its teeth into her as she tried to push the detonator into the soft substance.

With her lips tightly closed, Sarah took a deep breath, set the timer, and tried again. This time John lifted his hand to aid Dieter and the Terminator snapped its head up, attempting to grab him. Sarah pushed the detonator into place and then grabbed John, yanking him away.

Startled by her sudden move, Dieter pulled as hard as he could against the door, using his body as a weight. Once again he went flying as though smacked by God's pillow when the plastique blew. This time, in answer to the explosion, the Terminator's head flew into the cabin and bounced off the far wall. Bits of flesh and spatters of blood sprayed out into the cabin; not nearly as much as from a real body, but enough. Its massive body went pinwheeling through space, exploding in a magenta ball of flame just before it hit the azure blue of the water.

Dieter was slumped, once again unconscious, against the bulkhead. The door hung open.

Sarah raised her head and found herself looking into the Terminator's blue eyes. It snapped its teeth at her and wobbled on the floor, helpless to make itself move toward her.

"John?" she said, not taking her eyes off of it.

"Here, Mom," he said from beside her. He was watching the Terminator, too.

"We'd better get that door," she said.

Taking in her breath in a gasp that was too close to a sob for her liking, Sarah staggered to her feet and grabbed the door. John moved in beside her and pulled. They found that it moved better this time; at least the hinges weren't fighting them. It just wouldn't stay closed. Sarah tried to work the lock and got nowhere. Apparently something was jammed inside.

"Shit," she muttered. "I can't shut the door!" she shouted to the pilot.

"Right there," he said, a quaver in his voice. "Okay, got her on autopilot."

He came into the passenger cabin white-faced, a sort of crowbar in his hand. There was a slot in the floor into which he inserted one end, then pushed the other end into a similar slot on the door. "That's never happened before," he said weakly. "But it's good to be prepared."

He turned around to see John pick up the head. *My God,* he thought, *the kid really did want the head!*

"I'll need to make a Faraday cage for this," John said to him. "To cut it off from communicating with any of its friends. Assuming it has any. So I'm going to need some wires. Where can I take them from so I don't do serious damage to the plane?"

The pilot watched the head dangling by its hair from John's bloody hand with fascination. Then the head swung out, face forward, and clicked its teeth at him, its eyes rolling wildly.

From some place deep within, possibly the soles of his feet, the pilot felt a scream building, rushing upward until it blared out of his mouth. He leaped toward the pilot's cabin and slammed the door behind him, locking it and cowering in his seat, screaming.

Sarah tsked and looked around her, then went over to Dieter, kneeling beside him to feel his pulse. She looked up at John and smiled, giving him a reassuring nod. Peeling back one of Dieter's eyelids and then the other, she breathed a sigh of relief. The pupils were the same size. Pretty much. He should be all right.

"First the Faraday cage," she said briskly to John. "And then the pilot."

CHAPTER 21

TAMAULIPAS, MEXICO, NEAR THE TEXAS BORDER: THE PRESENT

Sarah tossed another stick of mesquite onto the fire and glanced over at John, at work on the Terminator's head in the uncertain light of a pair of Coleman lanterns. She watched him pull something out of the thing's skull with a pair of long-nosed electrician's pliers, holding it up in triumph under the brilliant desert stars.

Somewhere a coyote announced its presence to the night.

"This is a Terminator all right!" he said. "But it's primitive. Heck." He held up another bit he'd excavated. "This thing here is from a cell phone! It's nothing like Uncle Bob. Y'know? But the chip seems right."

At least it resembled the stuff he remembered seeing on Miles Dyson's computer printouts. This weird little-connected-boxes design had been all over everything. He turned it, studying it by the light of the lantern.

He'd been trying to get this thing out for the last forty-five minutes. The CPU was the first thing he'd wanted to take out. The damned Terminator seemed disinclined to stop trying to bite them all to death until he did so. Unfortunately the CPU had been buried deep underneath a solid steel cage and getting to it had been a long and nasty process.

Even knowing that the Terminator wasn't a living being, cutting into its head as it snapped its teeth and rolled its eyes at him had been pure nightmare fodder.

"And I suppose the power cell must be authentic, original equipment, too," John continued. "It sure wasn't running on a lawnmower engine! But the rest's like a cheap knockoff. Like something someone could do in a lab now. It's all a little different somehow. This thing was made out of here-and-now components, mostly. With the *essential* stuff from Skynet—from the future. It isn't Skynet's style, really."

Sarah smiled tiredly; they'd driven a long way through the desert today in the rather crappy Jeep one of her "friends" had sold them. Desert grit still made unpleasant little sounds between her back teeth, and itched in all the creases of her underwear.

"Now you're psychoanalyzing a genocidal computer?" she asked.

"What can I say—it's a long-term relationship," John pointed out. "You might say it's my mission in life. Hey! I'm supposed to be this great military leader, right? Did Napoleon's mom treat him this way?"

"She probably whacked him upside the head with a broomstick now and again. Of course, she didn't know he was going to be anything but a Corsican dropout."

"Yeah, but you do. So how 'bout a little respect?"

Sarah grinned and settled herself down, leaning her back against a rock and wiggling until the gritty desert soil felt a little more comfortable. "That thing from a cell phone," she said after a moment, "what's it do?"

"Basically it's the whole works," John said, "without the speakers."

She nodded, gazing into the fire. "So you were right to make that Faraday cage," she said grimly. "It was communicating with someone." She glanced up at him. "Any way to find out who?"

"Not without the right equipment." John's eyes grew dreamy for a moment. "Jackson Skye probably had stuff I could've used to find out."

"Hold on to it," Sarah said. "We may yet be able to find out."

"If it was communicating with someone it means there are more of them," Dieter said.

Sarah and John looked at him.

"We know," she said gently.

"The question is," John said, "another Terminator, or something else?"

"Like a T-1000?" Sarah said, her eyes distant.

John took a shaky breath.

"Yeah," he said.

"Or maybe just a better-made Terminator," she said. "If this isn't an original Skynet special, then something here is building them. It has to be. Something came back from the future, *with* the power units and CPUs. A coordinator, a manager."

"Sort of a master Terminator?" John said. He held up the board from the cell phone. "And this might have its number." He looked at his mother. "So, do we give it a call?"

A smile lifted one side of her full mouth. "Maybe, when we figure out how to get the number."

"I'm worried about the pilot," von Rossbach said suddenly.

"Don't go there, Dieter," Sarah warned. "If he's smart he'll go for therapy and within a month the doctor will have talked him into disbelieving what he saw. If he's not smart he'll take a lot of drugs or drink a lot of booze, and when they cart him off with the d.t.'s he'll have a therapist convince him it was all in his head."

"I think the second way sounds smarter," John volunteered.

His mother pointed a finger at him and he subsided, grinning.

"Thing is you can't concern yourself with him. We haven't got the time. Nobody will believe him anyway." Sarah said.

"Somebody will," Dieter warned. "Whoever is at Cyberdyne will. And they must be pretty well connected to the Web to have known we were in the Caymans."

John tapped his tweezers against the Terminator's metal skull in a hip-hop beat as he thought. "And if that's so . . ." he said, slowly, his eyes flashed up to meet his mother's.

"Then Sacramento is probably a trap," she said.

John nodded. "So? What are we gonna do?"

Sarah blew out a breath that fluttered her bangs. She shrugged.

"We go to Sacramento," Dieter said. "It's the only lead we have."

"Unfortunately," Sarah pointed out, "they know we have it."

"True," Dieter conceded. "But they don't know where we are, exactly, or when we'll arrive."

Sarah glanced at him and very consciously didn't say what she was thinking. Which was that *he* was the one who had wanted them to find the remote storage site.

Though, to be fair, she thought, *we did learn something fairly interesting. Which is that there's apparantly some sort of boss Terminator. Maybe something even smarter than Uncle Bob.* But what?

"Whoever, or *what*ever is looking for us," Dieter said, "can apparently find us very easily through the Internet. That means we can't use the credit cards or go near what might be computer-connected cameras." He stopped suddenly as though struck by an idea.

"What?" Sarah asked suspiciously.

"I was just thinking . . . Cyberdyne is on a military base. How difficult would it be for this person to get connected to an uplink and hack into the military's spy satellites?"

Sarah and John just looked at him.

"You remember how Mom said 'don't go there' a minute ago?" John asked. "Well, don't go *there* either."

Sarah shook her head. "Life used to be so much simpler," she said pushing her hair back from her face. "I liked it much better when all we had to worry about was the FBI and the CIA and Interpol and the Sector and stuff like that. Now we've apparently got a head Terminator who might be counting the number of sticks I'm putting on this fire. Well, here's one if you're up there!" She held her middle finger up to the stars. "And on that note, I'm going to try to sleep."

She pulled her blanket over her and settled down on the cheap plastic air mattress they'd bought in the village store. John looked up into the sky for a minute. Then he picked up the CPU and put it in his shirt pocket. The more suspicious looking of the Terminator's chips he gathered up and tossed into the flames. Dieter frowned, but said nothing as he watched the sparkles and flares they made in the fire.

NEW YORK CITY: THE PRESENT

Ron Labane was annoyed, glowering out his office window, fiddling with a cup of organic, peasant-grown, but cold coffee. It had been *days* and he'd yet to receive the courtesy of a reply from the CEO of Cyberdyne.

He chewed his lower lip as he worked on his press release about Cyberdyne's precious secret project. His followers would just eat this up. Secret military projects made the damn fools cream in their jeans. And since this would be just the first of many such facilities, a lot of precious manufacturing jobs would be going bye-bye forever instead of just going south. That should shake up the complacent, secure middle class. It also meant the more militant Luddites would get on board and stay the course until the issue was resolved.

He had a meeting arranged tomorrow with a group who would make the fab four look like the losers they were. This news would be at the top of the agenda. He'd received more information on the project, obviously from someone high up in the inner circle at Cyberdyne. Names, dates, places, logistics, even what had to be a general overview of the whole project.

Nice to have friends in high places, he thought smugly.

He read over what he had written.

Profit is good. Isn't it? Profit drives the economy; it's what provides jobs that allow us to have homes and buy the things that make life comfortable.

Of course, sometimes the profit motive can override common sense, or even common decency. As when medical care is denied to a patient because it might cost too much. Yes, it would save the patient, but . . . that's not really what health insurance is all about, is it? Health insurance is about profit, about dividends paid to investors. We all just think it's about our personal health.

What about when profit is so important that jobs are eliminated by the thousands?

What about a factory that's totally automated? A place that manufactures the machines it needs, repairs those machines, and sets them in motion twenty-four hours a day, seven days a week. No humans needed.

No such place exists, you say. Except perhaps in the daydreams of engineers.

Oh, really? Perhaps you should ask Cyberdyne Corporation about their plans to build such a facility for the military. Yes, it's a real project and it's due to be built . . .

To find the date Ron consulted the secret files he'd been sent. It was wonderful to stick it to a major corporation *and* the military at the same time.

He and his people would hit them seven ways to Sunday. Protests, lawsuits, and sabotage, maybe even a little bribery in the right places, maybe a few carefully placed bombs. Ron felt no guilt about moving to the next level. This thing was evil, he knew it, and it had to be stopped at any cost.

Humanity against the machines, he thought, *and their implacable masters!*

CYBERDYNE SYSTEMS: THE PRESENT

Serena read Ron Labane's article with pleasure. It was good. It might even motivate some otherwise rational humans to get involved in his cause. Labane and his ilk were the seeds from which the scientists who had created her and her siblings had sprung. It gave her what humans called a "warm fuzzy feeling" to see his progress. And encouraging humans to self-terminate was so . . . so *efficient.*

Besides, having protests and sabotage and sundry other dramas would make the president and CEO of Cyberdyne less inclined to keep her out of the loop from now on.

Serena smiled. One day she would make them very sorry that they'd tried to put one over on her. But she could wait—a lot longer than they could.

NEAR CHARON MESA, CALIFORNIA: THE PRESENT

Sarah drove with her eye on the gauges, ignoring the mesquite-and-scrub landscape that sped by in a blast of hot dry air. This Jeep was going to overheat; she knew it. They should have enough water to take care of it, but what with the Terminator and all, she felt they were operating under Murphy's Martial Law. So they'd probably blow a hose.

Still, they'd crossed into Texas and traveled through New Mexico and Arizona without raising the interest of the police. Maybe that was the problem; it had been nearly five days without any sort of incident. It was like waiting for the other shoe to drop.

She expected to come upon Enrique's small compound in a few miles. But she'd hate to have to walk there in this heat.

"Is your friend expecting you?" Dieter asked.

"My friend is always expecting somebody," she answered. "Assuming he's still there."

John looked up at that. There wasn't much in his young life that seemed eternal, but Enrique and Yolanda were two of them. What might have happened to them and their kids if they weren't there made his stomach curdle.

Don't borrow trouble, he warned himself. *Wait till you're there.*

The Jeep bounced and he almost fell off the seat.

"Yo! Mom, watch the rocks, okay?"

"You want to drive?" she snarled.

"Yeah!" John thrust his head into the front seat, grinning eagerly.

"Well, forget it," Sarah snapped.

Dieter laughed and Sarah frowned at him.

"Give the kid a chance, Sarah. He has to learn sometime," von Rossbach said.

Sarah narrowed her eyes. This part of the desert was beginning to look familiar.

"Well, not right now," she said. "I'd prefer to have a vehicle I can trust for one thing. Besides, we're here."

Von Rossbach stared at the clutter of stripped helicopter carcasses, Jeeps, and an old bus. Tumbleweeds rocked in a breeze too mild to move them. Everything else was deathly still and silent. "Nobody could possibly be living in this hole," he muttered.

"They're here," John said confidently.

Sarah drove on, saying nothing. She pulled up at the edge of the compound and got out of the Jeep slowly. She drew her pistol and looked around. Dust, weeds, and rusting wrecks. "Enrique?" she shouted.

They waited in the desert heat and silence.

"Hey!" John shouted, jumping out of the Jeep and running a few paces into the compound. "Anybody here?"

"*John?*" a disbelieving and familiar voice said. "Is that you, Big John?"

Enrique appeared from behind one of the helicopter bodies, rifle in hand. His hat was off, so they could see that his hair had receded and gone gray.

"Hey!" John said, smiling. He held out his hand and Enrique shook it. "We weren't sure you guys would be here anymore."

"Some aren't," Enrique said. "My cousin's moved to Austin. He plays a little guitar and I think he wants to be a rock star or something."

John grinned at that; he'd heard Carlos play. "Where's Yolanda?" he asked.

"Right behind you!" she said. She gave John an enthusiastic hug. As Sarah walked up she released him and reached for her. "So good to see you!" she said.

Yolanda hadn't changed at all; even her hair was the same length.

"Hey, Connor, you look like a schoolteacher," Enrique said.

"You look like a grapefruit farmer," she countered. They shook hands, laughing. Sarah's eye fell on a solid-looking little boy of about seven. "Paulo?" she asked, raising her eyebrows.

"*Sí,*" Yolanda said with motherly pride. "The last time you saw him he was just a tiny *niño.*" She ruffled his straight black hair.

Paulo ducked his head in embarrassment and cast an eye at Dieter, who stood at least a head taller than his father. Sarah took notice.

"This is Dieter von Rossbach," she said. "Dieter—Enrique, Yolanda, and Paulo."

Dieter held out his hand to Enrique, who seemed surprised and took a moment to respond. He glanced at Sarah and raised a brow.

"Later," she muttered.

"We heard a lot about you for a while," Enrique said. "Then nothing. Well, not nothing. Did you know there's a Web site with your name?"

"You're wired?" John said, surprised and delighted.

"Hey, everything up-to-the-minute with us! You know that!" Enrique said with a grin. "Don't let appearances deceive you, señor," he said to Dieter. "What you want, we got, can get, or can make." He looked at Sarah. "*Sí?*"

"*Sí,*" she confirmed. "I hate to break up our reunion with business . . ." she began.

"Oh, don't worry," he said. "Business is as welcome as company, always! What can I do for you?"

"Well, my computer needs its battery charged," John said.

"And this piece-of-shit Jeep Lupe sold me is ready to die," Sarah finished.

"Lupe, eh?" Enrique moved toward the Jeep and he started to grin. "*Ai, caramba!*" he said. "What are you doing dealing with that one, eh? You know Lupe is a capitalist at heart."

"Oh, he's got a heart now, does he?" Sarah said. "I'd never have guessed from the way he robbed me."

Enrique opened the hood and immediately started to dicker.

"Come with me, John," Yolanda said, slipping her arm through his. "I'll show you that Web site and we'll let these two hard bargainers go at it."

"Where's the tequila?" John asked.

"Ts ts ts," she shushed him. "We don't drink that anymore. I have Classic Coke, though, and Mountain Dew."

Sarah leaned over the engine, pretending she hadn't overheard. Enrique gave her a glance.

"I have a pacemaker now," he said. "So I watch what I eat and drink. Eh, we grow more stupid as we get older," he said. "Depriving ourselves of pleasure so that we can stay old longer."

Sarah laughed with him at that. She looked up at Dieter, who stood beside the jeep looking awkward.

"Would you mind taking a look at that Web site for me?" she asked him. "I'd like your opinion."

He gave her an ironic smile and followed Yolanda and John into the dilapidated school bus.

Enrique watched him go, then turned back to the engine. After a moment he glanced at Sarah. "He's different. Not so stiff like before."

Sarah's laugh was more a squawk. "You've no idea," she said fervently.

"So, how come he's 'Dieter' now and not 'Uncle Bob'?" He reached in and squeezed a hose, then gave her a significant look.

" 'Cause he's *not* Uncle Bob," Sarah said. The longer she looked at this engine the more discouraged she became. "But the resemblance is amazing, isn't it?"

He straightened up and wiping his hands on a rag looked at her askance.

"He's not the same *hombre?*"

Sarah shook her head. "They say everybody on earth has a double somewhere," she said.

Enrique shrugged. "They say bullshit a lot, too. What can you do, eh?"

Sarah laughed. "It's when I tell the truth that no one believes me."

"Maybe that's because for you the truth is always very strange." He held up his hand to forestall any protest. "About this Jeep," he said, "if it was a horse I'd put it out of its misery."

"Can you fix it?" she asked.

He looked off into the distance, then grimaced.

"You ask me can I fix it? *Sí,* I can fix anything. But with a car like this, you have to fix it every time you stop. You know?" He screwed his face up. "I got something better I can trade you for a few hundred. It's not pretty, but it will get you there and back again."

"Better let me see it," Sarah said.

He led her out into the desert and tugged a sand-colored tarpaulin off a diseased-looking Marquis. Sarah pursed her lips and walked slowly around it. The white paint had turned to chalk in places, exposing the underpainting, and the paint under that. It had a leprous look to it and rubber was dangling from the windows.

"That is one *ugly* car," she said.

"Like Lupe's Jeep would win a beauty contest?" Enrique challenged. "It's under the hood you'll see her value." He popped the hood and set it on its stick. "See?"

Sarah leaned in. She had to admit it looked a hell of a lot better than the Jeep. The hoses didn't look like they were going to melt, for one thing. And the interior looked pretty good for all its age.

"Air-conditioning?" she asked.

Enrique nodded proudly. "Works great." He held up the keys. "Want to try her?"

She snatched them out of his hand and opened the door. "Coming?" she asked.

■　■　■

Sarah leaned her elbows on the old picnic table, gazing out over the desert, watching the sun go down in opalescent fire. She let her eyes wander around the compound, resting briefly on the incongruous chain-link fence. Almost every open diamond formed by the crossing of the wires was filled with the head of a rattlesnake, jaws open as if screaming, fangs out in ferocious display.

She sighed, remembering when she'd first met Enrique and Yolanda. They were a young couple then, with only the trailer to live in. She'd been lost and thirsty and frightened, as well as big as a house with John.

They'd taken her in, fed and watered her and calmed her down, letting her stay as long as she wanted. They'd introduced her around and, in a sense, had gotten her started. Who knows how long it would have taken her to make the contacts she needed without them.

Sarah thought about the girl she'd been then. She'd led a sheltered life, protected, well fed, well cared for. Better than her son's actually. Until the night that changed her life the worst thing that had ever happened to her was her father's death from a heart attack when she was seventeen.

When she met Enrique in the desert she was still soft as a kitten, despite the loss of Kyle and the terror of being pursued by a Terminator.

Kyle, she thought wistfully, seeing his beautiful face in her mind's eye. *What a life he must have had.* And yet he'd remained a decent and gentle man. He'd touched her as though she were spun glass, impossibly delicate.

One night, she thought, not bitterly, but with an aching longing. Just one night to learn to love one another, to express that love, to conceive their son. Her throat tightened. She loved him still, and he deserved her love. *I wonder if he would love me if he could see the woman I've become.*

With an effort she pulled her mind from such maudlin thoughts. She was certainly a different woman than she'd been when she last sat here. Then she'd just met the T-1000, been saved by a Terminator, and was coming down from the drugs Silberman had pumped into her. Desperate to do *something* to stop Judgment Day. She looked at the words in the table before her, carved into the wood with a K-bar bayonet.

NO FATE.

"There's no fate but what we make for ourselves," she murmured, completing the thought. Kyle had told her that. John made him memorize it as a message to her from the future.

"That Web site is very strange," Dieter said, coming up behind her.

Sarah shifted, making a place for him on the bench.

"Why?" she asked. Sarah put her elbows on the picnic table and rested her chin on her fist, her eyes on the first faint evening stars. "What's strange about it?" She looked at him, and rubbed a finger over the time-smoothed words.

Dieter glanced at the graffiti, then swung one long leg over the bench. "Well, for one thing, whoever put it up thinks you're the victim of a government conspiracy."

Sarah laughed; it was so stupid she couldn't help it. "No kidding?" she said. "Are there UFOs?"

"How did you know?" he asked. "There seems to be a sizable group of people who imagine that the government is working with aliens to make your life difficult." Dieter hunched his shoulders, leaning his big arms on the table. "I find it disturbing that people that dumb can afford a computer."

"And they can vote!" She grinned at his expression. "Don't let it get to you. If they're busy on-line they aren't out making trouble."

"Not necessarily, Sarah. The ones that worry me are the ones who call themselves Luddites; they seem very serious. They had a private chat room, but I couldn't get into it. It seems to be by-invitation-only."

"So what are you saying? That I've got a following?"

"Just a feeling," he said. "I think somebody's manipulating these people. They attract them by using certain key words—'conspiracy,' 'aliens'—like ringing a supper bell for a dog—then direct the discussion. Whoever set up the site also set up the invitation-only chat room. It feels like they're picking and choosing individuals." He shrugged. "Big things have started from such small beginnings."

Sarah picked at a splinter on the table and thought about it. A Web site suggesting a government conspiracy would pull in a *lot* of discontented people no matter what the conspiracy was supposed to be about. *But my name on it . . .* Could that be a coincidence?

She sighed heavily. "It could be that 'master Terminator' we were talking about," she said, making air quotes. "If it exists it might just be smart enough to know that under the right circumstances humans could help it." She grimaced. "Interesting, but I don't see what we can do about it."

Sarah looked at him sidelong and watched him shrug again. She punched his arm gently and he looked at her.

"If it's some long term plan then the only thing we can hope to do is disrupt it by destroying said 'master Terminator'."

"What if there's more than one?" he asked.

Sarah rolled her eyes. "If you want a headache that badly, Dieter, just hit yourself in the head with a hammer." She stood up. "I'm going to check on John."

"Hey, sweetie," she said, coming up the steps of the bus.

He looked up from the keyboard and grinned. Sarah glanced at the arrangement he'd made on the tabletop. He'd stripped the Terminator's skull off the interior matrix, which he put in a smaller version of the Faraday cage he'd made for the whole head. The CPU was connected to Dieter's laptop by yet another jury-rigged contraption.

"How's it going?" she asked uneasily. "There's no modem . . ."

"Not as well as I'd hoped," he admitted. "In the movies they always break a code like this in a couple of hours."

"Ah, but this isn't the movies," Sarah said wisely. "Maybe you should take a break."

He shook his head. "Nah. I've got to keep banging away at this. I couldn't sleep anyway."

Wanna bet, Sarah thought. She seemed to remember sleep coming easily at sixteen, no matter what the circumstances.

"So what's the problem?" she asked.

John shrugged, drawing one corner of his mouth up sardonically.

"I dunno; maybe I'm just not cut out to be a hacker."

"My advice is to go for the simple solution," she said. "The machines probably aren't that big on innovation. Anything they used was undoubtedly based on human work. It might even be less complicated than something used for humans."

John frowned and nodded, his eyes on the screen.

"Let Dieter help you," she ordered. "He's been trained in cryptography."

John raised his head at the change in her tone.

"I'd like to see some progress on this by tomorrow morning," she said. Then she got up and walked away.

John blinked. He'd just been given a lesson, he realized. *Okay,* he thought, *so I'll get the big kraut.*

"First of all, I think we should disconnect this," Von Rossbach said. He pulled the clips off of the CPU and drew it out of its slot. "If it's functioning it might be altering any information remaining, or erasing it."

John slapped his forehead.

"Don't be hard on yourself," Dieter said. "Nobody can think of everything."

"Now here's what we're going to do." He began typing rapidly. The screen lit up and columns of numbers and symbols flowed past.

John leaned close. "What's it doing?"

"It's the latest decryption software from the Sector," Dieter said. "I've been told this is the best in the world." He gave John a look. "But then, they always say that."

The computer beeped and information began scrolling up in standard English. Dieter's face lit with surprise.

"Hey, maybe they were right!"

John leaned out the door of the bus. "Mom! Hey, Mom!"

Both Yolanda and his mother came running, both of them shushing him and making violent waving motions with their hands.

"For God's sake, John! The kids are asleep!" Sarah hissed.

"Sorry; sorry, Yolanda," he said, reducing his voice to a near whisper.

Yolanda ruffled his hair and rolled her eyes. "There's no point in whispering now, *hombre*," she said. "I'll go check on them." She cast Sarah one of those shared-between-mothers glances women do so well.

Sarah smiled and shook her head, then she approached the little table. "So what's all the excitement?"

"We cracked the code!" John said. "Well, Dieter did."

Sarah looked at him.

"The Sector did," von Rossbach said modestly. "We've got entry codes, a map of the facility—"

"Anything on this master Terminator we've been supposing," she asked.

"Uh, no. At least, not so far," Dieter said.

"There's a chance that the Terminator may have altered its memory, or erased stuff," John admitted reluctantly.

Sarah tightened her lips and put her hands on her hips. She stood in thought for a moment, then she shook her head. "We can't use this," she said bitterly. "And this . . . possible misinformation, coupled with the fact that they know we're coming, only makes me even more certain that we should go for the main facility first."

"No, Sarah. We need to know more before we can attack there." Dieter's voice held absolute conviction. "Nothing has really changed here," he insisted. "I still believe our best chance of succeeding with Cyberdyne lies in the Sacramento facility."

"And I still believe that going there would be a mistake," she said. "My gut tells me it would be a wrong choice."

"Sarah, we're not ready," Dieter said quietly. "We need the information that the Sacramento facility holds."

"Need I remind you that they *are* ready," she said through clenched teeth.

"But we know that!" John said.

Sarah rubbed her face, then slowly pulled her hands down and away. "So what you're saying is that we know that they know that we know, and that's supposed to make some kind of a difference?"

"Yeah, 'cause they *don't* know that we know," John said. "We only think that they know that we know. But do they?"

Sarah glared at Dieter.

"Don't look at me," he said. "I lost you the first time around. *My* argument is that Sacramento is the only place where we might be able to obtain entry codes and a map of the main facility. You know we'll need that. And we don't dare go on-line looking again.

"Besides, their main facility is on a *military base.* At the very least we need to know which one! Or were you planning to just hit them at random, hoping you'd get the right one the first time out."

Sarah blew out her breath and paced two steps one way, two the other, then stopped, her lips pressed into a thin line. "All right," she said reluctantly. Her eyes snapped toward John. "But *you* are staying here."

"Mom!"

Dieter nodded. "Fine by me."

"Well, it's not fine by me!" John protested.

"My mind is made up, John," his mother said.

"Mom, if you keep me from taking risks I'm never going to learn anything and I'm never going to lead anyone! This is my fight, too." He drew himself up. "And I *am* going."

"It's too big a risk!" Sarah insisted.

They looked at each other and said a great deal with their eyes.

"I think it's a bigger risk to leave me here." John shook his head. "You can't protect me forever, Mom. Skynet has to be stopped, and even if I am a kid, I have to try to stop it, too."

He startled her by pulling her into a hug and by doing so once again reminded her of how tall he'd grown. Sarah leaned her head against his shoulder and hugged him back. She could put her arms around him twice, he was so adolescent thin. Sarah let out her breath, and the last precious thread of her dream of a peaceful life for him slipped away in a long sigh. She pushed back and looked him in the eye, then she nodded once and released him.

"I want to go on record as saying I don't like this." Sarah muttered.

"We'd better get some sleep, then," Dieter interrupted, rising. "We leave at dawn."

CHAPTER 22

Serena frowned at the newly decanted pair of Terminators standing dripping on her improvised laboratory floor, amid the musky smells of the nutrient bath and the scent of damp concrete. Because she had needed them so quickly she'd put some of the tissue accelerant into their nutrient baths. *Perhaps a little too much.* They looked like weather-beaten men in their mid to late thirties. But they'd come out with full heads of hair and beards and a full crop of body hair, which was a convenience.

She walked around the two. No gaps, no flaws. But something niggled at her. *I've forgotten something,* the I-950 thought. As she came around to the front again Serena saw it immediately. They were identical. She gave an exasperated hiss.

This is what comes from having too many balls in the air, she thought. It was necessary to assign them both to the Sacramento facility and they were going to draw attention with their looks. *I suppose they could be twins.* No. Maybe brothers or cousins, but twins would cause too much comment.

Immediately she began planning what to do to differentiate them from one another. One would shave his head, the other his beard, and she'd apply a different hair color to the bald one's mustache. A Fu Manchu, she thought. She'd trim and color the eyebrows, too. *Some sort of stain to the skin to mimic a darker coloration should also help.*

The I-950 viewed the mock-up the computer part of her brain supplied with satisfaction. Then she applied dark glasses to one and half tints to the other. It would do. Especially if they weren't constantly lined up beside each other.

The next pair will look different from the get-go, she vowed. It wouldn't be hard, a few minor adjustments to the cartilage matrixes and different hair colors. She was pretty much stuck with the same bone structure. *But there's a lot you can do with that.* If you were smart enough to think of it first.

She relayed instructions to the two. After they were finished she'd set them to watching several talk and game shows that she'd recorded; then they would listen to a half-dozen radio shows of the same type. That should give them some idea of how ordinary people spoke and their body language. She'd already downloaded maps of California and information about the Sacramento target facility as well as a driving program.

Before doing their homework, however, Six and Seven started on the cosmetic adjustments she'd designed. Pity there wasn't time enough for corrective surgery.

Four she was sending to Two in the outback cabin where her own replacement was breeding. It would be taking the rest of the CPU and energy-cell packets with it. *With the way I'm going through Terminators, it might be best to leave a few in reserve for Serena Two,* she thought.

If it all worked out, the Connors and their allies destroyed and Cyberdyne safe, then she would probably keep the second fetus and abort the first as potentially unstable. If things went horribly wrong, she'd done her best to cover any potential outcome.

Five was young looking enough that it wasn't absolutely identical to the other Terminators; it just looked amazingly like them. Instinct prompted her to send it to Sacramento as well. There were probably cosmetic things she could do to it to further differentiate it from its cohorts.

The I-950 frowned. She could be giving the Connors more credit than they deserved here. Sending three Terminators, even this homegrown variety, after two humans was . . . *embarrassing.* Yes, perhaps she'd keep it with her at Cyberdyne.

Satisfied with her decisions, Serena closed her eyes and sat back in her chair. As the two Terminators worked on their hair and eyebrows, she sorted through the day's downloaded data. Still nothing from the Connors or their ally. They were definitely avoiding the Internet. Well, if they weren't updating her on their whereabouts and interests at least she'd deprived them of an important tool.

The last report she'd received from Three indicated that it had been captured. Serena had come as close as she ever had in her life to genuine rage. How had humans *captured* her Terminator? Destroyed, she could understand, all they'd have to do was knock it off the plane somehow. But captured?

True, Three wasn't one of Skynet's best. But it was a damn sight better than any three humans, especially when one was a smallish woman and another barely more than a child. Or it should have been.

Making the best of the situation, the I-950 had ordered it to erase certain portions of memory while she planted other information. Whether or not the Connors would fall for the false information remained to be seen. But they'd seemed dead set on attacking the Sacramento facility. *One can only hope that they'll remain stubborn about it.*

She wanted to go there herself. Very, very much. It would be exciting to pit herself against Skynet's two greatest enemies face to face. Serena imagined herself crushing John Connor's skull between her hands. Then realized she was smiling and smoothed her face to blankness.

Daydreaming. That was the sort of thing a human would do. She ardently wished for the stabilizing influence of Skynet, instead of the silence in her mind. *Another human response,* she thought disparagingly.

With an effort she pulled her thoughts away from that realization and the feelings that accompanied it. It was irrelevant. What was important was killing or capturing the Connors. Even more vital was defending Skynet from them. Which she would do to the last drop of blood in her body. She would not fail. Serena opened her eyes and watched the two Terminators work. *We will not fail.*

In the end, a day later, she decided to include the younger-looking Five. Serena gave him a haircut so distracting she was certain no adult human would be able to take their eyes off of it long enough to notice its resemblance to the others. It was an upright Mohawk roach dyed brilliant scarlet with green bars, and tattoos on the shaved sides of his head. A pair of tiny round sunglasses that made its face look wider completed the illusion.

The humans in the Sacramento facility might not like its looks, but since she'd sent it, they'd just have to rise above their feelings. One corner of her mouth lifted in satisfaction at the thought.

She ordered it to slouch and it looked like it was melting, its shoulders collapsing onto its pelvis in a move that even a human contortionist couldn't manage.

"Like this," the I-950 said, throwing out a hip and dropping one shoulder.

It imitated her perfectly.

"Now walk like this." Serena moved her shoulders as she walked, pushing her pelvis just slightly forward of them in a sort of James Dean dawdle. She looked astonishingly masculine. The Terminator duplicated her swagger.

She had him walk for her, adding little bits of business and then subtracting most of them. The others she left to themselves. "All right," the I-950 said, not satisfied, but resigned. She'd done all she could for now. "Get dressed. We leave in ten minutes."

CYBERDYNE SYSTEMS: THE PRESENT

"Jordan?" Serena's voice came smooth as ice cream from his intercom.

"Yes, Serena," he answered, laying down the report he'd been reading.

"Could you come to my office, please? I think I have something for you."

"On my way," he answered.

Jordan stood and slipped his arms into his suit jacket. When his boss said she thought she had something, she probably did.

He still couldn't get over how incredibly *good* her sources were. He'd taken a sneak peek at her personnel records and her work experience sure didn't explain it. If it was life experience that gave her the edge, she must have been one wild kid; because she was a lot younger than he was and his own sources were fewer and far less trustworthy.

Of course she was also damned smart. You could almost *feel* her mind going in a dozen different directions when you were with her. It was disconcerting. And she had a knowing air about her, as though she found the scientists she was guarding rather quaint as they groped their way toward things she already knew.

He nodded to Mrs. Duprey, whom he had discovered was yet another of Burns's infallible sources. She smiled at him as he tapped the door and entered to Serena's "Come in."

"Hello, Jordan," she said, smiling.

Three men seated on the couch rose as one. He glanced at them, then Serena called his attention back to herself.

"I need you to take a short trip for us," she said, her eyes bright with excitement. "There have been indications that the Connors are planning an attack on the Sacramento facility."

Jordan went still.

"Sacramento," he said after a moment. "Why Sacramento?"

Burns shrugged one shoulder.

"Apparently someone told them about it." She smiled. "Or maybe because Sacramento's a civilian facility. Who knows?"

Jordan's mind flew to Tarissa. Had she been in touch with the Connors? *Could it have been her?* It could well have been if she'd *had* the information. And it was perfectly possible that she did.

"When do I leave?" he asked.

"Now," Serena said with a smile. "I've arranged for accommodation for you in the Holiday Inn there." Her lips quirked and she said, "It's not luxury, but then, it *is* Sacramento."

He grinned in response.

"I'm also lending you some manpower." Serena gestured toward the three tall men standing in front of her couch. "Tom Gallagher, Dick Lewis, and Bob Harris."

The men nodded together, so Jordan couldn't tell who belonged to which name. He guessed they probably went left to right. As he looked at them he couldn't help but think of the ancient clay warriors who guarded the tomb of China's first emperor. The same bodies, lined up in the same postures, with different heads attached.

"Do you need to go home and pack a bag?" Serena asked.

"No," Jordan said. "I've got some things in my office."

It was an old habit he'd developed in the Bureau and it had saved him a lot of time and trouble over the years. He'd decided to continue it here until he knew just what this job entailed.

"Good," she said.

She handed him a folder, which on examination proved to contain addresses and phone numbers for the hotel and storage site as well as directions to both places.

"Let me know when you arrive," she said. She touched him lightly on the arm. "I wish I could tell you more than 'I think they're coming,' but right now that's all I've got. If anything else comes down the pipe I'll call you immediately."

"Okay," he said. He looked at the three men. "I guess you guys ride with me."

They nodded in unison. He smiled, a little nervously. *These guys are weird,* he thought. Formidable enough, certainly—they bulged with muscle, and they moved well despite their massive size—but weird. And they were all ironed, with shoulder holsters under a baggy sweatsuit jacket, a suit, and a leather affair with chains.

Stop echoing each other's movements, Serena sent. *Remember you're supposed to be individuals.* She almost sighed in exasperation as their heads turned toward her as one.

"Okay, guys, good luck," she said aloud.

The I-950 shut the door behind her minions with something like resignation. It was pretty much out of her hands now; what would be, would be. *I guess I'll have to be grateful that Dyson can't suspect them of being Terminators—because Terminators don't exist.*

She smiled. Being a figment of a deranged imagination made it *so* much easier to hide. Humans censored their own perceptions for you.

They didn't talk. Jordan had tried a few questions to loosen things up and they had answered, but as tersely as possible. *They weren't even personal questions for cryin' out loud.*

They were so quiet that he could almost forget they were there. Except for the way they moved their heads in constant overlapping arcs. They looked like a trio of lighthouses inexplicably built on the same promontory. Their bodies were so still that they might have been paralyzed from the neck down; no scratches, no twitches, no shifting. After a short while their constant head motion combined with their dead silence began to wear on him.

"Are you even breathing?" he said to the one beside him. *Bob,* he thought.

Seven consulted a subroutine in charge of imitating respiratory function. It appeared to be working at optimum; visual observation confirmed the monitor data.

"Yes," it said.

Jordan glanced at him. *Just yes?* he thought. What was their damn problem? Were they having a fight or something? Was this some sort of group sulk he'd walked into? *O-kay, that's about enough of this shit!*

"Look," he said aloud, and three heads turned, three pairs of eyes aimed at him like howitzers. Jordan's mouth twitched and he frowned. *Man! These boys have some attitude!* "I don't know if Ms. Burns briefed you on Sarah Connor, so I don't know if you're aware of what a tough, well-trained customer she is."

"We know about Sarah Connor," Bob said.

"Good!" Jordan said. *Cause I sure as hell wouldn't want to bore you gentlemen by repeating anything you've already heard!* "But you see, the problem is, I don't know what you know and I don't know anything about you three guys. And since we might be facing some pretty dicey situations together, I'd like to know a little bit about you. Okay?"

Bob looked at him. Jordan glanced in the rearview mirror. Tom and Dick looked at him. Nobody spoke.

"Don't all jump in at once," he said sarcastically. "Would anybody like to tell me how long you've been with Cyberdyne, or what your training is, or why I should have you as my backup team?"

"I have a headache," they all said at once. Then they returned to their lighthouse imitation. As one.

Then it hit him. Burns had introduced them as Tom, Dick, and . . . Harris. Was that some sort of joke? Had she hired some kind of freelance hit squad to take out the Connors? *Could she be a sociopath?* he wondered.

Not good, he thought. *Not good at all.* He could be wrong, he could be making mountains out of molehills, but these men were not normal. He knew nothing about them except their names and the fact that they were carrying Cyberdyne rent-a-cop ID and had licenses for the guns—Israeli Desert Eagle .50-calibers, at that, hand cannon. Usually he despised anyone who carried the things; the engineering was excellent—the Israelis were the world's best practical weaponeers—but the caliber was to big for accuracy, the sort of gun macho blowhards with little tiny dicks bought because they thought it made them baaaad. *These* gorillas looked as if they could actually shoot the damned things.

ROY'S DINER, JUST OUTSIDE SACRAMENTO: THE PRESENT

"Hey, something occurred to me," John said, pushing aside the second-rate huevos rancheros.

Dieter and his mother had been ignoring each other studiously; John hid his smile at the obvious electricity between them. *About time Mom found someone,* he thought. *I've got a good feeling about this guy. If a human could be Uncle Bob, Dieter would be it.* They probably thought it was a Big Secret, even from each other. From the smile on her tired face, even the *waitress* here was picking it up.

Now they looked at him. He unfolded his laptop, fingers flicking over the keyboard and trackpad, then swiveled it around.

"You know, one thing always bothered me. About this time-travel shit, the war against the machines, all that stuff."

"One thing?" Dieter said, raising an eyebrow.

"Well, a lot of stuff. But one thing that my . . . dad . . . told Mom. You know, those plasma weapons he wished he had? The ones that fried Terminators good?"

Sarah nodded, a brief flicker of sadness moving like a wave across the tight-held tension of her face at the mention of Kyle. "Yes?" she said.

"Well, when did they get *invented*? Like, originally Judgment Day was supposed to have happened by now."

Dieter frowned. "I hadn't thought," he said. "I just assumed that the future would have more formidable weaponry."

"Maybe Skynet invented them?" Sarah said, stirring the remains of her limp bacon around the plate with her fork.

"Maybe," John said. "But it's awfully advanced stuff, even so. Look at what I downloaded from the Terminator's memory—here's a schematic for a . . ." he pointed to the text below the diagram: " 'Phased plasma rifle in the forty-kilowatt range.' Energy storage cell, perfect dielectric—this is a Buck Rogers in the 25th century ain't-no-doubt-'bout-it *blaster,* man."

"Yes?" Dieter said.

"Well, it occurs to me—this information traveled back from the future, right? And we figure some sort of super-Terminator is watching over the . . . heck, the birth of Skynet at Cyberdyne, right?"

The older heads nodded. "So," John went on triumphantly, taking a bite out of a piece of leathery toast spread with pseudo butter. "I figure the information came back *with* the Terminators. Like, *nobody* invented it; it's in Skynet's memory because Skynet-in-the-future sent it back, and Skynet-in-the-future has it 'cause it was there because—"

"My head hurts," Sarah said plaintively. "I need more coffee."

They fell silent as the waitress came over with a pot in each hand, regular and decaf.

"Time to go," John said at last. "Let's get *radical.*"

SACRAMENTO: THE PRESENT

"Advanced Technology Systems," John said. "Or butt-ugly Bauhaus Office Building."

Dieter snorted. "Would you prefer fake gingerbread?" he asked softly. Then, his voice all business: "Go."

Sarah Connor crossed the street, looking as casual as a woman carrying a raincoat in a California summer could look. The bored rent-a-cop sitting at the semicircular security desk in the faux-marble lobby looked up politely as she approached.

The smile turned gelid as her combat shotgun came out from under the coat. "Hands where I can see them. Scoot back—yeah, right back from the alarm pedal you were about to step on, asshole. Do it *now!*"

She sat on the curved surface of the desktop and swung her legs to the other side, then held the shotgun one-handed as she pulled a roll of heavy duct tape out of the pocket of her khaki hiking pants.

"Lie down," she said as she stripped a length off with her teeth. "Time for a nap."

"Convenient," Dieter von Rossbach said as he put the bolt cutters against the pipe-enclosed conduit that ran down the aluminum siding of the building facing the alleyway.

"Welcome to California, where everything's aboveboard," John said. He turned his head as a shower of sparks spat out of the severed cables. Inside, the building would be dark except for a few emergency lights . . . and the phones would be cut off, and the datalink to the computers that handled Cyberdyne's storage. Not that it would matter much. There wasn't supposed to be anybody in the building this early except for the security staff.

"Go," he said, clipping the leads from his laptop's (highly modified) modem onto the bare wires of the exposed telephone line.

His fingers danced over the keyboard, dumping Cyberdyne's security codes and a set of very pointed commands into the machine's idiot-savant brain.

Dieter picked up the heavy duffel bag and slung it over his back, reached up, and began to haul his massive body up the pipe conduit hand over hand. At the second floor he swung out and kicked at a window. It was tough glass, and not meant to be opened; the impact thudded back into his torso, with a twinge that reminded him he'd never see forty again. A second kick, and the window frame and the shattered glass it had held punched into the corridor. Dieter swung through, the Heckler & Koch submachine gun in his massive fist probing about as if it were a toy pistol.

"Clear," he said, looking down at John.

The boy—young man, he reminded himself, remembering the Terminator on the plane—grinned up and gave him a thumbs-up.

"We've got to get into the office," John said. "There's a physical barrier, like I thought. But it should be pretty straightforward from there."

"All right," Dieter said, lowering a rope.

It's a good thing the Connor's aren't really *terrorists. They'd have given the Sector a run for its money.*

John swarmed up with a loose-limbed gracefulness. He handed Dieter the laptop, which he shoved into the knapsack slung across his shoulder and chest, and they moved down the corridor cautiously.

"Front's secured," Sarah Connor called from the stairwell. "We'll cover John from both ends of the corridor while he works on the lock."

John grinned again as he worked on the e-lock of a steel-slab door labeled ADVANCED TECHNOLOGY SYSTEMS.

"Insert stolen identity card here, trigger subroutine . . . there we go!"

Dieter had never seen a man move as fast as John did, when the door swung open and a massive figure who might have been Dieter—Dieter with a bald head and a Fu Manchu mustache—stepped through.

The younger Connor dove aside, his hand coming up with a weapon like a stubby shotgun; the Austrian knew it was a grenade launcher. It flashed with a hollow *tchooonk!,* but not before the big automatic in the Terminator's hand barked. The leopard grace of John's leap turned into a crumpled fall, one hand going to his side.

Things happened very rapidly after that. Dieter flung himself backward, emptying the full thirty-five-round clip of his machine pistol into the Terminator's chest and stomach. It staggered, turned, fired. The bullet struck close enough to Dieter's head to send chips of wallboard flying into his eyes; he rolled backward, blinking and shaking his head frantically as he slapped another magazine into the weapon, Sarah's shotgun boomed behind him. . . .

And two more Terminators came out of the office, guns extended, taking the heavy recoil of the .50-caliber automatics as if they were children's water pistols.

All three turned toward John. Dieter braced himself to hurl his own body between the young man and death, to give him a few seconds' armor. Behind him he heard Sarah's incredulous scream.

Another man came out of the office, a tall slim black man with a Glock in his hand. "Are you insane?" he shouted at the Terminator in the lead, forcing himself between the killer machine and the wounded human. "Get them!" he snapped. "I'll look after the prisoner. Now!"

He bent over John. The Terminators . . . froze. Motionless, their eyes on the black man, their guns halted in mid-arc.

A lifetime of confronting merciless necessity—and making the decisions he had to, had trained Dieter as much as the academies and courses. He dove from the concealing shelter of the office doorway and into the stairwell, scooping Sarah up as he passed and plunged downward to the lobby.

Dieter dragged her to the car and pushed her into the passenger seat. He pulled the seat belt across her body and strapped her in, then slammed the door and ran around to the driver's side.

Sarah closed her eyes and clung to the armrests, breathing through her teeth in harsh, tearing gasps as she tried to get her sobbing under control. Her throat felt as though she'd swallowed a sharp stone and after a moment she could neither indulge in the relief of weeping nor stop the pain.

When she opened her eyes she could see clearly, no tears obscured the road from view. Sarah concentrated on her breathing, on calming herself, on tearing her mind away from the awful repeated image of her son falling and the blood . . . *On to the next thing,* she ordered herself. *What comes next?*

"We have to destroy Cyberdyne's main facility, *now!*" she said to Dieter. Her voice was thick, and tense, but under the circumstances it sounded amazingly calm.

Von Rossbach's jaw worked. It would almost have felt better to have her throwing accusations at him. He glanced at her, then looked back at the road.

"I have no desire to commit suicide, Sarah," he said firmly. "If we're going for Cyberdyne I'll need a day, at least, to set it up. We still need to find out exactly where it is."

What do I need him for? Sarah wondered numbly, staring straight ahead. *Listening to him has screwed this up from the get-go.* If she was genuinely paranoid, as she'd been diagnosed, she'd suspect von Rossbach of being sent by Skynet.

But she couldn't blame him for this mess. She'd gone along with every suggestion, allowing herself to be persuaded against her better judgment. *There's nobody to blame for that except myself,* she thought.

Her eyes slid sideways, regarding the man beside her. He might yet be useful. She could scarcely walk onto Cyberdyne property all by herself.

Slowly she dragged herself back up onto her metaphorical feet. The wound might feel mortal, but she wasn't close to dead yet. Something those bastards at Cyberdyne were going to learn to their sorrow. Sarah Connor was a long way from defeated.

CHAPTER 23

As the lights went out Jordan knew that—once again—Serena's info had been good. His mouth began to go dry and his hand automatically went to the Glock holstered under his armpit, excitement pumping into his blood, and driving out the drowsy boredom of the stuffy, silent suite of offices.

Ideally he wouldn't have to use the gun; so far he never had. *But things are rarely ideal for the good guys when they're dealing with Sarah Connor.*

The Three Stooges stood around like furniture. They didn't move, they didn't talk. They watched the door. Occasionally, as if making a concession, they blinked.

Never thought I'd miss their scanning the horizon, Jordan thought. *They were downright lively then.*

The office had only one unblocked window, which was in the president's office at the back of the building. Feeling a need to get away from the creeps, Jordan decided to check it out.

They're just as likely to come down from the roof as up the stairs, he reasoned. In fact that's what he would probably do. Not that he'd ever gone in for that rah-rah commando stuff that some agents loved. He suspected that Sarah Connor did.

They'd sent the few employees there home and the dark office was full of suspicious shadows cast by the emergency lights and eerily quiet as he moved through it. Already the air seemed to be going stale. A rectangle of gray light shone through the frosted glass in the president's door and brightened the area around it slightly.

Jordan listened, then quickly opened the door and stood back, heart pounding, even though he'd really expected the room to be empty.

It was. He moved to the window, and standing back out of sight, studied the parking lot below. It, too, was empty.

C'mon, c'mon, he thought. *Where the hell are you?* He moved to the other side of the window and checked out the lot from that angle. Still nothing. With a sigh he started back toward the front office.

A flash and the percussive burst of a grenade followed by the sudden sharp pops of gunfire brought him up to a run. The front office had been miraculously spared—except for the receptionist's heavy desk, which was scrap. But there was no fire and his backup were all on their feet and heading through the door.

A sensation like a bolt of electricity shot through him when he saw a piece of shrapnel sticking out of the back of Lewis's naked head. Jordan fumbled a step at the sight. The three moved out into the corridor single file, then, as one, they each brought up their guns and fired. More gunfire met theirs in the hall. There was the sound of a machine pistol and a shotgun's heavy thudding boom, and the slight sharp nose-crinkling smell of burnt nitro powder.

Jordan sped up. He reached the door just in time to see the three of them aim at a boy collapsed on the floor.

"Are you insane?" Jordan shouted. He pushed his way between Lewis and the kid on the floor. "Get them," he ordered, pointing toward the stairway. "I'll take care of the prisoner."

Jordan felt the hairs rise on the back of his neck as the three froze. One he could take, but not three. If they decided to take him out—and it sure looked like they were thinking about it—there wasn't a damn thing he could do to stop them.

Then they turned and jogged down the hallway without a backward glance. The piece of shrapnel in Lewis's scalp came loose and hit the floor with a tiny *ping!* It wasn't until then that Jordan realized that Lewis's whole front had been a mass of blood, his shirt hanging in patches where it hadn't been pounded into the raw meat of his chest. Which meant that Lewis ought to be screaming, or possibly dying of shock and blood-loss. . . .

Jordan put the sight firmly from his mind and knelt beside the boy; Lewis couldn't be that badly hurt, or he wouldn't be moving so well. This had to be John Connor—her son. The boy who was supposed to save humankind from the machines.

The kid had crashed headfirst into the wall; the plasterboard was dented and there was blood in his hair and on the floor when Jordan turned him over. There was a wound in his shoulder, too.

No time for that, Jordan told himself. He hoisted the boy up and pulled him onto his shoulders in a fireman's carry. Then he headed for the back stairway. He didn't know just what was going on with those three, but he had no intention of letting them near John Connor if he could help it. He was—had been—FBI, not part of some cowboy kill-for-hire outfit.

As he came out into the parking lot he fumbled one-handed for his keys and hit the button on the key ring that unlocked the doors. He opened the back door and awkwardly laid the boy down on the backseat. He was pushing the kid's legs inside when Bob Harris came around the corner and froze.

Jordan jumped into the car and rolled himself over the seat into the driver's side. With a shaking hand he jammed the key into the ignition, thrilled that it was the right key, started the car, and backed up. Then he peeled rubber as he sped into the street, leaving skid marks and a low plume of black smoke behind him. The back door slammed shut and the kid half fell off the seat behind him. *Shit!* Jordan thought. *I should have just put him on the floor in the first place.*

He pressed his foot onto the accelerator and ignored everything he knew about responsible driving. Bob's big hand hit the fender with an audible thump. Dyson jumped and looked in the rearview mirror. His erstwhile backup's face was as calm as if he were having a cup of coffee with friends. His arms pumped and he came even with the car once again and reached toward the door handle.

Jordan checked the speed. Thirty-five. *Jesus, God!* he thought, and pressed down on the accelerator. Bob seemed to be keeping up with ease. Once more Jordan pushed the gas and they finally sped away from the big man. Forty miles an hour. Dyson's breath was hissing between his teeth and he felt light-headed, almost faint. *What the hell was that?* he wondered. *What in the* hell *was that?*

People could do insane things when hopped up on adrenaline, he reminded himself. *But why? What could the Connors possibly have done to them that's worse than what they did to me? What would drive a man to run forty miles an hour to commit murder?* Because they were going to kill John Connor, of that Jordan had no doubt.

And in spite of everything, I don't want to kill him, or his mother. See them in jail until they rotted, sure. He'd gladly see that day come. But he wasn't about to murder a kid! Not even Sarah Connor's son.

So where had Burns found these maniacs? They were stone killers if he'd ever seen any, which he had. Was she aware of what they were? Given her track record so far he had to believe that very little happened around Serena Burns that she wasn't fully aware of.

He plucked the cell phone from his pocket and dialed.

The phone rang once and was answered. "Burns."

"Would you like to tell me just what the hell is going on, Serena?" Jordan demanded, his voice carefully cold.

There was a pause.

"Isn't that what I should be asking you?" she said. "Did they show up? Or . . . they didn't and you're mad at me because of it."

In fact, she knew exactly what had happened: Six had given her a full report. Dyson had the boy, and if she wanted him—and she did—then this conversation needed to be handled very carefully. Jordan, she realized, would have to be eliminated as soon and as discreetly as possible.

"Oh, they showed up all right. And one of your boys almost blew the kid away."

"*What?* What are you talking about?" Serena put as much exasperation and confusion as she dared into the questions. "Could you please just tell me what happened? Because so far you haven't been very coherent."

Jordan drew a deep breath. Maybe that was true.

"Those three men you sent with me," he said slowly, "did their utmost to kill the Connors and their friend. They were so set on it that I can't help but believe that they were ordered to do so."

Maybe that's saying too much, he thought. If Serena had issued orders to kill, then he wasn't going to prolong his own life by making statements like that one. *I guess maybe I'm a little more panicked than I want to admit.* The image of a bland-faced Bob Harris reaching out and almost touching the car while the speedometer registered forty mph kept coming back to him.

"Whoa! Jordan," she said, sounding very indignant. "Slow down here! I did *not* give *anybody* orders to kill! Okay?" The I-950 paused for a count of ten.

"*Why* would I do that?" she said reasonably. "In what way would that make anything better? Huh?" Another pause. "Can you imagine what the papers would make of it? Can you imagine the questions we'd get asked?

"And why, Jordan? Why? I'm just as happy to have them in prison as dead! All I want is for Cyberdyne to be safe. But it's a company, Jordan. It's not my family, it's not anybody's family. There's no question of anyone having to die to protect it. Get real!"

He felt almost embarrassed. Serena was making sense here. *But what about what I saw?*

"Look, Serena, all I know is how they were acting. I mean, I never saw these guys before—"

"Well, neither have I. I sent down to the security shack for three guys who would be willing to travel overnight and those were the guys they sent up. I will check into it as soon as I hang up. Obviously we have a hiring problem."

She waited a moment then let out an exasperated breath.

"Jor-dan! What the hell happened? Did you arrest the Connors? *Are* they dead? Oh, God, please tell me they're not!"

"Nobody's dead," Jordan assured her. "Sarah and their friend, a big guy, got away. But I've got the kid in the backseat, bleeding all over the cushions."

"Oh, God," she repeated. It sounded right. "How badly is he hurt?"

"To be honest, I don't know," Jordan confessed. "I just got him into the car and ran."

"I suggest you pull over, now, and take a look," she said firmly. "I'll wait."

Jordan frowned. He didn't want to stop driving; he fully expected to see Bob come running up the road, even though he knew that was ridiculous.

"Yes, ma'am," he muttered, and pulled off the shoulder. Then he got out, opened the back door, and climbed in. The boy was unconscious, or mostly so; a bright, white line showed between his lashes. Dyson pulled him back up onto the seat and the kid moaned.

Jordan lifted the boy's eyelids. One pupil was noticeably larger than the other: concussion for certain. But his color was good and he didn't seem to be going into shock.

Dyson ripped the neck of John's T-shirt and looked at the gunshot wound: the bullet had gone straight through without breaking the bone or cutting major arteries. It was still bleeding pretty freely, though. Dyson tore John's shirt off completely and then ripped it in half, making two pads of the soft material. Then he stripped off his tie and bound the pads in place as best he could.

The head wound worried him. It was bloody, all head wounds were, but the cut was basically superficial. It was the evidence of concussion that bothered him. Anything might be going on inside the kid's head, there was no way to tell. He gently probed the area around the wound and sighed with relief when he felt solid bone.

Jordan shook his head. He needed expert help on this. Climbing into the front seat again, he picked up the phone. "Serena?"

"I thought you weren't coming back," she said, sounding relieved. "Well?"

Jordan hesitated. "He seems stable right now. But he has a concussion and that's not something to take lightly. I'm going to take him to the hospital."

"No!" Serena said, letting her voice shrill with alarm. "Jordan, you can't. You have to bring him here. We have a top-notch medical facility right here. We'll give him the best care available. Bring him here!"

"Serena," Jordan said slowly, "what are you thinking of? This kid is hurt, dammit! He has a head wound. Maybe you're prepared to take the blame if he dies or suffers brain damage, but I don't want that on my conscience."

"Jordan, his crazy mother is still out there somewhere. And right now she's probably very, *very* angry. Given her record, she's heading for Cyberdyne with blood in her eye.

"If we can show her that her son is alive and that we're taking good care of him, right here at what she might well consider ground zero, then maybe she won't hurt anyone. Do you want the deaths of who knows how many scientists and secretaries and who knows who else on your conscience?"

Jordan compressed his lips and thought. She was probably right.

Connor was probably headed toward Cyberdyne. And he personally knew what kind of mayhem she was capable of causing. But the one thing in her life that Sarah Connor had always been careful of was her son.

"Okay, look," he said. "I'll just get him looked over and I'll send him on to you by ambulance."

"Jor-dan! He's been shot! That means that any doctor or clinic or hospital you take him to has to report it to the police. Then the police have to come and question everybody, then everybody has to wait for somebody, somewhere to give you permission to send him down here. By then we could be a smoking hole in the ground."

"It's three *hours* to Cyberdyne," he snapped.

"If the kid is stable that won't matter. You said he was stable," Serena insisted.

Jordan rubbed his face with his hands. "All right, you mentioned the police," he said. "What are they going to say when they find out that I've dragged this boy down there and didn't report the shooting, and didn't take him to the hospital, and didn't stay here in Sacramento to be questioned, and didn't report his fugitive, *cop-killer* mother's presence in their town. You do realize that you're asking me to break the law, don't you?"

"I do," she said solemnly. "And I'll take the responsibility. Since we'll undoubtedly be shooting it out with Connor and her allies before the day is out, I think we can plead mitigating circumstances. Make him as comfortable as you can and bring him here. His presence in this facility is the only thing that will stop that maniac."

Serena stopped herself. It was time to stand back and see if she'd convinced him.

Jordan was silent, thinking about what she'd said, thinking about how Connor had killed his brother and destroyed his work. *Tried to destroy it,* he amended. Burns was right; Cyberdyne would draw Connor like a magnet. And this time she might very well not wait until the place was empty to strike. *Not if she's looking for revenge as well as serving whatever crazy cause she's into.* And the truth was, he wanted to be there when she arrived, not sitting in the police station answering questions.

"All right," he agreed. "I'm on my way."

It was wrong, and he knew it, but this was something he'd worked toward for six long years. it was easier to get forgiveness than permission.

Jordan stopped at the first store he saw and bought bandages, alcohol, a blanket and pillow, and some aspirin and bottled water. Then he rushed back to the car parked at the deserted far end of the parking lot and opened the back door.

Connor was conscious, but just barely.

The scalp wound was still bleeding, but sluggishly and it wasn't as deep as he'd feared. He poured some water on a sterile pad and wiped the blood away, then poured alcohol onto another and wiped the wound. Connor hissed through his teeth and his eyes flared open at the pain.

"Sorry," Dyson muttered. "At least you know you're alive."

"M'mother'd say 'at," the boy mumbled.

Jordan smiled grimly.

"From what I've read about her, I believe you," he said.

The shoulder wound was another matter, a far deeper wound.

Jordan wiped away the blood, then flushed it with alcohol.

"Sssshiiitt!" John shrieked, jerking upright, teeth clenched, muscles straining, then he flopped back onto the seat panting like a steam engine.

"Easy," Jordan said.

"*Easy?*" John rasped. "Easy . . . for you . . . to say."

Jordan gave him a quick look, he heard the boy's voice shaking and it worried him. But he wasn't looking any worse. If anything, he was looking more alert. *Of course, so would I if some bastard did that to me.*

"Why don't you just take me to a hospital?" John asked.

His eyes tried to catch Jordan's. This was a human. That was unmistakable, but from what he'd heard a few moments ago he was the super-Terminator's cat's-paw.

"I'm going to," Jordan said tersely. "You'll get the best care available. I just wanted to get you stabilized."

He pulled the bandage tight and John gasped.

"Easy! Easy," John said. "You're going to cut off the circulation to my heart! Loosen it up, let the blood flow."

"That's what I'm trying to prevent," Jordan muttered between his teeth.

"I know what I'm talking about. I've had some training in battlefield first aid."

"I'll bet you have," Dyson snarled.

John looked up and suddenly saw the resemblance.

"Miles?" he said, feeling weak. Weaker. He looked closer and realized the face was far too young. "No," he said sadly. "But you look just like him."

Jordan looked up from his work, his eyes blazing.

"Yeah, I do. I'm his brother. Correction, *was* his brother. Miles is dead."

John closed his eyes and nodded. "I know," he said.

Dyson frowned. There was a quiet dignity to this kid that moved him, completely against his will. He realized that he'd wanted the boy to be a jerk, a punk he could despise.

"Good field dressing," John said, his eyes closed.

"Glad you like it," Jordan said. "It's my first."

John smiled.

"What?" Dyson asked suspiciously.

"Nothing," John said. He opened his eyes. "Why aren't you taking me to a hospital?" He thought he knew the answer from what he'd overheard, but he wanted Dyson to tell him.

"I *am* taking you to a hospital," he said, looking down. He picked up the various medical paraphernalia and began putting it back in the shopping bag. "Just not in Sacramento."

"Who's Serena?" John asked. He kept his eyes on Jordan's face, willing the older man to look up.

"My, what big ears you have," Jordan snapped. He kept working for a moment, painfully aware of the boy's accusing eyes. "She's my boss," he finally said. "Chief of security at Cyberdyne."

That would fit, John thought. *Better than a scientist, even.* So this Serena had to be the super-Terminator. Interesting that it was a female. He wondered if his mother's reputation had inspired that choice. John tried to imagine a female Terminator and couldn't get beyond the massive chassis.

"What's she like?" he finally asked.

Jordan had watched the boy thinking things over and was waiting for his next question. This wasn't the one he was expecting.

"Younger than me, blond, very pretty, about average height . . . slender. Not what you expected, I guess," he said as John looked at him perplexed.

John shook his head. "No," he said. "I thought she'd be bigger."

Now it was Jordan's turn to be perplexed. *What the hell does that mean?* he wondered. He picked up the bag and began to back out of the car.

John grabbed his jacket with his good hand.

"Don't take me to her," he said. He tried to make Dyson meet his eyes. "She'll kill me."

"No, she won't," Jordan said disgustedly, pulling the boy's hand off his jacket. "There is absolutely no reason for her to kill you."

"Yes, there is," John said earnestly. "If I die, then Skynet wins."

"Who? Oh, wait a minute, that must be the monster computer that's going to take over the world, right?"

John nodded, then wished he hadn't as his vision doubled. He dropped his head back down on the cheap pillow. "She's here to protect Cyberdyne so that Skynet can be born."

"Of course she is!" Dyson sneered. "Why didn't I see that myself? What else *could* she be doing?"

"If she's really on the level, then why isn't she letting you take me to a hospital instead of dragging me to Cyberdyne?"

Jordan leaned closer to him. "Because she thinks—and I agree with her—that your dear old mom is heading for Cyberdyne with lots of explosives and no brakes. She's trying to keep her from killing anybody as much as she's trying to preserve Cyberdyne."

John licked dry lips. "Can I have a drink of that water?" he asked.

Jordan, looking disgusted, pulled it out and uncapped it for him.

"Thanks." John took a long pull, then plopped his head back down on the pillow, his eyes closed. He kept hold on the bottle when Jordan would have taken it away. "What's your name?" he asked.

"Dyson," Jordan said precisely.

John smiled slightly. "I admired your brother," he said. "He was a good man."

"And thanks to your mother, now he's a dead man."

John shook his head, then frowned at the pain.

"No. The SWAT team shot him. Mom never intended for anybody to die. He was too badly wounded to get out. Mom says he took the detonator and gave her a nod to go. Then he held on as long as he could before he let the place blow." John swallowed some more water. "He was a brave man."

Jordan felt the strength run out of him, as if someone had pulled a plug at the bottom of his spine. *The SWAT team shot him.* It was exactly what Tarissa had told him. Exactly. Except that she had gotten that information from the squad leader, while Connor here had gotten it from his mother. *Two independent sources,* he thought. *It could well be . . . must be true.* The thing about the detonator, though, that was new.

"You're telling me my brother committed suicide," he said aloud. He shook his head with a knowing smile. "That's not my brother. Miles wouldn't do that."

John looked at him. "It wasn't suicide. He was too badly wounded to make it; I told you that. He didn't kill himself, he sacrificed himself for his family and his friends. He died trying to save the world."

"That is insane," Jordan said straightening. "You are insane. You and your mother and her boyfriend kidnapped my brother and forced him to—"

"We didn't kidnap him—he *led* us to Cyberdyne. He willingly came with us, willingly showed us where things were, and he helped us set up the bomb." John closed his eyes again. He seemed to be less nauseated with his eyes closed.

"Why?" Jordan asked simply. He raised one hand and let it drop. "Why would he do that?"

"Because we had a Terminator with us who showed him some of its inner workings and he couldn't deny that proof," John said wearily. "Look, I know it sounds insane. Before I met a Terminator I thought my mother was crazy. But she's not. It's all true." He opened his eyes and looked at Jordan. "Call Tarissa," he said. "Tell her you have John Connor in custody and he's asking her to tell you the truth."

Jordan was silent for a moment, his mouth open.

"You want me to ask my brother's widow to back you up?" he said slowly.

"She'll confirm what I've told you," John said with perfect confidence. "She will."

Jordan tightened his lips and looked away. She would, he well knew it. He thought of Tarissa's message: *Remember what I told you.* And here it was again. "Shit!" he said. "Shit!"

John shut his eyes against the pounding in his head.

"Believe it or not," he said, "I know how you feel."

Dyson tightened his lips and glared at the kid. Then he dug into the bag and opening the aspirin bottle tapped out three tablets.

"Here," he said. "Knock yourself out."

Then he got out and slammed the door behind him.

He walked back and forth for a while, calming himself and trying to decide what to do. The kid thought Serena meant him no good. Given the behavior of the three "backups" that she'd sent with him, maybe he had a point.

But Serena denied it, seemed stunned when he told her about it, and there was nothing in her previous behavior to cause him to doubt her. Serena said she only wanted the boy at Cyberdyne to protect the people there. That seemed extremely believable to him. She said the three goons were strangers to her.

He stopped pacing. Getting beyond that was hard, maybe impossible. And in all fairness he had to give some credence now to the story that Tarissa had told him. Shrapnel dropping out of skulls, men running forty miles an hour. Unbelievable as it was, here it was again from a different source. *And what a different source,* he thought. The maniac's own son.

He wondered briefly if Tarissa might have been hypnotized into believing this insanity. *No. Even if she had, it wouldn't have lasted six years,* he thought. Not the way he'd kept her picking at it. And Danny wasn't even supposed to have known a lot of stuff that he . . . *claimed* to know.

Jordan ran his hand over his short-cropped hair. The more he tried to sort it out, the more tangled it became. He put his hands on his hips and considered his options.

Ralph, he thought. *Ralph Ferri.*

Ferri was a major in charge of base security. Serena had introduced them, very much as a matter of form, on his second day at Cyberdyne, and they had hit it off. Since there was something in Serena's manner that indicated she didn't want to encourage Ferri to take an interest in the complex under her care, Jordan had kept their friendship to himself.

Ralph's secretary patched him through with no difficulty.

"Hi Jordan," the Major said. "Wassup?"

Now that it was time to ask, Jordan choked. *How the hell do I put this?*

"Jordan?"

Oh, God. He rubbed his forehead. *This was a mistake.*

"Hello? Anybody there?"

"Hi, Ralph, sorry I, uh, dropped the phone." Jordan rolled his eyes.

There was a minute pause before the Major said, "Sooo, what's new?"

"I need a favor," Jordan said. "Uuuhhh. This is really awkward."

"Is it going to cost me my career?" Ralph joked.

"I honestly don't know," Dyson admitted. "Let me outline my problem for you." He went on to describe the situation, the three goons, the wounded kid, his notorious mother, and Serena's plea to bring the boy to Cyberdyne. "But I just . . . can't trust her," he admitted. "I just can't do it."

There was silence.

Then, his voice cautious, Ralph asked, "So, what do you want from me?"

"I want to put him in the base hospital under military guard," Jordan said.

"Aaawww, man!" Ferri was silent for a moment. Jordan could hear the rapid tapping of a pencil. "Let me get this straight," the Major said. "You want me to put a wounded sixteen-year-old fugitive, that your boss has *ordered* you to bring directly to her, into the base hospital."

"That's about the size of it," Jordan confirmed.

"I can't do that! Ask me for something I can do, man, and it's yours. But not this!"

"I'm willing to bet that Tricker would clear it." Actually, Jordan had no idea what Tricker would clear. He'd only met him once and hadn't seen him since. But instinct told him that mentioning Tricker's name in connection with something this hinky might work. The man was the personification of powerful, well-connected hinkiness.

"I'm willing to bet Tricker would put my ass in a sling for doing it," Ferri protested.

"No, he won't. Look, trust me on this man, it will be all right. I'm assistant head of security at Cyberdyne. Your department has been ordered to cooperate with Cyberdyne, right?"

"Riiight."

"So just do what I'm asking—cooperate with me. Okay?" Jordan waited.

"Yeah, but, Jordan, you just told me that your boss ordered you to bring this kid directly to Cyberdyne. To *their* med facility. Isn't that right?"

"Yeah. But you don't know that." Jordan waited a beat. "Do you?"

Ferri gave a long sigh, then he chuckled.

"No, I don't, do I?" he said. "Okay, bring him in. When can we expect you?"

"If I leave now I should be there in three hours. Depending on traffic."

"I'll stick around," the Major promised. "I'll leave word to expect you at the hospital. I'll have them call me when you get in. I'll expect a complete, if off-the-record, rundown on this thing."

"You got it," Jordan assured him. "Thanks."

"Hey, what are friends for?"

They hung up. Jordan grinned. Then he looked at the car. The kid was looking back at him.

This is going to be a loooong drive, he thought.

SAN JOAQUIN VALLEY, CALIFORNIA: THE PRESENT

"Left here," Sarah snapped.

Dieter looked at her from the corner of his eye. That was about all she'd said since the fiasco in Sacramento. "Turn right here, left, right, get on highway five." Her calm was beginning to get on his nerves. As was the way she was snapping out directions.

"Where are we going?" he asked as they climbed out of the heat and rectilinear farmlands of the valley and into high, dry hills.

"Friends," she said.

Five miles down the road he began to see things that looked familiar. When he signaled to turn just before she gave him directions, he knew he was right. It was a tremendous relief.

Ike and Donna Chamberlain would help settle her down. Her very stillness indicated that she needed to be doing something. They'd find something to keep her busy.

Sarah cast him a quick glance the second time he began a turn just before she told him to. Then she settled into silence. It didn't come as a surprise to her that they had some acquaintances in common.

Dieter honked three times, then twice, then once, then once again as he drove down a narrow dirt track that led to the Chamberlains' cabin in the woods.

Ike was a former Navy SEAL, and Donna was a former MP. Not surprisingly they had met in the Philippines one wild night when she'd had to arrest him. And tamed him in a heartbeat, so Ike claimed. They were survivalists first and foremost, making, growing, or hunting most of what they needed to live. For cash and anything else they had a sideline.

Ike was a gunsmith. More of a gun artist, really. He could re-create any gun ever made for a rich man's toy. Or he sometimes worked with the government, or an organization like the Sector, to produce high-tech models that would always be too specialized and too damned expensive for mass production.

The sideline was so lucrative that they could easily have retired to some tropical paradise to be waited on hand and foot for the rest of their lives. Such a suggestion, if one had the temerity to make it, was always greeted by a blank expression and the response, "Why, I'd just roll up and die if I didn't have nothing to do!"

Dieter pulled into the deserted clearing before the cabin. It was a large place; the Chamberlains had raised two kids in this out-of-the-way spot. Two kids who couldn't wait to get as far from the purity of the woods as their legs and the bus would carry them

They both worked in computers now and were doing very well. They called often, via cell phone, and never visited. It was almost as if they suspected their parents would keep them there by force. Which they were perfectly capable of doing if they thought it was the right thing to do.

Sarah looked around like someone coming out of a deep sleep, narrowing her eyes as she examined the two-story notched-log cabin. Dieter sat with both hands on the wheel and waited. Eventually a tall figure in a hip-length suede coat and broad-brimmed hat stepped from the woods, a rifle held under one arm, pointing downward. From the slenderness, Dieter thought it must be Donna.

"Never thought I'd see the two of you sharing the front seat of a car unless one of you was in handcuffs," Donna drawled. She grinned, her weather-beaten face breaking into a thousand lines, each one a welcome.

"Hello, Donna," Dieter said.

Sarah got out of the car and came around; opening her arms, she hugged the older woman, who returned the hug one armed. Donna's eyes dropped questioningly to von Rossbach, who tightened his lips and frowned in answer. She gave Sarah's back a pat.

"C'mon in, why don't you?" she said. "I'll put on some coffee and roust Ike outta the workroom. Then you people can tell us what's on your mind."

Ike and Donna blinked as they stared at Dieter and Sarah, then shifted nervously in their chairs and met each other's eyes in sidelong glances. They'd always worried about Sarah. Her strange crusade against Skynet, which Sarah herself said didn't exist—yet—was blatantly insane even by their relaxed standards. It made her a stand out even among the bizarre folk they tended to meet.

Visiting with them had always seemed to center her, though, to bring her back down to earth and the time and place everybody else was living in. She was actually very likable when she was calm and not talking about Judgment Day.

It was with regret that they'd watched her grow harder over the years. They tolerated her wrangy attitude mainly for John's sake. They saw how well she treated her son, even though they thought her discipline was a bit too strong. And they found John to be a delightful boy, they'd have done anything for him.

Dieter, on the other hand, they'd always liked, and by comparison to Sarah, he was very uncomplicated. Von Rossbach was unequivocally one of the good guys and that appealed to them. The few times they'd met had been fun and he was always welcome. If anyone had asked they'd have said he was one of the sanest, steadiest men they knew.

Now he was telling them that Sarah's wild stories were gospel truth. It was a hard mouthful to swallow. But the look Ike and Donna were giving one another now said as plain as words:

Shucks, the girl can't be that *good in bed!*

"So where's John now?" Ike asked.

"Probably on his way to the main Cyberdyne facility under a military base somewhere in California," Sarah said bitterly.

She put her face in her hands and breathed deeply for a moment. The other's around the table glanced at one another in embarrassment, not quite knowing what to do.

"Who'd be dumb enough to build a military base underground in *California?*" Ike asked.

"The army?" Donna answered, raising her eyebrows.

"Going to Sacramento was a complete waste of time," Sarah said bitterly, dropping her hands. "And way too expensive."

"Not entirely wasted, Sarah," Dieter said. He reached down and pulled up his backpack. Reaching in he extracted the portable computer. "John downloaded a lot of stuff into this."

"It never occurred to you to tell me about that?" Sarah snapped.

"I thought I'd give you some privacy," von Rossbach said calmly. He turned the computer on. "Now we can see what he got for us. Then we can go and rescue him."

"You're assuming he's alive," she said.

He stopped and looked at her, his gaze level.

"And what do you assume, Sarah?"

"I assume that if he was brought directly to the boss Terminator that he—" She stopped herself.

Letting her anger take over wouldn't help, and if she gave up hope there was no point in going on. Closing her eyes she took a deep breath, let it out slowly, and started over.

"I think we'd better find John before we blow the place up," she said grimly. "This whole rigmarole is pointless if we kill him ourselves." She looked at von Rossbach. "What did he get for us?"

One corner of Dieter's mouth curved up at that. He'd been worried. But this woman was, if anything, resilient.

"It's encoded," he said, and tapped a few keys. "In a few minutes the decoding program should bare all of Cyberdyne's secrets." Dieter shrugged. "Unless they've got something this program can't work its way around."

Sarah nodded. Ike and Donna looked at one another.

"Um," Ike said. Sarah and Dieter looked at him and he cleared his throat. "I don't like to sound inhospitable," he began awkwardly, "but was there a reason you came to us, specifically."

"Yes," Sarah said. "John indicated that he had plans for a . . . what was it?" she asked Dieter.

"A phased plasma rifle in the forty-watt range," he quoted.

"Yowza," Ike said softly, his eyes *very* interested.

"Not that I expect you'll be able to just whip one up, even with the plans," Sarah said. "But I had an idea and I think you might be able to help me with that."

"What is it?" Donna said. "You know we don't hold with killing soldiers just doing their duty, Sarah."

"I don't want to kill anybody," Sarah answered calmly. "I never have, and I see no reason to start now. But Terminators aren't people and weapons that would tear a human apart wouldn't stop one for more than a few seconds."

Ike and Donna both slid their eyes toward von Rossbach, who nodded grimly, his arms crossed over his chest. "The lady speaks from experience. Shared experience. I've seen it with my own eyes."

Sarah tightened her lips at their obvious doubt, then continued, "But they're robots. And robots have to have a power source. If we could interrupt that power, permanently, if possible, then they won't be as big a problem."

Dieter nodded, frowning thoughtfully.

"Yes, that would be good." He looked at her and shrugged. "Did you have something in mind?"

"I don't know if this is possible," she said to Ike. "But I was thinking, maybe, some sort of souped-up taser?"

Ike looked between them both, then at his wife, who shrugged.

"Sure, I could soup up a taser for you," he said. "But how souped up are we talking here?"

"At least three or four times what you'd need to drop a man my size," Dieter said. "Maybe more."

Ike blew out his breath. "The problem there would be battery power," he explained. "I guess I could work out some sort of back- or fanny-pack arrangement." He wasn't talking to them now, but to himself. He looked up suddenly. "When do you need this?"

"Tomorrow morning," Sarah said definitely. "I'd say tonight but that's just the mother in me talking."

Ike gave her a long look, then nodded. "I can have one, definitely. I'll try for two, but I make no guarantees."

"I'll accept that." Sarah smiled wearily. "It's more than I have any right to expect. And I thank you."

The computer beeped, and von Rossbach drew it toward him. He tapped keys and read, then tapped some more.

"There is no Skynet project," he said after a careful search.

"There's probably an artificial-intelligence project, though," Sarah said. She came to stand by his shoulder and read the text he was looking at. "Right now the things that will go into making Skynet might just be starting up."

Dieter started broadening his search, using "AI" and "artificial intelligence" as search parameters. Within seconds he had several projects listed. The first one he pulled up had a familiar name. "I know about this guy," he said. "He's a genius, but he's also a lunatic."

Sarah shrugged slightly. "In what way?"

"He's a Nazi for one thing; genuine article, no Haider pussyfooting. We watched him carefully in the Sector. We thought that he had terrorist leanings and that he could do a lot of damage if he put his mind to it. A very powerful mind."

"Maybe he's the one that taught Skynet to hate," Sarah said. *Maybe we should kill him,* she thought. *Stop the hate, stop the problem?* After all, there was no guarantee that destroying Cyberdyne again would stop the project. *Unless we get all the stored information this time.*

John's face was suddenly in her mind's eye, smiling, obviously about to crack a joke; she pushed it aside. She wouldn't allow herself to think about him until after they'd gotten him free. *If I think about him now I'll break down.* And then she might never get up again. So feelings and memories she didn't need. What she needed was something constructive to do.

"This is all great stuff," she said, "but not pertinent to our mission. We need to know how Cyberdyne is laid out, and if there are security codes needed to work the elevators, things like that."

"Yes," Dieter said. He tapped keys. A menu came up and he made a selection. A map of the complex came up on the screen.

Donna leaned in. "We've got a printer in the office that you can use," she offered. "In fact, why don't you go set up in there while Sarah and I get dinner ready."

Sarah's eyes widened and her nostrils flared. She was about to say something obnoxious like *My son could be dead and you want me to peel potatoes?* when she stopped herself. Actually, making supper might help. "Okay," she said. "Print out that map for one, Dieter." Sarah turned to Donna. "What would you like me to do?"

"Chop up some wood, hon, and I'll fire up the stove," Donna answered matter-of-factly.

Sarah smiled. She'd been right to keep her mouth shut. Hitting something with an ax was *just* what she needed right now.

CHAPTER 24

Serena sat absolutely still and concentrated on her breathing, trying to push every other thing in the world to the outer edges of her consciousness. The technique had been taught to her by Skynet itself and she had used it for as long as she could remember to focus her mind. Unfortunately, today it was terribly difficult to concentrate and she kept having to start over.

Today she was as close to murderous rage as she'd ever come in her life. The desire to kill was almost overwhelming. She positively lusted to tear a Terminator apart. Regrettably that was impossible; they were irreplaceable and not to be disposed of lightly, even if they were incompetent, moronic, bungling, inadequate, ineffectual, maladroit . . .

It didn't help that they were only following her orders. *I should have let them kill Dyson,* she thought bitterly. She was going to have to kill him anyway and she could easily have blamed the Connors for his death. Never in her life had she felt stupid. It was horrible. It was *human.*

Still, sending the Terminators after Connor and her accomplice had seemed more important—the more disciplined decision. John Connor was in her hands whatever happened. Catching his mother and the man with her was more logical than shooting some easily disposed of human who might still have some utility.

But the woman's ability to escape certain death bordered on the supernatural . . . unless she was the unknowing tool of a continuum that kept trying, with idiot persistence, to restore the original timestream. Once again she had slipped through their fingers.

Her own fingers squeezed the arms of her chair, making deep indentations in the hard rubbery material. Serena forced them to relax and she started the meditation process over again. A deep initial breath—

"Ms. Burns." Mrs. Duprey said, her apologetic voice interrupted Serena's solitude like a gunshot. "I know you asked not to be disturbed, but . . . Mr. Warren is here to see you."

I don't have time for this! Serena thought, irritation spiking. But one didn't send the president of the company away with a flea in his ear. "By all means send him in, Mrs. Duprey," she said mellifluously.

Serena stood as Warren entered the room, shutting the door behind him. "I'm sorry to interrupt you," he said, sounding subdued.

Is he still *regretting the loss of that bitch?* she wondered. "Not at all," she said aloud. "I have a slight headache and was taking a break."

"Oh, I'm sorry to hear that," he said. He looked for a moment as if he'd caught her with her shirt off. "It's just . . . this memo you sent around. I'd like an explanation, if you don't mind."

He'd surprised her. Serena thought of Warren as a nonentity, regarding Colvin as the real power at Cyberdyne, the one to work around. But the CEO was on a business trip to Dallas and wasn't expected back until Tuesday. She had hoped to have everything settled by then.

Serena smiled at the president and gestured him to a seat on the sofa. He sat and she sat beside him, her arm along the back of the couch. "I imagine the scientists are up in arms," she said, grinning.

"I've had a few calls," Warren said dryly.

"I wouldn't ask for this if I didn't think it was absolutely necessary," Serena said, turning serious. "We received some information—which turned out to be all too accurate—that Sarah Connor was gunning for us again."

The president grew visibly paler. Visibly to someone like Serena, that is.

"She's back?" he almost whispered. He put a hand to his forehead. Then he turned to Serena. "Tell me."

"She's made an attack on our Sacramento storage facility. I sent Mr. Dyson up there to take care of it and he gave me some good news and some bad news. The good news is that they stopped Connor from actually bombing the place. The bad news is that the system probably has a worm and/or a virus in it, and will have to be cleansed. It will probably be best to simply wipe the system completely and then reinstall everything. They cut a bunch of cables, too."

"That's actually pretty good," Warren said, looking shell-shocked, "considering what happened the last time she tangled with us."

"Further bad news," Serena said, looking regretful, "is that she and one of her associates got away."

Warren's lips tightened and he looked grim.

"I would have expected better from a former FBI agent," he said.

Serena leaned closer, smiling. "The good news," she said confidentially, "is that we have Connor's son."

Warren brightened, then his expression dropped.

"We have him, or the police do?"

The I-950 cocked her head to one side, smiling with satisfaction.

"We have him," she said. "I told Mr. Dyson to bring him here. But I don't expect him for a couple of hours yet." Serena gave Warren a level gaze. "That's why I sent the memo around. I don't want anyone getting hurt. Especially not these people; they're too valuable."

"Yes," Warren said thoughtfully. "I see what you mean." He put his hands on his knees and stared into space for a moment. At last he nodded decisively. "All right," he said. "At five tonight everybody goes home and stays there. Except for the security guards, of course," he turned, smiling, to Serena.

She nodded encouragingly.

"Um. How long do you think we'll have to stay closed?" he asked nervously.

"Not long," she assured him. "Mr. Dyson told me that the boy was wounded slightly. So I think his mother will come looking for him post-haste. Perhaps tonight, definitely by tomorrow. This nightmare should be over by the end of the week."

Paul Warren let out a deep sigh. "You have no idea how glad I am to hear that," he said. "I'm sure Roger will be too when I call him tonight."

"Do you think you should?" the I-950 asked, frowning. "This Dallas meeting is pretty important, isn't it? Mr. Colvin will probably want to come back and there's absolutely nothing he can do to help. And if he decides to stay down there he'll be very, and understandably, distracted." Serena tipped her head prettily. "Your call, of course," she said and smiled.

"I see your point," he agreed uneasily. Dallas *was* important. But he didn't like keeping his partner out of the loop like this. By the same token the whole thing might well be over, for good or ill, by the time Colvin could get back. And the Dallas meeting had taken months to set up.

"I'll take care of it," he said, rising. "Thank you, Ms. Burns. You have my complete cooperation on this. And"—he looked into her eyes—"good luck."

Serena looked up at him with a subtly moonstruck expression. After a moment he sort of shuffled his feet and nodded, leaving without a backward glance.

The I-950 rated her performance. *I did well,* she thought.

Now to more important matters. She would order the company doctor and nurse to stay after everyone else had left. By then the Terminators would be back and she could replace three of the six security guards with them. She would put Seven, the most conservative looking, at the front desk; the other two she would station near the boy. She'd tell the doctor that one of them was a trained nurse. Then she'd let the doctor and nurse go home.

And then I will sit back and wait for Sarah Connor to come to me.

This time, she wouldn't get away.

THE CHAMBERLAINS' CABIN: THE PRESENT

"Heeeeyyy! Ralph!" Dieter said heartily. "How's it going, buddy?"

Sarah watched him from across the room, her arms and legs crossed. A lot depended on this conversation.

"Dieter? *Dieter!* Whoa! What happened buddy? Cows getting dull?"

Major Ralph Ferri settled back in his chair, looking forward to an interesting conversation. He'd had the pleasure of working with the Sector agent earlier in his career, when he was a lot more active himself—Delta force, black-ops shit. They'd stayed friendly over the years, even though they rarely saw each other.

"You have no idea," Dieter answered. "All they do is chew. Even the bulls. They're all pretty boring compared to Srebrenica."

"So where are ya calling from?" Ferri asked. "Sounds like you're next door."

"Practically," von Rossbach lied. "I'm in L.A. I was wondering; can we get together?"

Sarah's heart gave a single bound, as though the Major were suddenly in the room with them and able to *see* the lies as they came out of von Rossbach's mouth. And how could he miss them? It sounded so completely false to her, staged, and insincere. So much depended on this conversation. John's *life* depended on this conversation. *Please, God, make him want to have dinner with Dieter!*

"Aw, man! I'm kinda tied up here. I don't think I'll be able to get away from the base for a couple of days, man."

"I could come see you there," Dieter suggested. "I'm not above eating in the commissary. I'd hate to be this close and not get to say hello. Unless you're too busy, that is."

"Oh, I think I can squeeze you in." Ferri chuckled. "We can eat in my quarters. I make a great Kung Pao chicken. After the way you carried me out of that place with enough jacketed lead in me to start a factory, I owe you a dinner. At least."

"Anything but beef!" von Rossbach said with feeling. "When should I show up?"

"Tomorrow's Sunday, should be a fairly easy day. How about six?"

"I'll bring the beer," Dieter said.

"Outstanding!" Ferri said. "See ya."

"Tomorrow," von Rossbach agreed.

He hung up and looked at Sarah. She seemed to be all eyes. He gave her a reassuring smile.

"We're on," he said.

ROUTE FIVE, JUST OUTSIDE L.A.: THE PRESENT

"Major Ferri, I'll be at the base in twenty minutes. That's seven-fifteen. Would you please meet me at the main gate?" Jordan asked, steering one-handed through the insane Southern California drivers.

Ferri sighed. "Sure," he said. "See you in twenty."

"Thanks Ralph. I owe you."

"You do," the Major agreed.

Ferri hung up, chuckling. He really did like having people owe him favors. Especially for things that weren't going to inconvenience him in any way. As for meeting Dyson at the gate, well, he was looking forward to a full rundown on this situation anyway and this would be the quickest way to get one.

Ferri never had taken to the Burns woman. She was a looker all right, too gorgeous to be real; you kept expecting to see some guy with an airbrush pop out of the bushes and give her a touch-up.

But the base dogs couldn't stand her and showed it, growling and showing their teeth. Ferri had been a dog handler early in his career, and knew that if the well-trained MP dogs couldn't keep discipline around that woman it had to mean something. What that might be he didn't know—yet. Maybe Dyson would be able to give him some insight.

Meanwhile, until he knew what was wrong with her, putting one over on that corporate snob was going to be absolutely delicious. And if it worked out that he could in some way embarrass Burns, or if fortune allowed, get her fired, well, that would just be the icing on the cake.

He glanced at the clock. It would take ten minutes to walk to the gate if he hurried, so he might as well start now and take it easy. This promised to be interesting, maybe even fun.

Jordan glanced in his rearview mirror at the boy. He looked a little more pale than he had when they started out, but not frighteningly so. He appeared to be asleep. *Should I wake him up?* he wondered. Head wounds were supposed to be kept awake, weren't they?

Whatever! He was an investigator, not a doctor. *Hey, he's breathing. And in twenty minutes he'll be in the base hospital getting transfusions.* He tried not to think of how he'd react if it was Danny bearing those wounds. *Of course, Danny wouldn't get himself into a situation like this,* he decided with certainty.

Then he remembered what Dan had told him about the Connors, his ardent young face making it impossible to misjudge his opinion. So maybe Danny would lend a hand at blasting Cyberdyne sky-high, after all.

Thank God the perimeter fence was finally in sight.

Ferri came out of the guard shack and hopped into Jordan's car. Then he pointed forward and Dyson took off.

"Whaddaya think?" Dyson asked.

The major turned in his seat and looked at Connor.

"What the hell do I know? I'd say he's asleep." He shook his head. "But for all I know, he's in a terminal coma."

"Jesus," Jordan breathed.

"The doc will tell us," Ferri said calmly. "Until then, just drive."

When they pulled up at the base hospital the Major went in and got a gurney and some attendants to take the boy out of the car. Inside he asked for two doctors by name. The second was on duty and was duly paged at the Major's request.

When he arrived, Ralph explained that the boy and his injuries were secret Cyberdyne business and that the hospital staff were bound to aid them as a matter of national security.

"Major, this boy looks to be under eighteen by a good few years and he's been shot! We can't keep something like this secret! At the very *least* his parents need to be notified," the doctor said reasonably.

"All I'm allowed to tell you, Doctor," Jordan interrupted, "is that this boy is in danger and must be guarded. I assure you, this won't be swept under a rug someplace. But sometimes timing can be more important than strict adherence to the rules."

"We're not talking rules here," the doctor insisted, "we're talking laws."

"If laws are being broken here, Doctor, I will take the responsibility," Jordan said gravely. "My object is to keep this boy alive. If you take it upon yourself to report his presence here, you may cost him his life and that will be your sole responsibility."

The Major and Dyson stared the doctor down. Reluctantly he agreed to abide by their conditions, then he got to work.

Jordan blew out his breath in relief and looked at the Major.

"I didn't think he was going to agree," he said quietly.

"Oh, he would have," Ralph assured him. "He was just trying to make me order him to do it. That way, see, it's totally my responsibility. But he's too good a doctor to let the kid lie there bleeding while he played that game." Ferri grinned. "Sometimes having a conscience can be really inconvenient, y'know?"

Jordan's mouth tightened. "Unfortunately, yeah."

"And now," the officer said cheerfully, "It's *your* responsibility."

"Thanks."

CYBERDYNE: THE PRESENT

Serena sat in her darkened office watching the digital readout projected onto her eyes count down the seconds, the minutes, the hours. It was nine-fifteen and twenty-seven seconds. She had sent the doctor and nurse home at nine.

It was obvious that Dyson wasn't going to show up. Serena had been sifting through police reports, looking for arrests or accidents, or even abandoned cars. Nothing.

Jordan should have been able to handle him as a trained agent.

The other and less palatable possibility was that Connor had subverted Dyson.

No! she thought. Not possible. Why would he aid and abet the people that he knows killed his beloved brother? Answer, no reason.

Still, he was human. Best to keep an open mind. The adult John Connor had a record of inspiring humans to insane actions.

She blinked and the time readout stopped. No sense in wasting time; she had work to do, her own and Cyberdyne's. If Dyson showed up, he did. If not, not. She thought that whatever had happened she could still look forward to a visit from Sarah Connor in the near future.

Two hours later, a considerable amount of report reading and writing had been accomplished. The phone rang and Serena patched in.

"Burns," she said crisply.

"Uh, Ms. Burns, this is Joe Cady of Aadvanced Security," a man said.

In the background she could hear shouting voices, trucks, running feet, a siren. Aadvanced was the subcontractor she'd hired to watch the automated factory site. The military had wanted to keep a low profile. Aadvanced—despite the misspelling that made them first in the phone book—had a pretty good record. Things did not sound good right now, however.

"What's happened, Mr. Cady?" Serena asked calmly.

"Some people came out of the night; they distracted us with a forest fire a few miles off. At least I think that was them. The fire-department guys said they thought the fire was arson. Then they snuck in and got the drop on us. They tied us up and locked us in the guard shack, took our cell phones, then they set bombs all over the place. Said they were the Luddite Liberation Army.

"When we got loose we sent a guy over to where the fire was to see if he could get us some help. They even blew our cars up, the bastards. So they've been gone a couple of hours at least." Cady's voice was shaking.

Serena gathered from this that he hadn't been sure the Luddites were going to leave them alive.

"How bad is the damage?" she asked. She quickly added, "I assume no one was hurt; you'd have told me if someone was hurt, wouldn't you?" She did, after all, have a role to play here.

"Yeah," Cady said. "I mean, no, nobody's hurt." He paused and she could hear him sucking his teeth. "The destruction is pretty near total," he said. "All the machinery, all the construction supplies and the company's trailer, the area they'd leveled—everything is busted up, burning, or crapped up somehow. I never saw anything like it."

"Did they leave a message?" she asked.

They must have left a message, this whole thing is a message, of course.

"If they did, ma'am, it's gone now. They didn't leave anything with us or tell us to say anything, like a message. You know? It's just fire and smoke and mess here." Cady's voice faded away. "I'll look around, though."

A messenger has left a parcel for the president and CEO, Seven, stationed at the security desk, said. *When I told her they weren't here she said she'd been instructed to give it to the next-most-important executive that was present.*

Serena sent Six to retrieve it for her. Probably it was from the LLA. *Luddite Liberation Army, of all the stupid names. These jerks wouldn't liberate their grandmother from backbreaking peasant labor by buying the old girl a washing machine.* But they all had to have "Liberation" in their name. Serena supposed *they* would feel liberated if everybody else was forced to embrace their ideals.

"Have you informed anybody else about this?" she asked Cady. Barely a second had gone by in real time.

"Well . . . Tony brought back some of the firefighter guys, and they radioed the police, of course." He sounded nervous. "I dunno if that was okay or not, but we needed help and they were the only people we could contact."

The general is not going to like this, Serena thought. *But I did warn him to let me handle security directly if he didn't want the army to take care of it.* She shrugged mentally.

"If the authorities have questions that you can't answer, Mr. Cady, you may refer them to me at this number. I'll be here for several hours yet."

"Oh, thank you, ma'am. Yes, I'll do that," he groveled.

Pathetic, the I-950 thought.

"Good night, then," she said. "Oh, um, since there's nothing left there to guard, I guess you and your crew can go home after the police are through with you."

"Great! Ah, yes, ma'am. I'll tell them. Thank you."

She broke the connection and leaned her head back against her chair. The I-950 was conflicted. This development was essential if she was to convince Cyberdyne and the military to move the factories far from human habitation. The I-950 had always preferred the idea of having the Army Corps of Engineers construct the facility. It wasn't traditional, but it would be cost-effective and very secret. *Maybe now . . .*

Serena sighed, almost contentedly. Each crisis gave her a greater margin of control. The fact that she had warned Cyberdyne that this might happen would count in her favor.

Except possibly with Tricker. He'd probably wonder about her prescience, her uncanny ability to read the future. *If he only knew,* she thought with a smile. The problem was that a professional paranoid like Tricker didn't believe in precognition, but did believe in people who made things happen.

The trick would be controlling this Luddite revolution. *But if the sites are remote enough it shouldn't be a problem.* And once the factories were operational she could direct them to build some advanced weaponry for self-protection. It would be good when the first HKs, those dear, old, reliable hunter/killers, rolled off the assembly line. Very good.

But for now she had this problem of her missing assistant and the equally, and more importantly, missing John Connor. *Supernatural,* she thought. *They're positively supernatural.*

Two made contact.

"Now what?" Serena muttered.

The I-950 clone has been harvested, Two announced. *It has survived the implant process.*

Excellent, she sent. *Keep me appraised of its progress. How is the other surrogate doing?*

Extremely well, Two sent. *Shall I terminate it?*

Not yet, Serena ordered. *Have you terminated this one's vehicle yet?*

Not yet.

Keep her for the first week, she ordered. *The I-950 organism will benefit from the mother's milk. In seven days it should be weaned and you can dispose of the human then.*

Understood.

Is there anything else? she asked.

Nothing.

Out, Serena sent.

Out, Two confirmed.

Serena sat thinking. It had been quite an evening; good, bad, and indifferent. Still, for the most part her plans were moving along just as they should. If only she knew what had happened to John Connor.

FT. LAUREL BASE HOSPITAL: THE PRESENT

Jordan sat in the too small, too short, and too hard plastic chair in the hospital waiting room and stared at the mayonnaise-colored walls as he thought.

How did this happen? How did I allow myself to be talked into this? He was feeling more than a little stunned. This was him? He was here? Really? Jordan sighed. *At least Tarissa and Danny will be happy.*

Ferri returned and handed him a cup of coffee from the machine down the hall.

"I got a flush, you got bupkiss," the Major said handing over the card decorated cup.

"Gee, thanks," Jordan said with a grin.

They sat quietly drinking the lukewarm brew.

"You are *so* gonna get your ass fired," Ferri said after a few minutes.

"Yeah, I am," Dyson agreed with a sage nod. "Yup, you got it in one."

The Major looked at him out of the corner of his eye.

"You don't sound too upset," he observed.

"I think I'm too stunned to be upset right now," Jordan said. He waved a hand. "This is the craziest thing I have ever done. I just can't believe I'm sitting here."

"So, what I'm wondering," Ferri said, "is where the hell you're going with this thing." He waved vaguely. "I mean, this kid should be turned over to the police. Ya know?"

Jordan nodded and took another sip. Then he shrugged.

"Eventually, yeah. See, the thing is, I agree with Ms. Burns that Sarah Connor is headed our way. I think that having John boy on hand might"— he tipped his hand from side to side, wincing—"make her a little less violent."

"That sucks," Ferri observed.

"Yeah, it does," Jordan agreed. "I keep thinking of my nephew."

The doctor came toward them and both men stood.

"He's going to be fine," he said. "I've given him something for the pain and he'll sleep through until morning at the least and probably most of tomorrow."

"The concussion?" Jordan asked.

The doctor's eyes moved from the Major to Dyson.

"I wasn't sure you cared," he said.

Jordan gave him a disgusted look. "So?"

"You're right, the boy does have a concussion," the doctor conceded. "A very minor one. I don't anticipate any problems, but I've got the nurses checking in on him every hour."

"Good," Jordan said. "Uh, I'd also like to keep an eye on him, so would it be possible for me to . . . bunk in with him?"

The doctor held his clipboard in front of him like a shield. "Hospital beds are for hospital patients."

"You can set up some kind of a cot," the Major said pleasantly. "Or maybe a reclining chair or something. We have to cooperate with Mr. Dyson on this. It's for the boy's own good."

The doctor opened his mouth to protest, saw the steel behind Ferri's smile, and relented. "Very well," he said stiffly. "I'll have the nurses set something up for you. Good night, gentlemen."

"I don't think he likes you," Ferri observed quietly, watching the doctor walk away.

Jordan shrugged. "I'm not sure I like me very much right now either." He grimaced, then turned to his friend. "Thanks, Ralph. You've gone way above and beyond on this one. I owe you."

"I know," Ferri said with a grin. "And one dark night I just might collect on it." He slapped Dyson on the shoulder. "But you've already made a partial payment by giving me a heads-up on this Sarah Connor thing. The doyenne of Cyberdyne security hasn't seen fit to let us grunts in on what's going on. If we're not on our toes for this it's my fault, not yours." He gave Jordan another pat on the back. " 'Night."

Jordan watched him walk away, then turned and headed for the nurses' station. *I am so gonna get my ass fired,* he thought.

NEW YORK CITY: THE PRESENT

Ron Labane studied the pictures on his computer screen in awe. *They did it!* he thought gleefully. *They actually did it!* Put a thumb in the eye of the military-industrial complex, kicked the legs right out from under the bastards. *And they had the balls to film it as they did it!* He didn't even need to be concerned that this would lead the police to him because they'd flooded the Net with these images.

Ron wasn't as happy about the forest fire they'd started and was prepared to be angry until he got a separate message to the effect that the area was already scheduled for a controlled burn. Very impressive, very satisfying.

The only difficulty, he thought, *will be in controlling them.* It wouldn't be the first time that early success also led to early imprisonment. *And I have plans for these people.*

CHAPTER 25

Dieter pulled up at the gate of Ft. Laurel and waited for the MPs on duty to come out. He felt a moment of nostalgia; going through perimeter security was something he'd done most days of his life for twenty years. Sometimes legitimately, on his way to work; sometimes under assumed identities, very illegitimately . . . also on his way to work.

He'd borrowed the Chamberlains' army-surplus Humvee on the off chance that Cyberdyne could identify him, and Sarah, by their vehicle. In the back he'd placed a case of the expensive (and very hard-to-find) Danish beer that Ferri liked. The man was a real connoisseur; he sneered at mere Tuborg as fit only for peasants, barely better than Swedish brews.

The MP at the desk looked him over thoroughly before he picked up his clipboard and came out of the shack, narrow-eyed and slow. He was backed up by another soldier with a rifle, who moved to the right fender and stood at the ready.

Dieter had his passport in hand and passed it over to the MP without being asked. "I'm here to see Major Ferri," he said.

Then he went silent, keeping his face turned toward the MP, who read the passport—as well as he could, it being in Spanish. The MP looked from the passport to von Rossbach several times as though comparing individual features. Dieter was amused by his thoroughness. When it all came down it wasn't going to be because this kid hadn't made sure of his identity.

"Are you boys expecting trouble?" he asked as the MP checked the backseat.

"Always, sir," the MP answered. He went around to the back and lifted the canvas cover. "What's in the box?"

"Beer." Which was obvious, the name was all over the case.

"I meant in the locker behind it, sir."

"A blanket, a tool kit, a flashlight," Dieter answered. "Some flares, stuff like that."

If it had been anyone else but the major's guest the MP would have asked the big man to open the trunk.

"You may proceed, sir," he said. Without waiting to be asked, he provided instructions to the Major's lodgings.

"Thank you," Dieter said amiably.

"You're welcome, sir."

Dieter glanced in the rearview mirror as he drove off and saw the rifleman watching the Humvee for a moment before going back to the guard shack. It gave him a sense of unease, as though they knew more than they should.

Calm down, he told himself. *The last I heard even the best MPs didn't have x-ray vision.*

"You okay in there?" he asked Sarah.

There was a sharp tap from inside the trunk in answer. The code was once for yes, twice for no. He'd be glad when she could get out of there. The very thought of her crammed into that tiny space was giving *him* claustrophobia.

And Sarah only mentally present was even harder to take than the silent accusation that had been pouring out of her when she was there physically. Not the least of the shock was realizing how much he cared about her opinion.

Ferri's place was relatively easy to find, one of a row of base housing looking like a marked-down suburb two decades out of date, with plenty of kids and dogs. The Major was sitting in a lawn chair out front waiting. He checked his watch.

"On time, as ever," the Major said, rising.

Dieter grinned and waved. Then he lifted the canvas and dragged out the case of beer.

Ferri's face lit up and he waved his arms in a mock bow.

"I'm not worthy! I'm not worthy," he said with a grin.

"You know what? You're right," Dieter said. "I'll take it back and get a refund."

Alarm flashed across the Major's face and he rushed forward to gently remove the case from von Rossbach's arms.

"No, no, no!" he said. "You just let me take care of these babies." He cocked his head toward his front door. "C'mon in, set a spell, tell me what you've been doing."

"In a word, cows." Dieter said surrendering the carton. He glanced at a grill by the corner of the house as he opened the door. "You're not going to barbecue anything, are you?"

"I thought you might be homesick," Ferri said innocently. "Kung Pao chicken," he said. "My best chicken dish."

The Major led him into a small, sparsely furnished living room. Ferri had never been one to put his imprint on his quarters. Probably because early in his career he'd been on the move so much. A lot of guys acquired souvenirs of the places they'd been, but Ferri found they lost their charm fast when you had to pack and move 'em twenty or thirty times.

In the kitchen, he put his prize down on a gray-and-red Formica table, then ripped open the box and pulled out a sweating bottle.

"Hey! It's cold!" he said in delight.

"Well, I knew you would want one right away," Dieter said.

He reached in and took one out for himself. Ferri produced an opener and they sat down at the table. For a moment all that could be heard was men swallowing good beer.

The kitchen was full of late-afternoon sunlight and smelled fantastic, suffused with the rich aromas of good cooking. The counter bore evidence of much meat and vegetable chopping having taken place.

"When do we eat?" Dieter asked, a greedy look on his face.

" 'Bout twenty minutes," Ferri said with a grin. "You hungry?"

"Now I am," von Rossbach said fervently.

Grinning, Ferri brought out a plate of cheese and a box of crackers.

"Don't eat too much," he cautioned. "But good cheese does go well with good beer."

Sarah waited for what seemed forever; ten minutes as the universe counted time. Then, when she heard no sounds from outside the Humvee, she pushed against the front of the locker with her hands and knees. It slid out slow and even and for a moment she just lay on her side breathing the sweet clean air that cooled her face and chest.

She rolled out, pulled out her supplies, and after a brief struggle in the semidarkness pushed the false front of the trunk back into place. Cautiously she sat up, lifting the edge of the canvas, she quickly checked the area around the car. People were visible in the distance, but their attention was elsewhere.

Excellent, they hadn't aroused the guards' suspicions. She could neither hear nor see Dieter or his friend. The coast was clear.

Sarah sat still for a while, letting the worst of the sweat dry from her face and hair. She'd been in the trunk only about thirty minutes but it had quickly become stiflingly hot.

Sensibly, she'd not donned her uniform blouse and it waited beside her to be put on. About her hair there wasn't much she could do. At least it was short. Maybe anyone who noticed it was wet would think she'd just taken a shower.

Ten minutes later she was striding away from the Humvee in the direction of the Cyberdyne facility; information John had teased out of the contaminated brain of the Terminator they'd destroyed. She carried a battered brown briefcase and wore the boxy cammo fatigues of the modern army, with an MP armband circling the sleeve, and a peaked cap worn level on her head.

In the briefcase were a set of detonators, timers, and several tools that would hasten her work. They'd made the fairly safe assumption that they would find everything else they'd need at the site.

We did the last time I blew up Cyberdyne, she thought grimly.

In the pocket of her fatigue jacket was a taser. It looked almost exactly like one of the bulkier cell phones on the market. The taser they'd adapted to disrupt a Terminator's electronics was clipped to her belt. She really didn't expect to find a Terminator minding the front desk after all and that one would fry a human—so she didn't want to get them mixed up.

Sarah crossed what felt like a mile of the compound before coming in sight of Cyberdyne. She kept her eyes front and by her manner indicated that she knew exactly where she was going and exactly what she was do-ing. No one gave her a second look.

She boldly approached Cyberdyne's glass front door and pulled the handle. Nothing happened. *I guess maybe they're waiting for us.* Her breath grew shaky and her palms began to sweat.

The glass was tinted; from four feet away it might as well have been opaque. Sarah leaned forward and made out a man behind a desk watch-ing her. She tapped on the glass and waved the security guard toward her.

He mouthed, "We're closed."

She took the taser out of her pocket and pretended it was a phone; lowering her head, she put it to her ear. She continued to wave the guard toward her, looking up at him from under the rim of her hat.

He kept waving his hands in a negative sign and saying they were closed, and she continued to alternately tap on the door and wave him forward. At last, looking intensely exasperated, he pushed himself up from his seat and came to the door. Unlocking it, he pushed it open a few inches.

"We—are—closed," he enunciated.

"Hold on, please," Sarah said to the taser. "I have an appointment," she said to the guard.

"There's nobody here," he insisted. "The place is empty."

"Check your appointment book," Sarah said. "I'll be listed."

He glanced at the MP armband and looked uncertain.

Sarah, holding the taser against her shoulder as though she didn't want it to overhear, sighed noisily.

"Will you just check. Please," she said. "I'm sure I would have been contacted if my appointment was canceled."

"We-ll," he said. "I guess Ms. Burns is still here . . ."

"That's who I'm supposed to see," Sarah told him. "Could you please just let me in and tell her I'm here." He stood looking at her uncertainly. "Sometime today would be good," she said sarcastically.

The guard stood back and gestured her in with his head. Then he locked the door behind them and led her to his desk. He sat down and called up a page on the computer.

"I'm sorry about this," Sarah said quietly.

The guard turned toward her and she triggered the taser; the twin cords shot out with an electronic *zzzzrrrnng*, hitting him full in the stomach. He went down and bounced and jittered on the floor while fifty thousand volts shot through his body and his muscles convulsed.

Sarah pressed the button that released the cords, snapped a new set into the taser's base, and stepped over his body before he even became still. Placing her briefcase on the desk, she opened it and took out some duct tape. Bending over the guard, she checked his pulse; fast, but steady. Then she slapped a piece of tape over his mouth and turned him over. With a few quick moves she had him bound, feet to wrists, and more securely gagged. Quickly she patted him over and withdrew his master keycard, then she shoved him under the desk.

Glancing at the computer, she noticed the page he'd brought up had been replaced by a prompt that asked what information the guard was looking for. She typed in "games," hoping that anyone watching over the system, if anyone was, would assume that a bored guard was looking for entertainment. The computer responded with a full-page scolding about playing games on company time.

Sarah raised an eyebrow. *They can't seriously imagine that anyone is going to go to the trouble of reading all that,* she thought. *It's a self administered spanking!*

She tapped in the sequence that John had given them and it brought up security; with a few taps she disabled the silent alarm. *Something I should have done last time,* she thought bitterly. Then she brought up the door locks and changed the entry code to test mode, one that only she, John, and Dieter knew. Then she shut the computer down and rose.

Sarah looked around. The guard's desk stood alone in a very unwelcoming lobby. No chairs for the comfort of waiting visitors, no plants to soften the harsh lines of the place. Just a polished floor and the desk, behind which was a short, wide corridor that ended in a pair of double doors. This led to the storage area, where she hoped to find her bomb-making materials. On either side of the corridor were a pair of elevators.

The desk itself was one of those that had a high shelf in front with the desk space consisting of another shelf below. Even when he wasn't tied up underneath it the guard would be very hard to see from the front.

Which is a plus, Sarah thought. *Some passerby glancing through the door wouldn't really expect to see anyone.*

She stood still, listening carefully: there was no sound but the sigh of the air-conditioning, and the air it put out had the utter sterility of a high-priced recirculation system. Apparently the guard hadn't been kidding; no one *was* here. *No one but Ms. Burns, that is, whoever she is.*

A group of monitors on the guard's desk showed her from several angles, so there were several cameras mounted around the place. But she saw no point in worrying about them. If she succeeded, they'd soon be so much melted plastic along with their tapes; if she failed, Cyberdyne would know who had invaded them anyway.

Snapping her briefcase closed, she took the key out of her pocket and jogged toward the storage area. The door opened smoothly on the first try. Sarah let out her breath in relief. She'd been half expecting an alarm to go off, or for some secret code to be required.

Sarah entered a warehouse-sized space and made a little sound of despair. *This is going to take longer than I'd hoped.* She looked around and noticed a bank of elevators along the front wall, flanking the corridor. The elevators had front and back doors. *How sensible!* she thought in surprise. *They've actually made it convenient for people to get supplies.* She'd assumed that she would have to drag everything out front, risking discovery.

This is going to be a snap, she thought.

FT. LAUREL BASE HOSPITAL: THE PRESENT

John looked around the room through slitted eyes; he was in a state of well-controlled terror, not knowing whom he was with or where he was. He couldn't see much, but he saw enough to know he wasn't alone: a man's legs with one foot crossed over his knee were visible off to his side.

He was in a hospital room, from what he could see. There was another bed to his left, but it was empty. The door to the hall was closed. He lay still, which wasn't hard; he was feeling very weak. *Better, though. Someone's given me fluids and a trank. I should hurt more. Head's a little fuzzy.*

The door opened and a gray-haired man with glasses came in; from his white coat he was a doctor.

"Isn't he awake yet?" the doctor asked, moving quickly to John's side. He took up the boy's wrist and checked his pulse.

"If he is, he hasn't said anything," Dyson said.

He sounded tired, but John was grateful to hear his voice. If Dyson was still here maybe he wasn't going to be turned over to the master Terminator.

The doctor reached over and lifted one of John's eyelids; he turned on a penlight and John blinked involuntarily.

"Aha! Playing possum were you," the doctor said cheerfully. "Well, I need to ask you a few questions, then you can go back to sleep if you like." He asked a few brisk questions to test memory and visual acuteness. "Are you in pain?" he asked finally.

"I'm comfortable," John said.

"Really?" The doctor glanced at his watch. "Some people have a pretty high threshold of pain, but yours is remarkable. You should be very aware of that shoulder right now, since you're due for a shot of Demerol."

"I'm fine," John said again. "I don't like drugs."

"I wish more of your generation felt that way," the doctor said, making a note on the chart. "Are you hungry?"

John nodded, his eyes closed. He wasn't hungry, but his mother would have insisted that he eat to keep up his strength. Besides, *he* thought he would feel better if he ate.

"I'll have them send up something, then," the doctor said. "Something light, some soup and some Jell-O."

"Thank you," John said.

The doctor gave him a quick, dry smile, then looked at Jordan. "You?" he asked.

"Yeah, please," Dyson said. "I haven't wanted to leave. I could use something to eat."

The doctor nodded, glanced at John one last time, then he left.

John turned his head and looked at Dyson. "Thank you," he said.

Jordan rubbed his stubbled face. "For?" he asked.

"For not turning me over to them." John's face was serious. "They *will* kill me if you do that," he said. He raised his brows. "And it may be a cliché, but I'm too young to die."

Dyson snorted. "Me, too," he agreed.

"Where am I?" John asked.

"You're in the base hospital at Ft. Laurel," Jordan watched John take a breath that was almost like a sob and then go still. "I haven't reported to my boss, if that's what you're wondering."

John let out his breath slowly and closed his eyes. "I was," he admitted. He looked over at Dyson. "Why not?"

Jordan grimaced. "Tarissa told me the full story a few weeks ago," he said. "I thought she was the victim of some sort of traumatic-stress/Stockholm-syndrome combination kinda thing. I mean she bought into your mother's delusion so . . . completely." He looked over at the boy. "I've known that woman since I was a kid, and I always thought of her as one of the most sensible, *sanest* people I knew. And then she dumps that on me."

"Only it's true," John said.

"Yeah, right," Dyson sneered.

There was a knock on the door and an attendant thrust it open with his foot.

"Dr. Huff ordered this for you," he said, holding out a tray.

Jordan got up and took it from him.

"Thanks," he said.

The tray held a bowl of soup, a dish of green Jell-O, a cup of orange juice, a sandwich, and a carton of milk.

"The sandwich is mine, I guess," Jordan said. "Do you want the OJ or the milk?"

"OJ," Connor said. "I need the sugar."

Jordan's brows went up. "If you say so."

John took a sip of juice and held it in his dry mouth.

"I know how you feel, you know," he said. "When I was ten, I thought my mother was a complete psycho. Then one day two Terminators showed up, one to kill me, one to save me." He shook his head, then closed his eyes and reminded himself *not* to do that. "It was the craziest forty-eight hours of my life. So far." John looked Dyson in the eye. "I don't *want* this to be true; it just happens to *be* true. If they find me, they will kill me. And I guarantee you they are looking for me. So what I need to know is, did you leave any kind of a trail at all?"

"What do you mean, like credit-card charges?" Jordan asked. "What, you think I was stopping in bars?"

"I was thinking of phone calls," John said.

Jordan bit his lip. "I called to make these arrangements from a pay phone, using a calling card. But that was from the last place I contacted Cyberdyne, so that wouldn't tell them anything. Oh, I called when we were about twenty minutes from here to tell my friend when we'd arrive."

"Were the card and the phone issued by Cyberdyne?" Connor asked.

"Ye-ah." Jordan bit into his sandwich and wondered where the kid was going with this.

"Get rid of them," John said. He could hear the tension in his own voice. "Anything that they've given you probably has the capacity to listen in or trace you."

"Well, they haven't so far," Jordan said casually. "And we've been here all night and all day. Which, if they were looking for us, they would have done."

"Maybe they're waiting for dark," John said, glancing at the window.

"They had plenty of dark last night," Jordan pointed out, his mouth full of apparently irreducible bread. He took a sip of milk. "So that doesn't work."

"If they suspected I'd convinced you," John said musingly, "they would assume you'd be too vigilant to attack last night. But tonight, your belief would be fading, you'd be wondering if you'd done the right thing, so you'd be a lot safer to attack." Connor looked at him measuringly. "Maybe it won't even *be* an attack. Maybe your Ms. Burns will just sashay in here and ask you what's going on." He raised his brows. "What would you say then?"

"I don't know," Jordan said honestly.

"Maybe something like, I got crazy, I don't know what came over me, the kid talked me into it?"

Jordan rolled up his napkin and tossed it into the wastebasket.

"When Serena Burns next sees me, the first words out of her mouth are going to be 'you're fired.' " He looked over at John. "After that she might ask me what the hell I thought I was doing, but since I'm fired it won't really matter what I say, now will it?"

"Would you let them take me away?" John asked. He had no idea how young he looked to Jordan at that moment, lying pale and weak in the bed, dark circles under his eyes, his hair tousled on the pillow.

Jordan thought of what Tarissa had told him. He thought of Danny and the look on his nephew's face before he slammed the door on him. *They* believed in this kid, and his mother. From what they'd told him, they had good reason to believe him. More important, Miles had believed in them. Could he do less?

"No," he said at last. "I wouldn't."

John almost wept with relief; his eyes filled and his throat tightened. He took a deep breath and forced himself to relax. *Nobody pays attention to a crying kid. Certainty. If you act certain, people pick it up.* After a minute he spoke.

"Then you have got to get me out of here, man."

Jordan looked at the door as though he expected someone to come bursting through it at those words. He leaned close. "Where do you want me to take you," he said quietly.

John thought for a moment. "How long have I been here?" he asked.

"All last night and all day today." Jordan frowned; he'd already told him that. Maybe the head wound was making him forgetful.

John blew out his breath.

"Then this is the day we were going to attack Cyberdyne," he said. He looked over at Jordan. "You have to take me there."

"To *Cyberdyne*?" Jordan asked. "Are you crazy? What about all those Terminators over there who want you dead?"

"My *mother's* going to be there," John said.

"Oh!" Jordan straightened up and rolled his eyes. "Why didn't you say so? I guess I'd better go find you some clothes. You can hide out in my office. No, wait; that won't work, because as soon as I show up, I'm going to get fired and I won't have an office."

John smiled. "Seriously," he said. "It's the last place the Terminators will be looking for me. They know I'm wounded; they'll expect me to be lying low. They might even be counting on my mother nursing me back to health in some remote location. But she'll be there. I swear she will."

Jordan tightened his lips. But he could see that the kid was serious.

"Like I said, I'd better go get you some clothes," he muttered.

■   ■   ■

Ralph's Kung Pao chicken was as good as it smelled. Dieter felt like a heel rewarding such a good dinner with what was going to be the mother of all headaches, but there was no help for it. While Ferri's back was turned he put the drops in his friend's beer.

Ralph turned back and put a brimming plate in front of Dieter, then set down his own.

He licked his thumb and said, "I think I made just enough. Which is to say enough for six." Ferri grinned, hoisted his bottle in a toast to von Rossbach and took a long swig. *"Where* did you find this?" he asked. "I've looked everywhere. I asked them to order it for me at the PX, but I knew when I did it they'd never be able to score the stuff."

"I have my ways," Dieter said mysteriously. He took a sip from his own bottle.

Ferri snorted and drank from his own.

"Actually, there's this place in L.A. that stocks it. It's called Ron's Imported Beers on East Alameda. They're in the book. Unfortunately they don't deliver."

Ralph grinned, already looking a little bleary.

"Even if they did I'm probably outside their delivery zone," he said.

They talked and ate for a minute more, then, without warning, Ferri's head hit the table. Dieter winced, then moved the dish of chicken out from under his friend's face. He leaned over to make sure the Major could still breathe, then headed for Ferri's bedroom.

In a minute he was dressed in the Major's fatigues and was headed out the door in the direction of Cyberdyne. *I wonder how far Sarah got,* he thought. He shouldn't be worried, he knew. Sarah Connor was very professional. But he was emotionally involved, whether he liked it or not. So he worried.

What if they have John there? he wondered. He knew Sarah thought that if her son wasn't dead he was a prisoner of Cyberdyne. *So, did she get right to work, or did she search for him?* Most mothers you wouldn't even have to ask that question, but Sarah Connor wasn't most mothers.

He couldn't help but be concerned. She had been absolutely cold since they'd taken John. So withdrawn she might have been living in another time and place—visible, able to interact, yet untouchable.

Dieter didn't think John was dead, because the man who had ordered the Terminators to chase them hadn't come after them. If the boy had been dead, he would have followed them and tried to help with the capture.

Sarah didn't buy it. She resisted the urge to hope, believing it a fool's game. You could almost see John falling—the blood, the boneless landing—in her eyes. She'd told him that if the first shot didn't kill him, then they would do it at their leisure, but that they *would* kill him. *If they have him, he's dead,* she'd said to him in a voice and manner that brooked no argument.

And so he approached Cyberdyne looking determined but feeling discouraged. From what Sarah had told him, if John was dead, then humanity's only hope was the total destruction of Cyberdyne. *And* that *looks damn near hopeless.* The place was like a Hydra; cut off one head and two more pop out.

FT. LAUREL BASE HOSPITAL: THE PRESENT

"No. I'll go out first, then you. I can steady you, and catch you if you fall. You don't want to risk that shoulder."

John frowned at Jordan's suggestion. Not because it was a bad idea, but because it was so obviously a good one. He felt strange, distant and distracted, which he supposed was due to drugs and loss of blood. But this was a bad time to be slow as an ox.

"Good thinking," he said aloud. "You go first."

Jordan slipped over the narrow metal windowsill without comment. The drop from the boy's room was about four feet. Not bad, but still enough to be bothersome if one arm was out of action. John followed him immediately, barely giving Jordan a chance to step back. Dyson put his hands on the boy's slim waist and eased him down. Then he looked around. The coast was still clear.

John was wearing his own jeans and sneakers, but Jordan had found a green surgical shirt to replace the bloodied and torn T-shirt he'd been wearing. Dyson looked down at his own rumpled and blood-stained suit.

We couldn't be more obvious on an army base if we were wearing rubber noses and orange wigs, he thought. Dyson looked around. It was just getting dark, things were getting hard to see, and the camp lights wouldn't be going on for a couple of minutes yet. There was no "good" time to do this, but right now was better than some. They started off.

By the time they reached Cyberdyne, it was full dark. There were pockets of shadow here and there around the building, looking all the darker for the arc lights surrounding them. They headed for a well of shadow at the back of the building.

John stumbled and nearly went down, but Jordan caught him—awkwardly because he was trying to avoid the wounded shoulder. To a passerby it would have looked like they were struggling.

In fact, to Dieter it did. He moved up silently behind Jordan, and clasping his big hands together, brought them down on the back of Dyson's neck. Jordan moved slightly at the last minute, reducing some of the force of the blow, but he went down in a heap, and John dropped with him.

"Ow!" John said, looking up into Dieter's grave face.

Jordan rolled over onto his back, his eyes wandered for a moment, then focused. "What the hell did you do that for?" he whispered.

"Dieter, NO!" John barked as Dieter brought his arm back for the *coup de grâce.* "He's on our side!"

Dieter relaxed, looking down at Dyson.

Looking up, Jordan could discern no expression in his attacker's face or eyes and he was ready to believe that this man was even more danger-ous than the résumé Serena had given him said he was. Assuming this was von Rossbach.

Then Dieter looked at John and smiled.

"Your mother is going to be relieved to see you," he said fervently. He offered his hand to help John up. "Let's roll."

John's eyes widened. "Terminal Mission Override XY74!" he snapped.

Dieter spun around and gasped in surprise. He was face-to-face with a Terminator, a thing with his face. He fumbled at his belt for the taser.

The Terminator was frozen by the dissonance of an imperative com-mand phrase uttered at the wrong time, by the wrong person, for the wrong purpose. Its processor worked furiously to reroute its command tree. For a second or two it stood helpless, so much inanimate metal and plastic.

Triggering the taser, von Rossbach stepped to the side, placing himself in front of the boy. Then they all scrambled back as sparks burst from the Terminator's eyes and mouth, its arms flopping wildly and legs stamping in place. Finally it stopped—frozen—with one foot in the air; then slowly, with the majesty of a sequoia, it fell, face forward, at their feet.

John looked around, then picked up a white-painted rock, and mov-ing over to the Terminator, began calmly slamming it on the thing's head.

"Thanks," Dieter gasped.

"De nada," Connor responded, never letting up the rhythm of his pounding. "I got the phrase out of the CPU of that Terminator we decapi-tated. I wasn't sure it was genuine, but looks like."

Shaken, but not to be outdone in cool, Jordan said, "We'd better get moving. Those fireworks might have attracted unwelcome attention."

Christ, it's real! He felt himself going into shock, and hauled back from the precipice with a gasping effort of sheer willpower. *I'll have the nervous breakdown later.*

"Can you really kill one of those things with a rock?" Dieter asked.

"No, but you can expose the access plate . . . here we go." John peeled back an arc of scalp, opened the plate, poised the pointed end of the rock, and struck twice.

"Sort of ironic—man's earliest tool killing his last." The big man looked at him, and John went on with a grin: "So I'm old beyond my years; so sue me."

John watched the red light of one eye flicker and fade, then dropped the rock.

"Yeah," he agreed. "We'd better get Bolts, here, out of sight before we go, though."

Dieter clipped the taser back onto his belt and leaned down. Grabbing one of the Terminator's arms, he tugged and grunted.

"He's heavy," he said in surprise, his voice showing the strain of dragging roughly three hundred pounds of inert mass.

Jordan took the other arm and they finally got it moving. They dragged, then pushed it into the shadows.

"Mom's already here?" John asked as they started off.

"She should be," Dieter said. "What do you Americans say? One big happy family."

"Christ," Jordan muttered.

CYBERDYNE: THE PRESENT

Sarah rolled the last barrel into the fourth elevator and took it to the lowest level, four. She'd already filled all the other elevators with the makings she'd flung together and sent them to the other floors.

Cyberdyne's equivalent of a quartermaster seemed to love ordering in bulk and she'd taken full advantage of his/her thriftiness. *I could come up with the makings for a bomb in a public rest room,* she thought; fruits of a not-so-misspent life, one the waitress-student she'd once been would have found incomprehensible and terrifying in equal measure. This abundance of *stuff* was pure luxury.

The one thing they didn't seem to have an ample supply of was dollies. She'd been able to find only one. When the door opened on four she tipped the barrel she'd loaded and raced for the far end of the complex. *Only fifteen more to go,* she thought.

Dieter tapped in the test code and the door lock disconnected with a harsh buzzing sound. The three of them pushed through the doors and rushed toward the desk. John slapped von Rossbach on the arm and pointed to the elevator indicator lights. One car was stopped on each floor.

"Hey, if a guy can't depend on his mother, who can he rely on? This is her most *excellent* MO, believe me." He went over to the elevators and pushed the button for the one stopped on four. Nothing happened. "She's got the door propped open," he said. Excitement seemed to be lending him energy. "I'm going down to three to help her spread the bombs," he said and headed for the emergency stairs.

"John, wait!" Dieter called out, but the boy was already through the door. He turned to Jordan. "Is there anybody else here?"

"Usually on a Sunday there are six security people and a few scientists working and maybe one or two eager-beaver executives," he said. He thought a moment. "If I know Serena Burns she's probably arranged for the place to be empty."

Dyson turned to the security desk and blinked at the sight of the guard, now slowly returning to consciousness, stuffed under the desk. Jordan shook his head and blew out his breath. *Get on with it,* he ordered himself. *Don't ask questions, don't think, just do it.* He set the monitors to show what was happening on each floor.

Most of the scenes shown were devoid of human presence. On four, something flashed by too fast to register.

"Sarah!" von Rossbach said, pointing a thick finger at the monitor.

"And John," Dyson said, indicating a monitor that showed the boy creeping through a door marked with a big "3."

The rest of the security cameras flashed views of the areas covered, showing two security guards and no one else.

"Those are the ones Serena sent with me to Sacramento," Jordan said.

"Terminators," Dieter growled, looking grim.

"We'd better tell John and . . . his mother," Jordan said.

"I'll take care of John," von Rossbach said. "Sarah has a taser with her that will take down a Terminator. The boy has nothing."

Just teenage hubris, Jordan thought.

"Is this Serena person likely to be here?" Dieter asked.

Jordan nodded solemnly. "The kid thought she might be the one in charge of all the Terminators we've been running into."

Dieter froze in thought, looking for all the world like the Terminator he'd disabled outside. "Can you distract her?" he asked.

Jordan rubbed his jaw, then shrugged. "I can try," he said. "I'll come up with some story about what happened. That might keep her occupied for a little while. I don't think she'll buy anything I come up with, though. That woman is *smart.*"

"If John is right, that woman isn't a woman," Dieter said. "Go ahead, do what you can. I'll go help John."

Jordan glanced at the elevators, then followed Dieter to the stairs. He wasn't sure what was up with that, but it wasn't an arrangement he wanted to mess with.

"Wait!" he said.

He went back to the guards' desk and shut each camera down individually. Then he fixed it so that they could only be turned on again using a new password: "fear." *Which I expect to experience more of tonight.* He stood up and blew out his breath. *I guess that means I've crossed the Rubicon for certain,* he thought.

"Okay," he said aloud. "Let's go."

Von Rossbach nodded and they headed out.

Serena sat behind her desk, hands primly folded before her, and worked the last conversation she'd collected between John Connor and Dyson through a series of filters. For some reason, once he'd entered the base hospital, reception had been extremely poor. The I-950 had been working on it for a half an hour now, using a reconstruction algorithm, and still couldn't make out what they were saying through the static.

Once Jordan had begun speaking again, shortly before he returned to the base, she'd been relieved. Knowing that the boy was at hand, if not actually in her hands, was satisfactory. She knew where he was and from what she'd heard he wasn't going anywhere in a hurry. *At least not pumped up with Demerol, he isn't,* she thought.

For now, she was content to ignore him. Serena had bigger fish to fry. Sarah Connor to be exact. *She'll be* here *soon.* Everything currently known about the woman promised it.

Five was patrolling outside, as were two of the human security guards. One of those she'd put near the gate with orders to report anything strange. The other she'd assigned to the hospital, where he was watching Connor's room. Six and Seven were on independent patrol of the complex. Now it was just a matter of waiting.

The I-950 looked up in surprise at the tapping on her door.

"Come in," she said.

Serena came as close as she ever had in her life to dropping her jaw in astonishment. She leaned back in her chair and crossed her long legs.

"Wellll," she said slowly. "This is a surprise."

He came in and slumped toward her desk, head down, looking tired, rumpled, and sheepish.

"So, what happened?" she demanded. "Speak to me, Jordan."

He leaned both hands on the back of the chair across the desk from her, pressed his lips together, and looked off to the side.

"Jordan?" she said, looking at him from under her brows. "Have you lost your voice?"

She upped her hearing level and found that his heart was beating rather rapidly. *Meaning?* she wondered. It could simply mean that he expected to be fired, or that he had hard questions for her, or it could mean something much more dangerous.

"No," he said, raising his hand. He looked her in the eye. "Let me tell you what he told me," Jordan suggested.

She raised her brows. "If you think it will help," she said laconically.

He blew out his breath and began to speak, his eyes keeping contact with hers. He told her about the Terminators and how they had ruthlessly pursued the Connors. Of how Connor was convinced that the three men she'd sent with him were nothing less than contemporary versions of the enemy they'd met before.

She listened quietly, taking note of the micro-tremors in his voice more than of what he was saying. *He's scared,* she thought. *Because he believes them or because he expects to be humiliated for that belief?* For a human, one could be as disturbing at the other. She had time; let him grab enough rope to hang himself. It wasn't as though he was going to survive this no matter what he said.

When he was finished Serena pursed her lips and steepled her fingers before her. "It's a remarkably self-consistent set of delusions." She looked him in the eye. "Isn't it?"

He nodded and slapped the edge of the seat in front of him.

"Yes, it is. So, am I fired, or what?"

She laughed outright at that and spread her hands.

"You still haven't told me what happened, Jordan. Give me something to base a judgment on, why don't you?"

He straightened, then looked to the side again as though gathering his thoughts. Now was the moment of truth: was he on her side or the Connors'? Did he believe Tarissa or Serena? Suddenly he thought of John telling him that Serena must be very, very smart, and it shook him. *Yeah, she is smart,* he thought. *And if Connor is right, then she might have resources that we don't.*

"He's a very persuasive boy," Jordan began. "And those guys you sent with me were *insanely* out of line." He rested his hands on the chair back. "Maybe I bought into it a little." He met her eyes. "So I brought him to the base hospital instead of here. I stayed with him last night and thought about it."

Serena looked at him, swinging her chair slightly from side to side.

"And what did you conclude?" she asked.

He shrugged, looking down. "To be honest, maybe I'm too tired to think straight, but the jury is still out."

She laughed again. "Yes, I'm afraid you *are* too tired to think straight. I suggest you not try to buy a used car today if you're capable of buying the crap that poor kid took in with his pablum." Serena uncrossed her legs and scooted her chair under her desk, folding her hands before her. "What did you tell them at the hospital?" she asked, all business now.

"That I didn't think our clinic could handle the kid's wounds. And that his life depended on his presence being kept secret." He shrugged. "I told Ferri that Tricker would want him to cooperate with us on this."

The I-950 looked thoughtful. He was telling the truth, at least for the most part, judging from the micro-tremors in his voice.

"Good!" she said with satisfaction. "You're probably right about the hospital having a better chance of treating him, too. We do have just a small clinic. So I'm not totally dissatisfied with your performance on this. I should have expected it, given your concern over the boy's wounds. And he is at hand if needed."

She looked at him, her head tipped to one side, then she lowered her eyes.

"I guess the jury is still out for both of us. How this all works out will determine your future with Cyberdyne," she said. "Now, why don't you go home and get a few hours' rest. I'd like you to come back in tonight; that's when I think she'll strike, sometime between midnight and dawn."

"Tonight?" he said.

Something in his voice alerted her. She extended her hearing and caught the sound of an elevator. Not her Terminators; they'd been instructed to use the stairs at all times in order to avoid human contact. The only human in the building besides Jordan was the guard on the desk. Who hadn't let her know she had a visitor. She checked the security cams and found them off-line. Despite her best efforts, she couldn't turn them on again.

She had gone so still that she might as well have been a mannequin. Jordan knew instinctively that something had gone very wrong. He took a giant step toward the door. His hand was on the knob when she flew over her desk toward him.

How he did it he never knew, but he was through the door and slamming it behind him before she could get her hands on him. He ran flat out for the elevators. Serena was through in a split second, her beautiful face completely expressionless, almost serene, as the door flew back hard enough to shatter the knob and tear the lock out of the plywood frame.

At first he flung things in her path, a chair, someone's computer, anything he could get his hands on. But he saw when he looked over his shoulder that she leaped over everything like a gazelle, her hair almost brushing the ceiling. After that he just ran, arms pumping, legs flying. It seemed miles.

There was one last door ahead, the glass barrier between the scientists and executive territory. He swished his card through the reader and a green dot lit, the door clicked, and he was through. The door slid shut behind him. He picked up a potted palm and threw it at the lock mechanism outside the door, which broke with a shower of sparks. Serena was nearly to the door.

He turned, crossed the corridor, and hit the elevator button; the doors opened and he flew inside. Jordan turned and pressed a button, any button, then watched helplessly as the demon approached.

Serena slammed into the door and bounced off, looking faintly surprised. Then, knowing she had him trapped, a slow, satisfied grin animated her face. She drew back her fist and punched forward, safety glass shattered into a thousand pieces, and she leaped through. As the elevator doors closed he saw her expression change to chagrin and the last he saw of her was her fingertips reaching for the door.

Then she was gone and the elevator was on the move. Jordan plastered himself against the side of car and gasped for breath, then he slid down the wall and sat for a moment, gathering his strength. Opening his eyes, he smiled, then looked to the side and froze. The elevator was full of bomb.

Serena hit the elevator door hard enough to dent it. She let loose a strangled cry of frustration, then quickly stifled it. *Where are you?* she sent to the Terminators.

Two, one of them answered.

One, the other replied.

The third didn't answer.

Serena watched the elevator indicator: Dyson was going down; he was already past two.

There's at least one human invader in the building, she told them. *Jordan Dyson. Terminate him on sight.*

Five came toward her from the far end of the corridor. A pity it hadn't been closer when Dyson ran; they could have cornered him between them.

"Go to the ground floor," she said. "Guard the elevators and the door to the stairs. Terminate any human who comes through them."

She looked up. Dyson had gone all the way down to four. There was a panel on the wall that controlled the elevators; she ripped off the cover and grabbed a handful of wires, then pulled them from their moorings. That ought to keep him where she wanted him for a while. She signaled Six to meet her there.

The I-950 turned and headed for the stairs. She had a small but powerful gun holstered at the small of her back under her suit jacket—a snub-barreled magnum that a human her size couldn't have controlled. Pulling it out, she clicked off the safety and made sure she had a round in the chamber.

Hunting humans, she thought. *How nice. Seems an age since I did this.*

CHAPTER 26

At the sound of the approaching elevator Sarah stopped what she was doing and ducked behind the receptionist's island. *Who the hell is that?* she wondered. Surely Dieter would know better than to use the elevator. She pulled her Glock from its holster and rested her gun hand on the desk, eyes on the elevator door.

The doors opened and Jordan braced his leg against one side to keep them there as he peeked out into the corridor. *So should I take the elevator back up, or use the stairs?* he wondered. Maybe he ought to check the indicators, see if Serena was following him. He edged out of the elevator slightly.

Sarah fired, aiming for the thigh of the leg inching its way into view.

Jordan went down screaming. He thrashed on the floor cursing and trying vainly to keep quiet. It hurt so damn much!

"Jesus! Jesus! Jesus!" he hissed, half cursing, half praying.

Sarah recognized him from Sacramento: the man who had said he would take care of John. She rushed from behind the desk to stand over him, her gun aimed at his head.

"Don't move!" she ordered.

Jordan opened his eyes to find himself staring into a small black hole. His breath stopped; it took five long seconds for him to make his lungs work again and he took his breath with a long, tearing gasp.

"Where's my son?" Connor said. Her voice and face were as cold as the moon and as distant.

"He . . . he's okay," Jordan stammered. He couldn't stop shaking and his leg *burned.* "He's on three, setting up bombs."

She appeared to think about that; after a moment she took a deep breath and let it out in a sigh. Then she almost smiled, looking younger in an instant.

"That's my boy!" she said proudly. "He can talk *anyone* around— even me." Sarah holstered her gun and squatted down to offer help to her victim. "The bullet went clean through, doesn't look like I nicked any veins or arteries from the way it's bleeding. Can I have your tie?" she asked.

"No!" Jordan snapped. "I already used it to bandage your son." *I will never again question why I have to wear that stupid strip of cloth to work,* he thought. He wished now that the unofficial dress code required him to wear two.

"Well, you'd better give me something to use unless you want to bleed to death," she said briskly.

Jordan shrugged out of his jacket and took off his shirt, with her help. Sarah used her knife to tear it into strips.

"First you shoot my brother, now you shoot me. What the *hell* have you got against my family, lady?"

"What are you talking about?" she asked, frowning.

"My brother was Miles Dyson," he said. He sucked in his breath through his teeth as a sharp pain shot through his leg.

"Miles," she said thoughtfully as she sliced away his pants leg. "He was a good man." Sarah smiled, her eyes on her work. "I guess next time I'd better ask questions first and shoot later," she said.

"Duh! Yuh!" he agreed. "OW!"

"Has to be tight," she explained.

"What about circulation?" he asked, glaring.

Sarah stood up and looked down at him.

"I guess that's your responsibility. Look, I've got things to do. Stay cool, I'll be right back."

"Stay cool? Hey!" he said as she walked away. "I'm being chased; that mommy Terminator you've been worried about is after me!"

She looked over her shoulder at him.

"Then I'd better work fast."

Dyson let his head fall back against the wall and closed his eyes.

"Yeah, I guess you better," he said softly. He swallowed and tried to fight down a sudden nausea. *Maybe it's time I tried to make a deal with God,* he thought irreverently.

Every agent does, sooner or later, Paulson had once told him. *So you should work out your terms in advance.*

Jordan lightly placed his hands on either side of the wound, just above the bandage, and wished he could ignore the pain. He felt a falling sensation within, and when he opened his eyes again he thought some time might have passed.

Off to his right, the door to the stairs began to open.

"Connor!" he shouted. He tried frantically to move, to back into the elevator, and couldn't seem to make his body work as a coordinated whole. "SARAH!"

Sarah dropped her screwdriver and ran toward his voice. She arrived in time to see a Terminator raise its gun, aiming at Dyson. Response was automatic: she plucked the taser from her belt, ran toward it, aimed, and fired even as it began to wheel toward her.

The results were dramatic: sparks shot from the Terminator's head and it flailed its arms and legs like a marionette gone mad. Its trigger finger convulsed again and again, firing the gun in uncontrolled bursts. Sarah threw herself to the floor and wished she could get lower. The machine kept firing until all that could be heard was the impotent clicking of an empty magazine.

Then, without warning, it was over. The Terminator crashed to the ground, frozen—sprawled like a giant doll, broken and abandoned.

After a moment's silence she crawled to the edge of the desk and peered around it. The Terminator lay inert. She moved over to it and tugged at the gun; it wouldn't let go, not without tools. She rifled its pockets for spare magazines and took those.

Dyson was flat on his back, most of his body in the elevator, so she couldn't tell if he was alive or dead. Sarah moved cautiously over to him, her eyes on the Terminator.

As she moved she snapped out the used taser cartridge, its wires still attached to the Terminator's torso, and replaced it. It was more powerful than the standard model, but it would be useless until it recharged. She quickly checked her watch; twenty minutes or so until it could be used again. She hung the unit on her belt and withdrew her pistol from its holster just in case. It wouldn't kill a Terminator, but it might slow one down—and it made her feel better.

She wished there was some way to be sure the Terminator was down for good, but the damn things didn't have a pulse she could check.

She glanced in at Dyson; he was looking back, seeming no worse for wear.

"You okay?" she asked, moving her eyes back to the quiescent Terminator.

"Just ducky!" he said sarcastically. "Incidentally, if you see a blond ho' with a very bad attitude who can walk through walls, kill her. That's Serena Burns, inhuman genius from the future. Sorry, I'm babbling."

"Shock," said the woman he'd hated for six years, and smiled.

He struggled to a sitting position and Sarah was reaching down to help him when the door to the stairs was thrown open, hitting the wall like a gunshot. Sarah straightened, saw a woman with a gun, and without hesitation raised her gun and shot.

Serena's head snapped back from the force of the blow and her vision went white, then black. She felt herself falling and had time to comprehend one word and to feel all the dread that accompanied it.

Failure.

Then she was gone.

Jordan leaned forward and watched with his mouth open in horror as Serena slowly crumpled, then fell to her knees, then forward onto her face. The right side of her head was a mass of blood, the pink gray pulp of her brain was visible, and the gold-blond hair was matted into spikes with it.

"My God," he said. He looked at Sarah, who was frowning at the fallen woman. "I thought you were going to ask first."

Sarah looked down at him.

"Everybody's a critic," she growled. She indicated Serena with her chin. "That the one you were talking about?"

"Yeah," Jordan said. "That's her. She dead?"

Sarah shrugged and put away her gun.

"Time will tell."

She glanced at Jordan, then went over and pried the gun from the woman's stiff fingers. Sarah touched her neck, feeling for a pulse. *If she has a brain,* which she visibly did, *then she must be human,* she thought. *So if there's no pulse she should be out of the game.* There was a lot of blood, too. Terminators didn't have this much in their whole massive bodies. Sarah frowned. The idea of a human running Terminators was mind-boggling. *No time,* she reminded herself. *Get going.* Returning to Jordan, she offered him the gun butt first.

"So you won't feel so defenseless," she said.

"Thanks," he said, accepting it. He looked up at her.

Sarah felt as though he wanted her to say something, but she had no idea what.

"I have to finish some things," she said. "Hold the fort and don't shoot my kid, okay?"

He raised the gun in salute. "You got it," he said.

He watched her go back into the office she'd come out of, then he looked around. His hands were shaking, so he dropped the gun to the floor beside him and clasped them, hard. Jordan grimaced at the bodies on the floor and let out his breath in a little huff. They looked so human.

What if they are *human?* he thought. *What if the Connors are delusional and I've somehow become infected?* Then an image of Serena making those fantastic leaps came into his mind's eye. He'd actually seen that with his own eyes. This might be the craziest thing that would ever happen to him, but *he,* at least, was not insane.

Jordan shook his head and slowly dragged his wounded leg into the elevator. He pushed himself back until he was leaning against the wall. Next time something came through that door he was not going to be a sitting target. He reached up; yes, he could touch the elevator's control panel; he could shut the door at need. He let his head lean against the wall and once again allowed himself to relax.

■   ■   ■

reroute. reroute.

Electronic components no human could have designed struggled to throw off their passionless equivalent of shock. They had been integrated with the biological half of their personality for a very long time. Autonomous reintegration took a long time; several complete seconds.

checksum. response: negative. damage—

neurological: central brain stem: nonresponsive. function terminated. terminated. terminated.

decision tree: restart autonomous functions from backup.

The corpse's lungs heaved, once, twice. The heart began to beat with an artificial steadiness. The computer analyzed how much function remained in muscle and organ; enough for a few minutes, if it controlled fluid loss from the ruined brain. But it had never been designed to move the organism in this manner. Complex calculation would be required.

Fingers quivered, clenched. A heel softly tapped the ground. An eye opened, and the pupil cycled from pin-sized to a black disk that swallowed the blue of the iris.

Serena Burns was dead. But her body began to move. . . .

"Last one," John said to Dieter, who shoved the dolly he'd found in the janitor's closet under the barrel.

"Okay," von Rossbach panted.

They'd been working well together, and fast, running back and forth to the lift every minute or so, it seemed. Dieter glanced up as he pulled the barrel out of the elevator.

"Oh, my God," he said softly.

John looked up at the indicator. There were now two elevators on four.

"Mom!" he said, and ran for the stairs.

"NO!" Dieter said, catching him by the back of his shirt. "Don't just run out there. *Look* first."

"Right," John said. He took a deep breath and gave the big man a rueful look. "Don't tell Mom, okay?"

"What do you think?" Dieter said.

Cautiously, they opened the door and listened. Von Rossbach nodded and they moved carefully down the stairs.

Jordan had fallen into a state of physical and emotional lethargy. His leg *hurt,* but he knew he couldn't do anything about it and on some level had accepted the pain. *Should I be worried about that?* he wondered.

When he saw signs of movement from Serena he thought he might be hallucinating—possibly going into shock. At first all he saw were random twitches, movements so small they might have been imaginary. Then there was a full-body convulsion.

Something postmortem, he told himself wisely. *Possibly brought on by all the fast food she's been eating.* And boy, could that girl pack away junk food. He'd always wondered how she managed to stay so slim.

Then her head lifted and he had a full-body convulsion of his own.

"Sarah!" he shouted. *This can't be happening. I'm going into shock,* he thought. "SARAH!"

Serena's head came up off the floor. Her face, streaked with blood, was utterly white, the eyes lifeless. She stayed in that position, motionless, for what seemed a long time. There was a dark hole just above her right eyebrow and blood dripped slowly from her chin.

"Sarah! She . . . it's alive, Sarah!" He could feel the blood draining from his face and he begged God not to let him faint. *Where the hell is she?* he wondered frantically. "CONNOR!"

Serena's head turned in his direction, but her eyes seemed unfocused. Jordan found he couldn't speak; his mouth went dry and his heart beat so fast it almost hurt.

Then Serena's body shifted, in an almost insectlike series of motions that first lifted her onto her hands and knees, then onto her fingertips and toes. Her head dipped and turned, in sharp, abrupt movements, as though adjusting itself to this position. A human couldn't have held her head at that angle without pain; a human couldn't have held her body like that without dropping to the floor almost immediately.

"*CON-NORRRR!*" Jordan screamed. Utter horror struck as he pushed himself back against the elevator wall with his good leg, until he was almost standing. "It's *aliiiive!*"

The thing that had been Serena Burns shifted its head to look in his direction, and Jordan pushed the close doors button frantically. Nothing happened; he pushed a floor button. *The elevator is dead,* he thought. *Oh, God! So am I!* He got himself onto his feet and half hopped, half slid his way around to the door and through it.

The Serena-thing scuttled toward him rapidly and he shouted in wordless terror, as he might had a spider the size of a wolf walked out of his dreams. Instinctively he put his weight onto his wounded leg and went down to one knee. He thought of the gun, still inside the elevator, and threw himself sideways; grabbing it, he rolled over and fired. It hit her in the shoulder and she folded back onto her knees, her head still up, still apparently watching him.

Jordan once again dragged himself to the side of the elevator, never taking his eyes off of the thing, and pushed himself to his feet. He wondered how he would get past it; it blocked most of the doorway. He and the thing looked at one another. The thought of it touching him made him want to vomit, and he swallowed bile.

Then she scuttled backward until she reached the desk. Slowly she maneuvered herself from a kneeling into a sitting position, her feet tucked under in a way that should have been agonizing. She pushed herself up until she was standing on her two feet; then she froze.

The wound in her shoulder didn't seem to bother her at all. The bizarre manner in which she climbed to her feet had brought no change to her bland expression. Somehow, although she was looking right at him, her eyes seemed blind.

Jordan noticed that she wasn't breathing. In shock, he tucked into himself as though someone had poked him in the stomach. *I've got to get out of here,* he thought, and he hopped forward, sliding along the wall once he was outside the elevator. He had to find Connor.

He risked a glance toward the office where Sarah had disappeared, and that's when the thing made its move. He brought up the gun, but it grabbed his wrist and pulled him forward. Once again his leg failed him and he began to fall. The thing struck him across the face hard enough to send him sprawling, then twisted the gun from his grip as he went down.

Sarah finished setting the detonator on time fuse. She had no idea exactly what was happening out there, but she did know that there was probably very little she could do about it. The taser still had ten minutes to charge. And this had to be finished. Cyberdyne was going up tonight, Terminators and all, even if she and Dyson had to go with it.

When she was finished she picked up the gun and stood. *Okay, minions of Skynet, here I come, ready or not.* She moved cautiously out of the office, thinking, *Dieter, find my son, keep him safe. Please, my friend. Please.*

She arrived just in time to see Serena knock Dyson off his feet. Taken completely by surprise, she froze for a second. Between the two of them, Dyson and the woman, this one was the least likely to be on her feet again. People with their brains blown out didn't get up again, and she'd *seen* the pink-and-gray jelly spatter.

The bloodied blond head whipped round and the woman raised her gun and fired in one sharp movement. The bullet clipped the bone at the top of Sarah's right shoulder and her gun went flying.

Sarah dropped down behind the desk as the blond woman fired once more, then stopped. Connor pressed down on her shoulder, her eyes tearing, and sucked air between her teeth. She was dizzy and nauseous and black-and-white spots danced at the edges of her vision. *Focus!* she ordered herself. *Focus!*

Sarah heard footsteps and looked around for the gun. It was under a desk, about twelve feet away from her. Gritting her teeth, she forced herself to crawl; her right arm was almost useless, but she pushed herself forward with her feet. Almost there . . . she reached forward and a bullet almost took off her fingers.

The I-950 continued to move forward, continued to work on readjusting its faltering visual equipment. It sensed that it had come very close that time, but the biological elements were failing and the implants could only compensate to a certain extent. When failure came, it would be an exponential process.

Sarah pushed herself backward on the smooth floor, back toward the receptionist's desk. The Terminator—it had to be a Terminator—had a gun in its hand, she was sure. She wished the damn taser would hurry up and recharge.

Finding its target gone the I-950 listened and heard slithering noises off toward the fallen Six. It couldn't run, at least not yet, but it moved inexorably toward its fallen companion. The human mustn't be allowed to obtain a weapon. This unit was vulnerable to guns.

Sarah stretched out her arm as far as it would go and grasped the barrel of the gun. She tugged and nothing happened; she couldn't even drag the arm closer to her. Whatever had happened to its internal circuits when she hit it with the taser had caused the machine to freeze into a single immovable piece.

Goddammit! she thought. Easing herself forward, Sarah brought her other hand into play, trying to wrestle the weapon out of the big hand as quietly as possible. She didn't waste much time on it; it took her a matter of seconds to realize it was hopeless. Sarah pressed her hands to the floor to push herself backward.

The I-950 fired and wounded Connor's left forearm. The human cried out in pain. It had to be content with that. Enough wounds, even minor ones, would kill the human with cumulative damage. Soon she would be incapacitated enough that the Infiltrator could kill her with its hands. Perhaps that was best.

Sarah pushed herself backward frantically, aiming for one of the desks behind its beige partition. *Maybe I can lure it into this maze and lose it long enough to get back to stairs or the elevators.* She'd like to get Dyson out of here if she could. Assuming he was still alive, that is.

She got herself onto her hands and knees and launched herself toward the clerk's den of cubicles before her. The Terminator fired, and hit her, creating a searing line of fire along her ribs. Sarah caught her breath in a sob; gritting her teeth, she moved on. She dived into a cubicle, separated the wall, then pushed them back together again, hoping the Terminator wouldn't know how to follow her.

The I-950 followed Connor into a cubicle but found her gone. It heard sounds on the far side of the wall and considered shooting, but decided against it. Its supply of ammunition was limited, while the target's ability to escape seemed unlimited. The Infiltrator had no doubt of its eventual success; it merely conserved supplies in order to ensure it.

Sarah moved as quietly as she could, which was difficult. Her wounds were relatively minor, but they all bled. She could feel herself growing weaker and she felt clumsy and disoriented. *I should go back toward the front of the office,* she thought. She could see the gun under that desk in her mind's eye. And she needed a weapon desperately.

The next turn brought her out onto a main corridor beside the wall. *Left or right?* she wondered. She couldn't see very much difference from here between either end of the corridor. *Left,* she decided, and began to stumble in that direction. She was almost there when she looked up and saw that she was heading the wrong way.

There was a sound somewhere behind her and she ducked into the nearest cubicle. Hunkering down and pressing herself against the soft wall, she listened, breathing through her mouth to quiet her breathing.

Outside the I-950 stalked by with no attempt to hide itself. Its head swung like a gun turret from side to side. Its eyes didn't seem to be working right. Maybe it was listening. The thought bumped Sarah's heartbeat up a notch and she grimaced. *If it can't hear that, it must be deaf.*

After the Terminator passed, she slipped out and crept to the other cubicle, ducking in there. She waited a few heartbeats, then risked looking out into the corridor. It was empty; the Terminator must have turned the corner. Sarah slipped out and ran as fast as she could toward the elevators.

The I-950 stepped around the corner and fired. A good solid hit this time in the target's leg. The human went down and thrashed on the floor for a moment. Then she was gone.

Sarah limped as fast as she could down the cross-corridor toward the far wall, blinded by tears. With every step that pulsed out more of her blood, her mind swore and raged. *I've got to bind this up,* she thought. Her worry was the trail she was leaving rather than her probable collapse. Sarah refused to contemplate such an eventuality.

When she got around the next corner she went down on one knee, and for a moment couldn't get up. Surrendering to necessity, she sat, her back to the cubicle wall, and pulled off her belt. She stuffed the taser in her pocket; still five minutes left until it could be used. *Unbelievable,* she thought. *It feels like I used it yesterday.* With shaking hands she bound her belt tightly around her leg. It wasn't much, but it would have to do.

The Infiltrator moved slowly down the corridor, expecting to find its target at any moment. Even the most slippery human was vulnerable to blood loss. Once again it tried to force more speed, only to find that slowed it more. The elevators were nonfunctional, it remembered, and with the wound in her leg climbing stairs would be slow going for Connor. Skynet would prevail.

Sarah struggled to her feet and found that it made her dizzy and brought a mouthful of bile; she spat it out on the floor and swallowed, the bitter fluid rasping at her throat. When she tried to take a step she found that her leg wouldn't bear her weight. Giving in, she allowed herself to collapse to the floor, and lying flat, crawled. It was easier.

Halfway along the corridor she spied a boxed fire hose on the wall. Above it was another box; behind its glass was a fire ax. Sarah looked at it stupidly for a moment, then she smiled.

Low-tech, she thought, *but serviceable.*

Beside the whole arrangement was a smaller box. If the glass on this was broken and the button pushed, the safety sprinklers would be activated. *Do I want to be wet?* she wondered. *Do I want to be alive?* she answered herself. Her mind seemed to be moving more slowly; the plan formed immediately, but it took her several moments to work out how to actually do it. The water first; that might help to hide sound and movement.

Sarah dragged herself up and hit the glass with its tiny hammer. She almost broke down and cried when the glass only cracked. She hadn't thought she was so weak. *What if I can't do it?* She thought of Kyle.

On your feet, soldier! she thought fiercely. She hit the glass again and it shattered. Pressing the button, she flinched when the first drops of water hit. It was *cold.*

The Infiltrator stopped dead as water exploded from the sprinklers above. There was nothing in its memory to explain this. What did it mean? Irrelevant, it decided. Something the enemy had done, though how or why it didn't know. Perhaps the intention was to obscure its vision or hearing. Looking out into a world gone gray, the Infiltrator thought its enemy had succeeded better than it could know.

Dieter insisted on going through the door first, which John had no problem with. He was wounded and therefore less able. John covered him, a gun in his left hand. There was a nasty, squeezing sensation in his head at the sight of the prone Terminator just outside the door.

Dieter shoved it with his foot, barely shaking it. Then his gun hand snapped up at the sound of a groan. Looking around, he saw Dyson sprawled in a heap by the elevator. He moved quickly over to him and John followed. He noticed a pool of blood beside the Terminator and looked around.

Von Rossbach knelt beside Dyson and gently turned him over. Jordan's eyes were open, but were as yet uncomprehending, and he groaned again.

Dieter tapped his cheek gently, whispering, "Dyson. Wake up. Dyson."

John crouched beside them, his back to the wall, eyes roving.

"Where's my mother?" he asked. "What's going on?"

Jordan caught that and tried to answer, the words came out strangled and garbled and he frowned. He licked his lips and tried again.

"Another Terminator," he said. "My boss. Sarah shot her." His eyes rolled toward Dieter and he shook his head slightly. "She came back to life. She . . . it got the drop on your mother. They're out there somewhere." He gestured weakly toward the semidark cubicles.

John and Dieter both rose to their feet, looking outward. There was the distant sound of breaking glass and then the water came on.

"This way!" Dieter said, and plunged toward the sound.

Sarah was sitting beside the doorway on the rolling desk chair, her back to the wall, waiting for the Terminator to pass. In her hands was the fire ax; she hefted it, holding it ready to strike.

The I-950 moved slowly down the corridor. It wondered how long this rain effect would last. It was diminishing its effectiveness. It paced on, head turning, listening.

Sarah watched it pass, then leapt up and brought the ax down as hard as she could.

John and Dieter rounded the corner in time to see an ax flash up, then down. It was a moment before John realized that his mother had wielded it. He ran toward them. The bright head of what must be Jordan's Terminator boss turned and its hand flashed back. He screamed as he watched it plunge that hand deep into his mother's abdomen in a classic knife hand.

Sarah's eyes turned back into her head and she went down. The Terminator readied itself for a deathblow, moving slowly but powerfully.

Dieter crouched, holding his Browning Hi-Power in both hands, and fired. The blond head bucked and the Terminator dropped to its knees. John fired, less accurately with his left hand, and struck it on the shoulder. Slowly it fell, landing athwart his mother.

John ran toward them and with a strength he hadn't known he possessed grabbed the Terminator and flung it aside. He gathered Sarah up in his arm and weeping called to her.

"Mom!" he sobbed. "MOM! Don't die, okay? Please, please, don't die!"

Dieter looked down on him, then turned to the female Terminator that was still moving weakly. He put his pistol against its head and fired several times.

John jumped and looked at him desperately.

Von Rossbach knelt beside them and checked Sarah over. The wound in her side was bad. Dieter had nothing on him suitable for making bandages, and neither had John. He glanced around and saw a scarf hanging from a coatrack in the cubicle before him. He grabbed it and bound it tightly around Sarah's abdomen. Then he picked her up and carried her toward the stairs, John trotting anxiously beside him.

Jordan was sitting up, somewhat revived by the cold water pouring from the ceiling. He gasped when he saw Sarah Connor's limp form in von Rossbach's arms.

"Can you get up if John helps you?" Dieter asked.

"I'd better," Jordan said.

He struggled to his feet and John slipped under his arm. They staggered a bit at first, then found a way to center their mutual weight. John pressed the elevator button.

"Not working," Jordan said. "I tried."

Together they struggled toward the stairs and began the long journey upward.

Dieter noticed a change in Sarah's breathing and felt his heart contract. Then he saw her eyelids lift and his heart did, too.

"It's me—Dieter," he said softly. "I've got you; you're going to be all right."

Her eyes closed slowly and he had no idea if she'd heard him.

Even he was gasping for breath by the time they came to the top of the stairs.

Jordan, so breathless he was unable to speak, touched von Rossbach's arm and signaled him to wait. Frowning, Dieter complied.

"Three," Dyson said, holding up three fingers.

Dieter's face lit as he comprehended the message. There had been three Terminators in Sacramento. Two, and their master, were destroyed. That left one unaccounted for. He gently lowered Sarah to the ground. She moaned and shifted a bit.

"Sarah," he whispered. "There's one more Terminator. I've got to take him out."

"P-ocket," she mumbled, and made a weak gesture.

He glanced down and saw the butt of the taser sticking out of her jeans.

"That ought to do it," he whispered, smiling down at her.

He kissed her on the forehead, then lowered her head. John was there in an instant, sliding his arm under her. Their eyes met and Dieter nodded, then rose. He was the only unmarked member of the team. This would be up to him.

Dieter cracked the metal door slightly to glance out into the reception area. Without warning, a barrage of bullets erupted. Holes punched through the metal and von Rossbach lent his strength to get his wounded comrades out of the line of fire.

The firing stopped and they heard footsteps approach the door. Dieter readied the taser. The doorknob turned, slowly, quietly, then it stopped. The tension mounted as nothing happened.

The Terminator held the knob in position; it sent out a call to Serena and to its fellows and received no answer. It was unimaginable that humans could eliminate so many of its kind. Perhaps a fellow Terminator, badly damaged and unable to communicate, waited behind this barrier. Humans couldn't do it serious harm, it decided. It pushed open the door.

Dieter didn't even have to aim; he fired and the cords flashed out. Von Rossbach grabbed the Terminator's hair and yanked it forward into the stairwell, where the inevitable pyrotechnics wouldn't be visible from outside. Then he popped out the cartridge and put the taser in his jacket pocket.

He bent and lifted Sarah carefully. Even so, she made a soft sound of pain. Then he led them to the front doors. They got a good way from the building and took refuge in the deep shadows behind the concrete-and-metal Cyberdyne sign. He and John laid down their burdens, then turned back toward the building.

"Do you think Mom finished?" John asked.

"T-mer," came from behind him, and he knelt beside her.

"I think she said timer," Jordan suggested.

"It doesn't matter," Dieter said, he held out a signaler—"I have this." He pulled out the antenna.

"Wait!" John said. He pointed. "The guard, under the desk."

Dieter sighed, then handed the signaler to John.

"I guess I'd better go and get him," he said. "Maybe we should set off an alarm or something in case anybody else is in there." It was what Sarah would want him to do.

He jogged toward the building, keeping an eye out for any wandering army personnel. Luck, such as it was, was with him. No one appeared. He tapped in the test sequence and the door lock disengaged. Dieter moved to the desk and found the guard fully awake. He pulled his knife and cut the tape around the man's head.

"Is there anybody else in the building?" von Rossbach asked.

"Ms. Burns, the chief of security, and two other guards," the man answered. "We've got to call the MPs; this is bigger than we can handle!"

"These guards," Dieter said, "one of them has a funny haircut and the other is bald?"

"Yeah! That's them," he said eagerly.

"They're already out," von Rossbach said. "Can you walk?"

"Yeah, I think so," the guard said. He rubbed his wrists where Dieter had cut the tape. "We should set off the alarm," he suggested.

"I tried that. I think they've disabled it. Let's get out of here, then we can call for help."

"Good idea," the guard said. He held out his hand and Dieter pulled him to his feet.

"Go!" Dieter said, giving the man a shove. He grabbed a handful of the guard's shirt and began to run, half carrying the man with him. "Keep moving!" he insisted.

He ran the man to where his friends were hiding. The man stopped, goggling, and hardly reacted when Dieter's hands clamped down on his carotids—risky, but still safer than trying to knock him out. The guard hit the dirt with a muffled thump and Dieter shook his head ruefully.

"He'll have a headache, but he'll live."

"Is there anyone else in there?" John asked.

Von Rossbach shook his head.

"Not according to him," he said, indicating the fallen guard. "At least nobody human."

John licked his lips and glanced at his mother.

"You do it," Dieter said.

John hit the ignition button and felt a shiver beneath his feet. Almost instantly the doors and the roof of Cyberdyne Systems blew out in a giant orange fireball.

They ducked, as fragments began to rain down, John covered his mother's head and shoulders. Then he straightened and looked at her. She was so still, her lips were pale, and she seemed to be barely breathing.

Dieter's hand came down on his shoulder and he jumped, opening his mouth in a soft gasp.

"John," he said, "we have to go." Dieter tightened his lips. "We can't take her with us," he said quietly.

John turned to him, his face streaked with tears.

"What?" he said. "We can't leave her! Do you know what they'll *do* to her?" John shook his head. "I can't let them put her back in that place. She still has nightmares about it!"

"John. She's too badly hurt. If we take her with us she will certainly die. If we leave her with Jordan they might be able to save her life. I promise you: we *will* come back for her."

John hesitated, clasping her hand tightly. Then he took a deep breath and let her go. He turned to Jordan.

"Take care of her," he said. "Don't let them drug her like they did before. *Promise* me!"

John's eyes were desperate, but the tears were drying.

Jordan nodded solemnly. "I give you my word," he said. "I'll watch over her as best I can."

"Come on," Dieter said. He looked at Sarah's face and clenched his jaw. *I will be back for you,* he promised her silently. *Don't lose hope.*

Then he and John ran. They got to Ferri's quarters without being seen, often by the simple expedient of running backward in a crowd, or in Dieter's case by issuing orders before people got a good look at them.

Von Rossbach stuffed John into the false-fronted trunk in the back of the Humvee and entered the Major's house. He changed, dropping the used clothes into Ralph's hamper. Then he went into the kitchen and shook Ferri's shoulder. Dieter propped him up in his chair and lightly slapped the Major's face.

"Ralph!" he said. "Hey! Ralph!"

Ferri snorted, then tried to push von Rossbach off him with fumbling hands.

"Wha . . . wassup?" he asked. Finally he opened his eyes, which promptly threatened to roll back in his head.

Dieter slapped him again, lightly.

"Something's happening," he said. "Listen. Something's up."

Slowly the Major came to himself, a look of confusion on his face. Then the sirens registered.

"Something happened," he said.

Dieter offered him some aspirin and a glass of water.

Ferri took them, his eyes meeting von Rossbach's. He popped the pills into his mouth and took a mouthful of water.

"You bastard," he said quietly and without rancor. "You owe me."

"I do," Dieter said.

"Get out of here," the Major said. He went to the phone and dialed a couple of numbers. "Ferri, here," he said. "What and where?" He listened for a moment, then glared at von Rossbach. "Okay," he said, "I'm on my way. I've got a friend visiting me. I'm sending him on his way; see that they don't hassle him at the gate. Dieter von Rossbach. Yeah. Okay." He hung up and turned to his friend. "I expect an explanation," he said.

"You'll get one," Dieter said. He held out his hand. "No hard feelings?"

"Hell yes!" Ferri snapped. He took Dieter's hand. "Right now, we're *even* for Srebrenica. But I always did hate those cyber-snots. Get lost," he said.

They left together, Ferri heading for Cyberdyne without looking back, Dieter driving for the gate, his heart in his throat.

I'll be back, he thought at Sarah.

They were close to the Chamberlains' cabin when Dieter's cell phone beeped.

"Von Rossbach," he answered.

"Dyson," came the clipped answer.

Dieter took a deep breath, but said nothing. He couldn't bring himself to speak. John blinked and came fully awake, shifting in his seat to look anxiously at him.

"Sarah's listed as critical," Jordan said. "But she's under the care of a good doctor. They think she'll pull through."

"Wait," Dieter said. He put the phone against his shoulder and turned to John. "He says it looks like your mother should pull through. She's in the care of a good doctor."

John let out his breath in something close to a sob and Dieter put the phone back to his ear.

"Thank you," he said.

"There's something else," Jordan said, sounding tired.

"Yes?"

"There was another backup storage site."

In the mountains of Montana, in a secret underbasement, a screen flickered and read: "Transmission terminated. No further download possible."

On a narrow bed, a young girl with Serena's face lay still, electrodes attached to her temple. Her eyes opened slowly.